DRAGON'S EYE

DRAGON'S EYE

DRAGON'S EYE

A CHINESE NOIR

ANDY OAKES

THE OVERLOOK PRESS
Woodstock & New York

First published in the United States in 2004 by
The Overlook Press, Peter Mayer Publishers, Inc.
Woodstock & New York

WOODSTOCK:
One Overlook Drive
Woodstock, NY 12498
www.overlookpress.com
[for individual orders, bulk and special sales, contact our Woodstock office]

NEW YORK:
141 Wooster Street
New York, NY 10012

∞ The paper used in this book meets the requirements for paper
permanence as described in the ANSI Z39.48-1992 standard.

Library of Congress Cataloging-in-Publication Data

Oakes, Andy
Dragon's eye : a novel / Andy Oakes.— 1st ed.
p. cm.
1. Police—China—Shanghai—Fiction. 2. Archaeologists—Crimes against—Fiction.
3. Murder victims' families—Fiction. 4. Americans—China—Fiction. 5. Shanghai
(China)—Fiction. 6. Mass murder—Fiction. I. Title
PR6115.A37D73 2004   813'.6—dc22   2003064707

Printed in the United States of America
ISBN 1-58567-495-8
FIRST EDITION
1 2 3 4 5 6 7 8 9 10

DEDICATION

In Memory of my late parents Eva and Len Oakes.

This book is dedicated to Jean, Annie Lucy Oakes and Tom Alexander Oakes.

A special thank you goes to my literary agent, Juri Gabriel and to the writer and teacher, Alan Fisher.

Chapter 1

THE BUND (*ZHONGSHAN LU*), SHANGHAI.
THE PEOPLE'S REPUBLIC OF CHINA.

A tide so low.   A night so dark.   A secret so raw.

The bodies of the eight, caked in black river mud and twisted around each other in the strange and silent choreography of death . . . could not be seen from the Bund, once the most famous street in the East.

Only when down amongst the debris that clogged the Huangpu riverbanks and away from the deep rooted shadows of the grandiose neo-classical edifices that skirted the old commercial heart of Shanghai . . . could their lifeless limbs be made out. And even more clearly, the dark steel links, the heavy chains that bound the weld of bodies together in death. Leg to leg. Neck to neck. A permanence about the chains, as if they had always rested there between the once living, the once breathing individuals.

★

A dazzle of headlight.   A car door slamming.

The Homicide Squad of the PSB. The tall shadow amongst the smaller shadows . . . the Senior Investigator. Eyes trained into believing that they had seen it all. Still, Sun Piao felt the shiver slide up his spine; wings of nausea flutter in his chest. With difficulty, moving forward. Swearing, cold mud oozing over the top of his shoe. A few more muttered to himself as his eyes fell upon the gaping holes. Black. Bottomless. Cleaving the chests of the corpses closest to him. Splitting them, neck to navel. Finding himself thinking of overripe peaches. Of a melon cut and halved . . . sticky centre of seeds spooned away.

7

Somebody's babies. Somebody's children.

Half turning to Yaobang who was following, and in a whisper,

"What a fucking way to die."

But the words swallowed whole by a freighter as it ploughed towards its deepwater berth south of the new Yangpu Bridge, the new Golden Gate; the sea-caravans of barges strung with tyres and the clumps of tethered junks, lifting, falling, lifting, across its insistent wake. He hadn't heard. Just as fucking well. His deputy didn't have the stomach for this sort of thing. He was, after all, from Kashgar in the north west. They didn't have murders in Kashgar, at least not like these. All that they had in the oasis city were hot dust driven winds and ice-cold Xinjiang beer. An exquisite embrace of opposites that surely proved that there was a God. Anyway, he would see it all for himself soon enough. There was no hurry, they weren't going anywhere, not these bodies. The limbs. The chains. The great curving black crescent moons of gashes.

They weren't going anywhere.

He didn't envy the Big Man. Better to be from Shanghai or Beijing and be used to such horrors; a civilised upbringing in an oasis town and a job as an Investigator with Homicide were not a complimentary pairing. Yaobang's passage through his career was not going to be hot desert winds and chilled beers.

The dim beam of the torch wavered. Yaobang was not built for such a balancing act as this. Too plump. Too belly-full. Thinking of dumplings, beer . . . bed. Moving forward only as Piao's urgently beckoning hand ordered. Shadows falling over shadows. The Senior Investigator hearing the Big Man retch behind him as the young detective caught a glimpse of the bodies. An instant reek of honey and vinegar invading the anonymous night air. Almost dropping the torch as he clumsily fled back across the broken foreshore to the tide worn stone blocks of the embankment.

"Headless chicken, throw the torch. How am I supposed to do my job with you halfway back to your mama's lap?"

Rough material of his cuff to his mouth . . . he threw the

torch across to Piao, leaving himself in a deep fold of darkness, the cold stone wall taking his weight. For a few seconds, eyes closed, but still seeing the horrors that the beam had illuminated. Subliminal cuts forming an inerasable film loop in his head. A part of his life now. A terrible part that would always be there. He felt sullied . . . despoilt.

Somebody's babies. Somebody's children.

"Boss, dump this fucking job. I mean look at them for shit sake. This has got to be state business. Fucking Party business. These are official . . ."

Wiping the jewelled cables of spittle from his lips, his chin.

". . . look, let me get on the radio, get Security to deal with it. This is their backyard. Let them get their fucking shoes shitty for a change."

The Senior Investigator stared back hard over his shoulder. The beam from the torch cutting harshly into the side of his slender face. Forehead. Cheek. Chin. Coldly chromed. Yaobang recognised the look etched into the tired features. He'd seen it before. Trouble . . . spelt with a capital 'S'. The Big Man's stomach rumbled again. Hoping that it was from the effects of the *Yoe Bing* . . . the large, flaky mooncake that he had hurriedly washed down with tea. But knowing, with regret, that it was not. His stomach, always an accurate barometer as to how much shit was heading his way. And right now the barometer readings were off the fucking scale.

"Get on the radio . . ."

Piao, almost absentmindedly, muttering the words, his attention nailed to the bodies. The frozen, intertwined arms, that seemed to reach out wanting to embrace a fingernail moon anchored in the crow's-nest branches of the trees in the neighbouring Huangpu Park.

The Big Man laboured through the rubbish. Up the slippery steps of the embankment. Mouth bitter with bile.

Every breath reminding him . . .

Somebody's babies. Somebody's children.

It was only as he stepped onto the road that the Senior Investigators said,

"Tell control that we need more men and floodlights. Lots

of floodlights. I also want Wu brought down here right away. The bodies . . . get them out of the mud and the area combed before the tide comes back in and we lose the fucking lot . . ."

A pause of seconds. Somewhere in the distance, in the night, a dog barking. A car refusing to start. A tug moaning as it passed down river . . . running lights in a constant fade to black.

". . . and Yaobang, tell them to keep it tight. No flapping mouths. This is police work. My work. I don't want those Bureau Thirteen security shits climbing all over my back, got it?"

He nodded, even though he knew that Piao wasn't watching him. His stomach grumbling more furiously than ever.

"Fuck it . . ." he groaned, loosening his trouser belt as he walked toward the car.

★

A cold, dark hour before the first batch of floodlights and men arrived. An olive green snake of police piling from an assortment of vehicles. Men extruded from the same mould . . . lean bodied and wide foreheaded. An hour and a half before the floodlights prised the darkness aside with an arc of white . . . blinding. Shadows, like sentries of razors. Two and a half hours before Doctor Wu arrived bleary-eyed and moaning onto the foreshore of a Huangpu that was beginning to turn. Yawning into life in a blush of palest baby pink. Three hours and ten minutes before Piao pulled the doctor out of the harsh arclight midday and into the splintered penumbra of the wooden pier for an initial report.

"We have eight who are no longer living."

The Senior Investigator moved deeper into the shadows where Wu could not read his face.

"You mean that they are dead. You have eight corpses to take back to your freezer doctor."

The cloak of Wu's smile slipped slightly; the passions pushed in, the outward impassivity drawn across his eyes . . . a heavy velvet curtain of constrained discipline.

"We have eight whom life no longer possesses."

Stupid bastard. A doctor for thirty years and he still can't use that word. That four letter word. Dead . . . they're fucking dead!

But he would get nowhere trying to bait him. Wu, who at one time must have had the looks and physical attributes of a proud and studious orang-utan, but who had since shrunk to resemble a wizened squirrel monkey, was a professional *Wenming* . . . a civilised man ruled by the old ways. Guided by the Book of Rites to conform, to meet the needs of life in society.

Piao felt the smile start to freeze on his lips . . . it laying across them as the dead dog does in the middle of the road, squashed, tongue sticking out. The society that he and other officers in the Homicide Squad moved in had no such restraints. He wished that it had. There were no courtesies in his society. No rules. No boundaries to adhere to. Just a carouselled blur of speed and colour. A head-on collision between the old ways and the new order. A society of guns, where no guns had been before. A society of swift retribution and death, where once the only pain that bled was from a dignity that had been wounded. He was glad that Wu could not see his eyes. They spoke no courtesies, they only said,

Your old ways are dead, old man – and now we're all fucked.

"Sex?"

The doctor visibly blushed, smile souring.

"What sex were they, doctor, these eight whom life no longer possesses?"

"One woman. Seven men."

Seven men. Not even the mask of a serene smile could hide the shock, the significance that the number seven bled onto Wu's face. The Senior Investigator knew the words that would be humming through the old man's head . . . the words that were already playing in the corners of his own mouth.

At Xun, there is a cold spring,
there, below that stream are your seven sons,
mother of pain.

Seven, the symbol of perfect prosperity. Did their murderers also know the very same poem from the Book of Songs?

11

As they ripped their victims asunder, shackling them together and then lowering them into the black waters of the Huangpu, had they also been mouthing the words . . .

Softly, the wind blows from the south.
Softly, the wind blows from the south.

A shiver racking him. Piao folded his arms, cutting it adrift.

"So, what else do you have? Time, cause of death? Any clues to their identities? Astound me, doctor. Astound me."

Wu shuffled uncomfortably. Cold, the mud. Filling his shoes, his soul. Thinking of the rubber boots back at the office. Thinking of the chains. The bodies . . . and the black, bloodless holes that spiked them and drew at his recognition, as the eye of the needle draws on the thread.

"There is nothing that I can tell you. I am a doctor. A scientist. Not a beachcomber."

Piao moved out of the shadows. Face to face with Wu. The old man smelling of mothballs, of an unreliable bladder. His mouth of pepper sauce and sticky words. Looking deeply into him . . . seeing the fear treading at depth in the doctor's eyes. Almost tasting it. Recognising it. And understanding it, but not wanting to. Never wanting to . . .

"What is it Wu, have you seen this before? What do you know of this?"

A small strained laugh from the doctor; a joyless hilarity closing tight across his face that gave the impression of steel shutters slotting into place.

"Don't give me this shit, Wu, don't pull this on me, not me. You know something, don't you? Don't you?"

Again, the laugh. A sound only. Edged glass across edged glass. Nothing in his eyes except for a secret and the root of an anonymous fear. Piao made a mistake and placed a hand on the doctor's bony shoulder, bridging the physical gap of courtesy . . . making all now possible. Unlocking Wu's anger. The passions thrown to the mercy of the elements. The old man hissed. His voice low. For the Investigator's ears only.

"I do not want this case. Not these bodies. I will not

examine them here or anywhere. They will not be admitted
to my laboratory . . ."

His eyes narrowed, his voice with them. Words, with the
heat of the blowtorch across the Senior Investigator's cheek.

". . . pass it on Piao. Pass this case on as I am doing. You
want nothing to do with it."

"Nothing to do with it? There's eight bodies out there in
the fucking mud. Seven sons and one daughter whom life
no longer possesses. You're the city Senior Police Scientist
for fuck sake. It is your job to poke around bodies . . . but
not these bodies? What are you telling me here, Wu, that
these are killings that you know about? Official killings,
sanctioned murders . . . down to Security, the State, the
Party?"

With a hiccup of shock, Piao realising that his hand was
once more on the doctor's shoulder; grip increasing as his
anger blossomed. He left it in place.

"Give me the bad news that's at the back of your eyes, old
man, or there's a tall building with a long drop waiting for
you . . ."

"You would threaten me, Senior Investiga . . ."

Cutting in, a sharp knife through fatty pork.

". . . tell me, or so help me . . ."

Cheek to cheek. Mouth to ear. Breath to breath.

". . . or you had better start growing a pair of wings."

Wu's smile fading to a grimace, as if he had just stepped
into a pile of shit.

"You are dangerous, Piao. You cause ripples where there
should be none. Watch out Investigator, those who cannot
swim can sometimes drown in ripples."

"Very poetic, doctor, but what the fuck is that supposed to
mean?"

"It means, Senior Investigator, that you should walk away.
As you have done before. As we have all done before. Walk
away. 'He who hammers out his sword and constantly sharp-
ens it will not keep it long.'"

Wu moved slowly out from the pier, zebra shadows falling
across his face as he made his way up the embankment to the

13

Bund. He passed Yaobang as he wearily reached the top of the stairs.

"That was fucking quick, doc. Alright to start loading them into the van?"

The old man raised a hand and waved him away as if dealing with a bothersome fly. A smile fixed across his face. Eyes averted. Looking inward and set upon some obscure horizon. Walking on. Not a single word passing his lips as night folded around him. A car coughing into life. Headlights panning fierce white. Shadows sprinting, shape shifting. A premature dawn. At speed, the old man driving away.

"Fuck, Boss, what's up with the old bastard? I never thought I'd see the day when he was scared shitless by some stiffs. I thought he'd just about seen everything?"

"He has . . ."

Piao moved out from underneath the pier. Shadow, light, shadow, light . . . across his eyes. Retracing the old man's footsteps.

"So what's up, Boss?"

"What's up, is that our esteemed doctor wants nothing to do with our muddy friends out there . . ."

The Senior Investigator spat into the wind, in the direction on the bodies.

". . . won't touch the job. He knows something and refuses to even examine them."

"Can he fucking do that, Boss? Refuse to carry out post-mortems?"

Deeper mud. Piao leading, the Big Man following. A faint reek of shit assailing their nostrils.

"Well, he has done it. What the hell do we do now? Eight fucking bodies and nowhere to take them. No idea who they are, how they died . . . and if someone of Wu's reputation doesn't want to know, then you can bet that no one else will want to know either."

"Fuck it. But you don't mean the Chief, do you?"

Mud over shoes and dragging at trouser bottoms. Black, iced with white arc-light.

"Look, country boy, I don't want to be the one to

disillusion you, let's just leave that to the job, but Chief Liping is like all other Police Chiefs, a politician before he's a policeman. He's got more feet in more camps than a centipede running a marathon. If this stinks to him of the Party, like it stinks to us . . . or he can't squeeze a back-hander out of it, he'll dump it. And us along with it."

"You're a cynical bastard, aren't you, Boss?" Deeper mud. Piao leading, the Big Man following. An oasis of blinding floodlight. Turning to face the squinting detective.

"It helps to keep me alive . . ."

Again, spitting in the direction of the bodies. The wind in his favour this time, the spittle landing within feet of them.

". . . cynicism is good for the health. I wish that I could have given them that advice."

Seconds of silence, punctuated only by the breath of traffic starting along Shanxilu.

"Dump the fucking case, eh Boss?"

Piao laughed. A throwaway laugh. The kind that seemed to have punctuated his life, his career, at depressingly regular intervals.

"Why not? What's eight bodies to a city of thirteen million. Besides, there isn't room in my icebox for eight stiffs."

"Nor mine . . ."

Both laughing. Yaobang the loudest. A laughter as free as a junk that had slipped its mooring. The Senior Investigator envied a man who could let loose such a laugh.

"Make it look as if we've bothered . . . get some of the preliminaries fastened down and then get shot of the job. Pass it on to Security. Another one for the back of the filing cabinet . . ."

The Big Man nodding almost too enthusiastically.

". . . get the photographer in to do his stuff and keep them sifting the mud for anything that's been missed. Also, get on to the hospitals. Try the Number 1 first. The Huangdong on Suzhou Beilu. See if they can take the bodies for the time being. If not, try Jiaotong and also Fudan University. Also the Academy of Science in Xehui. Just find me anywhere that will take the bodies without burying us in fucking questions, got it?"

"Sure, Boss. Anywhere that will take the bodies without burying us in fucking questions."

Making his way more confidently across the foreshore towards the car. On the Big Man's lips a constant tremble of half whispered words, repeated, repeated again, like a parrot with a compulsive disorder.

". . . take the bodies, no fucking questions . . . anywhere that will take them, no fucking questions . . ."

At the bottom of the stairs, stopping, looking back over his shoulder to the Senior Investigator. A figure stranded in a no-man's-land of mud, debris.

"Don't worry, Boss, you're doing the right fucking thing walking away. You don't want to be investigating this."

The Senior Investigator made no reply. He had not heard the words that had been stolen by the breeze and dragged off into the night. He had not heard the words, this time, or the many times that similar words had been used in the past. A freighter lumbered by. Came. Went. Noise. Lights. And then silence and darkness, as if it had never passed him. As if it had never cleaved the calm of the river in front of him. Piao walked to the Huangpu's very edge. The river lapping against the toes of his shoes.

"Shit."

Kicking at the river. Turning. Making his way back toward the noon of arc-lights; hurrying his pace as he spotted two un-uniformed figures, one standing, one kneeling, beside the bodies. The bodies . . . now fully unearthed from the cloying mud. Partially cleaned up. A string of clay limbs, torsos. Joined, steel link by steel link to each other in a paralysed dance across milky sheets of thick polythene.

Somebody's babies. Somebody's children.

"Hey, hey! This is a restricted area, can't you see? There's a police investigation going on here."

The men half turned, ignoring the shout from the Bureau's photographer who had also seen them; their slight frames casting the shadows of giants. The Big Man cut across Piao's path, intercepting him, a hand braced against his Boss's chest; moving into the area of foreshore where shadow became flesh and had a smell all of its own.

"Let me introduce you, Boss," he said with a wink and out of the corner of his mouth, before turning, striking up a more formal pose and tone of voice.

"Senior Investigator Piao of the Public Security Bureau Homicide Squad, may I introduce Comrade Zhiyuan, Chairman of the Shiqu, the urban borough that administers this area. May I also introduce Comrade Shi of the Party's Neighbourhood Committee."

"We've met before," Piao replied coldly.

The men smiled at him. Notebooks in hand. Fingers caked in river mud, which was also oozing over the tops of the sandals that they were wearing.

'Perhaps wet feet would persuade the bastards to piss off quicker?'

Piao moved forward, aware that his hands had already formed into fists. That balls and chains would drag behind every word that he would want to use. The taller man, Zhiyuan, a *tong zhi*, a comrade of the old guard, as gaunt, as stretched as an ancient knotted scar, stood as Piao's shadow cast across the first of the bodies.

"You are in my way, Senior Investigator. I was just studying these poor unfortunates."

"The story of my wretched life, Mr Zhiyuan, getting in people's way. But it can have advantages in my field of work . . ."

Pausing. Piao mentally cutting adrift the shackles that seemed to tie down every word whenever faced by a tong zhi of Zhiyuan's breed. It was still unfamiliar territory . . . dangerous territory.

". . . you don't mind if I call you Mister, do you? Comrade is so very rarely used nowadays. I even read that most of our schoolchildren have never heard of Mao. Imagine. I suppose that times change, don't they, Mister Zhiyuan?"

"Call me Comrade Zhiyuan . . ." the Shiqu Chairman corrected. A leer. Deep. Engraved. Teeth like broken headstones, etched in nicotine.

17

"... some of us are still proud of such a title. We fought for such a title. And you would do well to remember, Investigator, that getting in people's way can sometimes be bad for your health. I hope that you look both ways before crossing the street?"

Eye contact riveted in place. Piao standing firm, his shadow still eclipsing the corpses. Not sure that he'd heard the comrade correctly. A sudden chill to the air. An edge, glass sharp. What was it that the Shiqu Chairman was saying? Zhiyuan lit a cheroot. The smoke hiding his mouth. A pungent scent of secrets fanning against every question that Piao wanted to ask.

"What do you mean?"

"I mean, Investigator, that you are in my way. You are purposely interrupting my investigation . . . the Party's investigation into this matter."

"Oh, the Party's investigation, I see. I was under the misapprehension that I was the Investigator in this case. I must make a point of checking my wage slip next month. I wouldn't want the Party to be paying me for work that I wasn't carrying out!"

"You've got a 'fat job' and have been paid for doing nothing for years, Investigator Piao. This sort of thing is proof enough of that . . ."

The comrade turned toward the shadowed bodies.

". . . it is up to us, the people, the Party and the Security Services to move upon your role. You police have become lazy and have lost your way. You have not brought the values of the Party into your work and into your dealings with the capitalist driven crime wave that is threatening our people and our glorious way of life."

The Investigator caged the anger that fled to his temples.

"Nice speech, Chairman. Best to write it down and keep it safe for when your re-election comes up."

Zhiyuan laughed. A slap of a laugh that left Piao nursing its fine sting.

"You are a little man in a big world, Investigator. Just a little man with gold braid on his shoulders. You buck the system, the Party. You abuse your privileged position, but not for much longer. The people, the committees, they have many eyes, many ears. We are the Party, root and branch. We feed it night and day with all that we see and hear. The Party is thorough, Investigator, and getting more thorough as the days go by. Soon, Investigator, you will feel the Party's thoroughness."

"Like they did?"

Piao spat past the comrade and onto the island of polythene where the bodies lay.

Somebody's babies. Somebody's children.

Words free now. Restraints severed. Wondering what price he might pay for using them?

"Are you suggesting that the Party is involved in this, Investigator Piao?" Zhiyuan seized, the rabid old mongrel.

"No, not really. It's just that when you mentioned thoroughness, it got my mind ticking over. Homicide Squad Investigators are like that. A nasty little trait that I must have picked up from having this gold braid on my shoulder . . ."

He brushed a hand across an epaulette.

". . . you see, it's the word thoroughness that comes to mind when I look at these poor bastards. Thoroughness, and patience of course. Haven't you noticed, Mr Chairman? After all, you are studying these 'poor unfortunates' as you call them. I wouldn't want you to miss any of the more subtle details . . ."

Moving aside as the photographer got to work. Leaning back, filling the frame of the old black and silver Rolleiflex. An explosion of flash. Harsh. Cold. Mid-tones, subtle hues banished. From the mud, the plastic, the bodies seeming to rise and fall. Clay, patches of skin . . . alabaster. Wounds as black as the inside of a hound's mouth.

". . . come, Mr Shiqu Chairman, let me show you thoroughness. . . ."

Roughly, with resistance, guiding, pushing the comrades out of the path of the photographer's studied dance, to the other side of the bodies. Dead flesh just inches and eternity away from their muddied toes.

". . . thoroughness, yes, you'll appreciate the level of

19

thoroughness that is displayed here. Let me show you what I mean . . ."

A whine. A click. A blitz. Again, again, the photographer moving in for close-ups. Blue-white flashes squinting, piercing their eyes. Everything with its bright mercury taint. The eight, the bodies, turning to stone with each shot. Removed further and further from a life of flesh, of warmth.

". . . we have eight corpses in all, chained together by the legs and by the necks. Note the hands of the victims. A total of sixteen thumbs, sixty-four fingers, the top joints of which are all missing. Snipped off very neatly, wouldn't you agree? Very thorough . . ."

Another flash. Another. Illuminating the side of his face. Knowing that he would look as if he was fashioned from stainless steel. Waiting for seconds for an answer that he knew would not come. Thick seconds. Thinking of bolt cutters, cleavers, blunt knives. And wondering if they thought of such things also?

". . . the victims faces. Not much left of them, is there? Odontology, dental work, teeth . . . we can tell a lot from teeth. Age. Diet. Lifestyle. Social category. General health. Even nationality . . ."

Halting as the photographer knelt in front of him. Viewfinder filled with static heads. The caves of nostrils. Muddied, lank rope hair. Black wells of torn mouths. There can be a listless beauty in death sometimes. Sometimes . . . but not in these. No, not in these poor unfortunates. The flash of the large format camera. Another. Another. Naked death served as a main course, without the trimmings. Without the garnish.

". . . their mouths, their teeth, their jaws, have all been smashed. I would say by a heavy clubbing hammer. Their faces also. Smashed to bits to hamper identification. See, see? Fractured skulls. Cheekbones. Broken noses and jaws . . ."

Somebody's babies. Somebody's children.

Sweet mouths at the breast. Piao feeling his anger rise, hot and sour. Its wash creeping in to taint the edges of his words.

". . . finally, the eyes. But of course, Mr Chairman, you will

20

have already noticed . . . they are missing. Sixteen eyes, all removed. Gouged out, by the look of it . . ."

One, two, three, four, five . . . seconds. Pausing. But no questions. Not a breath. Lips still. The air still, and the river. As if time itself was waiting to be re-wound.

". . . what do you think, were they brown eyes? Or perhaps blue or grey. Maybe even green. I like green eyes . . . don't you, Mr Comrade Chairman of the Shiqu . . . ?"

Comrade Shi, Neighbourhood Committee notebook in hand, stumbled from the pool of arc-light. A thick trail of vomit marking his passage. Death and vomit, the two inextricably linked in Piao's mind. Death. Men think that it can be tamed. That they can become accustomed to its face as they can become accustomed to a strange and exotic foreign food. They see it every day in a city that does not kneel to hide it. Hot flowing blood in the long summer days. Cold and stanched brown in the grey winter hours. And then this . . . a sight that the rest of your life will be hung upon, pivot from. A sight only ever just a flicker of an eyelid away. Piao felt the bud of nausea unfurl its petals at the back of his throat.

". . . is this a brand of thoroughness that you recognise, Chairman Zhiyuan. A thoroughness that robs a man of the colour of his eyes?"

Zhiyuan turned his back to the cold bodies, lighting another cheroot. His fast hand covering the pages of his notebook with scrawl and ash as he talked.

"I am not here to play guessing games, Investigator . . . and even less to be taught by your kind . . ."

Smoke from his lips in a constant steel band.

". . . you have gone too far, Piao. Too dangerously far with your accusations . . ."

He drew closer. His lined skin resembling a city centre road map. His breath, its accumulated exhaust fumes.

". . . you forget who you are talking to. My words will find the ears of important comrades in the Party. And the Party has ways of dealing with . . ."

". . . what, comrade. Ways of dealing with people like me? And people like them also?" Piao interjected.

21

A single word piercing the coiled cheroot smoke as it left the old man's torn lips.

"Perhaps."

A hiss, and so close that Zhiyuan's breath intermingled with his own. Piao immediately thinking of meat-flies, puke, fatty pork. He suddenly felt very ill.

"Did you hear that, Detective Yaobang. A threat made to a serving Senior Officer in the police force of the People's Republic of China?"

"I heard it . . ." Yaobang replied. A tinge of reluctance plaited into his words. Spit, thick and white on his lips, Zhiyuan exploded.

"My Committee and the Central Committee will hear of your obstructive behaviour, Investigator, and of your vile insinuations that these murders were carried out in the name of the Party and of the State . . ."

The dark butt falling from his fingers. A hiss as it met mud. Its orange tip dying to grey.

". . . expect a knock on your door, Piao."

"Detective Yaobang, please escort Comrade Zhiyuan and Comrade Shi to their cars, they're leaving. They have a great deal of report writing to complete."

Watching their shadows shrink as they walked away. The darkness eating them. Piao chewing on the bit of his anger. Mouth tasting of polished metal. Of danger. He spat, but could not loosen its hold. Squatting, eyes closed for a few seconds . . . or was it minutes? Longing for sleep, but knowing that it offered no rest. Behind the dark curtains of his eyelids he could still see the policemen relieving their full bladders. The crescent moon now in flight above the river. And the paper white faces, with their smudged, eyeless sockets. They say that the eyes of the murdered retain within them a last burning image of who it was that killed them. Was it the Party that was robbing the bodies of this last old wives' tale?

The decision made, and made against the grain and every survival instinct that the fifteen thousand days of his life in Shanghai had taught him, Piao stood, shouting to a group of policemen who were smoking, gossiping, pissing onto the mud.

"Let's get to it, it's our case . . ."

A low moan of discontent. China Brand cigarette butts being flicked into the river. Flies being zipped.

". . . load them into the wagon and don't fucking drop them down the embankment, they've been through enough."

The dark figures peeled off from each other, crossing into the island of arc-light. A brief flurry of activity. The sound of bolt cutters meeting steel chain. Polythene sheeting being fashioned around bodies, now separated. Fibreglass caskets flexing, accepting their loads. Grunts as they were lifted. Eight caskets. Eight grunts. Eight bodies. A slow weaving line across soft shadowed broken foreshore. Staggering, stuttering up the steps to the Bund. The wagon doors being opened. Caskets slid in. The wagon doors being closed.

Piao meandered through the lines of waterproof suited policemen on their knees, sifting through the mud. A thankless task. He knew, already knew . . . these murderers would leave no calling cards. These murderers would leave nothing but their ravaged quarry. He looked up, across the stacked grey graduations of Huangpu Park. Clouds now rolling in against the moon, overtaking it and swallowing it whole. It was going to be a brushed steel grey of a day. He would be waiting for the leach of red rust to seep into it.

Chapter 2

Softly, the wind blows from the south,
Caresses the stems of the brambles.
Holy mother, good mother,
I was not your son.

WASHINGTON D.C., THE UNITED STATES OF AMERICA.

She had known that he was dead at that very moment, in that very instant; beyond her, beyond everything. The scream that filled her head waking her from a deep sleep. Her own voice crying out the name of her only child . . .

"Bobby."

As clear, as pure as a crystal sphere splintering onto a marble floor.

"Jesus . . . Jesus . . . Jesus . . ."

Shaking. Hearing her own words and pleadings, that seemed to pierce the night as the steel pin impales the butterfly. And all of the time his name burning inside her. An indigestion of loss, pain, and disjointed flooding memories. And knowing that it was too late. Already . . . too late.

★

Calm now. Reaching for the telephone. Counting . . .

ONE . . . TWO . . . THREE . . .

Brandy in one hand. A letter, his writing, the telephone number . . . in the other hand. And all of the time, reality and intuition in a fierce grapple for her attention.

"Bobby . . . Bobby."

Counting. Slowly . . .

FOUR . . . FIVE . . .

It can't be true . . . he can't be dead.

24

The telephone number, endless. Halfway through it, she realised that she had misread a digit. A five for a four. His writing had always been so poor, so chaotic; as if his mind was in a constant head-on collision of ideas, schemes. His brain working faster than his hand. A five for a four. The pain pressed harder. She re-dialled, counting . . .

SIX . . . SEVEN . . . EIGHT . . .

"Come on, come on."

The connection clicked into life. A ringing tone, replaying.

Be there, for God's sake be there. Let me be wrong, please. Please God.

A ringing tone, repeating itself.

Stupid. Stupid. He'll be there. The phone will be answered, the call put through to his room. He'll be there. 'Hi Mom, how are you?' Just like a few days ago . . . a week ago . . . a month ago. He'll be there. He'll be there, won't he, God?

A woman's voice answered. Draped in a Chinese accent, but her English starched rigid and oh so correct.

"Good evening, this is the Shanghai Jing Jiang Hotel. How may I help you?"

"Can you connect me to Mr Hayes in room 201. Thank you."

Seconds of silence punctuated by her own heartbeat.

"We have no Mr Hayes in room 201."

Putting down the brandy. Her ear pulsing, sweating against the plastic of the receiver. Again, counting . . .

ONE . . . TWO . . . THREE . . .

"Are you sure? Room 201 was his room, I'm positive. Maybe he checked out, or perhaps he's moved rooms. Can you please look again? It is urgent."

"Sorry, Madam, but we have no Mr Hayes in the hotel."

"Look, double-check. The name is Hayes.

H—A—Y—E—S. BOBBY HAYES."

A longer silence. Distant snippets of conversation in Chinese playing peekaboo behind it. With each second, it feeling as if an endless corridor of doors between her and Bobby were being slammed shut. Finishing the brandy. Relishing its burn. Counting . . .

25

FOUR . . . FIVE . . .

"Madam, we have checked our records thoroughly and we can find no mention of a Mr Bobby Hayes. You must be mistaken. He must have resided at a different hotel."

"But I telephone him at this hotel at least three times a week for Christ sake. I spoke to him just two days ago. I know the phone number by heart, 53—42—42. I have letters from him written on your hotel notepaper. Does that sound like someone who is residing at another hotel?"

The voice at the other end of the line, the other side of the world, was more insistent this time; almost brutal, slicing in its ice-cold certainty.

"No one by the name of Mr Bobby Hayes has ever stayed at the Shanghai Jing Jiang Hotel, Madam."

"Jesus, but I know that he's stayed there. Listen for God's sake, will you? His room number is 201. Check again. It's HAYES. BOBBY HAYES. He's tall, over six feet. And blond, very blond. You can't miss him. You just can't miss him . . ."

It was some time before she realised that she was shouting into a telephone that had been hung up on her. Only a tinnitus of electronic hum and buzz breaking up the featureless silence. Counting . . .

SIX . . . SEVEN . . . EIGHT . . .

She sat listening to it for a while, cradled in the heavy swell of duvet and sheet. The questions, the doubts, the informed perceptions, already nagging at her. Wondering. Wondering. Sitting, listening to the ocean of sound. The weave of babble, seeming to take on a voice, a faint voice of its own which seemed to be saying . . .

'BOBBY'S DEAD – BOBBY'S DEAD – BOBBY'S DEAD.'

Counting . . .
NINE . . . TEN.

Chapter 3

They moved south, then east, crossing the Nanpu Bridge . . .
the river, a black and thick cord below. City lights on either
side in a firm vice grip. On the Huangpu itself, nothing. No
life. No movement. A vast ebony axe blow cleaving Shanghai
in two.

Piao drove carefully, slowly, eyes constantly seeking the
rear-view mirror for assurance. The Big Man never knowing
the Boss to drive himself anywhere, not in four years. He
asked no questions, there was no point. There would be no
answers. Hitting Padong Avenue. A high spiking steel forest of
cranes flanking it. A thousand cranes. A thousand foreign cor-
porations staking their claims in the new market economy
zone. Fuelling, being fuelled by the bright economic renais-
sance. Five billion dollars of investment swilling around in the
manic rawness of a frontier town. The Great Leap Forward . . .
the trade and banking centre of the world by 2010. A fairytale
town of a thousand promises; dreams rising into the night sky
in the form of precast concrete towers, studded and pierced
with cold lights. The Senior Investigator shook his head . . .

The making of money, did it have to look so ugly?

Piao stepped out of the wagon, shoe sinking into a pile of
dog shit.

"Fuck it!"

Scraping most of it off against a wire fence that bordered
the edge of a construction site that seemed to have no end. A
jungle of bamboo scaffolding interlaced with strings of dirty
lights. Brown earth gouged to the surface in vast open
wounds. A deep flow of fetid mud water, yellow-edged and
slicked with rainbow oil spills. So tired, but if he'd closed his
eyes he would have still seen their neatly snipped fingers.
Their cracked faces. The dark, empty wells that were once
their eyes. He didn't close his eyes.

He pushed his hand inside the top of Yaobang's passenger window. The fruit of the photographer's dance placed in his palm. Four rolls of one hundred and twenty film, reassuringly large, solid. He pocketed them, a question on his face. The Big Man shook his head. Seven calls and not a hospital, a university, that would take the poor bastards that they had dug from the mud of the Huangpu.

"Fuck it . . ." was all that Piao said again.

Crossing the pontoon of planks to the new telephone box. A brief conversation. Animated, but brief. He was back inside the car before the Big Man had even lit his cigarette. Ten fen poorer, a thousand Yuan happier.

"Your brother . . ." Piao pausing to light his own China Brand from the Big Man's battered lighter.

". . . still at the Institute isn't he?"

"Mmm . . ." Yaobang drawing on the cigarette, his lips kissing at the nicotine clouds.

". . . he's doing a year's research into the human reproductive system. Probably the closest he'll ever get to fucking screwing . . ."

Laughing. A fit of amputated smoke, spit, and tobacco shreds.

". . . he's off to America in three month's time, some exchange programme with a big hospital in New York. Lucky bastard. I hear that American girls do it with the lights on. Doing it in the same fucking building would be enough for me . . ."

Laughing again. Piao pulling on his cigarette, it tasting of everything, but cigarette.

"He obviously knows his stuff."

"Top of the class, a real brainbox. Plenty up there, fuck all down here . . ."

Yaobang grabbed his crotch with both hands, smiling. Singeing his jacket with the furious tip of his cigarette.

"Not like you, eh?"

The Big Man nodded, laugh stalling in confusion. An insult or flattery? He was never sure with the Boss. Removing his hands from his crotch, examining the scorch mark on his jacket. It standing to attention amongst a parade of similar burns.

"Go, telephone him, now. Tell him that we'll pick him up at. Where does he live?"

"The Wenan Road. But why, Boss?"

"One hour, on Xizang Lu. The bridge as it crosses the Wusongjiang."

"But why, what do we want him for?"

The Senior Investigator tossing his half finished cigarette out of the window. Pressing the sweaty five fen aluminium coins into Yaobang's palm.

"Just phone him. And tell him to bring any equipment that he might need for examining a corpse. Is that clear enough for you?"

"But he's got no experience in that field, Boss. He wants to be a fucking gynaecologist."

Piao leant over, pushing open the wagon door. The Big Man asking no more questions. There was no point. He was halfway to the telephone box when the Senior Investigator shouted to him.

"And tell him to keep it to himself. We've found enough bodies in the Huangpu for one week."

Rain was starting to fall. Fine rain, that seemed half-hearted, exhausted, but which somehow managed to drench everything within its reach in a matter of seconds. Yaobang ran the gauntlet of planks, buttocks sluggishly swinging like two drunken sailors slumbering in their hammocks through a storm at sea. He was a large target. By the time that he made it to the telephone box, he was soaked. Mumbling.

"I just hope it's still pissing down when you have to wait for us by the river, little brother . . ."

Mumbling, as the drips ran down his neck. As the dampness soaked through the thin material of his jacket. Mumbling, as he dialled the local number.

The rain stopped the instant that Yaobang had finished the call and had got back into the wagon. Mopping his wide brow with his damp cuff. It depositing more water than it soaked up.

"Fuck it . . ." was all that he said.

★

Yanggao Road skirting the Padong Enterprise Zone, bowed in shadow. The towers, some finished, some not, lining its broken edge. Like dull needles reaching up to full bellied clouds.

"What are your names?"

Piao re-adjusted the rear-view mirror, looking deeply into the interior of the wagon; the question knotted into his eyebrows and aimed at the two PSB officers perched precariously, uncomfortably, on the stacks of caskets. They didn't answer. It was the first time that the Senior Investigator had addressed them since leaving the foreshore of the Huangpu. The Big Man hated silences, like he hated overcooked noodles. Like he hated women with gold front teeth. He answered for them.

"The old dog's Xin, the young puppy's Wenbiao."

Piao stared back to the road, the main artery of this new city . . . ablaze with lights, but devoid of the living of life. Feeling himself grimace as the headlights picked out the verdant glare of a rice paddy squeezed between the scraping range of concrete pinnacles. Ancient and newborn, silently arm-wrestling amongst the heavy machinery and the slosh of dollars.

. . . but workers will always need rice to fuel their labours, to aid us in the Great Leap Forward, to create . . .'

He wondered if words, like paddy fields, had room to breathe in this new age? If they had room to grow from the seed to the fulfilling of their promise? The shadows deepened, and they were in a valley tunnel of darkness.

"You will consider yourselves to be on special assignment. That means that you are answerable to me only. You will discuss nothing that you see. Nothing that you hear. Nothing that you think that relates to this case. Not with anyone. Is that understood?"

He checked the mirror. The PSB officers in the back of the wagon nodding like doggies, signalling their acceptance.

"From now on and until the job is over, I own what you see, what you hear, what you think . . ."

Again his eyes drifted to the rear-view mirror. Again they nodded. Yaobang had done his job well. They seemed to be a good choice. A grizzled old hound, eyes fixed upon his impending pension. Smelling of pipe tobacco and three day old newspapers. And the puppy dog, his mother's breast milk barely off of his lips. Too old and too young for the Security Services or Party activists to have bothered recruiting as informers.

". . . tell no one about this job. No one. Not even your wives."

Xin nodded. Wenbiao raising his hand as if in school, as if wanting to go for a pee.

"I'm not married, Comrade Officer, Sir. I don't even have a girlfriend, well not yet, anyway."

A smile creeping into the corners of his lips, but Piao cutting it adrift as his foot found the accelerator.

"Just as well," he said, and adding in a whisper lost in the drown of engine noise . . . ". . . a dark continent, women. The darkest continent."

★

An urban chameleon.
The venetian blinded towers. Harsh neons scrolling across the windscreen and onto the Senior Investigator's face in a constant shift of primary colours. Piao hated Pudong. He hated Shanghai, but at least you could hate the old whore in a familiar, warm fashion. But this new tart, gaudy lipsticked and spreading her legs across the east bank . . . she could only be hated ice-cold, in a detached way that mirrored her curves of steel and concrete. She didn't belong, but she was going to stay . . . and so fuck you.

He checked his watch, a fake Rolex. The grey base metal peeking out from beneath the worn gold coloured plating, as a nosey neighbour peeks out from the crack between the

31

curtains. Yaobang's brother would be nearing the bridge over the Wusongjiang and the fruit of his own telephone call would be ripening on the branch. Keeping to the back streets, he turned the wagon north.

★

They picked the student, Pan Yaobang, up on the curve of the bridge. He was not like his brother. Skinny, tall, bespectacled . . . a lank bean shoot, to the dumpling that was Detective Yaobang. Smelling different also. Not of a few days stale sweat and sloppily eaten *hundun tang*, the ravioli soup that all PSB Officers appeared to be addicted to, especially during those anonymous hours of patrol that never seemed to quite belong to the night . . . or to the day. No, he smelt only of alien odours. Of fake American trainers. Medical handwash. Freshly laundered jeans. And Coca-Cola lips. On settling into the back of the wagon he had said,

"This is a proper investigation, isn't it? An official matter?"

Yaobang had nearly puked with laughter when his student brother had leapt from the stack of caskets that he had been sitting on, narrowly avoiding a cracked skull on the steel roof of the wagon. The Boss had looked over his shoulder, pointed at the caskets and had replied, simply and with no ceremony.

"It's official. They don't come any more official than this . . ."

And had added, as he filled up the tank with diesel.

". . . we don't normally drive around the city with eight stiffs in the back of the wagon using them as extra seats, unless it's very official."

The student had asked no more questions. The student had insisted on standing . . . standing for the rest of the meandering journey to the *Patuo* of Yangpu and the festering port that scarred its boundary with the river.

★

A slash in the sky, vivid red . . . just above the horizon. The orb of the sun moving through it with the stealth of a street cat. The Senior Investigator watching it as he drove. Watching it, darting between the stop-start of stuttering warehouses and derricks that hugged both sides of the Huangpu for seventeen miles, as far as the point of confluence with the Changjiang, the Long River . . . the mighty Yangtze.

Dark now, Piao taking the wagon once more past the old warehouse. Only when he was certain that the shadows hid no other shadows, darker shadows, did he pull into the cobbled alleyway. A giant lattice of light thrown onto the yellowed brickwork as the headlights swung, piercing the heavy wrought iron gates. Three bursts of full beam, the walls of the warehouse seeming to rush out . . . a door in the corner of the loading bay opening. A man jumping down, sprinting to the gate, prising open one side of it before running back and leaping onto the apron of the loading bay. Piao drove in, swinging the wagon around, backing into one of the many bays. The man now pulling on a length of chain. Each heave, each arch of his back, the metal wall of the loading bay inching up. A wall of light, blinding white, replacing it. Xin and Wenbiao throwing open the wagon's back doors. The student bumping his head as he aimlessly wandered from the wagon and into the pool of arc-light. Squinting down at his trainers and weighed down by the two kit-bags that he was carrying. A throaty cough. The reek of spent gas filled the bay; the man now on a forklift, features sharply defined in knife-edge hard light. Narrow lipped. A single dark line of eyes screwed together. Rubber in a scream, as he wheeled the forklift violently around towards the pallet being loaded with caskets.

"Out of the way . . . out of the way."

The student, Pan, jumping to the side. The ungainly machine swinging into his path. Lifts slicing, skiing into position under the pallet of four caskets. Breaking the light . . . stilts of elongated shadow as it plunged into the interior of the warehouse. Piao and Yaobang stood out of the way, by the cab of the wagon.

"Who's the fucking monkey?"

The Big Man nodded his head toward the forklift, its butt shedding hard form to bruised hues of near white. Climbing onto the bay, the Senior Investigator stared beyond the gate, into the alleyway. Eyes narrowing. Shadows had fled, cobbles glinting dully in the floodlit barrage. Scales of the Dragon lighting a path to their door.

"Might as well place a fucking advertisement," he breathed.

"Sorry, Boss, what was that?"

Holding out a hand, Piao hauled the Detective onto the loading bay . . . thinking of carcasses of pork, sides of beef.

"I said that the 'fucking monkey' is my cousin . . ."

"Shit, sorry Boss, I didn't know, he doesn't look like you."

". . . my cousin on my mother's side."

Deep waters. Difficult waters. Yaobang excused himself, helping the others to load the remaining caskets onto an empty pallet.

The window that was set into the back of the wagon door was caked in dust, distorted, a crack running from the top left-hand corner . . . still, Piao could make out his features and recognize that they were not Chinese. Clearly, not a full breed. The rounded eyes, irises of beach-ball blue. The slim, sharp nose. The skin that was far too pink, far too white, to be rooted purely in Chinese ancestry. His father's features. Piao spat on the ground. His father's . . . a burst of brash American genes pushing aside a few hundred generations of Chinese. So easily pushed aside. Hardly a trace of his mother. Inherited only, the gifts, the curses of a diplomat on a long and unsecured leash. A sky-blue-eyed horny 'Yank', let loose in the candy store of no responsibility. No accountability. Stuffing himself with all that had been denied to him before. Was he, the disjointed reflection in the rear window of the wagon, still the sorry result of the union even after all of these years? Just the trail of vomit from someone who had fed for too long at the table?

Shame, it brands, it eats as a cancer does. Shame, a meal that not even a crow would choose. Piao kicked the wagon's doors closed, following the second pallet of caskets into the shower of floodlight.

★

The Yangpu Bridge Import Export Meat Corporation.

The vast interior of the warehouse . . . four rows of stainless steel benches that stretched for almost its full length. Running above each of them, a track, a carousel of meat hooks that would take the freshly slaughtered animal carcasses from man to man. Process to process. Bleeding. Gutting. Cleaning out with high pressure hoses. Boning. Dressing. Portioning. Before entering the packing department at the very rump of the warehouse. Beyond that, the river and the empty refrigerated cargo belly of a waiting ship. Blood and waste, byproducts of the butchering, would be sluiced from the narrow gutters that edged each side of the lengthy runs of benches. Also from the floor. Flowing, half liquid, half solid, into the large grates that led into down pipes. It running unimpeded, straight into the Huangpu River below. During a busy period, the New Year, Labour Day, or the Lantern and Dragon Boat Festivals . . . the waters of the Huangpu around the warehouse would be red. Day and night . . . red.

★

"There, put them on the centre bench."

Xin moaning as he eased his back into the work. Wenbiao lifting the bodies. Averted eyes. Trying to hold his breath, clamp his nostrils tight. Across sheets of polythene, smeared blood. Small pools of piss coloured river water. And then the smell as they were unwrapped. A smell that had been lost in the thick mud of the foreshore, the coldness of the river, but which now lived . . . sweet, bitter, earthy. A smell that sat at each end of a life, like book ends. A smell of birth. A smell of death.

Laying the polythene over the stainless steel bench. The bodies over the polythene. Toe to head. Toe to head. Toe to head. Eight times. Eight caricatures of the human form. Forty-four feet of humanity holed, laid to waste.

Somebody's babies. Somebody's children.

Piao spat into the gutter, taking a breath, deep, long. It had a taste, a reek, a signature of every death that he had ever stood over. There was no escape; the laid out bodies assaulted every single sense. Holding everyone in the warehouse in an almost hypnotic grip. No escape.

A throb of anger purred in the furthest backdrop of his hearing. He couldn't understand it. Did he really care about these broken bodies or was it just time to lift his head out of the sea of shit that he had been drowning in for all of these years? Time to make a stand? He wasn't sure. Not knowing, it made it even worse.

At least you should know why you are committing suicide. At least you should know why?

Tea . . . sweet, strong. Its bouquet brushing death from his nostrils. He reached out for the mug. Mao's face, scratched, fading, but still beaming, staring back at him from beneath the pin-holed glaze. Piao turned the mug around, his eyes focussing through the veil of steam on the student bracing himself against a worn, bare brick, blood-spattered wall.

"It's all yours . . ."

He nudged Mao's face towards the eight. Tea running down his fingers.

"Now?"

The Senior Investigator could see fear's brand in the dryness of the student Pan's lips. The dart of his eyes. The warm, pungent keynotes that now highlighted his smell.

". . . within the next week would be convenient. They're not going anywhere, but we do need to know about them . . ."

Drinking from the Mao mug, long and deep. The tea was too sweet, far too sweet. This was not a time for tea that was too sweet.

". . . and there are murderers to be caught and dealt with."

Another lick of his lips. Another glance, furtive, rabbit-like, over Piao's shoulder towards the bodies.

Shit . . . they're his first. He's never seen a stiff before.

"I thought that there was only one. My brother told me one."

"No, no, there are definitely eight. But just think of it as being one. One, but eight times. So don't look down the line, just concentrate on the one you're dealing with at that time. It's a lesson that I learnt a long time ago . . ."

"They don't teach us police psychology and training methods at the University."

". . . they don't teach us police psychology and training methods in the police. I learnt it when I was a cashier in my uncle's restaurant near Yichuan Park. Friday nights were fist fights and plates of fried noodles being thrown everywhere. My uncle would drum it into the top of my head with his best bone chopsticks . . . 'look at the cash register and the customer's money. The cash register and the money. Nothing else.'"

The student attempted a smile. It didn't work.

"But I have no experience. I have never examined someone who is dead before. I'm training to be a gynaecologist."

"Yes, your brother did mention it in passing. Okay, they're dead, but it can't be that different from examining the living. And look on the bright side, at least you won't get any complaints about your cold hands, will you?"

Piao, one arm around his shoulder, shepherded him toward the run of benches. Rivulets of brown-red water running from flesh to plastic to steel gutter.

"Detective Yaobang, get your brother a tea. It's the very least that we can do for our new police forensic scientist."

Walking the length of the bodies; moon crater knuckles whitening to bone as the student carried his kit-bags. The Senior Investigator taking Pan's hands into his own. Straightening the fingers, releasing the bags onto the bench as they stopped. So gently, the toes of the last body brushing against the imitation leather. The bright gold zip. Piao undid both bags, unpacking their contents. Towels, handwash, a pack of surgical gloves, a rolled-up wallet of surgical steel tools: scalpels, probes, clamps . . . a small torch, microscope slides, a large magnifying glass, a wad of self-sealing plastic bags, thermometers, sterilising fluid, swabs. But mostly books filling the kit-bags. Thick, well leafed tomes. Volumes on human anatomy. Forensic science. Thinner, less well leafed books on the study of changes after death. The calculation of the time of death . . . cooling, putrefaction, rigor mortis, cutis anserina, cadaveric spasm, lividity. Death, and its slalom through a universe of post–mortem events. All served up in black print on white sheet . . . so clinical. Not a body, not a run of skin anywhere within the books. Not a smell. Not a drip of stinking blood-tinged water.

"Impressive for a first timer. Wu used to get by on a therm-ometer, a pair of tweezers, a plastic bag, and a spare pair of socks . . ."

The student attempting another smile; it came into the world as a grimace. Piao walked over to the small office.

". . . just do your best. Try to give us some idea of the causes of death. Times of death. Some idea of their ages. Per-haps nationalities. Maybe even the sorts of lifestyles that they might have led . . ."

The Senior Investigator walked over to the small office . . . hard wooden chairs and discoloured walls. Looking for a re-fill of tea. Changing mugs. Placing Mao, beaming face to the grey wall, and swapping it for a mug with a view of Hong Kong imprisoned behind bars of streaky tannin stains.

". . . seeing death rots your soul. None of us ever get used to it, no matter what we might say . . ."

Taking a deep mouthful of tea.

". . . it's only that there are murderers to be caught that makes it bearable. That stops you from constantly wanting to throw up. So think of the murderers, that always helps . . ."

Another deep gulp of tea. Wondering why the second mug always tastes better than the first?

". . . just think of the fucking murderers."

★

River mud falling away. The clay dolls awakening. Yaobang's large hand diverting the jet of water, calming it. The cascade making clear the obscured, almost like a full moon slipping from between thick cloud cover.

Features perfect, features imperfect. A jaw that had been square, demanding. Proud, once beautifully defined cheek-bones. Eyebrows tapering to delicate brushstrokes. Hair, midnight black, set free and feathering an unlined forehead. A shadow of stubble. A pimple. A beauty spot. The pale ghosting stripe of an old scar.

And the mutilations.

Piao following the student, the student following the Big Man from body to body . . . to body. Yaobang muttering again and again, and again.

"Mother. Mother. Mother," as the waterfall from his hand unveiled the horrors. The horrors.

The student moving to the first body, slowly. The first body. Slowly.

No one ever runs to their first body.

His hands clammy. The first pair of surgical gloves splitting. Fastidiously smoothing a second pair on. Then cleaning his glasses. Anything that would dine upon the seconds, the minutes.

Not wanting to start . . . never wanting to start.

Another chorus from the Big Man. A tremble to his lips . . . as the water cleanses, unmasks, baptises the deep valley of wounds.

"Mother. Mother. Mother."

The Senior Investigator pulled out his notebook.

Ignore them. Ignore them. Look past it all. Concentrate on the small things. The things that seem to blend in, that seem normal, but which jar . . . nag. The little things that murderers have no time for. Seemingly less significant than fingerprints, faces, eyes, teeth, but just as telling. Don't forget . . . a murder for a murderer is just a means to an end, a signpost on the way to a final destination. His eyes already focussed on that distant horizon even as he went about the killing. Wielding the knife. The club hammer. The cutters. So, do not look for the big things. Look for the small things . . . they will be there.

A fresh page in Piao's notebook. The first heading . . .

HUANGPU 1 . . . H1.

H1 . . . FEMALE. ORIENTAL. AGE APPROX: 25. HEIGHT 5' 6".

Hair to just above shoulder, expensively cut. Attractive, good figure. Well-groomed. Eyebrows plucked. Ears pierced. Toenails painted (red), pedicured. No body hair. Tattoo on rear left shoulder (butterfly) . . . new, unfaded. Hands, knees . . . soft. No signs of manual labour. I think she's foreign. Database checks . . . Luxingshe. Also, CTS & OCTS. Visa, internal travel permit checks with foreign department. She could be a FIT. Check CITS. Known to Bureau Six?

H2 . . . MALE. ORIENTAL. AGE APPROX: *23.* HEIGHT 5' 8".
Hair, close-cropped. Newly cut, untidily cut . . . scissor or razor nicks to back of neck and top of left ear. Ex-user. Old track marks, collapsed veins in left and right forearms. One inch diameter birthmark on front of right shoulder. Three inch scar running above pubic area. Hernia operation? Army/Ex-offender. PSB database checks. Also, check with Mai Lin Hua, municipal prison releases.

On the periphery of Piao's vision, the student tiptoeing around the bench. Around the female, H1. A thermometer in his fingers. At last, pushing it deeply into the victim's rectum . . .

H3 . . . MALE. EUROPOID. AGE APPROX: 27. HEIGHT 6' 0".
Hair, blond. Wavy, shoulder-length. Athletic build. Muscular. The remains of a brace in his mouth. Must be American. Only an American would be confident enough to wear a brace on his teeth at 27! No scars . . . but several deep scratches over both forearms. Tanned face/tanned arms up to four inches above the elbows. Tanned legs to just above both knees. Elbows, knees . . . skin worn, callused. Rough skin and calluses also to both palms and what is left of the fingers. Must have been working outside all summer to get a tan like that. Construction? Too young to be an architect on a major project . . . Surveyor? Stone mason?
Check Luxingshe/CTS. Visa & internal travel permits . . . check on foreigners working on building projects. So blond . . . he'd stand out in a crowd, won't be hard to trace. Also check with Bureau Six.

. . . the thermometer eased from the rectum and cleaned with an anti-septic wipe. Held up against the light, the silver-black rise of the mercury level being sought for a reading, a 'peak of probability'; an estimate of the hour of death. With each span of sixty minutes, the bodies temperatures dropping by one point five degrees Celsius. Remember the water of the Huangpu, so cold . . . and so double the rate of cooling. Remember their nakedness, so cold . . . cooling when naked is half as fast again as when clothed. To the touch, they would have felt cold within five to six hours. By eight to ten hours their body temperatures would have fallen to the same as the environment in which they had been found. As icy-cold, as one with the muddy waters of the Huangpu.

H4 ... MALE. ORIENTAL. AGE APPROX: 40–45. HEIGHT 5' 3".
Balding . . . remainder of hair shaved short. Dragon tattoo on left forearm. Scars encircling both wrists/ankles. Prison/Asylum. Political? Check as H2.

H5 ... MALE. ORIENTAL. AGE APPROX: 29. HEIGHT 5' 9".
Shoulder-length hair/tinted brown highlights. Small scar splitting right eyebrow. Tattoos on both upper and lower arms. Right arm, top to bottom . . . a knife piercing a snake, an anchor and rope, a name (Zheng), four Xiangqi pieces, Ma and Pao. Left arm, top to bottom . . . Golden Dragon, a dagger through a Heart, four Xiangqi pieces, ju and jiang . . . a name (Yeman?). Not a user. Check PSB Foreign Department. Also CTS / OCTS. Seaman . . . merchant, fishing? Check arrivals from Hong Kong.

Latex fingers brushing torn lips. A nervous probe hovering over broken ranges of teeth, occasionally picking at the debris. Counting. Assessing. Measuring for wear. Probing in the hope of finding some exotic dental technique that will mark these teeth apart. Some odontological calling card that will wink and point the direction in which to travel. Transferring, with a weak, shaky hand, the mayhem of a clubbing hammer to the ordered progression of a dental chart . . .

H6 ... MALE. ORIENTAL. AGE APPROX: 30–35. HEIGHT 5' 6".

Prison haircut, short-cropped, two inch scar to back of cranium, centrally positioned. Face severely damaged. Another scar running down the bridge of the nose. Past user . . . old tracks and collapsed veins on left forearm. Right earlobe missing. Check as H2/H4.

H7 ... MALE. EUROPOID. AGE APPROX: 45. HEIGHT 5' 10".

Hair brown, greying to sides. Cut to collar length. Overweight . . . out of condition. Tanned (see also H3). Hands, knees, elbows . . . callused. White witness marks of three rings having been removed from right hand. Pressure marks to bridge of nose and behind both ears/spectacle user. Old scar, three inches, running down left shin bone. Faint scar running behind both ears . . . cosmetic surgery? Visa/Travel permit checks with Luxingshe. Also CTS & OCTS. Similar to H3 . . . working here? Could be a FIT. Double check with CITS.

. . . the breakdown of ATP after death. The quantity of adenosine phosphate increasing. Both lactates and phosphates accumulating in increasing amounts. Physical changes developing in the muscles as the fibres shorten, stiffen. The muscles becoming prominent, rigid . . . fixing the limbs. Rigor mortis . . . muscles now set in place by the flood of lactates; ten times more than is found resting in the muscles in life. Remember the water of the Huangpu. So cold. Remember their nakedness . . . so cold. The onset of rigor would have been retarded, slowed . . . the bodies of the eight retaining their flexibility for longer. But as the night comes . . . so would rigor have come. Firstly starting in the face at around ten hours. During, the next five hours, spreading to the shoulders, the arms. Finally to slip into the bulky leg muscles. At twenty hours, rigor fully established . . . not passing from the victim for up to four days.

The girl's face. Set. Her neck, shoulders and arms also fixed by rigor mortis. Down her trunk to her long legs, still flexible and unfixed. Fifteen to twenty hours; she'd been dead fifteen to twenty hours.

H8 ... MALE. ORIENTAL. AGE APPROX: 25. HEIGHT 5' 6".

Hair, cropped. Multiple scars to both wrists ... looks like several suicide attempts over a lengthy period ... Tattoo on top of right hand ... two swords crossed through a name (Shen?) Multiple razor cuts to backs of legs & buttocks. Self-harming? Full Luxingshe check. Also prisons/asylums/camps.

Piao passed on the coffee, preferring another sweet tea. Coffee, so American, so easy, so artless.

Stirring the tea. Watching the swirl of the liquid slow. Drinking. Some cases need you to be in touch with your most intangible thoughts. Tuned in, zipped to your feelings. Able to stop, put them in a hard place and prick them ... see if they bleed. And how they bleed. This was such a case.

Nothing was left in the tea mug except for a slick of black leaf powder. Piao placed the cup on the steel bench, aware that perceptions were starting to form. Seeing the eight in a new way. Not as eight at all, but as two quite distinctive groups of four. H2, H4, H6 & H8 ... inmates, still stinking of the prison, asylum, and of the corrective camps. Stinking of slopped out shit and the lightning flash of the razor down your buttocks in the shower. Its icy cut beading into a stream of blood running down your legs. Stinking of underpants that a hundred men before you had worn and soiled.

H1, H3, H5, H7 ... something that the Senior Investigator could not put his finger on, yet.

A girl who seemed Chinese only in the way a fake piece of Ming Dynasty Baoshihong 'bulls blood' porcelain is Chinese. The two westerners, most probably Americans. Their lives, secrets, and their deaths ... written in the Braille of calluses on the palms of their hands. And a Chinese. A Shanghainese most probably. The type that Piao could have seen on any of the crossroads along the Nanjing Road. A face that would always have been half in, half out of the shadows. The dragon of the illicit dollar breathing in his belly. A fake branded cologne over-lavishly applied to a neck stuffed into too small a collar. A wide boy. A conman . . . 'a stomach with two hands attached.'

Piao paced the office, slowly, deliberately . . . the leash short, for those who think too much. Stopping at the open door. A view, uninterrupted, to the warehouse floor. The benches. The bodies. Something binding these unlikely four together. Some glue that was strong enough, powerful enough, to hold these individuals in check for a single purpose. Holding them in life, causing their death . . . and still holding their secret in safe hands. And the quartet with their prison cropped hair, what was the common denominator that stood at the base of their equation?

Pacing again, the leash pulled tight. Chokingly tight. And these two groupings, what, besides death and chains, bound them together? That welded four with a prison pallor to four with a mocha tan. That welded four bearing the trademarks of abuse, to four with the hallmarks of the pampered. Piao knowing of only one such powerful flux, which came in the form of crisp green notes. Lots of crisp green notes.

Eight murders had to be worth a river full of them.

★

"I'm going, cousin Cheng. I need some sleep and then some time to try and sort out this mess . . . talk to my Chief. I also need a permanent home for these bodies. You don't want them cluttering up your warehouse, mixing them up with the pork carcasses."

The cousin smiled, displaying a grim set of teeth, but a brightness of eye that was enviable.

"I'm glad that you came to me for help, Sun Piao. It has been a long time, Chen and I have not seen you for a year now, not since Lingling left. The children miss you . . ."

Piao feeling the pain that was always present, press home. The Senior Investigator just two more words away from crying. Not daring to speak. The cousin seeing the hole of pain open up, filling it swiftly with more words.

". . . come and see us soon, for dinner. The children would love it, so would Chen. Besides, I have a case load of French

44

wine that swam over from one of the ships. It needs a dent putting in it, and I cannot think of anyone better at denting a case of wine than you."

"I'd love to, really. I'd love to. But you might not want to invite me for dinner after this investigation bursts open."

Piao's eyes moving across in the direction of the bodies. The eight. The cousin's following; a thousand questions to ask, but knowing that they would be blocked by the Senior Investigator. Frozen out of existence, probably for his own good. Cheng placed his arm around Piao's shoulder. The comfort almost unbearable.

"Nonsense. Family is family. Politics is politics and should be treated as such and flushed down the lavatory with the other shit . . ."

The swell of pain had peaked, ebbed. The Senior Investigator smiled.

". . . I have friends high up in the local Party machinery. If they can be of any help, Sun? I've even got a contact in the Politburo who is partial to a side of beef . . ."

The Senior Investigator fell silent. But the look, the look . . . Cheng knew it well, seeing it every day in the slaughterhouse just the instant before the hammer stunned. Just before the gentle stroke of the knife across the warm throat of the animal. Just before the blood flowed.

". . . shit. It's that bad, is it? You think that their death is . . ."

"Look, I must go, cousin. Send my love to Chen and the children. I'd love to dent that wine with you, but not yet, eh? Let me get the worst of this case out of the way."

"If you need any help, Sun Piao . . ."

But the Senior Investigator had already turned, walked . . . not looking back, not wanting to give any indication that he had heard his cousin's last words.

The student Pan was still examining the girl. Eyes welded to the gaping wound that now seemed the focus of all that she had been and now was.

"Stay until he's finished . . ."

The Big Man nodded as Piao passed, his shadow cast out

over the loading bay and across the mosaic of cobbles outside. Yaobang shifted his weight, the fibreglass casket that he was sitting astride, whimpering. Pulling the food bowl tighter to his greasy lips. Fried noodles, slipping into his mouth with chopsticks that never rested.

". . . my cousin will show you where the cold store is. Put the bodies in there . . ."

He nodded again. Chopsticks weaving.

". . . and then get off home. Take your brother and Xin with you, drop them off. My cousin and young Wenbiao will stay until I can sort something out with Chief Liping . . ."

Nodding again. Noodles from his mouth, hanging. Resembling New Year's decorations after the party has finished.

". . . I'll get a few hours sleep and then try to track Liping down."

The Big Man nodded again, lowering the bowl from his face. Inside his mouth, a scene of carnage. Open cast mining.

"The Chief's got a big place out on Taihu, hasn't he, Boss? Something to do with his cousin, the Minister."

"Fuck knows. He's never invited me for tea. He prefers to sip with higher ranking cadres."

"Only swims with the big fish comrades, eh Boss?"

The Big Man's words a dagger. Piao's thoughts flashing to Beijing. To sleek black cars. To a woman lost, a wife . . . her face, fast receding. And with it the pain. As fast as a songbird for the open door of the cage and as clawingly tenacious as a beggar who has seen the thickness of the wallet.

"The ocean that Liping swims in is full of big fish. Big fish, big shark, big turds."

Yaobang disgorged a half eaten mouthful of noodle back into his bowl as he laughed. The Senior Investigator could see his tongue, similar to a slab of city paving-stone littered with the detritus of modern day living. Laugh exhausted, the Big Man raised the bowl once more to his lips, continuing to push the noodles into the fleshy crusher of his mouth.

"Good noodles?"

"You fucking bet, Boss."

"Then I'll leave you to them, and Yaobang . . ."

"What's that, Boss?"

". . . don't forget the ones on your shirtfront and in your top pocket."

The Big Man pawed at the partially stiff ribbons with his stubby sausage fingers, grinning as he lowered them onto his tongue.

As he walked onto the loading bay, wincing at the light, the Senior Investigator swore that he would never eat another noodle again.

★

The Shanghai Forever Bicycle Company Limited produces three and a half million bicycles a year. A flood of chrome and tinkling bells that tidal wave onto the streets and avenues as the factories call the worshipful to the high altar of the new economic miracle. Gridlocking the city's arteries. In America they call the very same bicycles *Wind Catchers*. A romantic, heroic name . . . one of speed, space, freedom. In Shanghai reality roosts unchallenged, naked, devoid of romance or heroism. In Shanghai they are just called *Forever Bicycles*.

★

Daytime now . . . a sun, netted and unstruggling in a gauze of fog. Hauled across a city that seemed unprepared, ill at ease with itself. As if it were waiting for something. As if it wanted to, but couldn't quite sneeze.

Piao sat in a taxi marooned in amongst a sea of bright wheels and busy bells as the shoals of bicycles swept against the current, stalling all else. He swore . . . the driver who he was trapped with, ignoring him and continuing to sort out the problems of the People's Republic right there and then. Talk, incessant. Tinkling bells, incessant. An hour and a half to travel a handful of grubby miles. Stopping briefly to drop off the clutch of one hundred and twenty roll films for an urgent D&P at an out of the way back-street photographer's.

When the taxi driver woke him with a rough nudge to the shoulder, the bicycles had bled into the day with a shrug of quicksilver; the problems of the People's Republic still remained; and he was home.

★

A year now, over a year . . . but still Piao expected to see an envelope waiting for him on the floor. An envelope with a Beijing postmark and bearing the delicate curves and feints of once familiar writing. No letter was there. It happened every time, and every time he failed to learn.

In a city where the average living space for a citizen is little larger than a double bed, the flat was spacious. A living room. A kitchen. A bathroom. Two bedrooms. Too large for one. One . . . the space, oceans of loneliness. Leaving him with a constant sense of drowning. There was a photograph placed face down on the shelf beside the bed. The Senior Investigator picked it up. His arms encircling a woman. Small, so delicate. Protecting her as if she might break. Pretty? No, pretty was not the word that would come to mind. An edge, a coldness to her face that would banish such a word. But she was beautiful. Beautiful in the same sort of fashion that a cityscape can be said to be beautiful. An almond shaped face set in a frame of shining ebony hair, slightly tilted away from his embrace. Lips of a painted porcelain doll, almost too perfect to expect to kiss. And eyes that took no prisoners. Black, just black . . . their mid-tones sent running. Strange that he felt no anger. No bitterness. He still loved her. It was the worst and most useless dregs to be left with. He placed the photograph back onto the shelf, face down, and began to make his phone calls. It was Saturday. Everything came with a hefty price attached to it. Eventually tracking down Chief Liping's private secretary. A woman of few words. Lemon sucking lips. Guarded thoughts. And with breasts as cold, as comforting as anvils. Chief Liping was out of the city, she would attempt to contact him, although it might take some time.

Don't hurry yourself you bitch . . . it's only eight citizens that have been fucking slaughtered in the People's Republic.

She would call the Senior Investigator back. He walked into the kitchen, pulling a Tsingtao from the refrigerator. The beer, warm to the touch. As warm as tears. How was it that the Shanghai Xin Zhong Hua Machinery Factory could build one hundred and forty foot high Long March rockets that flipped satellites into orbit around the Earth, and yet also build refrigerators that failed miserably when attempting to chill a bottle of beer? The lager bit at the back of his throat. As smooth as razors. It was good. It would have been even better chilled. The beer beckoned tiredness. A wave of exhaustion that would not be denied. Sleep claiming him within minutes. The Tsingtao bottle falling from his grasp and onto the carpet, the remainder of golden lager forming a small puddle that slowly seeped away.

★

The telephone rang. He had slept for two and a half hours, seeming like two and a half minutes. He swivelled off the bed to answer it, instantly awake. Standing on the beer-soaked carpet.

"Shit. Shit."

Kicking at the spent bottle, sending it spinning into the hallway. Pulling off his sock. Dropping the telephone.

"Senior Investigator Piao, Comrade Officer Chief Liping has re-arranged his schedule and will see you in three hours time. A car will be with you in fifteen minutes."

The line went dead. Piao dried his foot with the bed sheet.

"And a nice fucking day to you too . . ." he said.

Chapter 4

She was a shaker, a mover . . . not used to shitted-up bureau-cratic machinery. Rarely, and only rarely, did she come across it in the vast swathe of responsibility that seemed to sit so easily upon her narrow shoulders. When she did come across it, she squirted her own unique brand of freeing oil into the situation. Sometimes laced with the charisma and easy long legged sex appeal that came so naturally to her. Other times, veined with the unstoppable energy and destructive power of a whirlwind.

Dealing with the Chinese Embassy, updating visas and requesting internal travel permits, simple issues . . . had proved to be a harrowing experience for her. She was powerless. Her last words at the end of her final fruitless assault upon the Chinese Embassy had been simple and to the point. Instead of the '. . . and fuck you too . . .' that some of her colleagues might have used, she had simply said . . . 'peace with honour and not peace with surrender.' Feeling quite confident in using Nixon's famous words of October '72. If a President could use them to heave America out of a war in which their butts had been kicked from Saigon to Yonkers, surely she needed no justification in using them to step out of a personal bureaucratic fire fight with some Chinese official who had more regulations in his head than brain cells. She rested her case, but still minus the visas and permits.

★

"Don't go . . ."

"I have to."

". . . put it off until the meeting in Beijing. The fuss about Bobby can wait. You know what he's like, it's probably nothing."

Barbara leant across his desk. So close. Her choice of per-

50

fume, immaculate. Carmichael would be dizzy with it. His favourite . . . Opium. And his eyes behind the oversize Yves St Laurent frames, they would be looking down the cream silk vee of her blouse at her tits. It would be a morning of pleasant sensations for him . . . even if his sexuality was as unpredictable as the Nasdaq.

"I have to go. Till now I've always put meetings, primaries, lecture tours, elections first. But this time I can't wait . . ."

She leaned even further forward. Her cheek almost bruising his. A whisper.

". . . this time I can't let him wait."

"But the groundwork for the next round of the Beijing negotiations, they're critical. The concessions that you want us to make, they've only just been approved. And what about the UN position? There will have to be some tough talking and private arrangements made."

Political words. Diplomatic words. Words for reports. Perfumed, preened words.

The reality. Tough talking . . . threats, pressure, intimidation, blackmail.

The reality. Private arrangements . . . bribes, backhanders, hookers, holidays, cars.

She pulled away, smiling that smile.

"And who better when it comes to tough talking, and even better when it comes to private arrangements, than you."

"Uh-uh . . . no way. No way."

Hearing them so often over the years, Carmichael's 'noes'. But hearing them now for what they really were . . . not so much 'no', as, 'so what do I get out of it?' Raising her hand, pale and crimson tipped. Always reminding him of Five Little Fishes.

"Whoa. Whoa. I'll owe you big. Very big. Do the groundwork and fixing of the concessions for the next round of talks, plus, cover my arse for me while I'm away, and we'll talk about it."

He removed his glasses, cleaning them. Delicately. Precisely. Eyes, a third of the size that they seemed to be when he was actually wearing the thick lenses. Tiny eyes. She had often wondered how he managed to see anything with such tiny eyes.

"You'll owe me?"

"And you'll have to fix my travel plans and documentation for Beijing. Their Embassy is giving me a really lousy time . . ."

"You'll owe me big?"

". . . keep it at a really low level. Call it just a personal trip. Play it down. Preferably, don't play it at all . . ."

"And we'll talk about it?"

". . . certainly will, especially if you can get me that shopping list of concessions that have been approved by the Whitehouse."

Carmichael replaced his glasses. Eyes instantly expanding by two thirds, his gaze averted from hers.

"You realise that this could all be connected, don't you? The talks. Bobby disappearing . . ."

She picked up her attaché case, ignoring his words. Forcing her attentions beyond the glazed confines of the office to the concrete and glass horizon melting to apricot.

". . . connected. Linked. How can you separate them? If the worst came to the worst, how could you ever separate them? Being a government official. Being a mother . . ."

The horizon, glinting like smashed safety glass.

"When it comes to it, if it comes to it, I'll know how to do the right thing . . ." she replied through cigarette smoke.

". . . I'll always do the right thing . . ."

She stubbed the butt out in the heavy glass ashtray. A single band of smoke rising, unbroken, like a sword blade across her face.

". . . now just do the shopping and leave the balance between politics and motherhood to me."

Carmichael adjusted his spectacles, his mouth as tight as a crack.

"Consider your shopping done, Barbara."

He was already dialling an out of state number as she moved to the door. A New York code . . . a contact at the UN.

His next call would be to the People's Republic's Embassy for a visa and internal travel documents. The call after that, to fix her flight. He was efficient. She had better start packing her case. She left his office, caffeine, nicotine, alcohol . . . calling her. None of which would have interested Carmichael; he was only a perrier on the rocks and waldorf salad sort of a guy. Hitting the interstate running, in a full flowing growl of confined and velour caged road rage. Tapping the steering wheel to an anonymous rhythm . . . its Morse posing her questions that she didn't want asked and couldn't answer. Didn't want to answer.

    . . . I'll always do the right thing . . .

    The right thing . . . but for whom?

★

Within two days she would be in the People's Republic of China. A visa . . . a bleeding red-inked sore at the very heart of her passport. On an unofficial visit. A personal visit. The most personal of visits to the only goddamn thing in her life that lay distanced, untouched by slur and backroom dealings. Untainted by the wash from fast-track political careers and dirt-digging. Family. Blood. Her son . . . Bobby. It was all that she had that was truly hers. Only recently understanding how her own needs and career had robbed Bobby of her for so long. How he had always been secondary to her driving ambition. Second, always coming second. A long way from home, but now he was first. Her son Bobby had her all to himself. At last, she was doing the right thing.

Chapter 5

She was surprised, expecting her first nibbles of China to be flavoured with rows of ordered queues and a sea of faded bluey-grey Mao jackets. She was wrong. Hongqiao Airport had the liveliness, the chaotic bustle of Kennedy on a snowbound Saturday. The terminal throwing wave after wave of faces at her . . . all seeming to have been peeled from the same mould. Tight-eyed. High cheekboned. She suddenly felt very tall. Very blonde. Very female. Struggling with her cases. Tugging at her too short skirt to lower it. Buttoning her blouse higher. Aware of her legs. Her hair. Her breasts. Her skin. Reminding herself of Marilyn in . . . 'Some Like It Hot.' Lazy glances. Studied stares. Without exception, every eye examining her. In D.C, New York, Dallas . . . she relished it. But here she felt as if every eye was a pin, and she the pincushion. She moved out of the terminal. A row of taxis jockeying for position in the periphery of her vision. Fat, angry meat-flies staking their portion of the action. She joined the queue, ushered to the front of it by a flurry of flapping hands. The air heavy with the smell of aviation fuel, old people, and rain about to fall. Stuttering into the taxi, manhandling the cases in front of her.

Damn it, I've brought too much. I always bring too much.

Skirt riding high above her knees. Lines of eyes with permanent questions riveted to their irises, following her every move as if she were a new and exotic spectator sport. "The Jing Jiang Hotel please."

The taxi pulled away. She settled into the plastic covered seat for the journey into the city's heart. Fifteen kilometres. The banner over the driver's head proclaiming the name of

54

the company whose taxi it was that she was driving in . . . the *'FRIENDSHIP TAXI SERVICE.'* It didn't feel very friendly. The driver's stare into the rear-view mirror not leaving her for the whole of the fifteen kilometres.

★

The main entrance of the Jing Jiang Hotel sits opposite a row of shops, the most exclusive in China. Amongst these is a supermarket that sells some rare treats . . . chocolate, cheeses, biscuits. Day and night there is a permanent queue at the checkout . . . such is the hunger.

★

It took all of her strength not to go over the same territory again. Not to grab the demure white bloused receptionist and haul her over the desk . . .

Where's my goddamn son, you bitch. What have you done to him?

And if an answer had not been forthcoming, which it would not have been, to do the same to the deputy manager. Then the general manager. And then the fucking shit of an owner, if she had thought that it would have done any good. But that had already been done verbally from many thousands of miles away; and on several occasions since the night when Bobby's name had javelined into the depths of her sleep . . . splitting her life away from all that it had previously been anchored to. She and Carmichael, bombarding the hotel with calls. Prodding. Probing. Slicing away at every polite response to their questions. Digging for an inaccuracy. Words . . . pinned. Sentences . . . dissected. Silences . . . analysed. Pressure, and a contact of Carmichael's at the China International Travel Service, resulting in the faxing of the Jing Jiang's guest registration book. Pages. Pages. Fifteen months of recordings. Room 201 had been busy, it was located in the prestigious north block, the preferred area of the hotel by those in the know; often frequented by dignitaries. Nixon in February of '72. Reagan, some twelve years later. But no Bobby Hayes. His name not appearing on the registration pages for room

201. His name not appearing next to any room number in the hotel. He had never stayed at the Jing Jiang, but Barbara could recall almost every telephone call that she had made to Bobby at that very same hotel. 53–42–42. Knowing the number by heart.

Approaching the desk, hand deep inside her raincoat pocket, fingers drumming against the thick wad of letters, postcards. Some written on headed hotel notepaper. Some bearing the hotel's name, its logo, stamped, black inked across dismal postage stamps. Words. Sentences. Descriptions of the Jing Jiang. His room. His view from the room. Flows of frantic scrawl. And still they said that Bobby had not stayed at the hotel whose lobby she was now standing in.

★

"Welcome to the Shanghai Jing Jiang Hotel, madam. How may I help you?"

Her English too perfect, as it had been over the telephone. Clipped. Polished. Cold. Perfect words, leaving her mouth as ice cubes.

"A reservation was made for me under the name of Hayes."

"Yes, madam, I will call a porter to carry your cases."

Punctuating her sentence with the placing of a room key next to the registration book. Its fob, heavy, large, unattractive. Their logic in reducing the risk of it being stolen as a memento of a pleasant stay in Shanghai.

"Your room, 210, is on the tenth floor of the hotel."

"201. I reserved room 201."

The girl's eyes fled fleetingly to the green scroll of the computer terminal as the porter approached with a trolley. She exchanged the key with another from the huge numbered board behind her and handed it to him. His uniform, pristine. But shoes scuffed, unpolished. Under his fingernails, black crescent moons of old engine oil. Hints of another life.

"Your room, 201, is also on the tenth floor of the hotel."

Barbara filled in the registration book, finding herself thinking, not in a flow, but in separate stills . . . and all of the time praying that they wouldn't zoom in on Bobby. Stills of his hand touching the same registration book. The same key fob. The same reception desk. And at the same time not wanting to push these feelings away either. Fighting, tooth and nail, against denying him. Needing so much to do nothing else but fill her every vacant second with his face.

The porter hauled her cases onto the trolley and moved toward the elevator. She hurriedly completed the registration details.

"Have a pleasant stay at the Jing Jiang Hotel, Madam Hayes."

The receptionist's words, snipped with steel shears. Barbara didn't look back. The elevator doors were already closing as she entered it.

★

201. The room, just as Bobby had described it. The porter leaving her sitting on the edge of the bed. Raincoat slipped off. The wad of letters, cards, spreading across the bedcover. A scrambled mosaic of whites and creams. Gaudy, retouched picture postcards and eagerly ripped open envelopes. Walking to the window, reading from a page of one of his letters. Gripping the window ledge until it hurt. Letting the page drift from her fingers, onto the floor. Looking out across the city. His words in her head, her ears, her eyes.

. . . I'm not much good at descriptions . . . all those technical archaeological reports that I have to write, I guess. But I'm looking out of the window of the hotel right now and wanted to tell you about it. It seems a long way from D.C or Boston. I can see the river beyond the elegant buildings that line the 'Bund'. String after string of junks tied up along its edges. Almost below me, next to the Sun Yaysen Museum (which is currently closed to those who do not have the right connections – but open to me, as I do) is Fuxing Park. I jog there every morning before breakfast. And by the way . . . they do a great western breakfast in the eighth floor restaurant of the hotel. Almost as good as 'Ed's', back home. You'd like the park, everybody does. It's a huge canopy of vegetation, a real oasis from the frantic city . . .

*especially on a hot day in the summer. It's big, nearly twenty-one acres
. . . but there's no risk of getting lost. The old folks really seem to love
this place . . . there's a group of them at least every fifty metres and
always only too eager to help a lost looking American boy. Remind me
to take you there if you ever have the time to come over . . .*

The green pool table foliage of Fuxing Park sat below her. She
could not make out the tired knots of old folks gathered
beneath it, but knew that they would be there. Perhaps some
of them would have seen Bobby, spoken to him? Perhaps one
or two of them had even wondered where the blond American boy, who always jogged in the park before breakfast, had
gone?

She walked into the bathroom reading a postcard that he
had sent on the 22nd; just two weeks ago. Creased . . . a view
of the Huangpu labouring under a sluggish, scaly skin of junks
and barges. Catching a glimpse of herself in the large mirror.
The tussle of blonde hair, fall upon fall of slow twisting loose
cascading waves. And the eyes . . . two dark blue sapphires that
surprised even her. An old college boyfriend had once penned
in a poem about her, that she 'looked like an angel who was
waiting impatiently in line for her wings to be repaired.'

It had been the only poem that he had ever written about
her, out of many, that had managed to catch at least the
shadow of a truth.

She filled the hand basin with water, bitter cold. Digging
deeply into it. Splashing it onto her face, her neck. And then it
was upon her, as if she had opened a trap door to it . . . loss, as
deep as a well. Thumping at the sides of the hand basin.
Ripples worrying across its surface.

*Jesus, Bobby. Jesus. Did you do this too . . . run the water down
your face? This room. This basin. This water.*

On her knees. His letters. His cards. Falling around her. A
snow storm of buff and scribbled ink. Inching her way across
the deep piled carpet of the room. Blind with tears.

*Damn. Damn. There must be something left of you Bobby. There
must be something?*

Searching for a hair. Long, wavy, blond. Just a hair. Tears

falling onto her arms, her hands. Nose running. Breaths . . . laboured, tortured. Racked by frantic spasms of sobbing.

Bobby . . . he had such lovely hair. The first time that he got it cut I cried. Watching it as his shorn locks being swept off of that dime barber's floor with that dirty broom.

"Jesus, Bobby. Jesus."

★

It was only when she was in the soft lobby of sleep's motel that she realised that the carpet that she had searched on her hands and knees, was new. Very new. Probably never been walked upon until she had entered room 201. Bobby's room.

The bastards have thought of everything, Bobby. Everything.

She fell asleep. His letters, his cards . . . her mattress, her dreams. She fell asleep, aware of only four words constantly repeating themselves through the sparsely strung necklace of night hours. Repeating themselves . . .

Is this my fault . . .? Is this my fault . . .? Is this my fault . . .?

★

In the fifty thousand characters of the Chinese language there is no word for privacy. There is no need for such a word, the Chinese, quite simply, do not recognise privacy. Neither is there a word for intimacy in the language.

In the People's Republic expect hotel staff to enter your room without knocking. In the People's Republic expect a doctor to examine you and offer you his diagnosis in front of six other patients sitting in that same room. In the People's Republic expect people to bump into you in the street and not offer an apology. In the People's Republic expect to bump into others in the street and for them not to expect an apology. In the People's Republic expect to see a three wheeled pedicab run over a young child and not stop.

Only *renao* is given credence and worth in China . . . a word, a value, that is the very flip-side of privacy, of intimacy. A word whose meaning cannot be found in the English language or in any other European language. Renao. 'Hot and spicy'. The pleasure of living life amongst a large group of friends and relatives. Renao. Chopsticks clicking. Loud voices jarring against each other. Plates of food being thrown unceremoniously onto the table. *Mah-jongg* tiles snapping to attention with the sound of stern, unforgiving applause. Renao. A life spent hot and noisy in a clamorous China where privacy is impossible except by the hazard of chance . . . except when thrust unwillingly upon you.

★

At exactly 7.00 am Barbara Hayes was awakened by a room boy in a crisp white uniform placing a bright red thermos flask of hot tea onto her bedside table. Rubbing the vestiges of sour dreams from her eyes, her mouth tasting of broken sleep and long-haul aircraft food. Holding the sheet up to her chin. She said nothing; he said nothing. He left the room. Settling back into the pillows, hoping that sleep would reclaim her and her it . . . only to hear footsteps outside, the door opening once more. The room boy, this time carrying a thermos of cold water.

"You could at least knock. It's 7.00am for Christ sake. Can you leave so that I can get some sleep?"

The room boy smiled, bemused.

"I come. I go. It is not important. You sleep. Sleep."

He left the room. She closed her eyes. Five minutes later he returned, a change of fresh towels draped over his arm. Barbara pulled a sheet around herself and entered the bathroom shaking her head; avoiding the mirror but catching an unwelcome reflection of herself in the glass shower cubicle.

At the urgent rush of the shower cascading into life the room boy smiled once more. He knew that there was no hot water.

★

The young man, blond, long wavy hair. Eyes, sky-blue and intense beyond his years . . . stared out from the photograph. Barbara couldn't recall when it had been taken. Who had taken it. What the smile hinted at. What the eyes spoke of. But she knew what they now said . . .

Find me, I am your child. Take me home.

Showing the photograph to the elderly Chinese in Fuxing Park. At first with confidence and hope. Expecting a nod of recognition followed by a few mangled words of English. How the Chinese love to speak English . . .

The American boy. Yes. Yes. He walk here many times. Very many times. He gone now. Gone to big hotel on other side of city. Other side. You find there. He there.

It would all be so simple. Easy answers. But as the eyebrows raised, the gazes turned away, the words failing to be born . . . showing Bobby's picture became a slow torture of erosion. The washing away of her confidence by the drop-drop rains of silence. She left Fuxing, her steps becoming more and more hurried, until she was running from the grasp of the foliage, the prune faces, the rotten teeth in their mouths of ginger and garlic. Back toward the hotel. Room 201. His room. At the back of her eyes, tears intensely hot; not daring to give them up, not until they blistered her with their intensity. Wanting to feel that pain, begging to physically hurt.

Running . . . not one Chinese seeming to stare at her.

Of the thirty-six ways of handling a situation . . . running away is best, goes the adage.

Making it to the room door. Slamming it shut. Fumbling with the heavy brass lock. Slipping it and muttering to every room boy in China . . .

"Try and get through that you bastards!"

The mahogany of the door cold against her back, unyielding as she slipped down it. Tears, in torrents, untethered. Down her cheeks. Her chin. As warm as babies' fingers.

It was some time before she could move, stand, walk. Rehearsing in detail every action before it was made. She opened the attaché case, hand still wet. Moving to the thin black diary. Page upon page of names and numbers. With each one, a story. With each one . . . a debt – a deal – or a favour. Remembering, at all times, the cardinal rule of amassing and retaining power, as her index finger travelled the black lines of digits. Never ask for a favour . . . only grant them or take them.

Slowly she dialled the number.

★

Debts – deals – favours . . . in that order. That is the oil of politics and diplomacy. The lubricant that ensures that its engine runs free and easy with no risks of seizing up.

Debts – deals – favours.

In the People's Republic, this lubricant it is known as *'guan-xi'* . The invisible but powerful threads that bind people. Moves situations along. That opens up back doors. It works well in China; it has to. It constantly oils a system that coheres a nation of one billion people. From the top to the bottom, it works. It can conjure up a dish of Sichuan fried chilli bean curd when every other restaurant diner has been assured that they had sold out of it. It can cut out waiting through three torturous hospital queues to see a frantic doctor . . . *zhou-hou-men*, 'taking the back door' to his home, after hours, to where the best and more leisurely medical care is given. It will give you access to the 'Friendship Store' . . . the department and grocery store reserved for foreigners and top graded cadre only, where goods not available to the ordinary Chinese abound.

Guan-xi. It has no rank. It does not know its place. It is there in the peasantry. It is there in the Politburo. It seeps, unimpeded, through the labyrinthine system of grades and ranks . . . the Chinese puzzle of twenty-four steps of government. The flex of its fingers takes all within its span. There is a joke in China that doctors, drivers and shop clerks are the 'Fat Jobs' . . . the professions that can make the most of guan-xi because of the access that they have to services or commodities that can be traded through the back door. They call these fat jobs the 'Three Treasures'.

Washington D.C. also has its three treasures . . . debts – deals – favours . . . in that order.

★

It was a private number that she dialled. A number that by-passed the bureaucratic regiments of the embassy . . . the hurdles that were set in place to upend or discourage all but the most persistent; or those with the necessary contacts. It was a private number that was relayed through its own telephone exchange and switching station. It was not foolproof, they were, after all, in China. But it was the best that they could do.

The name at the end of the line would volunteer his help to her because they were old friends. She had known him from a time when life was a lot less complicated . . . or so it seemed. A time coloured only by Leonard Cohen and Moroccan Gold. He would also help her because she had great legs.

With every digit dialled, a memory. Every memory tethered to his room at Harvard. Both students. Both learner lovers for two hours, never to repeat the clumsy episode over the next twenty-years as their lives frequently overlapped. If she closed her eyes tight, very tight 'like raisins', as Bobby had described them as a child. . . . she could still taste the cheap red wine. She could even feel his large hands upon her. The wrestling match with her bra. Her pantyhose. Her knickers. Pulling her reluctant fingers down towards his urgent, impatient crotch.

The telephone was answered. A measured and sort of sit on the sofa kind of a voice that you would imagine coming from the kind of man who only ever rose at the 'crack of lunch'. An American voice. Barbara could almost smell the blueberry pie. Could almost hear Cagney singing a chorus of . . . 'I'm a Yankee-Doodle-Dandy.' There was a pause before she spoke. That instant before a leap into space is made, is risked.

"Hi Edward, it's Barbara. How are you, Mr Ambassador?"

Chapter 6

A Hong-Qi, a Red Flag, is a car . . . but not just a 'car', you can't describe a dream of stretched black and chrome as just a car. In a country where the purchase of a bicycle can eat up two and a half years of savings and the flash of the silver from its forks or shopping basket exude status, germinate envy; the Red Flag is a hand-tooled wonder. A jewel in the crown of the elite; a social marker. A marker to be pointed at, one of the few that says. . . .

Yes, we have abolished class in China – but not rank, never rank.

The Red Flag is the transport of those drenched in rank. The high cadre . . . Generals, members of the Communist Party Central Committee, Bureau Chiefs, Governors of the Provinces, Cabinet Ministers, their wives and inner circle of hangers-on. Remember the proverb, old and Chinese, the ownership of a Red Flag breathing life into. . . .

If a man becomes an official, even his chickens and dogs will ascend to heaven.

★

Piao had never ridden in a Red Flag before. He was not a high ranking cadre or an official. Neither was he chicken or dog material. He could not have clucked or barked for some official even if his life had depended upon it.

Polished rosewood, heavily stitched creaking antique leather, contoured jump-seats, a fine lace antimacassar draped over the back of the rear seat, heavy brown curtains drawn across the rear windows. As a child, as every child, he had dreamt of being cocooned inside the moody, expansive coffin interior of a Red Flag. Less enthralled with the idea as he got older, seeing the blunt nosed missile of the Mercedes – Cadillac mix blood for what it truly was; a mongrel that could call its own tune, carving its unique path through the city. Cars,

64

bicycles, blocking its path, being shunted aside, out of its way. Red lights ignored, flaunted. The Red Flag excluded by special right, from the need to have to brake suddenly . . . in case the high ranking cadre in the back seat should be jolted or injured; even at the cost of maiming or possibly killing a pedestrian.

As an adult, Piao's tempestuous love affair with the Red Flag was over. Now, without even needing to concentrate, he could still see the star white face of his wife, the rear curtain slowly falling across it as the Red Flag pulled her further and further away. The traffic melting, dividing to let it speed ahead . . . robbing him of her. Her final glance back as an arm encircled her shoulder. A heavily gold-ringed hand bloomed with lines, teasing her face away from his gaze. . . . eyes looking forward now, towards Beijing and the cold bed of an old man. Without even needing to concentrate, Piao could still feel the rain licking at his face; could still taste the tears, salty and tainted by diesel exhaust.

The Senior Investigator drew back the curtains as they slid onto Huaihai Lu, brushing aside a red light and waved on by a policeman. The sun falling through the glass in a slow motion arc of amber, catching him full on the side of his face, its breath as warm as a satisfied lover. The ride was perfect. Silent, smooth . . . perfect. Perhaps he could learn to cluck or bark, he thought, teasing himself. Absentmindedly his hand ran over the leather of the seat . . . its softness, its smoothness. He remembered her thighs; the milk valley of the inside of her legs.

"It's your first time in a Red Flag, isn't it, Senior Investigator?"

Piao needed a chirpy, talkative driver, as much as he needed a toothache.

"Yes. How did you know?"

"Ah well, there you have it . . . you see I am a sort of Senior Investigator in my own right. Don't let this stupid chauffeur's uniform fool you. It's the person inside, I always say. The person inside. See, the first thing that anyone ever riding in a Red Flag does, is to draw back the curtains . . . so that they can be seen I expect. What's the point in riding in a Red Flag if nobody can see that it is you who is riding in it. Follow my logic?"

Like one of those toy dogs that you place on the rear shelf of your car, Piao felt himself nodding stupidly.

"But the real give-away is the leather. First time riders, they always stroke the leather of the seat. You'd think that it was a plump girl's thigh the way that they stroke it. As I said, a real give-away, if ever there was one . . ."

Piao slowly removed his hand from the leather of the seat.

". . . now this is what you call a car, it leaves the Zil streets behind. The Russians are fair enough engineers, but a car is more than that, isn't it? It's about style, lines, use of materials. Have you run your fingers over the wood yet? First timers always do that as well. As soft as your wife's cheek. Another give-away. Go on try it. The best available timber in China."

Piao felt obliged, he ran his fingers over the heavily varnished gold grain. It was as smooth as plastic. The driver beamed.

"Whose Red Flag is this?" Piao casually asked. The drivers eyes narrowed, his gaze moving from the rear-view mirror and onto the traffic scattering on the road ahead, the smile emptying from his features as if someone had pulled a plug. In its place, the passive stock face of the party chauffeur, with an answer to match.

"The limousine is the property of the State. This one is from the pool allocated to the Danwei of the Public Security Ministry."

Piao laughed in mock humour, his eyes not releasing their focus of the rear-view mirror.

"Very diplomatic, comrade. Your answer is well practised. I can see that you are a real *nei-hang*. It takes an expert of words to drive these high cadre around. I think that you are the one who should be sitting here in the back stroking the plump girl's thighs."

The driver's eyes cracked with laughter.

"Never were truer words spoken, my friend. In my job you

can't take a piss without wrapping it up in a box of tissue with a bow on the top. I can tell that you know how it is?"

"Yes, I know how it is, comrade . . ." Piao confided, moving slightly forward on his seat in empathy.

". . . my whole life, like yours, has been spent in making words look pretty. So, come on, tell me, who owns the car? It's not classified."

"In this country my friend, you never know what is *nei-bu*. They stamp classified on everything that moves and on many things that stopped moving years ago. They even say that some weather forecasts are now classified information."

"It's true comrade, it's true . . ." Piao confirmed with a shake of his head.

". . . maybe the Party is worried about us poor peasants finding the pot of gold at the end of the rainbow and realising that they got to it and spent it years ago."

The driver laughed in unison with his hand pumping at the horn, sending a flock of Forever bicycles sprinting into the dusty gutters with whirling mercury spokes, angry eyes and hands frantically wrestling handlebars.

"Yes, you're right. You're right. They want it all for themselves. Red Flags, even the fucking weather . . ."

He thought for a few seconds before continuing. His foot now hard down, racing for a break in the traffic as they intersected Zhongshanx Lu.

". . . ah screw them, it's the people that really own these cars anyway, so why shouldn't we all know who it is that take their wives shopping in them, and whose kids it is that piss on the back seat? This Red Flag is on permanent loan to your boss, Liping. Normally he wouldn't get his arse on the jump-seat of a Red Flag . . . not high enough up the ladder. No, it's his cousin's limousine, the Minister of Public Security himself . . . Kang Zhu."

Piao guessed as much, but the blunt nosed tones of Zhu's name still knocked him back against the leather of the seat. Trying to look calm, outwardly calm, the way that you do . . . but inside his head the cinema had already kicked into life. The images, black and white, parading in soft, slow flickers.

Her face . . . smaller, smaller. The limousine, a shadow jigsaw of street reflections, slipping into the night from which it had been delivered. An arm around her shoulder, as if she had always been his, never Piao's . . . always his. And just before the Red Flag was lost to him, the rear window curtain swept aside. A face of chiselled lines sculpted into a smile. Hair slicked and swept back into a tight fitting cap. Ebony keyhole eyes. Kang Zhu . . . the Minister Kang Zhu. The curtain falling back into place. The Red Flag becoming at one with the ink of night.

Piao spoke, but only a fractured croak came out. Seeing a reflection of himself in the window opposite. His face frozen into the smile of the imbecile emerging from the institution. . . . standing on the top steps, not knowing what comes next. So white . . . so fat, Kang. Only the high cadre can look like that, gorged on milk and meat. So white . . . so fucking fat.

"Nemma bai . . . nemma pang."

The driver half glanced over the red and gold of his epaulette, hooked by the words that had squeezed from Piao's fixed lips.

"You are acquainted with our Minister Zhu?"

He asked, a frown of worry eating its way across his forehead.

"I know him . . ."

Piao stared out of the window, it had started to rain, fast slanting spears of rain; the vista melting into identically changing worlds, all trapped within their own droplets.

". . . you don't need to worry. The Minister and I have what you might call 'a passing acquaintance'. I stand on the kerb with the rain pissing down and he passes by in his Red Flag with my fucking wife . . ."

The driver glanced around again, his mouth filled with a question. Piao chained it in place with a raise of a hand.

". . . don't ask. It's a very long story and it's classified . . ."

There was a slab of silence punctuated only by the wake of ripped air as they passed an old Shanghai Sedan slouching into the rain like a 1950's Packard, before the driver spoke once more.

"So, I don't suppose that a Senior Investigator with the PSB like you knows much about the Red Flag limousine?"

The driver squeezed his foot on the accelerator. Eyes fixed ahead. His mouth, a knitted scar. He said nothing more until they had arrived; until Piao had left the limousine. It was only one word when he did finally speak. . . .

"Bastard," was all that he said.

★

The zhau-dai-suo, the dacha guesthouse of Chief Liping, sat in a compound a flip of a stone from Lake Taihu. Only a slipknot of fishing boats to the south, the vast fertile plains beyond running to the horizon in a glide of easy greens and pinching yellows, fretting its surface.

Piao stood for a while smoothing down his uniform and watching the young women giggle and splash each other as they bobbed and floated in tar barrels harvesting the water chestnuts. There was no other sound. Above them, the lands of the north-west crumpled into hills. Soft, plump knots . . . a warm, generous land. Only when the dark darting eyes turned in the Senior Investigator's direction . . . the giggling into friendly taunting words, did he leave.

"Come give us blue-eyed babies, Comrade Policeman."

★

There was no number, no name to indicate that the residence was Chief Liping's. The zhau-dai-suo had none. Neither did it have an address. No telephone number was officially allocated to it. The road that it stood back from was nameless. That area of Lake Taihu, unchristened. It appearing on no maps. Piao pushed the buzzer. He'd seen it all before. It was the same in Beidaihe, Huang Shan, West Lake. . . . in all the country's favourite resorts, where the dachas of the high cadre had sprung up like desert blooms. In a country of deep secrets, the zhau-dai-suo were whispers; a *te-quan*, a 'special privilege' that the high cadre care to afford themselves, that are protected with an unparalleled jealousy. Those of the high cadre who use the dachas, never speak of them, except to

69

those who share the same inner circles of power and influence. To mention of such privilege is severely frowned upon. It is seen as. . . . *White eyebrows over red eyes.* A mistake. A glaring and very big mistake.

★

"Yes?"

"Senior Investigator Sun Piao to see Comrade Officer Liping."

Silence . . . and then an angry buzz of a lock automatically snapping free. Piao pushed the gate and walked down the long gravel drive. The architecture of the residence was brash western and seemed to shout out that it wanted to be seen, but the thick verdant gardens around it and the high security walls spoke in whispers . . . of lives lived apart and different. They also spoke of money. Other people's money. It all gave oxygen to the current saying about the high cadre, the saying that was tucked under the tongue of every other Chinese . . .

Our minds are on the left, but our pockets are on the right.

The elderly a–yi, who probably had a higher security clearance than he did, led Piao at a shuffle rather than a walk, through a long moody hallway . . . her mouth prised open by breathlessness. In a country where wood was in such short supply, the rich timber panelled walls were a rarity; the Senior Investigator allowing his fingers to trail against the lacquered, imprisoned grain. They arrived in a bright, large space of sun drenched apricot, the garden spilling in through huge open windows whose fine cream silk curtains gently undulated in the breeze. At the far end of the room French windows were expectantly ajar, alive with a constantly shifting lattice of shadow . . . all set against a lawn whose greenness made Piao want to shade his eyes. This was a woman's room. Marshmallow soft modern furniture, sugar–ice coving, delicate objets d'art, paintings of blushed pale strokes. None of it Liping. Even the light that filled the room seemed to be female. He could feel its perfumed fall against the stubble of his chin. He

70

looked across his shoulder, the a-yi had slipped away. When his gaze returned to the French windows, the shadows had stilled and the space was now dominated by Chief Liping.

He stood in a finely cut black Mao suit, his hands by his sides and stained rich tea leaf brown with soil . . . some of it falling from his fingers onto the cream carpet. For a Chinese he was tall, powerful. A harshness, a callousness about the bulk of Liping's body. An unforgiving, unrelenting nonchalance of posture that dominated a room. The way that the Comrade Officer seemed to be thrust forward, as if guarding the very edge of an abyss. His bony head under the close cropped bristle of hair. And the eyes that rested under their hoods of taut flesh; fixed in a permanent questioning look.

"Piao, so. . . . circumstances as unsavoury as ever. A trait of the profession."

A question, a statement? The Senior Investigator feeling his lips dry instantly.

"My initial report, Comrade Officer Liping. I regret it is hand written. Time has not allowed for a more formal report to be drafted."

The Chief took the papers and seated himself on a sofa. The loosely caked earth on his hands falling across them, onto the pale cushions. He was oblivious to the beauty of the room . . . the dirt falling from his fingers. The elderly a-yi on her hands and knees would have to clean it up; Piao felt a pulse kick into life in the corner of his mouth. He stood, not knowing what to do with his hands, as Liping read. The report, although consisting mainly of fluff and cotton wool, should satisfy the Chief. Liping loved paper. Put a report in his hand, no matter what crap might drip from its lines, and Liping was like a junk on the Yangtze, 'all sails set.'

"Stupid, stupid Senior Investigator . . ."

Liping's hands were crumpling the report into a tight ball as he spoke. He tossed it onto the floor, more soil being scattered. It arrived at Piao's feet, caught in a crossfire of shadows.

". . . you have a reputation, Investigator. You produce results. You are given the department's most difficult, most sensitive cases. And still you get results. But this. . . ."

71

Liping's head shook. Bubbles of spittle on his meaty lips.

". . . you should know better. No evidence. No facts. Yet you point with a finger that does not waver. You point at the Security Services. The Party. State killings. Stupid. . . ."

"Not evidence as such, Comrade Officer Liping, but I do have the behaviour of Doctor Wu who refused to examine the bodies, and the comments that he made to me. And I have seen enough of Security's methods in the past to recognise their work. And this was their work."

Liping brushed some dirt from his lap as he got to his feet. Piao had heard it said of the Chief . . . 'that he had ink in his stomach. He was learned but had no courage.' He now recognised that it was a comment that had been made by officers who did not have Chief Liping walking towards them.

"I cannot stop you being stupid. I only warn you against it. You have nothing, not even the basis of an investigation yet. No forensics. No autopsies. No details on the victims, their assailants. No why. No how. But you put your job, your life, where it should not be: at the end of a gun barrel. Wu . . . the old man is as dead as his clients. He breathes on his reputation only. Forget his actions, his comments. He was put out at having to get his shoes muddy. The man is incompetent. He has gone too far. He will be dealt with . . ."

Liping looked up from examining his huge muddied hands. Leaning across Piao's shoulder.

". . . Piao, advice. Take it. Don't build a case on Wu. Don't build a case on anyone. Evidence, build it on that. Sculpt your words from steel, not bamboo. Steel, nothing less. It is good advice. My very life has been built upon its walls . . ."

The Comrade Officer turned away.

". . . you will carry out a full, precise and organised investigation, Piao. More men will be assigned if necessary. I will personally arrange for the proper facilities to be made available for the bodies to be thoroughly examined. I want this case dealt with in a professional manner . . . no loose talk, no half truths. Facts, just facts. A string of bodies turning up and being left on the foreshore of the Huangpu is not acceptable.

72

Autopsies in a meat processing warehouse, a student doctor poking about. Unacceptable. Our city is to be our window to the west. Opportunity, Senior Investigator, opportunity. Do not forget that. And never forget, that to commit words to paper in a report . . ."

Liping looked down at the crumpled ball at Piao's feet.

". . . is to be the fish that places its self upon the barbed hook."

The Comrade Officer turned, leaning forward. His lips uncomfortably close.

"Cao-mu jie-bing. Cao-mu jie-bing."

The Senior Investigator knew the proverb that had been passed down from the late fourth century. Every school child did. It told of the rebel Fu Jian, who had raised an army of a million men to overthrow the State of Jin, which only had an army of eight thousand soldiers to defend it. But Fu Jian's rebel army had fled in terror, mistaking the moving grass, the swaying trees, as advancing state reinforcements. The four character phrase had become a parable for paranoia, every Chinese knowing it, every Chinese fearing its wisdom . . . its truth.

Cao-mu jie-bing . . . In the grass, the trees, everything seems a soldier.

Liping moved towards the French windows and beyond, the garden. . . . his hands seeking the malleable quality of earth.

"Daily reports Piao. You will not use the normal channels. I do not wish the regular procedures to be followed. Everything goes through me. I wish to lead this case from the front. If there are special, shall we say, implications to this investigation, I will deal with them. Not you."

Something deep in his eyes, alerting Piao's anxiety.

"It's highly irregular, Comrade Officer. Do you have any reasons for treating this case in this special manner, is there anything that I should know?"

Liping, his smile as tight as a clenched fist. If words could

73

melt, but Piao knew that they remained as epitaphs to folly and stupidity. He cursed the western genes that too often failed to control his tongue.

"I want a list of what men you are using. Who has been involved in the case to date? Who has seen the bodies . . ."

Liping noted everything. He noted the hesitation draw across the Senior Investigator's eyes.

". . . it is for their special protection. They might need it," he added, pulling a pad from the desk top, a gold pen from his top pocket and handing it to Piao.

Red ink on white paper.

Wenbiao, Cheng, Xin, Shi, Zhiyuan, Wu, Pan Yaobang, Officer Yaobang.

The names flowed. Red ink . . . Piao had always feared it. It felt dangerous, out of control, as if taking on a life of its own.

"Good, good Investigator . . ."

Eyes flicking down the list, smiling, folding the paper meticulously. Liping slipping it into an inner pocket of his jacket.

". . . if special arrangements are needed, I will see to it. Shi, Zhiyuan, the neighbourhood and Shiqu committee chairmen, they can look after themselves . . ."

Liping moved closer.

". . . they are no friends of yours, Senior Investigator. I have their reports. They speak anything but highly of you. Treason, treachery . . . strong words. You have a skill of making important enemies . . ."

It wasn't true. Important cadre had a skill of making an enemy of him. It was a subtle difference that had escaped Liping, but Piao kept his tongue still.

". . . their reports will go no further. A deep filing cabinet awaits them. What is it that the Americans say? 'The buck stops here . . .'"

The Comrade Officer laughed. Gold teeth at the back of his cavernous mouth winking dully at Piao.

". . . one consideration deserves another, Senior Investigator. My cousin, the Minister, he has been refreshed by your sensible attitude. You took my advice well. I am pleased.

Nothing would have been gained by a fuss. You, Kang Zhu . . . careers wrecked. And in the middle, your wife. A fish being pulled between two cormorants . . ."

The Senior Investigator bit the inside of his lip, the blood tasting of metal polish.

". . . you were wise, Piao, wise. A cadre of Kang Zhu's magnitude is best traversed. Face is saved. Besides, she was not an honourable wife. 'A good horse does not accept two saddles . . .'"

Liping approached the garden, replacing his pen; the shadows moving, playing across his face. His features imprisoned.

". . . remember. Daily reports, Senior Investigator. Don't make me chase you, I want this kept tight. With dead 'big noses' involved, especially Americans, there might be outside interest in this case, external pressures. Maybe political questions. I want to be one step ahead. I want to be in the driving seat."

Piao felt a chord resonate in his chest.

Big noses . . . wai-guo-ren. Westerners . . . yang-gui-zl . . . foreign devils.

Words that had a brick wall reality in his own life. Just look in any mirror, Senior Investigator, any fragment of reflection. See the face that is not as ours are. The eyes that can never truly belong. *Wai-guo-ren . . . external country person.* Foreigner.

A telephone rang in a distant room. It was quickly answered. The a-yi entered moments later, whispered to Liping, who left for a hushed conversation. While he was absent, Piao picked flakes of rich soil from the sofa cushions and the carpet. Liping was not gone for long.

"Senior Investigator, there has been an incident. You may take the telephone call."

Piao followed the a-yi to a room that was shady, its smell of secret gardens and guarded conversations. The telephone mouthpiece stank of Liping's breath, with its undertone of the fine reek of shit.

"Boss, you'd better get the fuck back here. . . ."

75

Yaobang, breathless, hot, running on adrenaline.

". . . I'm outside the warehouse. There's a fire, a fucking great fire . . ."

A pause. In the background, sirens cutting it. And all the time, Piao with a strong sense of what was coming next.

". . . I think that Wenbiao is still in there. And your Cousin Cheng . . ."

The Senior Investigator, eyes closed. Counting to three. The pulse in his ears racing.

"I'm leaving now, I'll be with you as soon as I can."

". . . thanks, Boss, we need you. It's hell down here . . ."

"Yaobang, the bodies, what about the bodies?"

". . . sorry, Boss, I can't hear you, there's more appliances just arriving . . ."

"THE BODIES, THE EIGHT?"

The Big Man shouting against a sob of sirens, frantic voices, a crack of timbers, bricks . . . licked by fire.

". . . FUCK KNOWS, BOSS. FUCK KNOWS."

The line died. The silence seemed to fill the world. Piao unclenched his fist; the mud from Liping's sofa and carpet, was still in his palm staining it reddy-brown. He dropped it to the floor.

★

The Comrade Officer was staring out at the garden from the French windows, his shadow, long. A black smudge cast deeply into the room. He didn't turn. His back remained to Piao as he spoke.

"Unfortunate. Fire has no preference for the living or the dead. Your eight bodies. Little will be left."

Liping stepped from the room and into the garden. . . . it was ablaze from a low and white sun. It seeming to eat him whole. Piao left, his mind racing ahead to a burning warehouse.

★

Beneath Lake Taihu's waters, suitable rocks are chosen and submerged. For decades they sit, the lake's pearls, as the waters

76

weather them to the point when they are highly prized for classical garden design.

Hidden and secret, they lay submerged.

★

The limousine started for the city. The engine a purr . . . the driver silent.

Big noses . . . Americans. Piao checked his copy of the report, knowing what it would say . . . knowing what it would not say. No mention of Americans had been made in his report to his Chief, Comrade Officer Liping.

Chapter 7

As black as her eyes.   As black as her words.

The smoke rose from the docks, striking across the river. A snake shedding its skin until its body was pale, paler. As he neared the warehouse the sky was changing. Black and yellow. Black and orange. Black and red.

The building that he had once recognised was almost gone; in its place the decayed stump of an old tooth. Yaobang's face was at the window of the Red Flag before it had even come to a halt. A full moon of charcoal smudges and inflamed pink marshmallow flesh.

"They're still fighting the fire on the roof. The bottom floors are gutted but too dangerous to enter. We've been told that we might have to move back. The whole fucking lot could come down at any minute. They're looking at it now."

Piao jumped out of the limousine, crossing the assault course of spaghetti hoses and swollen rivulets of black water. The Red Flag gliding out of the courtyard, out of the alley; a stream of fucks aimed at the Senior Investigator by the chauffeur who was already mentally struggling with a chamois leather to recoup the gleam of the paintwork from the fine ash that was drifting down from the sky like snow. Black snow.

"Looks like we've got company."

Piao nodded toward the Shanghai Sedan slumped against the wall of the far alley. Three men . . . dead eyes and junk breath, littering the gloom of its interior.

"Security shits. Why do they always travel in threes, Boss?"

The Senior Investigator was removing his jacket as they hurried toward the cordon, ducking under it. Toward the warehouse, removing his tie; the heat that it was already giving off burning his nostrils, drying his throat. He swallowed hard, but there was nothing to swallow.

"Don't you know, it's a top secret Politburo directive? One to read, one to write . . . the third to keep an eye on the other two intellectuals."

The Big Man didn't understand the joke, but laughed anyway.

Piao soaked his jacket from a fountain of water that cascaded from a holed hose, tying it around his head and face . . . as three bursts of a siren sliced through the organised mayhem. Everywhere, frantic but organised activity. Ladders being hastily retracted. Tangles of hoses slithering across the puddled backs of the cobbles as they were wound back onto their drums. A stream of fire-fighters, life extinguished in their eyes, washed past them; heading back to their vehicles. Only Piao and Yaobang moving forward towards the warehouse. The Big Man's eyes, white nervous orbs set into a face of smoky marble, watching the fire appliances back out of the courtyard.

"I think its the other direction we should be heading in, Boss."

Piao lengthening his stride. Yaobang hurriedly dragging his jacket off and through a filthy puddle . . . also wrapping it around his head. The dirty water running down his forehead and cheeks, like the melt of wax of a half burnt candle.

"Mother. Mother. Mother," on his lazy fat lips, pinching them into a tight scar, as the hand of a thickset fire-fighter, a Chief by the size of his epaulettes and the thick braid on his helmet, clasped hold of Piao's shoulder.

"Where the fuck do you think you're going? It's coming down. Can't you see its coming down?"

There was a cataract of fear across the fire-fighter's eyes. It surprised Piao, also unnerved him . . . but all the same, he said the words, not giving himself time to think about them.

"Homicide squad, this is official Party business. Out of my way or face the consequences."

The Fire Chief lifted his hand, a knowing look whittled in the gutter lines of his face.

"It's your fucking life . . ." he said. But Piao knew that already.

★

As black as her eyes. As black as her words.

The interior of the warehouse, a cinder . . . filled with the stench of charcoaled animal carcasses and the constant groan of timbers, bricks, whose own weight had now become too much to bear. Piao pulled his jacket tighter around his face. It was already dry and warm to the touch. The fierce oven door heat turning its attention to his exposed hands. He withdrew them into the flimsy protection of his shirt cuffs, as he and Yaobang bent their backs to meet the scorching heat. It was hard to know exactly where they were in the warehouse, the fire had sculpted its interior into its own image. A nightmare vista of twisted flowing steel, bulging fluid brickwork and blackened cracked wood beams, was all that met them. The concrete floor had also been transformed . . . now a wild ebony ocean of incinerated timber and debris from the three floors of the warehouse that had collapsed onto it. It was too hot, too urgent to pick a path. The Senior Investigator ploughed through its swollen tide, Yaobang close behind. The swearwords falling into the cracks on his lips. His shoes smoking, their plastic soles slowly melting.

Piao veered toward the area that only twenty-four hours ago had been an office. It was now just another fire pit of charred walls. Further along, the brickwork gave way to a steel frame and a heavy steel door hanging half open from it. The cold store. He trailed his fingers across its torched surface, pulling them back sharply. The metal was red-hot. The tips of his fingers screamed. Ice cubes, cold beer bottles, snow, frost . . . was all that he could think of. At that moment he would willingly have given a month's salary for just one chilled bottle of Tsingtao. Yaobang pulled the torch out from beneath his shirt and handed it to Piao. The beam sliced the darkness in half. He was only four steps into the vast store when he slipped, almost falling, the beam wavering sickeningly. He

80

steadied himself and pointed the torch at the floor. A thick lake of animal fat reflected dully back. He raised the torch slowly, illuminating the rows upon rows of animal carcasses hanging on their meat hooks . . . each one burnt to a crisp charcoal. A pungent clogging smoke pulling from each of them. Long waxy stalactites of fat hanging from them. Some so long that they bridged the gap to the floor, appearing to hold up the mighty bulk of the carcasses like delicate flamingo legs.

And this was where they had stored the eight bodies that they had snatched from the mud of the Huangpu. A cold store turned incinerator . . . *fire has no preference for the living or the dead. Your eight bodies, little will be left.*

Liping's words fuelling a nausea, deep and acid bitter, in the depths of his gut.

The Senior Investigator felt his skin tightening, his throat closing up, his eyes drying. He tied the jacket more firmly around his head, peering out from the most narrow of slits. He was drowning in the heat. It was everywhere. A part of everything . . . inescapable. He was dizzy, gasping for breaths that lacerated his throat. And behind him, Yaobang tripping, caught in the teeth of a coughing fit.

They stumbled through the forest of barbecued flesh, barely keeping their feet. The great carcasses swinging lazily as they careered into them. And all the time, the dread of what the beam of the torch would surely illuminate as they made the next turn . . . or the turn after that.

★

As black as her eyes. As black as her words.

It was at the far end of the store that they found them. Two more carcasses of charcoaled flesh strung up, run through with meat hooks. Now hardly recognisable as humans . . . yet hideously, clearly the bodies of the young puppy of a policeman, Wenbiao. And Piao's own cousin, Cheng. Hearing Yaobang retch behind him and the same words, time after time, dribbling from his cracked lips . . .

"Mother. Mother. Mother."

And at the same time, wondering how you tell your

cousin's children that their father is no more. Children . . . with wet kisses, warm breaths and wild strawberry lips.

Somehow Piao managed to haul the Big Man from his knees to his feet, easing back the cowl fashioned from his jacket. Yaobang's face, flushed, swollen by heat. A red balloon, over inflated and ready to burst. Piao's voice, a deep tortured croak that was alien to his own ears.

"You're going to have to help me. I can't leave them like this."

The heat drying the Senior Investigator's tears almost before they formed.

"And then we get the fuck out of here, Boss?"

Piao nodded, their gaze welded together in the raw horror of it all.

"You don't think we should look for the others . . .?"

Piao closed his eyes. The fires raging behind the purple midnight of his eyelids

Your eight bodies . . . little will be left.

"We'd never get out alive."

The Big Man nodded, reaching up, averting his eyes, his face almost pressed against a charred body. Trying not to breathe, trying to fill his mind with nothingness. He took the weight of the first corpse, the blackened body of the man who had been Wenbiao. Steel grating against steel. Piao released the first meat hook from the top of the rail and then the second, of the body of the man who had once been known as Cheng. Thinking of nothing, only the shards of questions from sweet mouthed children filling his head. How to answer such questions? How to wipe away such tears? He laid Cousin Cheng gently on the cold store floor, a single plume of foul black smoke winding from the coal hole that was now his mouth, and with it, a stab of realisation that he would have to learn 'how', shortly . . . very shortly.

And knowing that the questions that children ask do not soften and fade like smoke as it is taken up by the sky.

★

Leaving the warehouse. No memories, just a mosaic of slow

and laboured paces matched with slithers of mirage and madness. Light skewering darkness. Water piercing fire. Voices, as the fire crew reached them just inside of the warehouse loading bays. A blaze of sky spiked by a blunt needle of filthy smoke and falling from it a powdering of black snow. Everywhere, black snow.

Piao's eyes searched the alleys as they carried him on the stretcher, his vision, a constellation, a universe of fiercely bright pin-pricks. They were still searching as the ambulance doors met in a comforting clasp of steel on steel, but the Shanghai Sedan that had slouched against its scarred brickwork wall was gone.

Unconsciousness wrapped him in its soft dark glove. He gave in to its gentle embrace.

★

The Fire Chief had known fire well, but not intimately . . . by morning the warehouse was still standing and now cool enough for it to be searched. Inch by inch. Checked and re-checked. Amongst the incinerated animal carcasses in the Yangpu Bridge Import Export Meat Corporation's cold store, no evidence was found of any other human remains.

Chapter 8

The CIA Officer, McMurta, had resembled a ballistic missile . . . bullet headed, steel chinned, wire haired. The eyes, seemingly frozen behind the black glass blinds of the obligatory Ray Ban's.

The interview had lasted for a full three hours. . . . 180 minutes of unquenched, undiluted pain. Each detail of Bobby being ripped from her like a brace of ingrowing toenails. McMurta had worked to his own agenda, on the pretext of working to hers and Bobby's. It had left Barbara feeling raped, violated. And between each question, each answer, the only thing that made the experience bearable, sips of Xunhuacha . . . green Lucha tea, perfumed with chrysanthemum and rose petals. Served in cups that looked too delicate to hold. Its instant bouquet of rain soaked cottage gardens, of fruit lying in wet grass . . . in collision with the toothpaste and tabac, that was McMurta. Questions run out, he closed the folder and replaced his pen in an inside pocket, next to three identical pens of the same style, the same colour.

"I can smell a woman in all of this. There are lots of interesting diversions for a young man in China nowadays. Take it from me, he's gone native, nothing more than that. Right now he's probably locked away in some cosy little hotel room in the former French Concession, with a cute little *yeh ji*."

She put the cup down. Lipstick on bone china. Asking the question to an answer that she already knew.

"A cute little yeh ji, what the hell is that?"

"A yeh ji, a wild pheasant. A hooker. Christ, it's almost an obligatory part of the package deal."

Barbara poured more tea. Not wanting more, just needing to do something with her hands.

"Bobby isn't like that."

McMurta walked to the window.

"All men are like that, take it from me . . ."

The sky, a jaundiced yellow. River, cars, windows, reflecting back the same polluted hue.

". . . anyway, whatever's going on, you don't have to worry, ma'am. We're looking after you."

Anger in an instant blaze. Thumping the cup down on the table. Tea, across the saucer, her fingers, the train track grain of the chocolate mahogany.

"'We're looking after you'. What the hell does that mean?"

Still looking out of the window, McMurta blanching, his neck tightening with shock, wondering if it was right for a government official to swear. If a woman should swear. The shell of the 'new man' wrapped around the same Puritanism as a Pilgrim Father.

"The Agency. We're looking out for you. Making sure you're safe."

"I don't need 'looking out for'. I don't need the Agency making sure that I'm safe. Read my lips . . . I'll look out for myself. I'm safe."

"Well excuse me, ma'am, but you're an American governmental official and a vulnerable woman in the People's Republic of China. You're a long way from DC. You're involved in important negotiations with the representatives of this country. And now your son has gone missing. Maybe these are linked, maybe not. Personally speaking, I think your son's screwing around and will re-surface in a few days time. The US dollar goes a long way with a yeh ji. But whatever, the Agency are there to look after you Ma'am, whether you like it or not . . . that's what you pay your 'greenbacks' in taxes for."

His eyes followed the Huangpu to the east . . . a dull metal gash, splitting the old city from the new city. A division that no sutures of black brooding bridges could ever pull together. He placed his hands on the window ledge, drawing in a deep breath.

"I love Shanghai in the morning. Its smell. Its bustle. From ten floors up it's the greatest city in the world."

Barbara joined him. Below the city was alive. The heavily strung cord roads of black bead cars. A million dots picking their way along the Nanjing Road; a buzzing hive of pedestrians. Life . . . seething, bubbling over. Reaching out and up. Grabbing at her by the throat. Choking on its vibrancy; with a chill, feeling that she might never be a part of it again. She turned away.

"Bobby, I know he's dead. It's not true what they are saying . . . he was here. This was his room. I know from his letters what they serve for breakfast in the hotel restaurant on the eighth floor. I knew this room before I ever stepped into it. It's not true what they are saying. He was here. He's not with a hooker. He's dead."

★

As McMurta left the hotel room, she had noticed that he had a huge and flat arse: like Clinton's in those unflattering jogging pants. *Never trust a man with a flat arse . . .* had been a homespun philosophy that had been bequeathed to her by her ma. Her ma had never been wrong yet. McMurta. Barbara had seen tampons with more . . . more get up and go. She would get diddly, she knew it. He knew it. The door closed.

"Arsehole," she said.

★

Ambassador Edward Candy's voice was instantly recognisable. Its lazy drawl as welcome, as familiar as a bottle of Bud or a slice of pecan pie. The Ambassador talked about the weather, the primaries and the World Series back in the States. The States, it already seeming like a stranded shell of a past life. It was clear that he had no information on Bobby . . . she knew it. Candy was building up to say a huge zero. Barbara feeling a wave of panic wash over her. She stifled a scream and managed to twist it into . . .

"Edward, what about Bobby?"

. . . and then the steel shutters crashing into place.

"I've had two other agents on the case besides McMurta, but they've drawn a blank. Zilch. Their investigations show no record of Bobby ever having entered China. No

86

visas issued. No internal travel documents authorised. No registration ever made at any Shanghai hotel. According to McMurta's report, and the contacts that we have in the municipal Party machine and in the Luxingshe, your son has never been to Fudan University. Your son has never been in Shanghai . . ."

Candy paused, she could hear him sigh.

". . . officially Barbara, Bobby has never been in China . . ."

She wanted to respond, but nothing came out.

". . . we've taken it about as far as we can at this unofficial level, Barbara. Remember, we're in China and very limited as to where we can tread. My suggestion is that we involve the PSB. I have spoken to the Minister . . . he has arranged through Chief Liping, the head of police in the city, for you to see one of his best investigators . . . his name is Detective Yun. You will find him at the Hongkou Divisional Headquarters . . . that's near the corner of Sichuanlu and Haininglu. Lu means street. Take a taxi and be there for ten. I've already released some details of Bobby's file to Chief Liping, so they should be thoroughly briefed . . ."

The pen slipped from her fingers, the details of the meeting scrawled across the hotel notepaper. The Ambassador's voice trailed off, waiting for a response that she felt unable to give.

". . . but I'm sure that it's all explainable, Barbara. Just a series of bureaucratic mistakes, each one compounding the last. You know how it is?"

No response.

"Bobby will turn up, and when he does, you put a flea in his ear and then join me in Beijing for a celebratory drink. I'll put a bottle or two on ice . . . just like old times, eh?"

The call was ending and still she was unable to utter a word, only think them. And at the same time, picturing Candy straightening his tie, checking his breath as he spoke . . . an eye admiring a woman seated in the inner lobby of the penthouse suite, just out of reach. Checking her make-up in the reflection from the VDU. Pausing in mid-pout to give the Ambassador a half wave of pale perfumed fingers. Their tips, wriggling cerise fishes. Returning the wave . . . her signal to stand up, shimmy her tight skirt straight. She would be a Washington wife on the loose. A perfect bob-permed pink mannequin wrapped in Ralph Lauren. Smart, beautiful . . . with all of the weapons to win the war.

A host of questions suddenly crowding into Barbara's mind. In panic selecting one almost at random.

"What about Lazarus Heywood at Fudan, at the university? For Christ sake, he brought Bobby to China. He's worked with Bobby in the same department. Heywood can prove that he was in Shanghai, and that some sort of conspiracy is going on."

"Barbara, there is no conspiracy; your son is an archaeologist. Conspiracies do not stretch to include estate agents, tax inspectors, or archaeologists. Except, of course, in Hollywood."

"But Professor Heywood, has McMurta seen him, talked to him?"

The silence was long. A shiny bright barb of silence. Edward Candy, a fish hooked onto it. She could feel him wriggling. The mercury flash of the scales.

"Edward?"

Silence.

"Edward?"

The strike. Taught catgut, a whistle as it bit water. And then the words . . .

"Heywood's not been seen for two weeks. He's missing Barbara . . . he's also missing."

Chapter 9

The *fen-chu*, PSB Divisional Headquarters of Hongkou, sat on Sichuanlu . . . a frantic junction of whirring bicycle spokes, pissing dogs and belching traffic. The building was indented into a fussy parade of 1930s edifices. A mute, shadowed dimple of chipped marble and blind windows that shyly stood a step back . . . its posture stranded between defence and offence.

★

Polish . . . piss . . . testosterone.

The smell of the place reminded Barbara of home, of every police precinct that she had ever entered. Male territory. The kind of complex odour that lingered in the memory of every retired cop long after the faces of the framed, threatened and fearful, had long since faded.

"Detective Officer Yun is expecting me . . ."

The young policeman winced with discomfort.

". . . I have an appointment for ten o'clock."

Confusion knotted his eyebrows. He simply shook his head as if attempting to untangle them.

"Jesus Christ! What do I have to do to make myself understood in this country, hire a loudhailer?"

Her voice was growing. Rows of faces appeared staring from behind glass office partitions.

"Now get me Detective Yun before I really have to shout. I'm not nice when I shout."

"Yun, Yun . . . not nice?"

Barbara smiled.

"Get me Yun."

Still smiling, and almost as a whisper.

"Jesus, this is going to be hard."

The policeman also smiled. It was a living advertisement for the need for regular dental hygiene.

★

A book by its cover . . .

The man who followed the young policeman to Barbara's side was also young. Too young. A smile on his acne ravaged face.

"Detective Officer Yun?"

The Detective Officer nodded with a vigour that Barbara had come to realise meant that his name would be one of the few words whose meaning they would be able to share.

"You don't speak English, do you?"

The detective nodded.

"Yun, Yun." He tapped his chest.

"Yes, I know, I get the picture. You're Yun. Do you also know the word interpreter. *Interpreter?*"

"Yun."

Barbara felt the last vestiges of humour drain from her. All the tools that she possessed to lever, slide, oil information out of people, move situations along . . . seemed blunt.

Her voice rose. . . .

"What about the words sit on it, do you understand those?"

The veneer of control split. Words spilling from her lips, and all the time, the loose threaded stitches of Yun's smile, snagged and pulling from the seersucker complexion of his face.

★

Gauzed fingers lifting a chipped cup to cracked lips.

Piao sat in the canteen of the Divisional Headquarters. He had entered with a hunger, but his appetite now lay with its back broken, from the reek of old fat and earthy Panda Brand cigarettes. He scanned the report. Twenty-one pages to say fuck all. Twenty-one pages to point a finger at no one. Twenty-one pages to say that there had been a fire and that two had died. He already knew that two had died. The funerals would claim his Tuesday morning and his Friday afternoon.

"Shit. Shit . . ."

He folded the report neatly and stuffed it into an inside pocket. He would give it to Yaobang; it would make very acceptable toilet paper.

"Boss, what do you think, am I getting a little overweight?"

Piao looked up from his teacup, ignoring the ample stomach of Yaobang and the plastic belt that had run out of eyeholes.

"I've seen more fat on a butcher's apron."

He let loose the words and returned to his tea, stirring it vigorously and feeling no guilt. It was that kind of a relationship. The Big Man unwrapping a heavy doughy dumpling from its brown paper shroud, the grease oozing to its surface in flat black oceans.

"You got Pan out of the city?"

Yaobang pushed the paper into his pocket, grease spots blossoming on his shirt front, his eyes focussed on the dumpling which he held at chest height.

"Uh-huhh . . ."

"To your uncle's house?"

"Mmm . . ."

He was slowly, steadily, raising the dumpling to his lips, his eyes fondling the great white pearl.

"He'll be safe there?"

"Yeah, yeah . . ."

"You're sure?"

He could smell it, almost taste it, almost feel its bland texture across his tongue. He lowered the dumpling from his lips, still in one piece.

"Boss, I'm sure. It's a small village. Any sign of strangers and the alarm goes up. If it's not fat geese, it's skinny old women or the chairman's old Red Guard. They're the best early warning system in the country. Between them they might not have a fucking tooth in their heads, but, believe me, they could scare the shit out of anyone with those gums."

The mention of teeth, gums . . . he thought of his own and drew the dumpling toward his open mouth.

"And you gave your brother the photographs of the bodies?"

"Yes, I gave him all the prints."

"And you reminded him of when and where we are meeting?"

"Boss!"

Yaobang drew the dumpling away from his lips one last time.

"You already know the answers to these bloody questions. Now can I get on with my meal. I haven't eaten all day."

Piao raised his eyes from the cup.

"You haven't eaten for an hour and a half."

"Okay, okay. A day, an hour and a half, does it matter? I was a big baby. I need regular feeding."

He launched into the dumpling, lips glistening grease, a dreamy look washing across his wide face. When he spoke, each word was muffled and punctuated by a peppering of sodden dumpling shreds.

"As fucking good as a fucking orgasm."

"How would you know?" Piao countered.

The Big Man coughed, spluttered and then swallowed hard. He reached into a trouser pocket retrieving a fistful of crumpled notes.

"The collection money for Wenbiao's mother, three hundred Yuan so far . . . not bad, eh? The boys thought that we should get the old woman one of those new barbecue sets; every time she uses it she could think of him."

Steel on steel . . . black snow. Piao closed his eyes for an instant and could still feel the knifepoint heat behind his eyelids.

"I know, I know, Boss. Bad joke, bad taste. It was Yantan. You know what animals these Kazakhs are."

The Senior Investigator stirred his tea once more. It was already cold. He had never had any intention of drinking it; stirring it, watching it . . . that was enough.

"Yantan's an imbecile. His mouth writes cheques that his brain can't cash."

Yaobang bit into the dumpling once more.

92

"Whatever you say, Boss. Whatever you say. Shit I nearly forgot! Boss you're needed at the front desk, Yun is having his balls chewed off by some American woman. Last I saw he was screaming for an interpreter, so was she. I volunteered you."

Piao pushed his cup across the tabletop.

"Thanks."

"Had to Boss, Yun had that look on his face, like the time his patrol car was stolen on Yishanlu."

Piao remembered the look: dog shit all over my new shoes, kind of a look. The Senior Investigator was already leaving his seat.

"What's the story?"

"Spilt rice, Boss. The word is that she's a big-wheel politician. They say Liping's promised her the earth and she doesn't look the type to be fed on just promises and plain fucking noodles. Not this one. Besides, it's more than just a lost handbag . . ."

The Big Man rolled the last of the dumpling into a tight ball and tossed it into his mouth, his palms glistening with grease.

". . . they say her son's gone missing."

Perfection, the number seven. Perfection, the form and white fragrant flesh of the lychee. And her.

And her.

He hated her the moment that he saw her. She reminded him of how sour his life was, sucked through the tear bitter pith of a lemon. She reminded him of the dirt that sat underneath his fingernails. Also, other things he knew as soon as he saw her . . . with a certainty. That her son was dead.

Remembering the cascade of crystal water meeting mud and washing it aside. The desperately white skin revealed. The fine feathering of corn dolly hair. The broken lips kissing at a secret agony. Yes, he knew the secret. Her son was dead. There was no turning back now; the rail track home had been ripped up.

"Are you Chinese, the interpreter?"

Piao moved closer. A perfume of expensive flowers laced by steel wire about her.

"Are you American, the client?"

Barbara's eyes narrowed, reminding the Senior Investigator of ships running lights on the Suzhou Creek in winter.

"Your English is very good for a Chinese."

"Your English is passable for an American."

She snapped her head back, her hair flicking as a sharp breeze does when it rolls across a field of heavy corn. Every move she made speaking a thousand words in English and ten thousand signs in Chinese.

"Can you tell the detective that I am Barbara Hayes. Chief Liping has spoken very highly of him and has assured me of his full assistance in attempting to find my son. Can he tell me where his investigation is at present?"

Piao interpreted. Each word adding to the acned fire that blistered across Yun's face.

The Senior Investigator knew this look also . . . *The bastard hasn't even glanced at the report. He'll stall . . . in an investigation that hasn't even started yet. Shit. An investigation that will never start.*

Yun's reply was very well rehearsed. Words that were not his own; practised in the reflection of a mirror as he poked and preened the pucker that was his face. Who was the Lord of Yun's heaven? Piao knew for sure that he would be a merchant who would not give, if he was not paid.

"I, as representative of the Public Security Bureau, welcome you as our esteemed guest. We are humbled to have an American government official of such magnitude visit us. However, it will be our pleasure to demonstrate to you our efficiency in dealing with your difficulty and bringing it to a satisfactory conclusion. The police force of the People's Republic of China is known throughout the world for its unwavering thoroughness and ability. You will be in a position to witness this at close quarters and to take this experience back to your own country . . . our esteemed trading partner, the United States of America."

It was only after Piao had fully interpreted Yun's speech that the assembled detectives, with Barbara at their epicentre, had applauded. Applauded politely. Applauded gently. It sounding like the waters of the Huangpu lapping onto its foreshore. As it had done on that night.

★

It was only when Barbara had left the *fen-chu* and was on the street, that she realised that she still had nothing. Just words. Words, as sticky to the plate as caramelised sweet potato fritters and as filling as candy-floss.

'Stupid . . . stupid.'

She walked, hands clasped together in a tight cage; knuckles white, shaking her head. Sichuanlu wrapped itself around her, assaulting every single sense. All of life strewn out to view. A garbage of cooking, arguing, selling, shouting. A vast and constantly changing mosaic of darting children, urinating dogs, tight knots of women, and streams of concerned-eyed men. . . . and through the middle of Sichuanlu the constant roar of a metal river of traffic in a full flood of diesel fumes and cracked windscreens. It was a madhouse. She raised a hand and a taxi veered towards her in a salvo of horn blasts. But with a jolt, she was being propelled away from the kerb, across the sidewalk and toward an alley. A hand, huge, hard, across her mouth . . . silencing her terror. Large arms around her, making her think of bear paws . . . almost lifting her under her armpits and thrusting her forward through the crowd. Her arms hanging limp. A wash of faces accelerating past her, none of them lifting up their eyes to hers. The sunlight was gone and suddenly it felt very cold. At the far end of the alley a car clung firmly to the shadow. A limpet of steel, bald tyres, peeling chrome. The door opened and she was levered in. An odour of cheap cigarettes, sweaty groins, filling her nostrils. Danger and bad news, both have a smell . . . this was it. She clawed for a door handle; her hand parried and then held. Then the words that she knew that she would have to come face to face with. The moment that she heard them, knowing them to be true.

"Your son's dead."

The cars engine gargled into life, the driver turning around to face her. Blue eyes set into a soft mask of diluted Chinese.

95

"I'm sorry,' Piao said. But the words were lost to her as they pulled out of the alley and into Sichuanlu, the tide of hot metal taking them to its heart.

★

Chinese women are liberated, but unequal. China is a man's world. Look to the fields. A wife is no longer a *neirer*, an 'inside person' . . . as represented in the ideogram for peace and harmony, a woman sitting under a roof. Women are outside, in the world. They plant beans. Harvest rice. Feed the animals. Cut the corn. They are outside, in the world. But they do not drive the tractors. On CAAC, women will be your air stewardesses; but almost all of the passengers will be men. In restaurants you will be waited on by women; but it will be men who will be eating the dishes of pork and mustard greens. In hospitals, it will be women who will bandage your hand; but men who will direct them how and where to apply that bandage.

No longer the broken arch and curled toes of the 'Lilly Foot' . . . "Obey heaven and follow fate." But for women, who Mao had drawn to his side by putting words to the promise that they, "held up half the sky" . . . a disregard, a using.

As a baby girl you will be told that you are "a thousand ounces of gold" . . . but that a baby boy is "ten thousand ounces of gold." As a teenage daughter who will eventually be given away in marriage, no longer of any economic benefit to her family, you will be told that you are as "spilled water." As a bride you will go to your marital bed knowing that, ". . . if a woman marries a chicken, she should act as a chicken; if she marries a dog, she should act like a dog."

For women in China, it is the existence of the invisible touch, the silenced word, the lowered eyes, the tiptoed presence. It is an equality that never reaches *gao-chao* . . . the 'high tide' mark.

★

He could see her reflection in the rear-view mirror. Her

96

temple brushing the side window . . . hair flashing corn yellow. When Chinese women cried it was as if the world would crack, but this woman cried silently. As if each tear had a hefty price attached to it.

Piao knew of no way of handling death other than laying it wide open to view. You vomited it out, as you would overhung duck or sweetly putrid pork. For your own health, you vomited it out.

There was no detail that he left out. She deserved at least that, and so did the spilt life of her child. From beneath the driver's seat he handed her the heavy brown envelope with the pin-sharp, full frame monochrome prints. Watching her in the rear-view mirror as she studied each ten by eight inch print through the melt of tears. The prints of torn, wasted, discarded flesh. She said only one word . . .

"Bobby."

That was enough.

★

The lobby of the Jing Jiang Hotel was full of stripe shirted, check trousered Americans. Round, grizzly shouldered men slung with exotic black cameras, and craggy thin lipped women whose hair never moved, and whose mouths never stopped moving. Piao and Yaobang brushed past them as they followed Barbara to the elevator. Their smell was of syrup sweet candy and dust, of opulent pensions and prescription drugs. Piao crumpled the packet and pocketed it. It was his last Panda brand. Tomorrow would be a bad day, it would be back to the local shit.

"A Senior Investigator in the Homicide Squad, is that good? Are you good?"

They were the first words that she had spoken in thirty minutes. Eyes now dry, but washed out . . . almost white. Like cold and distant stars that had been plucked from Orion's Belt. Piao exhaled.

"Good?"

Smoke curling from his nostrils.

"I suppose that it depends on what good means to you.

97

Good in Washington might be shit in Beijing. Shit in Beijing might be acceptable here in Shanghai."

"Are you good?"

Steel in her voice. Her eyes darkening now to the hue of granite. The elevator door jerked open.

"I'm the best you're going to get."

She walked into the corridor, Piao's eyes following her legs.

★

Room 201 was warm, but felt cold, as if sheltering under the wing of some vast and unexplained beast. Barbara sat on the bed, legs folded under her like a graceful gazelle. Head lowered. Hair forming a golden curtain to her eyes, her thoughts. Yaobang stood at the window picking his nose, picking his teeth, scratching his arse. At the desk, Piao read the report on Bobby and the dead son's letters and cards to his mother. It took forty-five minutes. Two thousand seven hundred seconds without a cigarette. Occasionally he walked to the window, shoulder to shoulder with the Big Man . . . postcard in hand, lifting his eyes to where cityscape met sky. The sun high, a yellow drawing pin holding up a sheet of colourless sky. When the Senior Investigator closed the report, Barbara raised her head.

"What do you think?"

Piao winced. He hated having to give an instant appraisal. He was a homicide detective. Builders gave instant appraisals, so did tailors. But detectives . . . their words had to be measured in thousandths, and snipped from heavy gauge steel plate.

"I think that your son had an enemy with a long shadow and a secret that fell under it. To make someone disappear in this country is not difficult, but to erase a life, to rub out its path as if it never existed, that is another thing. To do that, to influence the Luxingshe, the PSB, the Internal Security Services . . . now that is another thing. You have to be highly placed, powerful."

Piao was on his feet, pacing. The implications of his own words driving him towards the bed.

"You're saying that there is a conspiracy . . . you're saying

98

that I've been screwed since I stepped off the plane, lied to?"

Yes, you've been screwed. When does the screwing ever stop. Whoever assigned Yun to you, with his pretty speech, knew what they were doing. Brush it under the matting. A detective who couldn't find his dick in his own pants . . . in a fen-chu that couldn't arrest a dog on heat. Yes, this is screwing . . . high cadre screwing.

Piao nodded. Turning. Moving once more toward the window. Aware that this was a woman who intended to skin the whole snake and not give a shit about the gore left on the kitchen floor. The Senior Investigator felt a headache inching behind his eyes. Enough. This had to be where the screwing stopped. Resting his hand on the window frame, he felt a rash of paint drips hunched under its lip. Sloppy workmanship . . . he hated sloppy workmanship. Piao pushed a fingernail into one of the plump tears, removing it, leaving a soft edged crescent moon . . . his nail bleeding sticky white. Fresh paint.

"Yaobang."

The Big Man followed Piao to the door and out into the corridor. A room boy was several doors away. The Senior Investigator nodded in his direction and Yaobang fetched him by the elbow, stifling his complaints with the glimpse of a red and gold badge. Yaobang pulled the long chain of keys from his pocket and nudged the room boy to indicate which ones were to be used for the room doors either side of room 201. With walnut knuckles, the Big Man gently tapped on each door before opening them. The taps were not answered. The rooms empty. Piao spending no more than thirty seconds in each room before leaving, gently closing the doors and retracing his steps back to room 201.

"What the hell was that about?"

She moved from the bed. Something in her walk that reminded Piao of the sway of a reed bank. He was no expert . . . it had been years since he had seen a reed bank. Eighteen months since he had even looked at another woman.

"I needed to be sure that this room, your son's room, is the only room that has recently been redecorated."

"And?"

He walked past her toward the bathroom. She followed him straightening her skirt, turning to face him.

"And?"

Again she wanted words that he could not measure, did not have time to carve from stone. It left him uncomfortable, almost fighting for breath.

"I am sure. They have done a thorough job. We will see how thorough."

Piao started to pull the side panel of the bath adrift. Yaobang got to his knees to help him, panting . . . a sweat already pushing its way onto his forehead.

"It's almost impossible to remove every detail of evidence . . ."

The side panel was off, the Senior Investigator starting to dismantle the piping around the large U-bend.

". . . evidence gets everywhere. Where people have spent time, something always remains . . ."

A pipe, rusting steel, flaking paint . . . fell heavily to the floor. A brief sound of water. A vicious stink of sewers.

". . . people, slugs, they are no different. Both leave a trail of slime wherever they go . . ."

Piao carried the pipe to the hand basin as Yaobang straightened, grumbling.

". . . check out the other room."

The Big Man nodded, his large hands massaging the base of his spine as he limped from the bathroom. The Senior Investigator rolled up his sleeves and flushed the U-bend out violently with a stream of cold water. A fat slug nosed from the other end of the pipe. Congealed hair, spent matches, nail clippings, cigarette butts. He eased the mass from the pipe with his fingers, fully exposing it. The stench filled the room. Bile rising in Barbara's throat, her hands automatically seeking her mouth . . . clamped across it in a grill of white knuckles and pink blush nail paint. But the fascination of what Piao was involved in, holding the sickness at arm's-length.

With a pen in each hand he slowly dissected the mass. Teasing it from itself. Exposing its fibrous innards and soft underbelly.

"Jesus," he heard Barbara breathe across his shoulder. A thick stratum of long blond hair amongst the black, being teased away and apart. A rich vein of Bobby's hair, all American golden candy yellow . . . encased in a mesh, a confusion of oriental ebony black. Piao placed some of the hair in a small polythene bag and sealed it. With tweezers he removed other objects from the hair-ball's guts and dropped them into another bag.

"Something always remains," he breathed.

He turned and walked into the bedroom to be greeted by Yaobang's arse squirming from underneath the bed. If arse ever became as expensive as pork, the Big Man would be sitting on a fortune.

"Anything?"

Yaobang sat like a Buddha, brushing the fluff from his jacket, the buttons of his flies straining at their buttonholes.

"One condom, used. Three cockroaches, dead. At least a hundred cigarette butts, but fuck all listening devices. The Sixth Bureau wasn't interested in this *wai-guo-ren*, Boss. There's no signs they've ever given this room the treatment. The cleaners weren't too interested in this room either."

"You're sure?"

"As sure as my stomach's telling me it's lunchtime."

You couldn't get more sure than that. Piao returned to the window. The city was moving. Slow trickles of reflected glass semaphoring in and out of shadow. Once more he searched for Huangpu Park . . . the embarkation point for river trips, knowing that he would be unable to see it from room 201. Again Piao read two of Bobby's postcards. Confirming. There was no doubt. *You must recognise the sun for what it is when it shines.*

The view written about could not have been glimpsed through 201's windows. The view written about could not have been seen from the Jing Jiang Hotel. When Bobby Hayes had written these two cards he had been sitting in another room in another part of the city . . . with another view filling the window. Another view filling his eyes.

★

101

Warm fingers stroking through cold water.

Piao could not see her eyes but knew that she was crying. A lock of Bobby's hair held in her fingers, dancing to the flow of the running water.

"Do you have children?"

He could only just hear her above the cascade of the water.

"No. I had a wife, but no children."

She turned slightly. A tear on her cheek, followed by another.

"Don't. Losing them is too painful to bear. Better not to have had them."

"But all the memories you have . . ."

Barbara turned the tap off, facing him. Drying her hands and folding the wisp of hair into a handkerchief. The depth of the silence like a knife held to Piao's throat.

"Memories . . ."

Piao thought that he'd never heard a word, any word, said so sadly.

"Sorry," he said, leading her from the bathroom, her hand as cold as frost.

★

The hotel restaurant was closed, but the red and gold on Piao's badge got them in; Barbara's dollars bought them coffee . . . bitter and lukewarm.

"Did you know your son?"

Barbara lit a cigarette. She was so close that he could taste the smoke, leather and honey. He would have given a middle finger for just one American cigarette.

"I think so, well . . ."

She pulled at its long filter as if it were a lifeline. It's tip firing to the hue of a ripe tangerine.

'. . . I know that he always hated wearing diapers . . . used to pull them off every time. I know that he had an allergy to peanuts when he was six. Put him in hospital twice. When he was eight his dad left. I know that he took it bad, but has never talked about it. I know that from ten years old, when he found a Cherokee arrowhead in his grandpa's backyard, that he wanted to be an archaeologist . . ."

Her lips melted around the cigarette butt. Soft, calm rivers, encircling, embracing a stone island.

"You know your son as a baby, a boy, perhaps even as a teenager, if you're lucky. But as a man, who knows men?"

Smoke across her mouth. Smoke across her eyes.

"Men tell women nothing of importance. Sons tell mothers only the things that they want them to know. Does your mother know when you are visiting the hospital to have the dressings on your fingers changed? Does your mother even know that you were injured?"

The Senior Investigator's hands found his trouser pockets.

"See what I mean?"

He buried his hands deeper. Point taken.

"The telephone calls that you shared, did he ever mention a girl, even once?"

Barbara shook her head.

"No, never . . ."

"You are sure?"

". . . mmm, positive. He never mentioned a girl."

Piao's gaze wandered, an elusive shadow of a thought passing through his mind. Although the Jing Jiang was Shanghai's most prestigious hotel, it looked dusty, jaded. A favourite aunt who was slowly fading away in a shrug of washed out red velvet and threadbare salmon and yellow patterned carpet. He watched a group of tourists pass the double doors, faces glowing from showers that were too hot, too fierce. Not a single crease on tee shirts or slacks. It would have cost him three months' salary to afford just one night of luxury at the Jing Jiang. He looked away.

"You know something. What is it that you're not telling me, Senior Investigator?"

He already had the small polythene bag in his hand, its contents falling onto the page of his notebook. Six crescent moon nails bleeding with bright red nail varnish. And with it . . . the smell of that night on the foreshore, upon him. And the mud . . . its heavy black veil slipping aside to reveal the albino toes with their red painted toenails. Like overripe cherries.

"The girl that your son never mentioned."

Piao poked the red varnished nail clippings with his pen.

"A prostitute?"

The Senior Investigator wondered why a mother should automatically think that the girl who had shared her son's bath should be a *yeh-ji*. Perhaps the red of the nail varnish was a little too red? The coating of the varnish a little too thick? Perhaps she thought that only prostitutes trimmed their nails in the bath?

"No, not a prostitute. Wild pheasants are too busy to spend their time manicuring their nails while they are at work. *Yeh-ji* are either on their back or in the back of a taxi heading for a tourist hotel to spend more time on their backs. Time is money. Money is fucking."

She didn't blush. Piao felt cheated. Barbara could see the logic. Her hands found her pocket, locating the lock of Bobby's hair; weaving it between her fingers. Secrets upon secrets. The onion skins peeling away.

"No, this was a girl relaxed, at home. This was not casual. This was playing at mummies and daddies. This was playing house . . ."

The hair intertwined between her fingers felt like razor wire.

". . . there was a girl amongst the eight pulled from the Huangpu. Pretty. Her toenails were painted red. The same colour of red. I remember them, they reminded me of sweet cherries. It has been a long time since I have eaten cherries."

Piao chased the nail clippings back into the polythene bag and re-sealed it; standing, flexing the stiff joints of his fingers.

The walk to the restaurant's double doors felt perilously long. His teeth clenched upon half secrets and half truths. All of the time, aware of her following him . . . their shadows spilling into each others. As he neared the doors he could see the tourists herding through the corridor. They would smell of soap and leather . . . 'greenbacks' and dreams. With luck it would drive the stench of river mud and secrets from his nostrils.

★

104

Secrets . . . the hint of a meal not yet cooked.

She lost him to the weave of tourists, but the elevator slowed him . . . catching him as its black mouth engulfed them in a press of plaid and mock leather shoulder bags.

"Tomorrow . . ."

Piao turned to face her. Blue, her eyes . . . unbearably blue.

". . . I suppose we'll be going to Fudan University to see if we can get an angle on Bobby and Lazarus Heywood?"

"We? I do not think that you fully realise the situation, my American guest. This is an investigation of a multiple homicide. Strict protocols have to be adhered to. There are regulations to consider, regulations that forbid us from including you in such an investigation as this. We do not need a, how do you say it . . . a 'sidekick'? This is Shanghai. This is not Seattle."

Piao reached into his pocket for a crumpled cigarette from a crumpled packet. A jolt of realisation, none left.

Fuck it.

"Look, I want to be included. I need to be involved . . ."

Trying to catch his eye as he let the carton fall to the worn square of carpet.

". . . I think that I might already be involved. That this murder, Bobby's murder, might be . . ."

Thinking too much. Saying too much. Her fingers moving to her lips, as if to hold the words in place with their pale spanning web.

"Might be what? Are there things that you have not told me?"

Marking her silence, his fingers tapping out a nervous rhythm across the brushed steel of the elevator's clamped doors.

"Barbara Hayes, are there words that you need to say? If there are, I must hear them."

Silence. The Senior Investigator shaking his head.

"I have already said. There are strict protocols, especially for a tourist to my country. Even though you are a privileged guest. Regulations. Rules. This case, it is complicated. So very complicated. Your involvement, it is not invited. It is not required. It is not recommended."

The elevator door staggered open, spewing them out. Barbara at Piao's heels, chasing, snapping, a hand on his shoulder pulling him round; now firm, cool against his chest. Barring his way. Her eyes were grey, stainless steel and beyond influence. No words from her, just her look . . . fire and rain in her face. A dead son . . . ten thousand ounces of gold.

Piao shook his head.

"I am not going to Fudan University tomorrow. I am going to my cousin's funeral. The cousin who died for keeping your son's body in his warehouse."

He moved down the stairs towards the car, aware only of her beside him. Her hand on his arm, the rough material of his jacket between her fingers.

"I am sorry, it was selfish of me. If I may, I would like to come and pay my respects?"

He pulled away. She let go of his arm. Watching as he stepped into the car. Watching as he turned the ignition key. Piao winding down the window as the car slowly moved off.

"Wear white," he shouted above the slaughter of traffic noise.

"In China, white is the colour of death."

Chapter 10

The city, the countryside. Both have lives that are different. Deaths also.

In the city, if you die, you will be cremated . . . it's mandatory. Land that can grow rice and cash crops cannot be lavished upon those who life no longer possesses. In the city, the elaborate and costly funerals, the very substance of China's native religion, the cult of the ancestors . . . have been simplified; pruned back to the heartwood.

In the countryside, the party's edicts slow in the mud of the fields; mellow in the nicotine yellow fingers of the peasantry. At sixty, the number of years considered to be the normal life cycle, the grandmother will still save for the eighty Yuan that will purchase the fine camphor wood coffin, storing it in readiness in the corner of the family's single room. And when the grandmother is no longer in possession of life she will be laid out for the traditional three days in front of the Buddhist star that was so carefully hidden from the Red Guards during the shudder of the Cultural Revolution. Her favourite foods will be placed in three clay bowls around her. At night her spirit will be guarded by her sons and grandsons. The last night before the funeral, she will be placed in the camphor wood coffin which will be propped up on a chair . . . the oldest son will sleep beneath it. The demons kept at bay. A practitioner of the ancient wisdom of Feng-Shi, the geomancy of the 'spirits of wind and water', will decide the favourable site for the grave. The funeral procession of close relatives dressed in white robes, white caps, strips of white paper over their shoes, will wind their way above the village, and she will be buried amongst the fir trees on the hillside.

Above the lakes, above the valleys, beyond the confines of the starry spheres.

For seven days close relatives would be forbidden to eat

107

meat. For forty-nine days the sons and the daughters, would be forbidden to bathe or wash their hair. If you died before reaching the age of sixty, the intricate scaffolding of the funeral rites would be brutally demolished. You would be called a 'short-life devil'. Someone who must have committed some terrible misdeed in this or in previous lives to have been cut down at such a premature age. Your body would not be honoured within the family house. It is known for peasants who have died young, run over by a truck, to not be honoured with a funeral at all. Their bodies left where they fell.

The festival of Qing Ming, in early April, honours the ancestors. It is a time to visit the low brick tombstones of the ancestors . . . sweep them, clean them of weeds, tell the stories out aloud, make the children aware of the rivers that flow through their lives also. Underline the reality of the days now being lived by what has gone before. It is a comfort. A thumb in the mouth.

When you leave the tombs you place a paper flower on them to mark them out, to show that they have been visited, cared for. That the ancestors are still with us; they breathe, they live.

Red flowers, blue, green, yellow, white flowers.

The Party do not give the peasants a holiday for the festival of Qing Ming. It is a superstitious custom. It honours the ancestors. It raises the hanging tree of religion. Above all, it interferes with work. But go to Quanzhou on the day of Qing Ming, to the hillsides hugging hillsides. Each lazy arc a darker grey than the last. See the paper flowers?

Red flowers, blue, green, yellow, white flowers.

★

Gashed to the colour of worn leather; running to a horizon obscured by pillow hills, the fields had been worked, ploughed, planted to within inches of the cemetery boundary. Inside the graveyard, it was as if the heavens had opened up and wept, spotting each tomb with paper flowers of red, blue, green, yellow, white. There was a rustle with each breeze.

Paper on paper. Colours colliding. Polite applause of gratitude from the ancestors.

★

The line of mourners, like doves, moved through the graveyard, across the fields, back toward the house sitting at the edge of the village. The smell of the house was of wood fires and tears. Piao refused tea, preferring Dukang. It was where it always had been. He helped himself. The rice spirit was fire, it would dull the knife-edge of pain within him.

★

A dull light played from the ceiling of the attic, swinging on a flex tethered by cobwebs. Piao gently placed the bottle of Dukang onto the floor, the glasses also, beside the sleeping bags; empty bottles of Qingdao beer, bowls of congealed rice with slicks of red pepper sauce, littering the wood boarded floor.

"I see you're out of beer?"

A bottle spun from Piao's foot, rolling against Yaobang's sleeping bag. The Big Man stretched his back; bones colliding and crunching into place.

"Out of beer, out of patience, out of fucking vertebrae."

He grimaced. His teeth looking like the soles of shoes.

"Out of toothpaste?"

Yaobang rubbed his front teeth with a discoloured finger.

"Toothpaste?"

He examined the finger carefully.

"Never use the stuff. Bourgeois shit, used by queers and capitalists . . ."

Piao could still taste the mint from his own toothpaste on his tongue. The Big Man wiped his finger across his shirt front.

". . . what was the funeral like, Boss?"

Piao finished his drink, filling his glass and the other two. The Dukang's hue, that of smelted lead.

"Funerals. Just filler to cover over the waste. Depressing. Fucking depressing . . ."

He took the drink through clenched teeth, across his tongue; a rye and sorghum bushfire out of control.

109

". . . the only good thing about funerals is the drink."

The Big Man nodded in agreement, raising his glass and draining it before slamming it down for a refill; the tears haemorrhaging to the corners of his eyes.

"Nothing to be gained by being depressed Boss. What does it fucking give you? Only the shits and the sleepless nights?"

"It gives you less distance to fall," Piao whispered. There was silence. A silence as if he were already falling. The Senior Investigator re-poured.

"Dukang, or do you only drink Coca-Cola, like other students?"

The Senior Investigator held the third glass of spirit towards the shadow beyond the Big Man. The liquid as grey as wet slate. Pan Yaobang shifted uncomfortably on his haunches, the side of his face catching the light. Piao knelt in front of the student, pressing the glass into his fingers; his own hands wrapped around Pan's.

"Let us play a game. I will be honest, completely honest for two minutes. I would appreciate it if you would too . . ."

Between them, from the rafters, dust in a slow and balletic fall. Dark to light . . . light to dark. Piao continued.

". . . you are scared, alone, and angry. So angry. One moment you are a student, university is simple. Minimal study, no responsibilities, no ties, the future looking secure, safe. And the girls . . . 'the girls'. The next moment you are in a world where people are torn in half like so much waste paper; crumpled up. In the night you are moved from safe house to safe house. Shut away in rooms that have no windows. Living with strangers. What is the future now? Life is dark . . . under threat. You are being followed. People around you are being killed . . ."

The student's eyes were closed. Tears . . . hot, fierce, clamped tight. Piao could smell their warmth, the salt in their sting, the fear at their root.

". . . and I am the one you blame. It is my fault . . ."

Pan's eyes opened, the tears set loose.

". . . drink the Dukang. Alcohol can help, when you do not need it to help . . ."

The Senior Investigator raised the student's hands to his lips. Drinking, coughing . . . tears running into the rice spirit. Piao wiped Pan's face with his cuff.

". . . my fault student? Eight bodies split like bean pods and thrown into the river. Two men, one my cousin, buried outside. Strung up like pork carcasses on meat hooks. Two hours, that is all. If you had been in the warehouse two hours longer you would have joined them. But you were not, and so there are more days in which life has possession of you, of us. More days to seek those who kill . . . and who would kill us. That is all that I wish to do . . ."

A breeze sighed through the large loft. For a few seconds they seemed to be held solely in its grasp. There was no world. No sky, no earth. No broken bodies.

". . . I am no hero, but I know heroes. They are too scared to be cowards . . ."

He reached down for his drink, it had spilt, the glass tipped to the floor. A mercury pool slowly shrinking through the floorboards. A gift to the ancestors.

". . . so what do you do, close your eyes, walk away? We live in a country that 'kills the chicken to scare the monkey'. I know, I have killed enough chickens in my job. But there comes a time when one can't close one's eyes, when someone has to say 'enough'?"

Piao looked away, his attention summoned by a distant car horn. Knowing that the Shanghai Sedan that had followed them would still be parked in the shadows on the twist of the Lushin Road. Its occupants taking turns to sleep. One always awake, watching. In the hours that deserved respect, cigarettes would burn angrily. Talk would be of disembodied tits, pussies. And there would be a smell that cars with such passengers always smelt of . . . cold noodles, cold sweat, and the hint of violence served cold. Now, right now, they would be watching. But watching for what, an Investigator, investigating? Or watching an American, an American with official status who still had the cold tears of a dead son in her eyes? Perhaps a Senior Investigator in the Homicide Squad was just the side-glance, a flicker of disinterested attention. But such an

American, now there is an object worth the full and studied glare.

Pan raised his head. Eye contact for the first time. He looked tired. It was obvious that his sleep was ragged. His words slow, strung out, like clothes hanging from a washing line on a still morning.

"Have you ever seen cowboy films, American films, westerns?"

Piao shook his head, feeling the effects of the Dukang. Giving every word an echo, every movement of his eyes a feeling of nauseous acceleration.

"No, I do not care for American films. I saw one once, *Love Story* . . . my wife's choice. A film for a woman. I remember that she cried a lot."

"I like cowboy films. In cowboy films the bad men wear black. Always black. Even their horses are black. The good men wear white. Always white. White hats, jackets, and they ride white horses . . ."

He stopped to lick his lips. Dukang makes your mouth feel dry . . . so dry.

". . . what are we?"

Piao laughed. A half Chinese cowboy detective riding a white horse through the cityscape of Shanghai. It would have had interesting possibilities if he had been able to ride.

"Senior Investigators do not wear hats, neither do students. But we are the good men . . ."

He halted for a second, the laugh fading, but its memory etched into the blue of his eyes.

". . . in this case."

"But we will win. The cowboys in the white hats always win in the end?"

"Winning might be several different things, in this case. If you are really asking me if you also will end up in the river or hanging from a meat hook, I can answer you, if you want me to?"

Pan nodded.

"You will live, student. I promise it, live to an old age. Live to see the Party crumble and every family realise their dreams

112

of owning their own video recorders, their own cars, their own overdrafts . . ."

He patted Pan on the cheek.

". . . you will live, cowboy. *Ku-hai yu-sheng.* Alive in the bitter sea. Now get on your white horse and talk to me of the words that dead bodies speak."

★

Estimated times of death. So much to take into account. Cooling when naked is half again as fast as when clothed, and when in water, in the Huangpu, twice as fast. The physique of each victim to be noted. The ventilation and temperature of rooms, if that is where the body has been discovered. Allowances to be made for all of these corrective factors. And all adding up to nothing more than a 'peak of probability.' All of the eight sharing the same peak of probability. Eighteen to thirty-six hours. Rigor had still been present. The skin markedly wrinkled on the hands and feet. No discoloration at the root of the neck. No discoloration or swelling around the face or neck. Yes, eighteen to thirty-six hours. That was how long they had been dead.

Pan took some more Dukang, coughing. His notes flapping in his hands like the wings of baby birds.

The girl, she had been pregnant, probably around twenty-one weeks. A needle mark still visible on her abdomen from an amniocentesis that would have been performed between the sixteenth and eighteenth week of gestation. The Senior Investigator finished another drink, the Dukang wet on his lips . . . his fingers suddenly nervous, not knowing what to do with them. He poured another glass.

"If it's such a common test, how come I've never heard of it?"

The student looked up. At last, a subject that he knew.

"They are getting more common, yes. Twenty to thirty millilitres of amniotic fluid is withdrawn from the amniotic sac. It is then bio-chemically analysed and foetal cells are cultured for chromosomal analysis. From this, foetal abnormalities can be detected. Down's Syndrome, as well as helping us to detect some genetic disorders . . . haemophilia, cystic fibrosis, Tay–Sachs Disease . . ."

He looked back to his notes, his spectacle lenses now taken up by lines of writing . . . words, like black beetles, scrolling across the glass.

". . . from this test you can also determine the sex of the foetus. That is why it is becoming more popular in our country. It gives the opportunity for early abortion. Male babies are wanted. Female babies are not . . ."

"Spilt water."

Pan looked up, recognising the Senior Investigator's words; the sarcasm lettered through them, and sharing it.

". . . no need for an abortion here. She was carrying a male foetus. It had not been expelled, it was still in her womb."

The Big Man spat, long, phlegm . . . chasing it with a shot of the rice spirit, as his brother moved on, shuffling his notes.

"The older westerner, around thirty-seven to forty-five years of age, he was American and afraid of getting older. The scars around the backs of his ears were from a cosmetic facelift. But it was what was left of his dental work that tells us of his nationality. He had an apexification. A root-end closure induction to a non-vital tooth. A calcium hydroxide paste dressing is applied to the canal which produces a calcific barrier across the root canal, or allows an immature permanent tooth apex to continue root formation."

The student looked pleased, allowing himself the seed of a smile.

"And we couldn't do that in the People's Republic, little brother, when we launch satellites into fucking outer space?"

The seed blossomed; Pan smiling fully at the Big Man, aware that every double act needed a stooge.

"We could, but we wouldn't bother. We would let the tooth rot or pull it out. In the People's Republic we care only for satellites. Take a look in the mirror at your own teeth sometime, big brother."

Yaobang turned away, running a thumb around his mouth, muttering . . .

"Nothing wrong with my fucking teeth."

Piao slapping him on the back.

"Nothing that an American dentist couldn't put right."

The student was already continuing, attention welded to the next page, the last page of his report. He seemed to be the sort who would leave the best for last. Eating the rice first, next the dumplings . . . saving the slices of aromatic duck on the side of the plate.

All had died from trauma and blood loss due to the massive wounds, lacerations and mutilations to their stomachs and chests. Also the lacerations to their lower backs, only visible when the bodies had been further sluiced down. The mud pouring thickly from the wounds, the rips, in dark winking globs and flows. But there were abnormalities, seemingly a pattern to the apparent chaos of lacerations. Procedures to the mutilations. Marks that he could not explain. Trails of hidden techniques that he felt lost in. He was just a student . . . so much of this beyond him. Text books could only provide so much help. Detailed pictures, sketches, samples, swabs, he had sent to a trustworthy professor he had studied under at the Institute, who was now a government advisor in Beijing. The Senior Investigator felt the air whistle between his teeth.

"That is very risky. I would rather have your analysis or at least your educated guess."

Pan looked up, for the first time the Senior Investigator really seeing the pain displayed in his eyes.

"No, no. This is beyond me. No analysis, no educated guesses . . ."

He stopped to drink, pulling off his spectacles. The tears bleeding to the corners of his eyes; wiping them away with his cuff. Just like a boy, just like a little boy.

". . . because Senior Investigator, nothing at the Institute trained me for this. Nothing could ever have trained me for this . . ."

Replacing his glasses. Regaining his self-control. Folding his report neatly and handing it to Piao.

". . . you see, none of the eight bodies that you pulled from the river had any kidneys. None of them had any hearts. Someone had taken them."

Chapter 11

The city morgue and forensic laboratories were housed in a rambling 1920s building a step back from Zaoyanglu. Beside it, the Wusong staggered listlessly; hiding, seeking, beneath the rib cages of bridges. Its surface colour stolen from its surroundings . . . black, grey, black. Until it decanted its arterial waters into the greater body of the Huangpu in a blossoming cloud of avocado that was on the turn.

The interior of the city morgue had been ripped out and replaced; a bloody autopsy of an excavation that had left a structure that was scarred with an architectural un-adventure that would be meaningless, worthless, within twenty years. A suspended ceiling, plastic veneers, nylon carpets, the hum of an air-conditioning breeze that smelt only of the faintest hint of burnt electricity. Was this design more suited to the handling of death? Perhaps it was.

★

Piao logged in at the new reception area. Within a minute a large Kazakh appeared, a huge bloodhound of a man . . . eyelids hanging with the certainty of heavy steel shutters. Following him as they spoke.

"I was expecting to see Wu."

The man coughed politely, a Pekinese snuffled sneeze of a cough from such a huge frame.

"Doctor Wu is on sabbatical at present."

The Senior Investigator felt the smile slide across his features, at first trying to anchor it in place, and then deciding to allow it free reign.

"Sabbatical. New words come into our vocabulary every day. And are sabbaticals normally as sudden as being run over by a truck?"

Again the cough, the avoidance.

"I am Doctor Shangyin. I have been seconded from Beijing to cover for Doctor Wu."

Seconded. Another new word. A high cadre word. A word that dripped from the lips of the military, the security forces. Not a word used by doctors. Never doctors. Piao felt the smile start to stall.

"Seconded. Well, let me wish you a very happy secondment with us here in Shanghai. And I hope that it will be a very long time before you too are volunteered for a sabbatical Doctor Shangyin."

The Kazakh blinked. The steel shutters falling and rising slowly across eyes etched yellow by jaundice. Moving through a doorway, and then another. Arriving in a large space, everything within it moulded from stainless steel, soft cornered, flowing . . . as if the ritualistic equipment of the autopsy were organic. It was as if a tidal wave of mercury had borne down upon the room; the enamelled autopsy tables with their chipped guttering that had run with laboured rivulets of scarlet, discoloured tiled white walls and open gutters that had taken the fall from the tables and which had criss-crossed their way across the stone floor in deep, brown lacerations . . . all swept away. Even a different smell haunted the space. Antiseptic, iodine, surgical handwash . . . replacing the all pervading reek of shit that Piao had always associated with the morgue. The stink that lingered in your nostrils long after you had left the building. Lingering for hours. Sometimes days.

The doctor walked to the door set in a wall of frosted glass bricks, a walk of precision . . . a measured march that could only have been fashioned on the parade square. As he opened the door the Senior Investigator noticed the Kazakh's fingers. The inside of the right forefinger, a ring of hard skin. A trigger callous. The results of friction between the flesh of the trigger finger and the metal, that repetitive use a firearm produced. Its braille was not lost on the Senior Investigator.

The door opened, revealing a stainless steel wall of deep drawers containing the bodies of those who life no longer possessed. Piao feeling a shiver deep inside of him, start to move through him to his limbs. Shangyin checked the number on the large drawer before pulling it out from the steel wall. A faint chill of air. The smell of damp earth.

"D-1150," he said.

"He has a name."

"We don't deal in names. Names are for beyond the front door."

The Kazakh moved away from the drawer, flamboyantly flipping aside the thin cotton shroud, his fingers brushing against a cold cheek . . . but not even noticing the contact. He retreated to the centre of the room, knuckles trailing the contours of an autopsy table.

"You can make a positive identification, Senior Investigator?"

The woman who lay in the drawer was perhaps sixty years old; her face, pulp, but her body screamed the passing of each year. A railway junction of silver tracked stretch marks, converging and then dispersing to separate destinations. Her breasts milkless, shapeless. Seemingly hollow pancakes that fell between her upper arms and torso.

Piao turned the cardboard tag that was tied to her big toe. L-901.

"You have screwed up doctor. Your own sabbatical draws closer."

Shangyin's snatched the tag from Piao's fingers. No words, just controlled rage.

"A bad day at the office?"

The Kazakh glared at Piao, his forehead flat, shiny. Reaching past the Senior Investigator for the steel drawer behind him. Piao ducked. A sigh of chilled air. The cotton barrier snatched aside. The doctor fumbling for the toe tag.

D-872. Male. Bloated, stinking. A river floater . . . flesh on the turn like the waters. Age, perhaps forty, forty-five.

The Kazakh reaching for another drawer . . . and another. His breath coming faster.

*L-907. Female, a child, eight years old? Face, torso, limbs . . . black
. . . swollen with a storm of bruises.*

*L-740. Female, mid-twenties. Road accident. Red nail varnish and
red lacerations to face, torso.*

Another drawer wrenched open, almost off its hinges.

D-1101. Male. Fifty year old. Knife wounds to neck, chest, stomach. Black slugs of un-bleeding punctures.

The sixth drawer yanked open, sliding on runners to its stops.
Shangyin checking the tag and pulling it adrift for correction;
facing Piao, breathing controlled now. Relaxing. The ghost of
a smile.

"Now can you make a positive identification, Senior
Investigator?"

Piao fought against the desire to close his eyes once more.

*How many bodies of the dead can you look at before they mark
you, scar your soul?*

*D-1150. Male. Twenty-two years old. Student. Multiple gunshot
wounds. Two to the head. One removing the left side of the jaw and
half of the bottom lip. The second shot, dead centre of the forehead
. . . obscenely neat. The entry, a blood blister . . . the exit, a ragged
crater that had robbed the back of the skull of its substance. A hole
decanted with blackness and a shock of bone . . . so white. Two more
shots had also found their target, one clipping the right shoulder, just
a snip. The last shot taking out the throat in one great red angry
bite.*

"A positive identification Senior Investigator, we need one. Is
this D-1150?"

Piao's eyes not leaving the corpse's forehead. The symmetry, the size, the neatness of the hole passing through it,
intriguing him.

"What size round was used?"

"I do not know . . . it is too soon. One was dug out here.

Several at the scene. They only went up to the lab this morning."

"They were 7.65mm, weren't they? Type 64. Rimless, unique . . ."

"I said that it is too soon Investigator . . ."

". . . too soon for an experienced eye like yours, doctor?"

Piao grabbed Shangyin's hand, pinning it to the steel wall, spreading out the fingers and running his thumb across the trigger callus; hard, dead skin, tanned by nicotine and sitting like a discarded segment of juiceless orange.

". . . too soon for a good Party member like you who spends so much of his spare time on the firing range?"

The Kazakh pulled his hand away, the sweat from his palm leaving an imprint against the stainless steel skin of the wall.

"7.65mm. They were 7.65mm, type 64 and you fucking know it. Standard issue for security . . ."

Piao pushed the drawer, it coasted on runners closing flush into the metal wall with a gasp of air. He walked to the door.

". . . I will be seeing you again, Comrade Doctor, you can depend upon it. That is, if you are not also sent on a sabbatical."

The Senior Investigator swung open the door. An urge, sudden and bottomless, to run and not stop . . . through the streets like when he was a child. Pavements sprinting. Leaving the pain behind.

"D-1150. His name is Yaobang, Comrade Doctor. Pan Yaobang."

The door closed. He ran.

Huangdong, the Number 1 Hospital – Suzhou Beilu.

"We left four hours after you, like you said, Boss. We couldn't have been seen, not in that darkness. There was fuck all on the road, and we'd seen those bastards leave following you in their Sedan."

A room stormed with white light. Deep shadows . . . as if cut with shears. A steel framed bed dominating the small space.

"It was a two hour drive. We were just outside of Tunxi. I know the road. I walked the 'Back of the Carp' to the peak of Tiandu once. You know they call it the 'Capital of Heaven'? I was thinner then. I didn't see God . . . and he couldn't have fucking seen me."

Shoes, a nurse's stout legs planted in them . . . walking in the corridor outside, just beyond the room.

"I stopped the car halfway down the hill, between the hair-pins. I needed a piss, I was nearly doing it in my pants. I walked partly down a bank, it was just starting to rain. I remember it on my face. I got my cock out and began to piss. Then lights came on moving past our car, down the hill. Another car, a Shanghai Sedan I think, its engine turned off. There was no sound, except for shots. Silenced shots, like sneezes, a fit of sneezes; and the piss running onto my shoes."

A saline drip running into a vein. Colourless liquid moving down a colourless tube.

"I don't know how many shots. The rain was heavy now, the shots were a part of it. Maybe twenty, twenty-five. I got to the road, my cock was still out, my trouser leg was warm with piss. My pistol was already in my hand, but there was nothing to shoot at, just the darkness and the silence. I could see Tunxi below us, all those people . . . but it was as if I was the only person left in the world."

The canullas plastic head blooming from flesh. Tethered by plasters, its steel root sticking the vein, pricking like a face that you recognise . . . a name that you cannot.

"He was dead when I got to him, I knew it . . . but I still talked to him. I held him. I could feel his blood soaking through my clothes like the piss on my trousers. I felt angry that I couldn't separate them . . . his blood, my piss. He was twenty-two years old for fuck sake and I was holding his head together like I was gluing a toy model. And all the time I was thinking what I was going to tell our mother."

A man so big standing up, so small in the tuck of the bed. Seemingly so fragile in the handshake of starched cotton sheets and medical ritual. The tears cutting down his cheeks . . . looking as if they might wash him away.

Yaobang's arm stretched out, straining on the drip. They touched hands . . . flesh upon flesh.

"Save the bastards for me when you find them, Boss. They've killed my brother. The fuckers. They've killed my little brother."

★

It was cold as he left the hospital. A bitterness about it that chilled the soul. Piao reached to his jacket collar to fasten it. The button was missing. Who was there to sew a new one on?

Chapter 12

As if a crumbling tooth had been extracted, the dark gap filled the *Kung an chu* . . . taking up most of the second floor. The Computer Centre . . . now a ransacked hole. Amputated trunking, stripped conduit, sprouting cables bleeding copper. And against each roughly hewn wall, grey cabinet against grey cabinet . . . dented, chipped tinplate. Each spewing thick plaits of wiring. Gaping innards of vacuum tubes. On the floor surrounding the obsolete main frame computer . . . a fine dusting of powdered glass. A seedling scatter of delicate filament wire. And through the only window, a light so weak that it died without reflection across the floor in front of the Senior Investigator's feet.

At the centre of the space that Piao no longer recognised, an island of dark grey workstations spotlit . . . new, protective plastic sheeting still covering their flanks. A thick umbilical cord of bundled wiring snaking from the innards of the VDUs and keyboards. One disappearing down a roughly chiselled hole in the concrete some metres away. The other, to a two metre high sentry of grey sculptured steel. A single flash of red holed by a chrome lock. A logo picked out in white lines . . . *IBM*. The workstations were empty except for one man, his face dominated by over large spectacles. As Piao drew closer, also came the smells. Smells of a thick wallet, filled with illicit yuan notes. Smells of the heat of a man's body through pure cotton . . . and the breaths that concentration brings. Short, stale . . . hardly breathed at all.

"Welcome to my new kingdom Sun Piao."

Rentang, known to all in the Kung an chu as, 'The Wizard', turned slowly in his swivel chair. The man revealed. Pallid. Mean featured. Not a wizard at all . . . just a man. A man who was good, very good with computers. Piao lit a Panda Brand and, through the smoke, looked around.

"The old main frame was stripped out a month ago. It was a first generation electronic computer . . . American, Sperry Rand. It weighed over thirty tons and all that it had was the computing capacity of a five hundred dollars personal computer of today . . ."

He laughed. A laugh as generous as a chicken carcass. And all the time, his fingers across the keyboard in a precise ballet. The VDUs fever across his spectacles.

". . . it never worked anyway. For the last fifteen years we've been mainly dependant on manual filing systems for the retrieval of information. A city with modern crime and a basement full of ancient filing cabinets . . ."

Nodding toward the sentinel of grey steel.

". . . now we have a new American baby. An IBM S/390 Parallel Enterprise Server, Generation 3. It weighs just nine hundred and thirty-eight kilos and takes up two square metres. It can feed a console on every desk, in every *Pai chu so* in the city with the details of any criminal and dissident in the Republic within the time that it takes to say 'filing cabinet'."

He stroked the screen of the VDU, almost breathless. Rainbow pixels haemorrhaging blurred across his bitten nails.

". . . a sweet, plump American baby. It can do anything that we want it to and won't shit in its pants."

Piao dropped the cigarette butt to the cold concrete, his foot coming down upon it. Death throes of smoke winding around his shoe.

"Anything?"

Rentang swivelled his chair, removing his glasses and revealing eyes of black with nothing in them.

"You want something of me Investigator. Something that will pay back the favours that I owe to you."

Piao pulled out the envelope from the inside of his jacket; the five full frame monochrome prints scattered onto the desk. Smashed, broken faces. Bone, blood. And seeming to pin each face . . . craters that held no eyes, bleeding, weeping mud.

"You're supposed to be a wizard. Give them back their faces."

★

The wizard with vomit on his breath returned from the toilet, fingers still dabbing at a stain on his tie. Tears pressed into the corners of his eyes. He stabbed a finger at the prints.

"Give me some warning next time, yes, Investigator? Unlike you, we're not all used to seeing the fruits that the Homicide Squad feeds off."

Fruits that the Homicide Squad feeds off . . . an unusual phrase to describe such a harvest of tortured, dead bodies. Piao suddenly thought of overripe avocados. Halved and mashed melons. Squashed and pitted lychee.

"A warning. What, a day, a year, ten years?"

Rentang would get nothing from this conversation. He put a peppermint in his mouth. The taste of bile fading slowly from his tongue. Sitting at the workstation, an unbearable urge to rip off his tie, discard it and have a shower.

"So, you want me to give them back their faces. Is that all?"

"And run them through your new toy. I need to know who they are."

"And who are they, Sun Piao . . . Politicals, non-conformists, dissidents? There's no security involvement here, is there?"

The wizard's eyebrows, a tight slipknot of concern.

"They're just the fruits that the Homicide Squad feeds off. Can you do it?"

Rentang's finger traced the outlines of the monochrome faces.

"See the angles of the jaws, the lack of definition, the mis-alignments . . . all would suggest severe damage to the skeletal structure. The mandible, body and ramus. Damage to the temporal bone also, as high as the zygomatic frontal process. On some, the noses seem completely unsupported due to crushing or splintering of the maxilla and nasal bone. Some of them have collapsed completely into an enlarged anterior nasal aperture. And damage to the frontal bones of the skulls is quite marked and severe, in some cases as deep as the lesser wing of the sphenoid, the superior orbital fissure and the optic canal. They did a good job on them; their skulls are jigsaw pieces. What was used?"

Through the smoke of a new cigarette . . . "A club hammer has been suggested."

Piao remembering the colours in the mud. Hard, harsh in camera flash. Bone, so white. Gash and gouge, so black. The Senior Investigator drew deeply on the butt, forcing the memories away. Rentang turned. The smile on his face, a paper cut.

"You seem surprised at my knowledge of human anatomy, Sun Piao. It's nice to rock a Senior Investigator back on his heels. I trained as a doctor for three years."

"Why change, you sound as if you were a promising student?"

"You're correct, Senior Investigator, I was a very promising student. But a doctor, I ask you, would I have made a doctor? No, no . . . it was once a 'fat job', but not now. But this . . ."

He stroked his fingers across the VDU screen. A paleness. A stark skeletal quality about them that reminded Piao of a river crab.

". . . computers. Now this is a fat job. One of the fattest."

The Senior Investigator leant forward.

"Remember, I know just how 'fat' your job is and how fat you have become in it . . ."

Closer, closer, the smell of bile on his breath as sweet as toffee apples and Guerlain on a warm summer's evening.

". . . don't tell me about jigsaw pieces. Can you give them back their faces?"

"Their faces. Yes. I will have to brush up on my anatomy, and there is a professor in the Institute Medical School who has a reputation for rebuilding the fragments of skulls found in archaeological excavations. A strange way to spend your evenings, but it could be of use to us especially in the restoration of the structural damage . . ."

He must have seen the question in Piao's eyes.

". . . and of course I will be discreet. I know how to be very discreet . . ."

Rentang smiled, as reassuring as a snake draped around your neck.

". . . I do a little freelance work for some of the other Security Bureaus, most of it to do with the preparation of cases against suspected dissidents. Some of it a little more political. Fat cadre jockeying for even fatter jobs. Mostly image manipulation, placing people next to other people in photographs, people who they had rather not be associated with. Putting them in places that they should not be. Putting them in, what should we say . . . indiscreet situations? Anything can be done to an image nowadays. It's become rather a speciality of mine . . ."

Again, the smile.

". . . I use a Macintosh PC with a world standard photo design software package. We could use the Layer Mask facility to anatomically reconstruct, to the professor's instructions, the skull and facial bone damage . . . and then lay muscle and flesh across this without destroying the original image data. Plus it also has ninety-five special effects filters that I can use to sharpen, style, or remove blemishes from the image."

"Meaning what?"

Piao almost spat the words . . . drowning in the sea of technobabble that seemed to be the common denominator among every computer expert that he had ever met.

"Meaning that you will get your faces Senior Investigator."

The VDU faded grey. Pixels imploding to form a silver star at its heart.

"And what we will get will be realistic, accurate?"

"Yes. But of course we will never know the true colour of their eyes . . ."

Lazy figures of eight. Rentang's index finger tracing around the monochrome, empty eye sockets.

". . . you can't have what you never had Sun Piao. And talking about having, what is it that I get out of all of this?"

The Senior Investigator was already making for the exit, the blind-eyed reflection of the monitors tracking his shortening frame.

"What you get is my amnesia. My continued amnesia."

Rentang shouted . . .

"Investigator, you're fucking with me. You're cutting my legs off."

His reply was only a whisper as he moved into the corridor, but Piao was sure that the wizard would hear it. He did.

"Every cripple finds his own way of walking."

★

The car sat on wasteland behind the Nanjing Road, once the spilling rears, the working entrails of restaurants, tailors, bakers; now home to western named shops. Gucci . . . Pucci. Gold blocked letters growing from marble. Cool neon blues spilling onto pavements. Their backsides wiped clean and as pristine as their grey minimalist shop spaces. Garbage bins with names on. Loading bays whitewashed and swept clean.

★

A shaft of sunlight skewered the car against the far wall. A slither of sharp edged yellow-white slicing against dirty paintwork and across Barbara's face. She brushed her hair, eyes lightly closed. The sun lazily warm. It could have been California, or Tampa offseason. She opened her eyes as Piao slammed the car door shut, still brushing her hair. But it was Shanghai.

"He'll help, this computer whiz?"

Her hair was gold. Piao's gaze returned to the road; a photograph being summoned up from his childhood. The only photograph that he had ever seen of his father. Such golden hair. His father. The stranger. The man who had screwed his mother.

"Golden hair," he breathed, as a taxi sounded its horn and let him become a part of the swollen wave of traffic moving north up Xixanglu, past the Park of the People.

"Excuse me?"

Barbara's face tilted gently towards him.

'Golden hair . . . . a little piece of heaven, a little piece of hell.'

"The Bureau's computer expert, if he cannot give the dead back their faces, nobody can," Piao said, as the road tumbled between cliff faces of offices once more. The sun's edge dulled. The colour of her hair turning from gold to tarnished brass.

★

The buildings that made up Fudan University sat like so many discarded shoe boxes . . . hemmed in by clipped lawns cut into jigsaw pieces by a web of narrow concrete paths. At the intersections nearest the buildings, policemen stood; olive green uniforms mimicking the grass in shadow. From a distance they could have been mistaken for bushes growing out of the cold concrete base.

"Why so many police?"

Piao reluctantly returned a salute as they neared building Number 4. A banner, red on white, draped above the double doors, stating, in Mao's own words uttered at the outset of the Cultural Revolution, that . . .

Youth must be put to the test.

It had been hurriedly erected, paint still wet and running into drips. The Senior Investigator smiled, reaching up to pull the banner to one side . . . the gauze on his fingers bleeding red paint. He translated the graffiti that lay underneath it on the brickwork. Red on brown. More words from Mao's lips, the dictum . . .

To rebel is justified.

"Mao is elastic, he is used in a similar way to your Bible. His words can be used to support any argument."

The Senior Investigator said only one more word to Barbara before they were met by a university official, who would escort them to the office and laboratory area that had once been the domain of Professor Lazarus Heywood.

" Tiananmen."

Barbara nodded. It explained everything.

★

129

"I told you. Expect little or nothing."

The large space was stripped totally bare, cleaned, repainted. It was dark, no windows. Lit only by two gently swaying yellowed bulbs hanging from ceiling cords, giving the room a sense of gentle movement, as if it were adrift on a great and deep swell of ocean. Barbara moved to the centre of the space, her shadows lengthening and shortening on alternate walls.

"Is this it? You said that it was a laboratory and also Heywood's office."

"It was."

Piao joined her, his eyes not leaving hers.

"This was also where your son would have worked."

She turned away unable to speak, her eyes lost to Piao. The official shuffling forward in shoes that were shiny, but which pinched, as Piao circled and re-circled him.

"I take it that you have no knowledge of an American by the name of Bobby Hayes?"

"I have no knowledge of the person to whom you refer."

The official, a medium ranked cadre, was controlled, a mask of a smile levered onto his face.

But the calm of the surface of the ocean belies the sharks fighting in its depths.

"But you do have knowledge of Professor Lazarus Heywood whose laboratory this was?"

The official gave a small strained laugh. He was sweating. Piao could smell its garlic taint oozing from his pores.

"This is not a game. Let me explain clearly what I am doing here. Why I am talking to you. I am the Senior Investigator with the Homicide Squad of the Public Security Bureau. I am investigating two fistfulls of murders . . . and you, Mr University Official, are getting in my way. Now we can do this here, informally . . . or we can be more conservative about it at the kung an chu. But be warned, if you force me to take you to the city headquarters you will not be out to celebrate the New Year, which is still some time away. So think of your family and answer my questions. Do you understand the point that I am making?"

The cadre was weighing up threats. Plusses and minuses.

Which to grasp, which to shrink away from. Piao knew the look, he met it every day, like a sweaty handshake that you could not wipe off.

"Professor Lazarus Heywood, tell me about him?"

"He, he worked here in the university. Professor Heywood lectured in Chinese history. And in um, archaeology. Yes, also in archaeology."

"Where is Professor Heywood?"

The silence was long, but full. Nothing more valuable than such silence. Experience had taught Piao to allow the fish more line.

"It is not known where the Professor is. The university alerted the Luxingshe as he is an American national. He failed to attend to his university lecturing commitments. We were . . . we were concerned. This is a very worrying, a very unusual situation. I understand that the Luxingshe are still investigating the matter."

The official had dull eyes. You saw such eyes on the fish that were left on the market stall long after a full day's trade had passed. The fish that would never be bought. The Senior Investigator moved closer, his shadow eclipsing the cadre.

"Life no longer possesses Professor Lazarus Heywood. And in the zealous nature in which you have gone about 'tidying up' these rooms which once belonged to him, I would suggest that you were fully aware of this fact?"

The cadre's laugh was grating, like rusty cogs.

"I repeat what I just said. Professor Heywood is dead. I should know, it was me who fished what was left of his body out of the Huangpu . . ."

The official took a step backwards, the cold wall now against his back.

". . . I need to see Heywood's personal belongings."

"I, we, do not have them. A team from the Luxingshe took official control of this area. The room was sealed off to university staff while it was searched and cleaned . . ."

He stopped to clear his throat, his Adam's apple bobbing. Lowering his voice in false sincerity. Lowering his eyes in honest fear.

131

". . . it is all a question of Professor Heywood's political activities and his contact with dissident student groups. It is *nei-bu*, classified information, but the Luxingshe were gracious enough to tell us that much."

Piao walked to the centre of the room, the light from the bulb directly above him elongating his features. His eyes drained of colour, shadow running down his cheeks.

"I was in contact with the Luxingshe this morning, before coming to your university. The Luxingshe have no record of such an operation ever having taken place. They have no knowledge of any action being taken in regards to Professor Lazarus Heywood. The Luxingshe were not even aware that Professor Heywood was missing."

"Bu–but I saw the Luxingshe officers myself. I . . . I examined their documentation. They had full authority. Their paperwork was in order. Th–they had full authority."

"They might have had full authority, but they were not Luxingshe."

Spit on the cadre's lips, reminding Piao of the discoloured foam discharging from the Suzhou at low tide.

"But n–no one impersonates Luxingshe, no one w–would dare to. And who could g–get the documentation that I examined, the au–authority?"

The cadre smelt of cheap aftershave, Hong Kong piss water packaged in gaudy imitation boxes.

"Security? Or the murderers who robbed Professor Heywood of his life?"

Again the whisper into the perfumed ear . . .

"Perhaps the two are the same. Security and the murderers of Professor Heywood?"

Silence, this time long, empty. Nothing is less valuable than such silence. The official was rallying his defences, Piao would get nothing more. Barbara was already walking toward the door, her eyes too dark to read.

"Is there anything that you need to tell me, Mr University Official? Do you still not know of an American called Bobby Hayes? Do your students not know of an American called Bobby Hayes?"

"I know n-nothing of a Bobby Hayes and now I know n-nothing of a Professor Lazarus Heywood. Neither will the s-students of this university."

To recognise the thirst must also be sometimes to recognise that the well is empty.

The Senior Investigator pulled on his jacket and fastened it, the top button still missing.

"Go back to your office, Mr University Official. Let me know when the Luxingshe men call again. Let me know when you remember an American boy called Bobby Hayes."

★

Fudan is large. It took over two hours for Piao to show Barbara its every corridor of beige, its every lecture hall with black heads bent in study. Barbara had never made a good tourist, her feet were tired within twenty minutes. The flooring hard, unforgiving. Her head light with a constant churning of unanswerable questions, untangleable thoughts. Piao, the Senior Investigator from the Homicide Squad, an enthusiastic guide. It had surprised her, he didn't seem the type. It was only his insistence that had carried her along, when all that she had really wanted was a beer. And to lay under a duvet, as dark as a cave, and give permission to herself to be eight years old again.

★

The central square of Fudan University was empty. They walked its perimeter. The sky undercoat grey, the air ripped with a bitter cold wind. A siren interrupted their footsteps, and then there were students spilling from every doorway, every corner of the square. The noise of their feet on concrete, swamping the electronic shriek. They were like any other students, perhaps a little neater in appearance. A tide of denim-blue creases. Baseball caps. Hooded sweatshirts. Girls with hair slicked alluringly over one eye. It surprised Barbara. Had she still really expected Mao suits and little red books held at head height?

"Christ, it could be downtown New York . . ."

She was pointing with one hand, her other hand brought to rest on Piao's. Its softness, its coldness . . . at that instant, nothing else in his universe.

". . .Coca-Cola tee shirts, Minnie Mouse jackets. Look, there's a Laker's baseball cap. It's unbelievable. It really could be the States."

"Yes, your country has given us the very best that its culture has to offer. We are all enriched by the experience."

But he was already moving away from her, hands no longer touching. Any PSB Officer would also have sensed it. Incoming danger and the excitement that is its carrier oil. It had a scent, the ashes of roses. It had a feel, gloved finger tips across the nape of the neck. A crowd of students were congregating in the centre of the square, off the pathways. To hold such a gathering was prohibited . . . counter-revolutionary sabotage. Since June 4th '89 . . . Tiananmen . . . such an act had been prohibited. Students had now been forced into being nothing more than a generation in waiting for Deng Xiaoping and his high cadre cronies to pass on.

A period of waiting, is not dying, is not living.

A banner unfurled. Yellow on red.

Build once more the Goddess of Democracy.

A violent red bloom in a foliage of baseball caps, Minnie Mouse jackets and the flailing olive green arms of the PSB. More police rushed towards the banner, but another group of students had assembled in a far corner of the square . . . and then another group. Hoods across their eyes. Caps pulled down. Banners meeting the breeze in lacerations of scarlet. The Senior Investigator had hold of Barbara's elbow, moving her firmly down an exit, out of the square towards the car.

"This is bad. We cannot be involved. We must go."

It was cold, getting colder, but Barbara felt the perspiration shock her forehead. The car doors barely closed, and they were shooting toward the main gate. Students spilling into the road. Piao wrestling with the wheel. And a roar of a thousand voices pitched in protest. A PSB officer was in the distance, arm raised. Behind him the gatehouse barrier lowering. The Shanghai accelerated with a jolt. The Senior Investigator pulling his badge from an inner pocket and slamming it against the inside of the windscreen; head out of the side window, roaring . . .

"Homicide. Homicide. Homicide."

The PSB officer straining to make sense of the oncoming vehicle. His eyes, a dark slash across his face. A hand moving to his hip, to the pistol buttoned into its small, neat holster. But a sudden realisation. A recognition. A thump of adrenaline. Waving the barrier up with both hands; barely escaping the charge of the bumper's peeling chrome. Getting to his feet and brushing down his trousers. The red and white candy stick barrier lowering behind him as Piao joined the flow of traffic into Hongkou's belly, toward the stadium. The high-rise cityscape falling back around them. Still in the Senior Investigator's hand, in a tight clasp . . . his badge. A five pointed star embossed in his palm. He replaced it in his pocket. The red and gold eclipsed in darkness.

★

People's Square swirled with colour. Peasants bussed in from outlying villages, dressed in traditional regional folk outfits. Long Magyar dresses. Embroidered silk kimonos. Ladakhis robes of silk on broadcloth, quilted with fur. Boots of thick felt. Turkestan full-length dresses of orange bleeding to yellow and into white. Long jackets of vertical and horizontal stripes; candy stripes. . . . black, red, blue, yellow. The New Year would be full of dance, beckoned in by the music of the provinces. The New Year would be a parade of earthen and fired hues; of slashing sky bound fireworks. But above all . . . the New Year would be organised.

"Slow down, slow down. I want to see this."

Barbara put a hand on Piao's shoulder; the Senior Investigator put a foot gently on the brake. She wound the window down. Drums and high pitched pipes on the breeze. Her hair in flight.

"So much colour and look at the different costumes. When

I see this I realise just how bland Fifth Avenue is. How dull the States can be."

Piao turned to look out of the side window as the vista slowly passed. The lines of costumed peasants being shepherded into order; choreographed into their precise place by serious-faced and stern-voiced comrades . . . *Smile, smile. You're not on the pig farm now!*

He'd seen it all before, every year. The Senior Investigator pushed his foot down firmly on the accelerator.

"So. America is bland. Dull. Even with Coca-Cola, tee shirts and Minnie Mouse jackets?"

Barbara wound the window up, the music truncated. The silence suddenly felt threatening, Piao wishing that he had not spoken.

"I did say it, didn't I? An America official putting down God's own country. Back in the States that's treason, I guess you'd call it counter revolutionary sabotage. I could get twenty-five to thirty years solitary in Disneyland for saying such things."

The Senior Investigator looked at her, startled.

"Really? Such severe sentences exist also in America?"

"No, no, I was just joking, making fun."

Barbara threw back her head and laughed. It reminding Piao of the sound that water makes lapping over pebbles.

"It is the very first time that I have heard you laugh."

"It's the first time that I've laughed in a long time. I use to laugh a lot. I guess lately that I've not had much to laugh about."

The words, Piao knew . . . such feelings, he also knew.

"Laughing can be more difficult than crying. To laugh is to realise a little of what God had in mind when he created the world."

Barbara's hand was on his shoulder once more. He never wanted it to leave.

"That's lovely. So beautiful. Where did you hear it? Is it from Confucius?"

"No, it is not from Confucius. I read it in an old American book. I think that it was called the Reader's Digest."

She laughed again. Piao ploughed the car into the Jinling Road, drinking from her laughter, but with no idea as to why her laughter had occurred. It was true. Americans could be very complex people.

★

The Shanghai Jing Jiang Hotel was busy. Coaches end to end on Maominanlu. Piao double parked, a coach driver suggesting that he fuck off, until spotting the gold and red of the Senior Investigator's epaulettes. The driver returned to his three day old copy of the 'People's Daily', his eyes hidden from view by an editorial diatribe on the latest production figures for Liberation Trucks.

"If you would not find it offensive or a great inconvenience, I would appreciate it if you could perform an important function for me?"

Barbara leaned, bracing herself against the frame of the open car window, eyes narrowing on Piao inside. The last person to ask her to 'perform an important function for him', an obese Congressman from Iowa, in the cramped confines of the Washington Hilton elevator, was still nursing a bruising knee to his nuts.

"My cousin Cheng who was killed, his children have a love of chocolate. I would like to give them some, but it is difficult. I do not have a card for the 'Friendship Store', and the hotels will not accept money unless it is from a tourist. Would you feel able to get me some chocolate?"

A sense of relief washed over her. A man for all seasons this Investigator. Pumping a car underneath the blunt nose of a pistol and a fast descending barrier, an hour later, wanting to buy chocolate for his cousin's tearful children.

"Sure, sure. I'd be glad to. It's a lovely thought. The hotel shop over there is great. What did you want, Twinkies, M&Ms, Hershey bars?"

"They have Swiss chocolate, or English . . . Cadbury's?"

"Cadbury's? Yes, yes I suppose so. I'll see what I can do."

The Senior Investigator pressed the neatly folded bed of bills into her hand. Feeling a sense of guilt in accepting them.

137

She earnt more in an hour than the Homicide Detective made in a month. Barbara was moving up the steps of the hotel, amongst a flock of Italian tourists, their hands flapping like flightless birds, when Piao caught up to her.

"Barbara Hayes, this case, your dead son and the others. Nothing is moving. Sometimes, when it is like this, we must 'turn the dead cat'. Change the situation. Our approach. Perhaps take a risk . . ."

Noticing that his hand was on her shoulder. Not knowing why, but it concerning her in the same way that lilies did. That breaking a mirror did. But at that instant, she couldn't have stood him removing it.

". . . we are being followed. You or me. I am not sure where their interest may lie. But I can't help thinking that an American government official is more of a catch than a Senior Investigator. And particularly an American government official still crying tears for her son found dead in the Huangpu."

Saying nothing, but in the knots of her eyebrows, questions . . . and answers.

"Is there anything that an American government official should be telling the Senior Investigator who is conducting the case into her child's murder?"

Saying nothing. Her lips, soft gateway of secrets.

"Then I want to say to you that you should be vigilant, aware of everything. Accept nothing by its face. Accept only that which you know by name."

Barbara moved up a step, her eyes, ice and fire. His touch, lost.

"You've already done it, taken a risk. Christ, what have you done?"

But Piao was already beyond her words. When he looked back in his rear-view mirror she was alone on the hotel steps, the last in a long line of tourists being swallowed by the revolving doors of the hotel.

The dead cat turned.

He accelerated into the snarl of Fuxing Park . . . *Cao-mu jie-bing . . .*

Barbara slept for three hours. Devoid of dreams. The room boy had silently visited, a flask sat on the bedside table. She poured the tea when she had awoken. *Wulongcha.* Sips of its bitterness before and after showering. Sips of its bitterness while dressing. She answered the telephone before it had rung three times, drawing back the curtains, the room flooded in a light the hue of under-ripe lemons. A pause at the other end of the line. The caller reticent, hiding behind the anonymity of distance. And then a man's voice . . . whispered.

"Madame Hayes. This is Madame Hayes who I am talking to?"

"Yes it is. Who are you?"

Another silence. Longer, full and plump with expectation.

"Your child, Bobby Hayes. I knew him, he was my friend."

His name coming from the lips of someone else who knew him; it seemed to make Bobby breathe again. The words propelling Barbara backwards to the bed. She asked the questions, but her voice seemed to belong to somebody else.

"Who are you? How did you know Bobby?"

"The telephones, they are not safe. It is best that my name is not said."

"Sure, sure, I understand. But how did you know him?"

His voice lowered even more. Barbara straining at the earpiece, aching with concentration.

"The university, Fudan. I am a student. Bobby, your son . . . he was my friend. He gave me cigarettes. Marlboro. He gave me a Los Angeles Raider's cap."

She closed her eyes tight, so tight until they hurt. She could see the Raider's caps. Silver and black. Bobby was never without them. Surely, only someone who knew Bobby could have known his cigarette brand; could have known about his Raider's caps.

"How did you know that I was in Shanghai . . . how did you know where to find me?"

"You were in the university today, yes? I saw you pass my lecture hall. I saw Bobby in your face . . ."

139

The dead cat turned.

The son of a bitch. I was the bait. He knew exactly what he was doing making me walk around Fudan. It was a shop window.

". . . I knew that it would be Bobby's hotel that you would stay in. The Jing Jiang. We joked, we call it his hotel. Room 201, it was his room, yes? For so long he stayed there. Long enough to own the room. You know that?"

"Yes. Yes I know that."

She could feel the pump of the blood through her heart. So many questions to get out of the way, so many answers to embrace. And truths.

"You know that my son is dead?"

There were no words, just time interspersed with gagged breaths and distant voices on crossed lines.

"Dead?"

He was sobbing. Its openness, its honesty, shocking.

"He was found in the river. He was murdered."

"I did not know. Forgive me. Forgive me. He was my friend and I did not know."

The crying lessening, its tide on the wane and replaced with a deep well of anger.

"Bobby was not at the university, it was sudden. When my friend was no longer there we were told strongly, warned . . . 'do not talk of the American boy. He was not at Fudan. He was never at Fudan . . .'"

He paused to blow his nose. Barbara counting the seconds.

". . . one day Bobby was at Fudan, the day after that he was not there. But it was *nei-bu*, we must not talk of it. All that was your son, my friend, was now classified. To talk of such things could mean *laodong gaizhao*. In the west you have no knowledge of this. In China it is the unspoken words; *lao gai*, 'reform through labour'. *Lao jiao*, 're-education through labour'. Many, many die."

Barbara was on her feet; pacing seemed to ease the anger. She spun the top from the bottle of brandy, pouring two fingers into the heavy glass, spilling a little onto the table. Drinking deeply. Its effects immediate and centring on her forehead.

"Who warned you, who told you not to speak of Bobby?"

"I did not know the men. They were not of the university. But not to know the face, does not mean that you do not know the threat . . ."

She understood. Her silence being all that she could give him.

". . . Madame Hayes, I would like it if I could see you. I would wish to give you the Raider's cap that was Bobby's. Your son would think that good, right. I know that."

"Yes, Bobby would think that good. And so would I."

"But I cannot come to the Jing Jiang Hotel, you understand? It is well that we meet outside, apart from the hotel. Perhaps the corner of Maominanlu and Shanxilu. The tea shop is a good place. Is one hour enough time Madame Hayes?"

"Yes, an hour from now is enough time. That would be good. Could I bring a PSB Homicide Officer along with me, he's investigating Bobby's murder? He's a good man. A Senior Investigator. He can be trusted."

An edge to the callers voice. Not anger. Just fear. Undiluted, real.

"No. No PSB. There are no PSB that can be trusted. I know this . . ."

His voice trailing off, re-balancing itself. Softer this time, trying to comfort.

". . . no PSB, Madame Hayes, but if you would wish you may bring Bobby's girlfriend to the tea shop. I would like it if I could offer her my sad wishes."

The glass slipping from Barbara's fingers, its crash distant, her thoughts focused on crescent moons of cherry-red fingernails.

"A girlfriend? Bobby never told me."

It was some time before the caller spoke again. His words a sigh through the uppermost branches of the trees.

"But Madame Hayes, did you really not know? Your son, Bobby, he was to be a father. His girlfriend was pregnant with his child."

★

The supermarket that slept under the shadow of the Jing Jiang was fat bellied, full of expensive delicacies from all around the world. But there was no aroma of food . . . just polish.

"Do you have Cadbury's chocolate, it's English I believe?"

"Yes we do, Madam."

"Give me as much as this money will buy."

Barbara unfolded Piao's notes, placing them on the counter. The assistant, starched blouse, starched accent, instantly calculating the total and converting it into bars of chocolate. The few fen in change was pushed towards Barbara. She left the light alloy coins as a tip. The assistant smiled, said nothing, and continued to gift wrap the bars of milk chocolate.

★

Barbara ordered a mooncake and a Coca-Cola. The sticky dough lodging in her throat.

The *Xinhuizhai* was unexpected; Pop art, chrome tubing, and waitresses dressed in the Chinese perception of 1960s' western clothing. During the whole of the 60s, Barbara had never, on any occasion, met a hippy wearing a Stars and Stripes bandanna around their forehead. It had taken a trip to Shanghai to fill that yawning gap in her experience.

She sipped her Coke. Its taste too complex, evocative of everything sad, everything about Bobby and home. The student was late, very late. She paid the bill, five dollars for a tea and a cake. A factory worker's daily wage. The feeling of guilt etching into her. She was just about to leave, but staring across to the other side of Shanxilu, and in an instant recognising him . . . and the cap in his tight hand. Silver and black. A Raider's cap. She had moved from the *Xinhuizhai*, the 'New Taste', and onto the pavement. Watching him as he crossed from Shanxilu. Wanting to run to him, embrace every word that Bobby had ever said to him. But in the corner of her eye a ramming blunt shadow, black . . . accelerating across her vision. Eating its way into the carousel of traffic. When the car hit the boy, everything slowed. His body in flight, already limp. An oncoming bus slewing across the road, blocking the black car's forward momentum. A gear change. The car reversing back over the body, with not an instant of hesitation. And the sounds. The race of an engine. Tyre rubber burning. Brakes. Clashing gears thrust into reverse. Screaming metal. The car shooting back in the direction from which it had come. As if a film were being rewound. And the sound. A skull colliding with the road. A sound, never to be forgotten.

Barbara ran toward the body. A second car passing her at speed, also in reverse. Piao at the wheel, hands frantic. Head turned violently across his shoulder. His face, a mask of blurred concentration.

Turn the dead cat . . . turn the dead cat . . . a rhythm that replayed, as if on a tape loop in her head, with every step that took her closer to the student's body. And when she finally reached him, only a single question. How was it possible for such a compact body to have so much blood? And so warm, across her arm as she cradled him. Across her chest as she held him.

Barbara picked up the baseball cap from the road; also the gift wrapped bars of chocolate that she had dropped. They were broken.

★

You can appreciate the beauty of the Tiger even as it leaps at you.

Piao had sensed the onrush of something just about to occur, but when it did . . . the speed of the event, its grotesque efficiency; he was left cold, dazzled. The Shanghai Sedan was passing him at speed, in reverse. He could do nothing, just a glimpse of shooting black and silver. Piao rammed the car in front to give himself more space. The road ahead blocked by the side-on bus. Throwing the car into reverse. Foot hard down. Spinning the Sedan around a parked Volkswagen, clipping its bumper. A smell of tyre rubber. Half spent fuel. His head wrenched across his shoulder, looking up Shimenlu. A steel ribbon of oncoming traffic, with the black Sedan weaving violently in and out of it. A gap in the parked cars . . . Piao slicing through it, aware of the speed of his own hands. A

143

vicious thump as the car hit the kerb and mounted the pavement. People screaming. People scattering. One hand permanently on the horn. The pavement ahead clearing, shop doorways jammed with faces. A blush of shock across his forehead. Temples aching. The colour drained from his sight. Images only in the harshest of monochromes. The incident, the murder, replaying in his head. And still an edge of disbelief . . . to kill in the centre of the *Patuo* of Huangpu, in the middle of Shanghai. What sort of men are these? So fast. So hard. So cold. I could not do this . . . never could I do this.

Are they stronger than me because of it?

A junction ahead, on the fringes of Huangpu Park . . . the busy flow of Zhongshandonglu biting across their path. Suzhou Creek, just north, lumbering into the Huangpu in a wash of mud driven undercurrents. The junction was wide, perhaps he could pull a handbrake turn, throw the car in a 180 degree arc. Facing forward. By the time they hit the creek he would have caught them . . . and then what? Knowing that the other driver would be thinking the same, exactly the same. Brains linked, their hands also joined . . . as Siamese twins. Piao thrust the Sedan down the kerb and into the madness. The black Shanghai just twenty-five metres ahead. No plates. Tinted windows. A hint of three shapes, maybe four. The Shanghai making a sudden weave across the lane, a gouging smudge of an arc against a stuttering shift of pastels moving down Daminglu. No room to turn, both Sedans still in reverse. The Senior Investigator following. Engine shrieking. Shoulders on fire. Neck locked. The Shanghai, two car lengths in front, hitting a series of bumps. Four wheels leaving the road, meeting it again with a dislocating jolt. Piao's stomach rammed into his throat as his Sedan met the first bump and then in freefall as the stubby car took off. Occasional disjointed views of the black Shanghai's roof, its wheels and flexed suspension as it bounded past the new industrial areas of Hongkou and Yangpu. A tight bend taken on two wheels, screaming wheels. Plumes of smoke lazily drifting across the fringe of the river. A race of oncoming traffic thrown into confusion. A wall of breaking steel. Sichuanlu impassable . . .

cutting hard right with Piao on the Shanghai's bumper. A carousel of sprinting colours. The road leading only one way. The buildings of the Shanghai Port Facilities looming above the dock walls. A single breach in the weathered brickwork, Gate 12 . . . a long articulated red lorry poking from its mouth. There was a narrow gap between the lorry and the dock wall, the Shanghai slamming through it. With arms of lead, the Senior Investigator plunging the Sedan murderously into the dark alley, slamming it heavily against the lorry's towering wheels. A yelp of torn metal as the rear bumper was wrenched off. And still no room to turn from reverse and into forward gears . . . the alleyways between the yellow bricked wharves too narrow. An expanse of water opened up to view. Grey, metallic, lifeless. The only roads a series of narrow bridges crossing that water. Dangerous. Precarious. The tyres picking up a rhythm from the steel grated road base. Piao, head jammed across his shoulder, tearing backwards . . . staring into the blind windscreen of the Shanghai. Both cars occasionally out of control and clipping the steel parapet. A machine gun of thumps. A flail of dull yellow sparks. The water on both sides of the narrow bridge gazing back blindly. The bridge spilt onto a slim warehouse apron of oil stained concrete, which pushed them toward another bridge, more substantial with great pectoral arms of girders. A tilt bridge crossing an inlet of the Huangpu and leading to the deep water berths . . . home for fat-bellied tankers. In the distance, the derricks of the Zhonghua Shipyard on Fuxing Island, sitting like a black steel bed of nails. Through the gaps between the warehouses, flashes of river . . . the colour of an old man's tongue, and rusting red and blue paintwork as a Panamanian tanker was hauled by tugs up the inlet, heading toward the bridge. At the lip of the dock embankment, where the concrete of the apron was grafted to the steel of the riveted structure, four red eyes blinked into life. The bow of the tanker already breaching the half horizon of brick. The bridge already dividing at its centre. The road not a road at all. . . . but two dividing lengths of steel arm, cranking slowly from horizontal to vertical. Sky, widening between them. There was no

other route. Options all run out. . . . water through cupped
hands. The Senior Investigator expecting the Shanghai to
brake. But no. Running up a hill, a hill becoming a cliff. Piao
following. Ridiculously following. The breath frozen across
his lips. A fist in his chest, clenched around his heart. The
Shanghai above him . . . and then gone. Leaving a black edge
of iron against sky. He grounded the accelerator, but there was
no response. The Sedan losing traction. The incline steeper.
It's passage to the vertical speeding. Rubber scarring steel.
Smoke billowing . . . as the car slipped back. The Panamanian
tanker almost breaking the water that the bridge spanned. Its
bow baring down, an iceberg of pitted red paint and blue
paint. The Sedan slid, skewing to the left, wheels still power-
ing against the skid. Piao thumped his fists on the steering
wheel. The Sedan falling back and coming to rest, straddling
the concrete apron. Its interior flooding magenta to the pulse
of the bridge's warning lights.

The Senior Investigator wrenched open the buckled
driver's door. Bracing his neck with both hands. Stretching his
back against the strength of a girder. The tanker . . . a wall of
red, sedately slipping by. The only noise, a deep throated
cough from the tugs; the wake of disturbed water splashing
against the stone of the dock embankment. He kicked at
a punctured tyre, two, three times, as the realisation started to
set in.

*You have to go home. Go home Barbara Hayes. The blood is
getting closer. Closer. Flowing in your direction.*

Raising his eyes. Across the water the black Shanghai sat on
the apron of concrete backed by warehouses, its engine
switched off. Piao's body started to shake uncontrollably. He
lit a cigarette, hardly able to hold it . . . hardly able to taste it.
The Shanghai's engine started up. Behind the tinted glass
would be smiling faces. Slaps on the back. The promise of
Qingdaos all round. And jokes . . . of course, the jokes. And
the professional pride of a job well done. To kill a boy in the
middle of Shanxilu as the afternoon turned sour; there was
much pride in that for men like these.

The Shanghai had found room to turn, moving in forward

gears now, it crept down the dockside's edge. The Senior Investigator examined the Sedan. A write-off. He spun around, eyes taking up the anger and burning with tears that he wanted to deny. His hand around his cigarette lighter, and with all of his remaining strength, throwing it in the direction of the black Shanghai. He saw the lighter plop into the deep waters. Its ripples spreading out. Weakening, calming, until they were as one with the greater body of water that filled the dock. When Piao looked up, the black Shanghai Sedan was no longer there.

★

A dress discarded on the bathroom floor. A stain spread across its front . . . old blood, leather brown. A smear across the floor tiles . . . old blood, but still red. Traffic light red.

The water was hot, steaming hot; cascading, plunging onto Barbara's face. Rivulets down her breasts, the flat plane of her stomach. The bloodstain being cleansed. A stream of discoloured water the same tincture as spilt Coca-Cola, running down her legs. An indolent spiral in the shower tray to the plughole. But bloodstains still on the soap, on the thermostat, on the inner and outer door handles. And all of the time, as constant as the flow of water . . . an almost unbearable drive to run back to D.C. Grab the next plane seat. But not before pinning the Senior Investigator to the nearest wall. She'd seen a boy murdered today, dead in her arms. And for what? The dead cat turned. A little knowledge. A Raider's cap . . . nothing else. To find a murderer, more murdered. How could she ever balance that? How could she ever balance so many things, now? And yet, a balance would be needed. A balance would have to be achieved. Power. Politics. Somehow, in the coming days . . . the perceived needs of America would have to be balanced with a child split like a vanilla pod. Her child. Bobby. That was politics. The art of balance, no matter what rocked the equilibrium of the cradle.

She fell onto the bed, the duvet drawn around her as if to ward off ghosts. Her stomach aching with a pregnancy over twenty years distant. The brandy, Japanese and undefined, had done its job. She was asleep within five minutes.

★

"Go home."

Barbara's hair was almost dry; she ran her fingers through it.

"Yanks go home. It's not an original line. Not for you Senior Investigator."

"Yanks?"

"Americans. Americans go home. It's been used from Vietnam to El Salvador. Grenada to Somalia."

"You make fun of me Mrs American government official. You do not understand. I care for your well-being. That is why I say go home. This is not about you being an American."

Barbara shook her hair back. A fluency in the movement, not unlike the twist of raindrops down a windscreen.

"You don't like Americans do you?"

Piao turned to the window. The sun as violently red as the streak of blood on the cream of her dress that he had seen heaped on the bathroom floor.

"I do not wish to talk of Americans, just you. The blood is getting close. Leave China. There is something in all of this that is about you. It is water through the gaps between fingers. I cannot tell you what it is, but I feel it. You, the American government official, part of you is a part of the puzzle. Perhaps you know this already?"

She said nothing. Always, the American politician part of her, saying nothing.

"Leave China."

"No. *No* . . ."

Standing between him and the sun. Angry. The words coming too slow for the feelings.

". . . no. The blood is coming closer, I know. I don't need you to tell me. Jesus, the boy died in my arms."

She pushed the wet towel into Piao's hands and walked into the bathroom.

148

" I'm not leaving. Us Bible belt gals don't frighten easily. My great-granddaddy shot and skinned buffalo for the railway."

The Senior Investigator raising the towel to his face. American women. Chinese women. They all smelt the same . . . scent and steel and babies never born.

"You should know every part of the picture before you decide to stay in China. As you come from a long line of ancestors who do not fear anything, I am sure that a little more knowledge will not alter your decision to stay. What is the knowledge of another death in comparison to the skinning of a buffalo?"

"Another death!"

Folding the satin gown around her she stormed from the bathroom. In her fingers, the delicate ties forming a bow. Just a glimpse . . . such long legs. The delicate curves, arcs of a swan's neck. Feeling so empty. Knowing that at that moment, he would have given anything just to run his hands up their smoothness.

"Another death?"

The Senior Investigator moved to the far side of the bed, placing a barrier between them.

"A student, about the same age as the boy today. He was to be a gynaecologist . . . very promising. We could get no one to examine your son and the other bodies found in the river. I volunteered him . . ."

Piao pulled out a battered blue pack of cigarettes, a soulful Panda staring from its sides; offering Barbara one with a tilt of the carton. She declined. He held down the smoke until it burnt, releasing it slowly.

". . . we needed information, any that it was possible to obtain. The student did well . . ."

Another deep drag.

". . . I met him after the funeral. He was taken to my cousin's house and hidden in the loft. We were very careful."

"So that was where you disappeared to. You were seeing this student, getting a report from him?"

The Senior Investigator nodded.

"Your cousin's wife. Chen? I was looking for you. I asked where you were. She gave me a recipe for Aubergine and Chicken."

Piao smiled.

"Cheng is known for her aubergine and chicken . . ."

"And her diplomacy."

"That also . . . and I thought that we had been so careful. So thorough. But they are thorough also. The student was taken from my cousin's house long after we had left. It was dark. Near Tunxi a Shanghai Sedan passed. It was the Shanghai Sedan that killed the boy today . . ."

The Senior Investigator stubbed out his cigarette. A single plume of silver lost against the cityscape.

". . . they shot and killed the student. It was very quick, thorough."

"You seem to admire their professionalism?"

"No, I admire no such act as this. Catching killers, that is to be admired . . ."

Piao felt a chill, his hand going to his collar to fasten it. To the button that was missing.

". . . yes, catching such killers as these, that is to be greatly admired . . ."

And adding, as a painful afterthought.

". . . the student, he was Yaobang's brother. His baby brother."

★

The bar on the ground floor of the Jing Jiang was awakening. An elderly trio of musicians in the far corner playing 'Mexicali Rose.' Each note, just a hint off-key. The booth was dark, but Piao still felt conspicuous; slipping off his jacket, turning it inside out, hiding the epaulettes. Feeling exhausted . . . shoulders, back, arms . . . it was an effort to move, to sit, to talk. He would have, should have slept, but knew that its minutes would be spiked with subliminal cuts of black Shanghai Sedans, tinted windows, numberless plates. And behind it all, the thudding volley of a skull making fierce contact with a

150

road, over and over again. He drank from his glass of Dukang, its scorch turning the tide.

"So. You will leave China now?"

Barbara embraced her drink. Her lips with the smelted gold of the Scotch.

"No, I won't be leaving China now. Would you?"

They both knew the answer, the Senior Investigator stepping over the question.

"Then I will have to look after you even more closely Barbara Hayes. It means that I will not let you beyond my sight."

"Suits me fine," she said.

Her eyes, playfully blue over the rim of her glass. Piao drained his drink. Dukang and exhaustion, friends that should never share beds, the alcohol had gone straight to his head. Everything more intense. The lights, the music. Her fingers, her neck, the snow lace edging of her camisole.

"Tell me what the student said to you. Everything."

The glass woven into her hands. The Scotch slowly swirling.

"He told me about Bobby staying here at the Jing Jiang, in room 201. That they were friends at Fudan. When Bobby disappeared the students were warned not to talk of . . . what was the name that he used now?"

Her eyes closed as she hunted the words down.

" 'The American boy'. That was it. They were warned not to talk about Bobby, the American boy. 'He was not at Fudan . . . he was never at Fudan.' He didn't know who they were, but they scared the shit out of him."

"But we know that they drive a black Shanghai Sedan. What else did he talk about?"

"He was shocked, he cried a lot when I told him about Bobby's murder. He wanted to meet me but didn't want any PSB involvement. He didn't want you there."

The Senior Investigator studied his fingers. The gauze was sticking to them in honeyed stains. The dressing needed changing.

"Of course you told him what a trustworthy and good man I was?"

151

"Of course. He still didn't want you there."

"Us PSB, we are very misunderstood. Not even an American politician can make us more popular."

She smiled.

"Do they hurt?"

She took Piao's fingers in her hand, rubbing a thumb lightly across the discoloured gauze. He wanted to say that they didn't hurt anymore.

"What other words were there between you and the student?"

Not letting go of his fingers. An anchor to something real. An anchor to somebody else's pain.

"He said that I could bring Bobby's girlfriend to the meeting if I wanted to. That he wished to offer her his condolences."

"The girlfriend, did the student give you a name, an address, any details?"

"You want to know if she was the girl with the red toenails that you hauled from the river along with Bobby."

"And Professor Heywood."

"How do you know Heywood was one of the other bodies?"

"Pan Yaobang, he did well for a student gynaecologist. Dental work. It was conclusive. Heywood was the other western male found in the Huangpu."

Barbara's hand was away from his fingers, playing with her glass. The pain in his wrist remained.

" The girl in the river. That wasn't Bobby's girlfriend, she couldn't have been. The student told me that Bobby's girlfriend was pregnant. She was having his baby. Bobby was going to be a father . . ."

Piao's hand reached for hers. Gauze on skin. Pain on pain.

". . . lots of young girls paint their toenails red. You know that, don't you? A Senior Investigator like you must know that."

She turned her head, the tears already upon her in a wave of salt and warmth. The lights of the bar melting. Already knowing the words that he was about to say.

"Barbara, I am sorry. The girl in the river was also pregnant. Five months pregnant. The girl in the river was Bobby's girlfriend."

★

"Peace?"

Piao rubbed the back of a hand across his eyes before focusing on his watch. 3.05am.

"Barbara Hayes, do you know what time it is?"

"Barbara."

"I do not understand."

"Barbara. You keep calling me by my full name. You've earnt the right to call me Barbara."

Cars, lights, bridges, tinted glass, a puppet of a body falling through the air. Piao could still see them. The residue of dreams nailed in place, clinging on.

"You have telephoned me at this early time to tell me your name, is this an American custom?"

" 'Peace'. The student said it to me when he was hit by the car. He said it three times."

"Peace. That is all?"

"That's all. It doesn't sound like it, but I know that it's important."

"Anything that a man struggles to say in the few seconds before he dies is important. And to say it three times . . ."

Piao sat on the edge of the bed sipping water. Its taste of chlorine and dust.

". . . to understand what he said, we need to look at and decide what it would be that he would feel such a need to say to you . . ."

He pulled a blanket around himself.

". . . what would you have asked the boy first when you met with him?"

"About Bobby I guess. The last time he had seen him. How he was. What he said. How he looked . . ."

A pause.

". . . no, no that's not true. I'd have asked him about Bobby's girlfriend. Her name. What she looked like. Where she lived."

"The boy is laying in your arms. You are telling him that it will be alright. But death is close, he knows it . . ."

The Senior Investigator was on his feet, pacing. The blanket draped around his shoulders.

". . . peace. He was not at peace, so why use the word three times? He was burdened. He needed to tell you something about the girl before his time ran out. Her name? Where she . . ."

Discarding the blanket. Piao already slipping on his trousers before she could speak.

"You've got something, haven't you? You know why he said peace . . . why he repeated it?"

The Senior Investigator fumbled his keys from the table. The telephone cord taut. Buttoning yesterday's shirt.

"I will be outside the Jing Jiang in twenty minutes."

And not waiting for a reply before he put the phone down.

★

170 Nanjingxilu. The hotel straddling the corner. Art deco and pigeon shit. Its lobby, gaudy yellow, like a mouthful of high cadre gold capped teeth.

Piao had never stepped through the hotel's doors before. The building was a part of him, of every Shanghainese, like speaking the distinctive accent that made Shanghainese Mandarin almost unintelligible to outsiders. Like the food with its abundance of rapeseed oil, the culinary quirk that Shanghai cuisine turned upon. And the utter conviction that every Shanghainese held, that beyond the city limits only darkness was to be found.

The reception area was bright, garish. Wincing, the Senior Investigator straightened his tie. It was 3.45am. The huge space empty, just a night porter. Fingernails bitten to the quick. A hip-flask in his pocket, just used. Maotai, the fermented must of corn and sorghum . . . its subtle scent still on his lips. Barbara was two paces behind . . . reaching for Piao's arm, grabbing him back.

"What are we doing here?"

The words almost whispered, but Piao continued to the desk. A pad of hotel notepaper sat next to the registration book. The Senior Investigator twisted it around toward her. The flowing letters in gold, pallid in yellow light.

HEPING . . . THE HOTEL OF PEACE.

"Would you really have got him pushed out of his job for drinking, if he hadn't given us what you wanted?"

"I would have reported him to his Danwei. They would have done the rest. Would you have expected less from a good citizen?"

Piao pushed the elevator button, top floor. The doors groaning closed. A hiccup of movement before it started its slow, steady haul.

"Would you have expected less from a good Homicide Investigator?"

Barbara checked herself in the wide mirror, Piao's reflection across her shoulder.

"You were lucky, his drinking. How else would you have got the information out of him?"

"All night porters drink, as certain as room boys will look through your underwear drawer. If that did not work, I would have broken his arms, then his legs . . ."

She stopped in mid-motion, fingers frozen in the stream of her hair.

". . . if that did not work, his flask of maotai would have been next."

The elevator slowed, came to a halt, the doors opening. Barbara turning to face him. The dregs of a smile still in the corners of his mouth.

"It could be a coincidence, the boy saying 'peace' . . . and this hotel? The girl on the top floor, the night porter wasn't sure that she was pregnant."

The elevator doors started to close. The Senior Investigator's arm forced them open.

"It will not be a coincidence. Coincidences do not live in a room that faces due east, with a view of the embarkation

155

point in Huangpu Park. A view that your son wrote about so many times in his cards to you."

She squeezed through the gap between his arm and the door. A glimpse of his face as the elevator slammed shut and fell. He was right. She knew that coincidences did not live in a room with a view overlooking Huangpu Park.

★

Can you not see the waters of the Yellow River descending from the heavens, hurrying irrevocably down to the sea?

The emergency lighting pinned fuzzed shadows to the run of corridor. The heavy carpet shrouded in milky plastic sheeting. A gantry of painting platforms supported by step ladders. Wallpaper half stripped, hanging in frayed tassels. And the smell of paint, turpentine, varnish . . . and *Jiaozi*, the doughy triangles of meat and vegetables eaten during hurried meal breaks. Almost palpable, the fine burn of indigestion.

The corridor was long, the occasional door of dark wood furnished with polished brass, breaking it into equal dashes. Ornate icing sugar art deco plasterwork being re-touched. Frozen climbs of ivy. Bursts of trumpeting lilies. Statuesque females clasping fiery torches. Everything in a state of flux and re-decoration.

"This is some place; I've never seen anything quite like it. Well, except for the Plaza in New York or the Deauville in Miami."

She turned to look at Piao, the light sparse, his eyes lost in penumbra. Fingers trailing the wall, a door, the wall.

"The money from the ugly trade, drugs, can buy many beautiful things."

"This was built with dirty money?"

"Opium trading. It was built by the Sassoons in the early years of the century. They were a great trading house, like Jardine's . . ."

He stopped next to a door, Suite 315. The key in one hand, his other in an arcing flourish.

". . . this was the place to stay in before the war came. The

Cathay Hotel. It had a private plumbing system that was fed by a spring on the outskirts of the city. It had marble baths, silver taps, vitreous china lavatories that were imported from Great Britain. The finest and most elegant art deco in China . . ."

He inserted the key.

". . . Noel Coward would stay here. He completed 'Private Lives' in this hotel. Do you know it?"

"Is that the one with the ex-wife who's a ghost?"

He pushed the door open.

"I think the English have much style. Noel Coward. Vitreous china lavatories . . ."

". . . and Cadbury's chocolate . . ."

Even in the near dark Barbara could see him smile.

". . . such confidence, such style. These cannot be easily found in China today. The Sassoons who built this place had these qualities. They were Jews. 'There is only one race greater than the Jews, and that is the Derby.' "

"Who said that, Noel Coward?"

"The Sassoons."

"They were wrong."

"Why, are not the Jews a great race?"

"Sure they're a great race. But the greatest race isn't the Jews or the Derby . . . it's the Kentucky."

The spotlights of the suite sparked into life . . . puddles of warmth. A tide of pink veined marble and of a thickly bevelled mirror riding on its back. The Senior Investigator followed Barbara into the suite, watching the light trickle across her shoulders, her cheek. Kentucky, he knew, wasn't in China. It could be in America or Britain. Wherever it was, he wondered if they had vitreous china lavatories.

★

The suite was in organised disarray. Dunes of dust sheets covering furniture. Plastic sheeting. Step ladders, planks, paint tins, brushes . . . stowed neatly in a far corner by double picture windows. Below, the city, with only the arterial lights of the roads spiking across Pudong towards Beilai, breaking its raven blackness. The girl who had been staying in Suite 315 must have had money. To live in such luxury could cost over two hundred yuan a night. It was only within the range of diplomats, company executives, politicians ... the rich. Such people would be worth listening in on. The Senior Investigator knew where to look. As the dog finds the bone, Piao found what he was looking for. Behind the electrical points in two rooms, crystal controlled UHF transmitters. Mains driven and operating continuously. Immune to 'bug sweeping' devices. Transmitting on very narrow bands to dedicated receivers. Behind the telephone junction boxes, UXT 'wire taps.' Energised from the line. Maintenance free. Electronically invisible. Transmitting both sides of a telephone conversation as soon as the handset was lifted. State of the art. Neat, reliable ... unfussy. Only Bureau Six could have commissioned such equipment. The rest of the Ministries thirteen Bureaus depended on human intelligence gathering. It cost little ... a scrap here, a threat there. No, this was Bureau Six. Piao refitted the last junction box and tightened the screws into place. Technology such as this was a good sign. At the end of every transmitter, perhaps kilometres away, would be receivers. Beside the receivers, sleepy, bored operatives. Thinking of food, beer, bed. But beside each operative, immune to such diversions ... a reel to reel would be slowly unwinding. Its full attention given. Each word caught on tape. Each conversation etched onto Chromium Dioxide. The girl, perhaps even Bobby, both would live on tapes. Numbered, catalogued, scrawled with black marker pens. Sitting amongst a bank, a wall of other tapes.

Barbara was looking out from the window. The horizon strung with lights, meshing with her hair in haloes of cold white.

"What did the night porter say that her name was?"

"Ye Yang."

She repeated the name to herself, levering aside the images of mud, eyes gouged out, red painted nails ... that now seemed welded to it. Thinking only of the pregnancy, the baby. The words that Bobby had never spoken of. Had never written of. Her eyes followed the line of the Bund far below. Its dark incision into the flank of Huangpu Park. Where verdigris turned to slate grey.

"This is the view that Bobby wrote about in some of his postcards, isn't it?"

Piao at her shoulder, breath into her perfumed hair.

"This is the view. This was also his home. Here was his girlfriend who was having his child. You know that this is true. If you wish I could take the bath apart, show you his hair in the pipe. Perhaps we would also find more nails that are painted red?"

"There is no need for that, Piao, thank you."

"Please do not thank me for this message that I bring you. Its pen and its paper are pain. To know that Ye Yang was Bobby's girlfriend, is also to know that she was the girl in the Huangpu with the others."

Her eyes were already misting. Lights forming stars. The river, the Bund, an inseparable smear. Fighting against the tears, she took one last look at the view. Bobby's view. Being his eyes, his senses. Wanting to own the view also . . . forever. Turning, she walked to the door, the Senior Investigator following.

★

Nothing was said between them until the hotel was left behind; its windows lost amongst a multitude of others. The early morning was cold. A cancerous cold eating into the bone. Weakening resolve. Bleeding the soul. The sky lightening and fixed in bands of cloud that resembled a rack of thick-bladed butchers knives.

"You're a Homicide Investigator, tell me how anyone could kill a pregnant young woman?"

The Senior Investigator started the engine, its racked bronchial cough sounding like he felt.

"Professional killers do not have likes or dislikes. They do not ask questions. You are a professional politician, do you ask all of the questions that you should before signing the order or negotiating the deal?"

"But that's not the same. This was a pregnant girl, for Christ sake. It's not the same."

Piao pulled into the Bund, trailing the finger of Huangpu Park as it stretched tight against the river, seemingly one and the same. Lights moving through the trees. A freighter approaching, slipping past, disappearing into darkness. The Senior Investigator wound down the side window, moving into Fuzhoulu, away from the park. Away from the river. Were there worse sins than others? He put his foot down sharply on the accelerator, a draft of bitter wind across his face watering his eyes, everything falling into grey.

"Politicians think that it is never the same," he said.

Chapter 13

Piao didn't sleep. The light in the flat, too harsh to allow asleep. Albino. Severe. It carried movement from the *long* below. And sound. Cars, bicycles, snatches of Mandarin. They all said that sleep had been left behind and that day awaited. He wrote reports. Each word shaped by Chief Liping's imposing shadow. At eight he washed. The water cold, unsweet. The mirror prominent and demanding; making him think that he was looking older. Tired. Gutters of lines around his eyes. A permanence about them now that made it impossible to call them laughter lines.

Could she ever find me attractive?

He dressed and went to the bottom drawer of the tall cabinet. The bundle at the back in amongst bed-linen, was wrapped carefully. Soft cloth. A sparse fall of lint. An acidic waft of light machine oil. Piao undoing the parcel with care, as if it contained a crystal vase or some delicate relic that might crumble on exposure to the air. The pistol felt lighter than he remembered, but more clumsy. A Type 59. A crude copy of a Soviet Makarov PM. Blowback design. Double action derived from the Walther PP. Piao slowly, carefully, placed the cold black barrel in his mouth. Metal against teeth . . . metal against flesh. Removing the slide-mounted safety-catch that locked the firing pin. A sharp click as he squeezed home the trigger. Reverberating through his head. Reverberating down the years. He withdrew the barrel and pushed the magazine into place. Eight shot, detachable box. Nine millimetres. It fitted with a reassuring snugness into the leather shoulder holster. A second magazine he placed in an inside jacket pocket. He massaged his neck and shoulders before heading for the door. Tense and frozen, they had the feel of an anchor chain, taut and straining on the turn of the tide.

Piao saw the photograph on the wall as he pulled the door

161

open. Her hair touching his cheek. A wisp across his lips. A sable finger crossing his mouth, warning of lies. He closed the door, locking it all away. Walking down the stairs and into the street.

We are all bitterness here . . . it's our only device.

★

The meeting lasted ten minutes. Ten minutes seeming like ten hours.

"In!"

Piao marched up to the white line on the floor, exactly one and a half metres from the front of Chief Liping's desk, and saluted. He didn't expect and was not offered a seat. His lack of expectations were fully justified. Several seconds of silence, the Chief's eyes downturned, towards a sheet of typed paper.

"Two hundred and seventy five thousand yuan, Senior Investigator. A substantial amount of money. Damage that you have caused. You are a careless driver."

More silence, overflowing the brim. Liping's eyes rising. Their full attention on him . . . like headlights through a fogbank.

"What the fuck were you doing?"

Hot words served cold. Piao had never heard a swearword said with so little emotion. Its impact all the more searing.

"It is in my reports, Comrade Officer Liping."

Pointing to the neat pile of papers on the leather topped desk and standing back. Black shoes behind the pristine white line.

"I have read them. I asked for daily reports, Senior Investigator. A report a day, not a collection of daily reports up to a week and a half late. This is not good enough . . ."

Liping tapped the paper, the rundown of figures in front of him.

". . . and this is not good enough Senior Investigator."

"I was pursuing the known perpetrators of a planned hit and run . . . a murder, Comrade Officer Chief Liping. I believe the occupants of the vehicle to be also responsible for

162

the murder of Officer Yaobang's brother, our Comrade Officer Wenbiao . . . my own cousin and possibly the eight victims that we found in the river. It is all in my reports, Comrade Officer Chief Liping."

"Yes, Senior Investigator, all in your reports . . ."

His hand across the typed pages. Hard fingers. Cruel.

". . . all in your reports, Piao, except for a single description of any of the three occupants who were in the black Shanghai Sedan . . ."

On Liping's face, the jigsaw pieces of a smile. He stood and moved around the desk surveying his office. Dark wood. Brass. A marble bust of Mao. No sound, except for his footsteps on the polished wood floor.

". . . I am underwhelmed, Piao. You still believe in the conspiracy theory? I know of your stubbornness. I did not expect stubbornness to extend to stupidity."

He walked slowly toward the desk, rounding it; the ease of a big cat who had just made a kill. Hands braced on the back of his chair, taking his weight. Everything about him immaculate, preened. His uniform of standard design, except its cut, the quality of its material, its hand stitching. It would be custom tailored at the Paramount on the Nanjing Road. Expensive. Beyond even Liping's pocket, surely? Unmistakable quality. Quality for the highest of cadre. Piao feeling dull, grubby. Aware of the mud on his shoes. The hole in his trouser pocket. The taste of shit in his mouth.

"You are off the case, Investigator Piao. You are personally involved. Unsound. You have no proof to substantiate any of your assertions . . ."

The Chief sat. The heavy leather bound upholstered chair creaking. His jacket taut against his bulky shoulders. The muscles grouped, flexed, in some anonymous anticipation.

". . . you are no nearer than you were a week ago. The trail is cold, Piao. You are getting nowhere."

"With respect, Comrade Officer, there have been recent developments which I feel justify my continued involvement in the case. I do not believe that the trail is cold and feel assured that we can move forward with certainty. It is all in my reports."

The temperature rising around his collar. His palms, his feet, itchy . . . wanting to scratch them until they bled. He had said little, but with a lot of words. Liping was no fool, he would recognise what was water and what was silt cupped between his hands.

"Recent developments. Continued involvement. Moving forward with certainty . . ."

The Chief nudged the reports away with his knuckles.

". . . you sound like a politician. You say much with little content. That is my job, Senior Investigator. Your job is to say little and provide results. Is that understood?"

Liping's eyes fixed on him. Black burning into blue. Piao nodded.

"You speak of recent developments. What recent developments, Investigator?"

"Three of the bodies that were found in the Huangpu have been identified, Comrade Officer."

"And?"

"Two are Americans. One, Professor Lazarus Heywood of Fudan University. The other was an archaeologist involved in a research project at the same university. His name was Bobby Hayes . . ."

Liping's face as still as the waters of a lake. His hands at rest, fingers interwoven.

". . . the third is a female by the name of Ye Yang. Nationality unknown at present. She was the lover of the American, Bobby Hayes. She was pregnant, three months pregnant."

The Comrade Chief Officer's gaze not weakening its hold. The words female, pregnant, not causing a ripple across the waters.

"The identification of the Americans is positive?"

"Yes Comrade Officer. Dental and positive witness identifications."

The hands parted. One moving to his scalp, across the bony roof of his skull. The bristle of hair bowing to the palm and then flicking back to attention.

"Is that all?"

"The girl, Ye Yang, she was staying at the Peace Hotel. The

164

room and telephones were wired. The hardware was very sophisticated, expensive."

"Bureau Six?"

"I believe so, Comrade Officer."

"And you want the tape recordings?"

Piao nodded.

"You are aware of how many hotels in the city the Bureau would have an interest in?"

"Eleven Comrade Officer."

"Over five thousand hotel rooms. Half of these would be fitted with listening devices. Only ten per cent of these monitored and transcribed. And you still want the tapes, if they even exist?"

"It is vital to the investigation, Comrade Officer. They could provide links to the other victims. Possibly a motive for the murders."

"I am aware of what such tape recordings could provide, Senior Investigator . . ."

He was on his feet, thumbs tucked into his pockets. A strength permeating from every aspect of his posture.

". . . it will take time, it will take effort also, but I will make sure that you have the tape recordings that you require . . ."

He said nothing for several minutes. The silence as sharp as razor wire. Piao counting each second.

". . . you have a reprieve, Senior Investigator. Make sure that you 'move forward with certainty'. You may go."

★

It was only when he was outside that Piao realised that he had not taken a breath since leaving Liping's office. His lungs a brazier of amber coals. When the breath came it was long and ragged, like that of an old cadre snoring through a Politburo committee meeting.

Liping, the man was deceptive, reminding the Senior Investigator of the old saying: *The buffalo of the County of Wu does not suffocate under moonbeams.*

In other words, he was not what he seemed. Piao had expected a fight about the tapes. A struggle over every detail

165

of his reports. Perhaps even an official investigation into his own theories of Pan Yaobang's murder and the killing of the student. The Senior Investigator pulled in a deep and ragged breath, purging the Chief from out of his nostrils.

Liping was not what he seemed. Ye Yang, the tapes from her hotel room . . . would they be?

★

As he walked, he smoked . . . half a pack before he even realised it. The tasteless smoke becoming his breakfast, his lunch, his evening meal. And thinking, and replaying every word that Liping had uttered. Only when he found a substantial enough bone to gnaw upon, did the smoking stop . . . crumpling the packet into a tight ball as he replayed the words. The Chief . . .

'. . . all in your reports Senior Investigator, except for a single description of any of the three occupants of the black Shanghai Sedan.'

How did Liping know what was not known? Not known to Piao and not hidden in the turned and re-turned pages of any of the reports that he had submitted to the Chief? That there were 'three' occupants in the black Shanghai Sedan?

The buffalo of the County of Wu does not suffocate under moonbeams.

A second time to know what was not known. A first time . . . a mistake, a guess? But a second time? The Comrade Chief Officer Liping, he was not what he seemed. He knew things that he should not know.

Chapter 14

Ni nar – *"Where are you?"*

Chinese telephone conversations will always start with this. A Chinese will be asked this rather than his name when he goes somewhere new; a place in which he is not recognised. It will be the first question at the top of any hotel registration form.

Ni nar – "Where are you?"

"What is your unit, your Danwei."

Every Chinese belongs to a Danwei; through the place of work, the office, the commune, the factory, the school. The Danwei are the building blocks of Chinese society. A second citizenship braced firmly in tandem with the first. The Danwei can be so well equipped as to provide a cradle to the grave service. It can furnish every need. Where you live, where your children are educated, the clinic for when you are sick, the authority to purchase food, 'industrial goods' . . . bicycles, radios, tvs. But the Danwei is not just a provider. It has a hunger too. It has needs that must be met. When you want to marry, you are requested to apply to the Party Secretary of the Danwei for their permission. They will run a security check. Depending upon its result, you will be given permission, or denied it. If you wish to transfer to another job . . . the Danwei have to give their consent. As a Chinese, if you wish to meet with a foreigner, you are supposed to seek permission and then report back to the Danwei about what was discussed. Before taking a journey or leave of more than a day's duration from your place of abode, approval from the Party Secretary of the Danwei must be sought and given. When you die, it is the Danwei who will bury or cremate you. It is a womb that you can never be born from. A level of control by the authorities over the Chinese people that could never be understood by the *yang-gui-zi* . . . 'the foreign devil'.

167

Each personnel department of each Danwei holds a sealed envelope on every employee; biographical information, work records, educational records. But the sealed envelope will hold much beyond this. The stains of any political accusations made by neighbours, however unfounded. The Party's evaluation of the individual as an activist, or as a possible or suspected counter-revolutionary. The Party's 'Bloodline Theory' committed to type . . . a dissection, a family tree of the Danwei member going back three generations. Were the fathers, grandfathers, great grandfathers . . . landlords, capitalists, or peasant workers? Only the high cadre can know the contents of the dossier on the individual. Your eyes will never read it. Theirs will.

Only the high cadre, through the Danwei, can map out your life before it even arrives. Can escort you through that life, their traffic lights showing red at every major intersection of that life . . . if they so deem it. Your funeral planned from the day that you were born.

The cradle to the grave. Their shadow across yours.

"Ni nar" – "Where are you?"

You know where I am . . . you are always with me.

★

"You look like shit."

Yaobang pulled on his cigarette butt.

"Thanks Boss, nice to see you too."

"When did you come in?"

"Six. Since Pan got shot it's fucked up my sleep."

Piao sipped his tea. It was already cold.

"Doctors have pills for everything."

"I tried them. They gave me wind and the constant shits. I'd rather have no sleep."

"I'd rather you had no sleep as well. I appreciate your social conscience."

The Big Man smiled. Teeth as grim as the inside of a tea pot.

"They didn't fix your teeth while you were in then?"

"I asked. Fucking doctors . . ."

168

He opened his mouth, a black coal chute. Prodding the decayed back teeth with a finger.

". . . not economical. How can a citizen's health be 'not economical'. Fucking doctors."

Piao poured the remains of the tea into a sorry looking pot plant. It seemed to wilt even further.

"You shouldn't be in. You should be anywhere but here."

"There isn't anywhere but here."

The Senior Investigator recognised the words, the feelings, the sense of belonging nowhere. He didn't pursue the subject.

"Luxingshe, Bureau Six. Have they reported back to us yet?"

"Yes, for what it's worth. The reports are on your desk. Only standard stuff on that Heywood. Visa documentation. Entrances, exits, internal travel permits. Shit all on the others."

"What about Mai Lin Hua at Gongdelin and the Chief Warden at the Municipal Prison?"

"On your desk with the others."

"Anything positive?"

The Big Man rifled through the stack of files, smiling. His tongue caught between his teeth, like a mouse trying to squirm from the trap.

"Here it is . . ."

He held the paper aloft in triumph.

". . . a handwritten note from Hua inviting you to tea at Gongdelin. Besides that, fuck all."

He let the note drift from his fingers and into the bin.

". . . I've got the old dog Xin and three others that were drafted in by the Chief going through the files of prisoners that have been released over the past month. It's endless, but you never know . . . something might even come up on some of those tattoos that the victims had . . ."

"The three that Liping drafted in, do you know them?"

"No, but they've all got dirty shoes. It's normally a good sign."

Piao slid open a desk drawer, placing his cup into its depths. Four other cups were already in there.

"Let them do the spade work . . ."

He closed the drawer and pushed over the pile of reports. They spilt across the desk in buff landslip.

". . . but don't let them know too much of what they're digging for."

"Sure boss. Give them the fucking spades, but not the seeds . . ."

Yaobang pulled a creased slip of paper from his pocket.

". . . and Boss, you got a call. No name and from a public call box. He said to meet him at the Huxingting Tea House, Yu Gardens."

"What time?"

"Half an hour ago, Boss."

Piao hurriedly took the paper and pushed it into his pocket.

"Yaobang, do a bit of spade work at Fudan, eh? I want the names and details of any students who were friends with Bobby Hayes. Anyone who was close to him. Hung out with him. Anyone who shared a tea with him."

The Big Man rubbed his hands together and tested his breath. As sour as a bull's bladder.

"Just my sort of fucking job, Boss. Student girls are my favourite . . ."

He tightened the greasy knot of his tie.

". . . what do you want them for, onto something?"

Piao moved from the desk, buttoning his jacket. It was cold outside, unseasonably cold.

But whatever season, he always felt cold.

"No, not really. You just never know . . ."

He tapped the side of his nose.

". . . I just have a feeling that they might be of use at some point . . ."

He was halfway through the door when he stopped and looked back.

". . . your brother, Pan . . ."

"There's no need Boss, we've already said it all."

Piao nodded, stepped out into the corridor and closed the door gently. It was only when he was halfway to Yu Gardens that he knew that it could never all be said.

Every day should be so sharp. Every piece of bone china so white. Every death so dark.

It had been five years since Piao had last visited Yu Gardens; suddenly finding himself dipping into the memories as if they were a box of chocolates. The soft centres . . . her small hand, cold, fitting neatly into his. Her lips as she drank Xunhuacha . . . rose petals set in alabaster, and on the flight of her breath, jasmine. The hard centres . . . the ones that you never choose. The argument. The spilt tea, its stain spreading across the desert of the tablecloth. The words, the name-calling . . . indelible and still indigestible, even after all this time.

★

Yu Gardens was unnaturally quiet. Too early for locals. Too out of season for tourists whose buses usually crammed Hen-anlu. The Huxingting Teahouse was close to the Bridge of Nine Turnings, he remembered. The Heart of the Lake Pavilion, set in waters filled with emerald algae and lotus leaves. The Longjing Tea would be expensive here. Cheaper at the Wuxingling . . . only fifteen fen a pot with as many refills of hot water as you wanted. At the Huxingting you also paid for the view, the bone china cups and the white linen. When you're in love you don't mind, it is a part of the foreplay. When you're not in love, when you're just chasing the job . . . such things have no importance. The view, the bone china, the white linen . . . they aren't worth the extra fen because they don't matter a fuck.

Rentang sat in the far corner of the Huxingting, drinking tea and eating quail's eggs. His face dominated by the large black rimmed spectacles, as if each eye were centre stage on two individual television sets. As he drank, one lens frosted grey with steam. He didn't look up.

"Who's the woman?"

"You do not need to know."

Piao pulled out a chair for Barbara and then seated himself. Rentang peeled a quail's egg, the fine shell forming another layer of skin to his fingertips. Still not looking up.

"I don't need to know! I wish I knew nothing about this case of yours. This fucking mess . . ."

He drank his tea almost to the bottom of his cup; charcoal shredded leaf slicking the snow of the bone china.

". . . *Dao-mei*, Piao. *Dao-mei* . . ."

His eyes lifted. Black, nervous, trapped behind glass and the reflections of strips of decapitated dark trees from the window opposite.

". . . that's what they're calling you at headquarters. 'Bad luck'. Everyone's dying around you. It's that Huangpu case, the one you've stuck me with. No one knows about it, but they're all talking. You can't get any details, just rumours and names. Names of all those getting fucked around you . . ."

He leaned forward. Unborn quails on his breath.

". . . you've got me by the ball's Sun, but don't get me involved. You can still leave me out of it. I don't want to talk to you about this, nobody does."

Dao-mei. Piao felt the sting of the words. Dao-mei, the colloquial term for menstruation. And in turn, for 'bad luck.' He'd used it a thousand times himself to put a woman in her place. He'd used it to her in this very place. With regret, remembering the single tear in travel down her cheek, behind a fan of jet hair.

"You want details, I will give you them. You want to know why I am pushing so hard, I will tell you."

"I don't want to know. I don't fucking want to know. I shouldn't be here. If you've been followed it'll be me who ends up."

He was moving from his chair, a palm raised, warding off the Senior Investigator's words.

"Sit."

Piao's hand firmly on Rentang's forearm, pulling him back into his chair. Quail's eggs rolling across the table.

"Is everything okay?"

Barbara concerned, shielding her tea with one hand, chasing the eggs with the other. Piao ignoring her. His face so close to Rentang's forehead that it touched the frame of his spectacles.

"Details. I am investigating eight bodies found in the river. I know the identities of three. The other five is why you are here. In the process of my investigations another four people have been murdered. One was Wenbiao, a young PSB officer. You heard about that?"

Rentang nodded.

"And Yaobang's brother?"

Again a nod.

"The other two. One of them was my cousin . . ."

The Senior Investigator pulled Rentang's face around with both hands, holding it firmly in front of his. The lenses of the glasses misting with each word.

". . . no one has followed us, I was very careful. I should have been as careful before. You are safe from them, they cannot harm you. But I can . . ."

He tried to pull away, Piao increased his grip; Rentang's cheeks transforming into ripe apples embraced by too hot a sun.

". . . you are right, I have you by the balls and I am about to start squeezing. One letter from me to the Party Secretary of our Danwei and you will be investigated. Using your position, influence, Security Bureau time and hardware, plus highly confidential information for the benefit of a commercial enterprise. These would be regarded as very serious charges . . ."

The Senior Investigator released his grip. Rentang was safe, tamed. The blanch of his cheeks whispered it. The dullness of his eyes shouted it.

". . . there was a similar case in Nanking a year ago. It was a showcase, they made an example of him. He was executed."

"What the fuck's happened to you, Sun. You'd really do that to me, over this?"

"What the fuck has happened to me is pulling eight bodies from the river with their eyes gouged out. Their stomachs slit like *Wawayu*. Have you ever heard the noise that the fish make when they are pulled from the waters of their favourite river banks? They cry like human babies . . ."

173

The Senior Investigator picked up a quail's egg, rolling it gently in his palm. Pinching it violently between thumb and forefinger. Letting the debris fall onto the white linen tablecloth.

". . .I do not want to, but yes, I would do this to you for the twelve whose deaths are now up to me to put right. They deserve at least that."

Rentang reached into the deep inside pocket of his coat to retrieve a large folded manila envelope.

"Fuck you too," he said, as he placed it on the table and slit it open.

★

Monochrome prints spilling onto lace white. Five prints. Full portraits . . . ten by eight inch. Faces marbled in river mud. Rentang pushing the teapot, the cups, aside. Placing the photographs across the table in some unexplained order. Reaching deep into the envelope. Five photocopied reports. Black trenches of type headed by report numbers. And in bold print at the top of each page.

PUBLIC SECURITY BUREAU . . . SHANGHAI HUNG AN CHU.

In the bottom right-hand corner of each report was a copy of a photograph, passport size. Faces staring out in harsh black and white. Expressionless. Eyes stolen of light. Vulnerability frozen into prints just a handful of centimetres square. Rentang placing the reports in turn, carefully across the faces of mud. Death given names. The mud washed away. Pulling from the envelope five more prints. Five more faces. Shiny, new, unblemished. Each laced together with faint guidelines, drawstrings . . . latitudinal, longitudinal, snap-to rulers and guides. Across the top of the page, icons forming a computer programme menu and toolbar. Reconstructed faces. The same faces pulled from the Huangpu, but made new. An exterior complexion of a million computer generated pixels, glowing a healthy steel

174

grey. And in the eye sockets, ball-bearing orbs of matt silver, holding no reflection and no fire of dreams burning in them.

Rentang checked the code at the back of each graphic before placing one at the bottom of each report. Vague in their similarity to the faces of mud. Unmistakably a match to the faces framed in the copied passport size mug-shots. His hand brushed against the first report.

"H2 . . . the first face that you gave me. Wei Yongshe. Age 25. Born Sichuan. A string of previous convictions. They are all in the report. Nothing serious until the last one. He stabbed another *liu-mang* in a street fight. He was sent to Gongdelin."

Rentang's hand moving to the next report, fingers spread across it in a web of pale knuckles and fingernails bitten to the bloodied quick.

"H4 . . . Hu Feng. Age 43. Born Shanghai. A history of mental health problems and violence. He was also in Gongdelin. He killed his sister with an axe."

The monochrome eyes passing beneath Rentang's palm. The next report, the next face, coming alive with a double tap of his index finger.

"H5 . . . another thug. A long history of petty crime and violence. Liu Qingde. Age 27. Born Shanghai. An-up-and coming little shit. Put away in Gongdelin for threatening behaviour and extortion. And then you have this beauty."

Piao's eyes moving from image to image. The passport print . . . the man that he had been. The face of the body pulled from the Huangpu, slipped in mud . . . the man that he had become. The computer enhanced image, a face generated by blips of power and pressure on keyboard keys . . . the man that he now was.

"H6 . . . Pei Decai. Age 33. Born in the Henan region. Drug trafficker. Caught coming over the border from the New Territories and into Shenzhen with pure heroin. Very tough, but used to money and luxury. He didn't find them in Gongdelin."

Rentang's eyes shifting to the next report.

"H8 . . . the last of your beauties. Age 27. Born in Shanghai, almost next door to Gongdelin. He didn't make it very far. Name, Yan Ziyang. Ex-asylum. Totally mad. Cut off the balls of one of his cousins, who died of blood loss. Then he tried to cut his own off. They should have let him. Imprisoned in Gongdelin."

He rubbed his hands together and then wiped them on the corner of the tablecloth, as if there was shit over his palms rather than sweat.

"You are sure, these are them?"

Rentang looked up. Anger scribbled into the corners of his mouth. The pale yellow yolk of quail's eggs sitting in the cuts and lines of his teeth.

"I'm sure. This is what you're threatening me for, isn't it? Faces made whole. Positive I.D.s."

Piao poured Barbara and himself tea. Its aroma, of Monday mornings.

"I am making threats because nobody, including you, will do their jobs without them being made."

"Well, now you've got what you want and where the fuck does that leave you? They're still dead and I'm released from your threats and your friendship."

The Senior Investigator's eyes found the window. Beyond the lake, the slow wave of the ginkgoes, the curve of the park's walls . . . the city was building to a lunchtime marked by Yellow Dragons, the sulphurous mustard clouds that poured from a hundred thousand factory chimneys. The peace of the garden, the mayhem that stamped just beyond its walls, how could the two opposites ever be reconciled? And something in Rentang's words, nagging at Piao. Something feeling wrong, out of mesh. Also irreconcilable.

"How did they get to be in the Huangpu? These were serious crimes that they had committed. Four out of the five you have told me about would have been serving lao-gai . . . life sentences. That is if luck had smiled upon them. Why had they been released from Gongdelin, what were they doing as free men?"

Piao thinking aloud. The words mainly for himself and for a God who never seemed to answer. Rentang stood to leave, pushing the chair back rudely. Fishing deeply into his trouser pocket and throwing some crumpled notes and loose change onto the table.

"I don't even want you paying for my fucking tea . . ."

He rounded the corner of the table, his shadow, his head across Piao's shoulder. A warmth about his smell. A heady mix of streaky pork, expensive tobacco and too much sleep.

". . . read the reports, Investigator Piao, who said that they had been released from Gongdelin Prison? Only one was on the outside. Qingde. Your deputy, Yaobang, he should know all about him. He was the one who put him inside in the first place. Perhaps you should be asking those closest to you, why it is that they said nothing when someone they recognised was being pulled from the river?"

Rentang's voice a needle inserted into the Senior Investigator's inner ear and beyond.

"The other four, Yongshe, Feng, Decai, Ziyang . . . they never left Gongdelin prison. 'Officially'. As you said, their crimes were serious. The State thought so as well. They were executed for these crimes a day before you dragged them out of the Huangpu. Officially, their bodies have not yet been released. Officially, you could never have found them in the river. Officially, you are investigating the murders of men that never could have taken place. Officially, they had already been executed by firing squad . . ."

He adjusted his spectacles.

". . . where does that fucking leave you, my dangerous friend?"

His footsteps made no sound. When the Senior Investigator looked up, Rentang had left. The only sound was in Piao's head, a thousand questions, each with a busy tongue. And laced through the labyrinth, a single red thread. The name Gongdelin. *'Virtue Forest.'*

Chapter 15

The Nanjing Road stretches for six miles. A razor slash of windscreens running west to east and spurning twenty-six side streets . . . splitting the city into two chunks. Four huge department stores ride its back, including the No.10 store at 635 Nanjing, where the Chinese themselves buy. The No.1 store at 830 Nanjing, on the fringe of the People's Park . . . the largest store in the country. Its floor space packed with every item available to the Chinese worker.

Many other shops also vie for the trade that is generated by a million pedestrians a day. At 257 Nanjing, silk. At 428 Nanjing, jewellery. The Xinhua Bookstore at No.345. Porcelain, pottery, at No.550 and 1698 Nanjing. The Yangzhou Restaurant at 308, with its wild duck and tofu. Scrolls, wall hangings, at No.190. The wood panelled dining room of the Cantonese Xinya, at 719 Nanjing. At No.546 the Xin Xin Barber's Shop. Eighty cutters permanently occupied. Men on the ground floor, women on the first floor. Five yuan buying a traditional massage in the lap of their special vibrating barber's chair. On the corner of Sichuan Zhonglu, the coffee bar Deda Xicaishe, with its renowned chocolate buns. Or a couple of doors down at No.143, the Donghai Fandian with its minted coffee. Around the corner at 952 Nanjing, the 'Face Friend' cosmetics shop. On the counter top, their famous 'nourishing powder.' On the back shelf, a central display of their lipsticks. Next to it a large mock-up of a fingertip crafted in shiny plastic. On its long elegant nail, such red, red varnish.

Blood red.

★

The bar was at the wrong end of the Nanjing Road. Away from the most prestigious shops, the most expensive hotels. This was the rump of the horse, the end where the shit poured out. The Nanjing that the tourists stayed away from and which led onto Hongqiao, the road to the airport.

It was easily missed, a door with no sign. It led to a hallway, poorly lit and rich with the stink of piss and the embrace of subtly scented maotai, fifty-three per cent proof. The bar was downstairs. A place to be lost in, in a country that constantly watched each face. It was a place of contagiously fierce drinking. Although still early, the dustbin behind the counter was already full of bottles without labels. Two of the empty bottles were Yaobang's.

The Big Man bought another bottle from the bar. Piao's eyes following him. Noticing how shiny his shoes were, as he placed a hand across the top of his glass as Yaobang bowed the bottle in his direction.

"What about you Mrs American, yellow wine, you try some?"

Piao interpreted.

"Is it good?"

The Senior Investigator shrugged.

"Some think so. I do not. It is a clouded wine, old. We bury it in earthenware bottles for many years, then we mix it with a young wine. It is like your western drink, sherry. If you like to drink a sweet syrup, you will find it good. But it is nineteen per cent, it will make your beer seem as water."

Yaobang smiled, ready to pour. Barbara shook her head, her fingers, an ivory cage across the mouth of her glass.

"I think I'll have some more water."

Piao poured some more of the Qingdao beer into her glass, its amber flush seeming to warm her fingers.

"This is very pleasant, Boss. Very pleasant. Even if the New Year is still a few weeks away. We should do this more often . . ."

The Big Man took his drink down in one, eyes closed, tongue like an over boiled hot dog, set between his teeth. He poured himself another yellow wine.

". . . I could always arrange for a Liberation Truck to move our office over here, Boss. I could take the table over there."

It was the table nearest to the bar. The Senior Investigator smiled on cue.

"Talking about work . . ."

They weren't, but he had to introduce it.

". . . I need some names checked out. Full reports. I want to know everything, nothing left out."

"You mean what colour turds they shit, eh Boss?"

"That is not exactly how it is put in the bureau's training manual, but I think that you have the general idea."

The Big Man smiled, taking the list of five names and browsing down it. Placing the paper in his pocket. Not a hint of recognition at any of the names. And all of the time, the Senior Investigator's stomach in a bottomless fall.

"Another drink, Mrs American?"

"Sure, why not. I'm amongst friends, aren't I."

"Boss?"

Piao shaking his head. Unable to find any words, as if his tongue was screwed to the roof of his mouth. The bottle's neck lifted in mid-flow, dripping across the table and stranding a spangle of yellow wine stars on the off-white chipped formica of its surface. The Big Man setting the bottle back down as he strained in his pocket for the list. Eyes marching back down the names.

"Liu Qingde. Boss, I know this fucking little shit. A *liu-mang* that I put away about a year ago. What's the story here?"

Piao suddenly feeling that he could breathe again. Find words again.

"Five names. The five who were unidentified from the river."

"You sure, Qingde was one of them, Boss?"

The Senior Investigator nodded.

"Fuck it. I should have recognised him, shouldn't I?"

Piao drank his beer, only noticing its sweetness now, not its bitter aftertaste.

"He was mutilated. He had no eyes. Face broken with a clubbing hammer . . ."

Letting the Big Man off the hook; a sense of exhilaration that there was no cover-up. That Yaobang was still his man.

181

"... and the mud, and the swelling from the river."

"But I still should have recognised him, Boss."

Barbara sensing the tenseness, not understanding it, but wanting to diffuse it.

"A *liu-mang*, what is it?"

The Senior Investigator looked up from his glass.

"A gangster. A heavy . . ."

Looking back into his glass avoiding eye contact.

". . . yes, you should have recognised him. But you did not. It has cost us time. What the cost of that is, who can know? Just get me the reports and we will take it from there. Now tell me about Liu Qingde."

"You were testing me, weren't you Boss,? Fucking testing me!"

Piao pushed the glass towards the Big Man's fist.

"This case is testing all of us. Drink with me and test this new bottle."

He nudged the glass into Yaobang's palm, shaping the Big Man's fingers around its coldness. The warmth of his flesh. How could he ever have thought that of Yaobang? *Fuck it. A case like this will shake anything loose that is not bolted down.*

The Big Man thrust his glass against Piao's, a rain of beer and wine falling to the table.

"Shit. You and me against the fucking world, Boss. Here's to Pan and to your cousin."

"And Wenbiao."

"The young puppy. Yes, Wenbiao."

"And Bobby."

Barbara's glass clinked against the other two. A second's silence, marking a boundary, almost as if it signposted a rite of passage. Piao's arm fell around her shoulder.

"Your understanding of Mandarin is improving. We must be more careful about what we say . . ."

He smiled, Barbara's smile following in its footsteps.

". . . here's to Bobby . . ."

The Senior Investigator refilled the glasses.

". . . now let us test more of the bottle while you tell

me about the tough little shit, Liu Qingde, that you put away."

Yaobang drank deeply, swallowing hard.

"He was small time, Boss, but with big time dreams. I remember he smelt like a yeh-ji. Sweet perfume around his neck, puke on his tongue."

"A yeh-ji, a wild pheasant, a hooker."

Barbara seeking Piao's nod of affirmation at her interpreting skills. He nodded. The Big Man threw back the rest of the drink. A drip of yellow wine running from his lips, onto his chin, onto the table.

"You know Li Zhen, he owns restaurants and a few clubs? Also pimps and runs the protection rackets in the French quarter . . . most likely the drugs distribution as well, although we've never proved fuck all. Qingde was working for him and at the same time trying to carve out a little of his own territory. Protection mostly. All we could get him on was extortion and threatening behaviour. We thought we'd be able to squeeze the little bastard, get to Li Zhen. I have to hand it to him, tough little fucker, never said a single word . . ."

The barman wiped the table. The cloth more dirty than the gutter outside. Yaobang remained silent until he was gone.

". . . Zhen and Qingde, they're distant cousins. It's a family firm. Everyone's a fucking cousin or a cousin of a cousin. It's as tight as a camel's arse in a sandstorm."

Piao drank his beer.

"A small fish in a big pond, Zhen. A legend only in his own toilet."

"They've been trying to get him for fucking years, Boss. They say that he moved from pimping and protection to drugs. Now they say he's always been in drugs. The other things were a front."

Piao finished his beer and placed the glass on the table, streams of foam racing to the bottom of the glass.

"Zhen, they cannot get hold of him because its not the other activities that are a front, its him, he's a front."

"Always the way, Boss. And where does the fucking trail lead back to? Where it always does, some fat, rich shit high up in the Party. Probably the loudest speaker when it comes to complaining about corruption in the government."

"Slugs. Their trail of slime always leads home."

"Or to other slugs," Barbara added.

The Big Man smiled as he tried to wring the last few drops from the bottle. No sense of embarrassment in the lengthy wait for their fall into his glass. He shook his head.

"A voice of experience from our Mrs American, yes?"

She nodded, raising her glass.

"Yeah, Boss, tough little shit that Qingde. Always gave me the feeling that he was overstretching. That he would either end up as the top liu-mang or on a slab in the city morgue . . ."

Yaobang held the rim of the glass above his tongue, the yellow rain drizzling down onto it.

". . . poor little bastard. Missed out twice."

"Zhen, is he around?"

"Sure Boss, saw him the other day on the Fuzhou Road. He was in a Hong-Qi, can you believe it, a shit like him in a Red Flag?"

"Most of the shit in Shanghai is not in gutters, it is sitting in Red Flags. What is new?"

The Big Man laughed, head tipped back. Nostrils black, round, reminding Piao of the entrance to the vehicular tunnels that passed under the Huangpu near the Longhua Pagoda.

"Where can he be found?"

"Most of the time he's at his restaurant on the Wenan Road. The street market end. It's got a stupid name, the Duck something. What the fuck is it? The Roast Duck. The Big Duck. The Sick Duck, that's it, the Sick Duck . . ."

Yaobang shook his head in genuine concern.

". . . how can someone own a Red Flag and then call their restaurant the Sick Duck? Such persons should be under constant surveillance. They are a threat to decent citizens . . ."

The Senior Investigator nodded in polite agreement. His own uncle's restaurant next to Yichuan Park was called the Crying Dumpling. He considered, for an instant, telling

184

Yaobang this, but thought better of it. His uncle was not a man who would appreciate constant surveillance.

"... perhaps we should pay him a little visit Boss, what do you think?"

Piao watched the spilt stars of yellow wine run into each other and dribble off the end of the table.

"It is the very least that we can do for the decent citizens of our city," he replied.

★

Hours and bottles.   Bottles and hours.

"What the hell did Bobby have in common with five Chinese thugs in a prison in Shanghai?"

Barbara's fingers moved across her eyes, brushing aside a hook of yellow curl.

"It just keeps going around and around my head. What's the link, Piao?"

His finger traced the edge of the beer glass as he spoke.

"A steel chain binding eight bodies together in death, that is a link. It says that something else, something with much power was shared by these eight ..."

Piao looked away. The honesty in her cerulean eyes too much to bear.

"... they had a secret. Your son was a part of this."

"Bobby had no secrets."

Her voice louder, but with a broken edge of uncertainty.

"You forget, I am a policeman. The most cynical of professions. Everybody hides something. Everybody has a secret."

"Not me, Mr Policeman. Politicians haven't got the time to hide things. We're too goddamn busy finding out what everybody else is hiding."

"It is the opposite in China. Our politicians are so busy hiding their own secrets that they do not have the time to discover the secrets that anybody else hides. Is this more honest?"

"Honest?"

She laughed. Her teeth were white. He had never seen teeth so white.

"What the hell has honesty got to do with it? But tell me, Senior Investigator, as we are talking about honesty. Tell me about Bobby's secret. About the secret that they all shared. I'm sure that a cynic like you has an opinion?"

"I have an opinion about everything."

"I bet you do, so put it on the table."

She would not like what he had to say. He drew a breath, holding it in the well of his throat. Pumping up the words with it.

"Drugs, only drugs create such violence. We have a problem with shipments and gangs crossing the border from the New Territories. There has been much violence. Not like this, but still considerable. We have been highly successful. Many arrests, many severe punishments. In most of the cases government officials had been involved, issuing passports, visas, travel permits. Theirs were the most severe punishments."

"But you've no evidence of any drug involvement with Bobby or the others."

"We know that two of the Chinese found in the river were drug users. A third was working for Li Zhen, a suspected dealer. We know nothing of Ye Yang, yet. We are awaiting reports. Heywood and your son, they do not seem to have been users, but they were in a position to be able to travel in and out of the country at will, from province to province without internal travel documents being issued. This is very unusual, but in the drug's trade very necessary. Having people in responsible positions, trusted, respected, who can move freely . . . that is of unimaginable importance."

A rage in Barbara's eyes. Blue fading to grey, the colour of knife blades.

"You don't miss an opportunity do you? I asked you to put your opinion on the table, not chop it up for firewood. Two junkies and one shit who was associated with a pusher does not turn it into drug murders. Christ, if you locked up everyone who mixed with junkies and pushers, half of the American Senate and Congress would be doing time."

Piao's eyes narrowed.

"You joke with me, yes?"

She ignored him.

"And just because Bobby and Heywood were in positions of authority and could travel freely, that means diddly. It certainly doesn't mean that they were in the drug's trade. You're wide of the mark, Senior Investigator. Off target completely."

He looked puzzled.

"Diddly?"

"Diddly. Diddly. It means that it doesn't mean anything at all."

She longed for a conversation with words that she didn't have to simplify; didn't have to repeat.

The Senior Investigator looked even more confused.

"Anyway, Barbara, my opinion, I have not finished it."

"You have very long and wild opinions, Senior Investigator."

"Yes, many say that, and many more are not brave enough to say that. I thank you for your honesty."

"We seem to keep coming back to honesty. It's not a subject that politicians like me know a lot about."

"But it is a subject that an officer like me can recognise when he sees it. In your son's death, the death of the others, I recognise the honesty of something going very wrong. The cadres who are the shadows behind this, sensing the rifles of the execution at the back of their necks. They panicked. They feared being caught and so destroyed the evidence. Your son, Heywood, Ye Yang, the others . . . just evidence. Nothing more than evidence. Not sons or daughters. And still they destroy the evidence, trying to cover the path back to them. Pan, Cheng my cousin, the student . . ."

His hand was on her shoulder. On material. On skin. Feeling rough, dirty against her softness. Wanting to keep his hand there, but feeling that he should remove it.

". . . it was simple, like the drug's trade. Not complex. There was what you call a deal. It went wrong. The cadre took a decision, a business decision. It was about money, percentages. Profit and loss. They wrote off what they could not salvage. The drug's trade has a dishonesty about it that is almost honest. It was drugs, Barbara. Your son, he was selling drugs . . ."

His fingers, tight across her shoulder."

". . . the mother of an addict might say that he deserved to be found in the river."

A flame in her eyes, dangerously fierce.

"Damn you, Senior Investigator."

Pulling away from his hand with a sharp turn. Moving out from the doorway and into the alley. It was raining outside, plump mercury tears. She would be soaked within seconds, but she didn't seem to care. He did, but knew that he couldn't have stopped her even if he had tried.

★

Piao and the Big Man cowered in the doorway of the bar. It was still raining. They had been there for twenty minutes, waiting for it to let up. Yaobang hating rain, fearing it more than a liu-mang with a knife in a dark piss stinking alley. An adult, a detective with a fully paid up pot-belly, afraid of a few drops of rain. It had always amazed Piao.

"Woman trouble?"

Yaobang's head nodded in the direction of Piao's car.

"She still has some painful things to hear, painful things to accept."

The Big man picked his nose, examining the result of the excavation with amusement.

"A bit like a bogey, eh Boss?"

He held up his index finger.

"Things always look clean and neat from the outside, until you poke around too much."

The Senior Investigator felt a ripple of nausea wash against his forehead.

"Is that an ancient adage passed down from your family's ancestors?"

Yaobang was indignant.

"No Boss, I thought of it myself."

It was true, the black gapped smile said it all.

"Talking of painful things to hear, Boss, Liping's old crow,

the secretary with the tits like burst paper bags, she was looking for you. She looked like she'd been trying to suck a snake
from its skin. Ugly old sow."

Chief Liping. Painful things to hear, painful things that
would wait until tomorrow. The rain seemed to ease, they
weren't sure, but they made a break for the cars anyway. The
windscreen blasted in silver dribbling shot; almost impossible
to see Barbara's face through it. He opened the door, got in
and drove. She said nothing until they reached the Jing Jiang,
and then only as she stood on the hotel's steps. The rain
beading her hair. Across her face in a scatter of pearls.

"You don't know Bobby. He'd never be involved in anything to do with drugs. His father died of drugs. His own
father."

She was walking up the steps, a curtain of rain between
them, dividing them. Turning once more and almost
shouting.

"You don't know Bobby, you don't even know me."

A heavy drum roll of fierce drops against the car roof. Her
outline lost in grey, as if she were slowly being washed away.
And all along the Nanjing Road, the spattered beat of the
windscreen wipers labouring against the torrent, seeming to
echo the rhythm of the question that was repeating in his
head.

So, who are you? . . . So, who are you? . . . So, who are you? . . .
So, who are you?

★

"Serious charges, Senior Investigator Piao. Extremely serious . . ."

The letter was still in Piao's hand, unopened. As soon as it
had been handed to him it had burnt. He had recognised the
type, the envelope, even its smell. He knew the sort of coated
tongue that had sealed its contents in place. He had never held
a letter that had felt so threatening. . . . that had stung with
such malevolence.

". . . to have made an enemy of such an important *tong zhi*,
stupid. Stupid. Comrade Zhiyuan is powerful. He is of the old

189

guard, the accusations that you made that night on the fore-shore would not be forgotten or passed over by such a man as this . . ."

Liping's face marble. Eyes unblinking. He stood, striking a formal pose.

". . . Comrade Zhiyuan has raised the following formal charges with the Danwei of the Public Security Ministry. That you made counter-revolutionary statements about the Party and Government of the People's Republic of China. That you made serious accusations against the security appar-atus and services of the Party and Government of the People's Republic of China. That you engaged in language and behaviour that besmirches the pride of the Chinese people and which strikes at the heart of our great sense of national-ism. That you threatened a Chairman of a Shiqu, a favoured citizen of the People's Republic of China and an honoured member of the Party . . ."

Liping let the letter float from his fingers to the desk. Piao's eyes following its fall.

". . . Comrade Zhiyuan and the Party Secretary of our Ministry's Danwei were together during the 'twenty tortuous years'. They were comrades in the Red Guard . . ."

He walked around the desk, his shoes, hand stitched, foreign.

". . . the charges will be answered behind closed doors in two weeks from now, in front of the Central Committee of the Danwei. It is unavoidable, Investigator. You will be found guilty on all charges. However, your past record will be taken into account. It will lessen the final punishment. Expect as the minimum, a severe reprimand. A demotion from Senior Investigator. It is likely that the Danwei will also insist upon your transfer for 're-education' . . ."

The street below in full flood, Liping's eyes constantly shift-ing and dissecting the flow.

". . . enjoy the traffic Senior Investigator, I do. It is com-merce, business. The future . . ."

He turned.

". . . you have pissed your career away, Piao. In Xinjiang the

190

only traffic that you will see will be donkeys and camels heading across the Mountains of Heaven . . ."

The Chief was silent for half a minute, its intensity underlined by a background of white sound from the traffic jammed streets below.

". . . you will run down all your cases pending the investigation. Detective Yun will familiarise himself with them. Your full co-operation will be needed and given. Is that understood?"

Yun, a career based on *pai-ma-pi* . . . 'patting the horse's arse'.

Piao nodded.

"Good. Good. Let us make this as painless as possible. Expect a call from Detective Yun . . ."

Liping's eyes not leaving him for a second.

". . . before you go, I should tell you some good news. There is always room for good news, is that not so, Investigator?"

Piao nodded.

"Your wife, she is pregnant. She and the Minister Kang Zhu are most happy. It is best that you should know this, and do not learn of it in a more insensitive fashion . . ."

There was a faint smile. Liping not bothering to hide its trail.

". . . as it is said, it seems as if your bad luck comes with a lover in tow, Senior Investigator. You may leave."

★

Wood. Marble. Their coldness through the polycotton weave of his shirt. The sweat on his back drying instantly, and with it, feeling as if his strength, his life force, had evaporated. Making it into the office. Jamming the door closed with his body. In a slow slide against the lacquered mahogany, slipping to the floor. Every detail, in razor sharp relief. Lighting the cigarette, on automatic pilot, but not feeling its welcome slash and burn. Not even tasting it. And through the tears and the tremble of his lips . . . Piao saying, over and over again the same words.

"My baby, it should be my baby. My baby, it should be my baby. My baby . . ."

The rain had stopped. Sunshine pissing through the shredded clouds and onto the dented car bonnets. Yaobang was waiting in Xingyelu; a blanket of steam rising over Fuxing Park. Everything damp. Everything bled of strength and on its knees.

"How many men?"

"Six including us, Boss."

He started the engine. The air, hot and breathless with diesel fumes, pouring from the air vent.

"What's the letter?"

Piao had been unaware that it was still in his fingers, unopened, corners so sharp. So sharp. He pressed it into the Big Man's hand.

"It's just toilet paper, that's all."

"It's a bit hard and rough Boss. It will spread the shit around rather than wipe it off . . ."

He stuffed it into his pocket.

". . . you know what they're calling toilet paper now, Boss? *Hou-men-piao* . . . 'back-door tickets.' Fucking back door tickets! What a country. You need a ticket for taking a holiday, a ticket for shopping, a ticket to have a baby, now a fucking ticket to wipe your arse."

The Senior Investigator slumped into the passenger seat. Back-door tickets. He could be given a thousand, it still wouldn't clean up the pile of shit that covered this case from top to bottom and back again.

★

The Sick Duck Restaurant had three exits; four if you counted the side door into the filth choked alley. Piao didn't count it. A liu-mang like Zhen was not the sort to try a runner, and even less the sort to screw up a four hundred yuan suit. So . . . three exits, six men. They could cover it comfortably.

The radio communicators were broken; they always were. A series of hand signals from an officer in the building opposite told the Senior Investigator what he needed to know. That

Zhen was in his office on the first floor. He was alone except for a secretary. Great legs, no tits. And a desk littered with banknotes. Zhen had seemed more interested in the piles of notes. The surveillance officer, in the secretary's legs.

The restaurant was full. A fifty seater jammed with diners. Renao, 'hot and spicy'. Waiters throwing dishes onto tables. Bowls held high to hot pepper stained chins . . . chopsticks clicking. Frantic, snapping conversations. Extra orders shouted from rice filled mouths. Noodles anchored to lips.

Piao and Yaobang, in plainclothes, moved through the restaurant, around the tables. Not too fast, not with purpose, but never too slow, never seeming to linger. Pace was everything. It could give you away or hide you. A bead curtain covered a damp stain on the wall and the entrance to the stairs . . . they swept it aside, moving through it without a glance back. It fell behind them. A brief rattle of ceramic bead against ceramic bead. The stairs were bare, stained with food. The smell of fried rice and old banknotes following them. Zhen's office was a flight up. Accommodation on the next floor. Beyond that, the roof and Heaven.

On reaching the landing, they moved swiftly. The door pushed open. The Senior Investigator moving to Zhen. Yaobang to the secretary.

"Who the fuck are you?"

A protective arm thrown around the piles of banknotes on the desk. Zhen's other hand stealing inside his jacket, but Piao was ahead of him. An arm around the liu-mang's throat. His hand wrenched from his jacket. A brief glimpse of leather and the black diamond cut of a pistol butt. The Senior Investigator pulled the weapon from the holster. A Type 67. Its body neat . . . its permanently attached Maxim-pattern silencer seeming to throw it off-balance. And in the sweaty air, an immediate acidic tang of steel, oil, aftershave strong with sandalwood. Dropping the pistol to the floor. Piao spinning Zhen around on his chair, his breath hard against the liu-mang's face.

"Naughty. Firearms can be very dangerous for your health and for the health of others."

"Fuck off."

The Big Man laughing, hand across the secretary's face, almost covering it. His knuckles white. Her eyes rolling wide above the stub of his fat thumb.

"Not much of a vocabulary for a big city crime shit, eh Boss?"

"He must be upset. It happens at times of stress. Are you feeling stressed?"

Zhen strained in his chair, bucking against Piao's arms.

"What are you bastards, some kind of double act come for an audition?"

"This is no audition Mr Restaurant Owner. Mr Drugs Pusher . . ."

The Senior Investigators lips almost touching Zhen's perfumed cheek. But through its musk, the stench of fear cornered and looking for a way out.

". . . the show has already opened, and you are centre stage. Can't you feel the heat of the spotlight on you?"

Yaobang reached across, locking the door.

"Who the fuck are you?"

"I think he said that before, Boss. Must be that stress that you were talking about. Personally I'd just call it the fucking shits."

Slowly he removed his hand from the secretary's mouth. Lipstick, as red as tomatoes, smeared across his palm. Smeared across her pale face.

"Not a word . . . nothing."

His eyes locked to hers, an understanding struck. Yaobang swapping with Piao, the grip tightened. The liu-mang now swamped in the Big Man's sweaty embrace. No chances being taken. Zhen was strong, a neck as thick as a rice pot and a PSB record studded with a clutch of violent acts never quite proved . . . never quite disproved. The Senior Investigator moved to face him across the desk. The piles of banknotes forming a half built wall between them.

"We are PSB Investigators, but just regard us as an enthusiastic audience looking forward to your performance."

"I've nothing to say to shits like you. If you're PSB, take me in. I'll guarantee you that I'll be out within two hours, and that this will put your safe little careers back ten years."

"Tell us about Liu Qingde?"

"Never heard of him."

"Your cousin, he worked for you."

"Never heard of him. Take me in if you don't believe me."

The Senior Investigator emptied the wastepaper bin and stood it at Zhen's feet; taking a half full bottle of maotai from the side table he poured a quarter of it into the bin. Alcohol, its pungent aroma filling the small room. Piao took a pile of banknotes from the desk, edges filthy, tattered. A washed red, green, brown, block of ten yuan notes, with the look and feel of dusty moth's wings . . . and a smell of old trouser pockets. He dropped them into the bin.

"They say that in the Kaxtax Shan region when it is a bad winter, to keep warm they will burn anything. Nothing is of worth, nothing has value unless it gives out heat."

The Senior Investigator struck a match. Zhen's eyes flaring with its burn. Sulphur and alcohol, a smell to fix the memory to a single moment in time. Zhen struggled in the Big Man's arms.

"What are you doing for shits sake, what are you doing?"

"Qingde. Tell me about him?"

"I told you, I don't know him. I don't fucking know him."

A yellow flame, burning its way up the match. White to black. The Senior Investigator dropping it into the waste bin. A slow tumble as it fell, meeting a fireball of ignited alcohol. A thump of orange . . . air being sucked in. The smell of old paper and unpurchased dreams, riding on the back of spit drying heat.

"No . . . no, no, no. You bastard. Bastard."

Screaming, fists clenched. Eyes, complexion, taking on the fire's fanning hunger. Yaobang jerking him back into his chair.

"You fucking maniac. That was two thousand yuan. More than you PSB shitheads make in four months."

Piao picked up another bundle of banknotes.

"Pimping and pushing pays well. Very well. They would be

very satisfied in the Kaxtax Shan with your efforts, Mr Restaurant Owner. The result is good fuel, with a brief, but strong heat. . . ."

The veins in Zhen's temples, like annealed links of tangled chain.

". . . Qingde, your cousin, tell me about him?"

"I've already told you, I don't know him."

Piao dropping the bundle of notes into the fire.

"Not again you bastard. Not again . . ."

Edges browning, shrivelling. Orange flame under passive faces of viridian ink.

". . . I want your names, your fucking names, you bastards."

"Tell us about Qingde."

Picking up another bundle of ten yuan notes. Spreading them across his palm. A fan of aged, paled tattooed colours.

"Okay, okay. He did a little work for me. A bit of this, a bit of that."

"What sort of work?"

No reply. Piao letting a few notes tumble into the flames.

"A bit of running. Collecting monies. Small stuff. Shit stuff."

"Nothing else?"

Zhen shaking his head. More bills meeting the blaze. Green, to yellow, to black.

"You bastard. Alright. Alright. He did a bit of heavy stuff. Protection, setting up and collecting. He had a skill for it. Mean little fucker."

"But you haven't seen him for a while, have you?"

No reply. The Senior Investigator's hand moving across the flames.

"He got greedy, fucking greedy. They all do in time. He was ambitious, wanted his own piece of the action. We fell out, you might say. Anyway, what the fuck is this about."

Piao placed the remaining handful of bills back onto the desktop.

"Liu Qingde was found in the river, minus his life and any identification. Minus his finger tips. Minus his eyes. Sounds like drugs to me. What about you?"

196

Zhen instantly nervous. The words coming fast. Each syllable underlined by the sweat slicing down both sides of his face.

"We fell out, but it wasn't like that. Not like that. I had nothing to do with it . . . I don't run an operation that kills people. Not even people that cross me. Sure, I shook him up a little. Scared the shit out of him for trying to screw me. But to cut him up like you said you found him, no eyes, no fucking finger tips . . . forget it, that's not me, I don't do those sorts of things. Check my record."

The fire had died, embers of dull rubies amongst filo pastry layers of black paper. And amongst the shit that Zhen spoke, sparks that Piao recognised as the truth.

"I know your record. It is what we don't know about you that concerns me. A man like you is capable of anything when it comes to this shit."

The Senior Investigator scattered a pile of yuan bills. A tabletop full of banknotes sliding in an anaemic inked avalanche. Money . . . it was both sweet and sour to Piao. It held dreams; it crushed dreams. But always, it brought with its mention, memories. Memories. Remembering her sigh, as her eyes half turned away from him . . .

Why are we always poor? I can't spend ten yuan on myself without feeling guilt . . . worrying that it should have been spent on food. I dream of perfume, new clothes . . . and babies, fat babies.

And babies . . . 'nemma bai, nemma pang.' So white, so fat.

"You're not hanging this on me. I haven't seen Qingde for a month. He wasn't exactly fucking popular around here. There must have been a thousand who would have liked to have murdered the little shit. But I wasn't one of them. I have too much to lose . . ."

He nodded towards the tabletop, the banknotes, smiling. Teeth immaculate, newly capped. A wall of bleach white porcelain.

". . . you should talk to some of them. I'll give you a fucking list. Start with Qingde's half-brother. He's probably crossed him as well, which would have put him in the shit. Xie

197

is a powerful man, not the sort to turn a blind eye, half-brother or not."

"He was working for Xie?"

"I heard rumours."

"What was he doing for Xie?"

"The usual. Girls. Protection. Xie runs about everything in Hongkou and Pudong. With all those foreign companies coming in across the river, it's sale time."

"And drugs?"

Zhen nodded, but with a sudden realisation lighting in the backs of his eyes. Relaxing in the restraint of Yaobang's arms. A swagger in his expression.

"You didn't know that Qingde and Xie were half-brothers, did you? Fucking PSB, and you didn't know."

Piao felt the anger rise to his neck, his collar a steel band. Needing to rip it open. The case was moving fast. Too fast. Like a lorry ploughing down a hill out of control. He should have known about Xie, about every member of Qingde's family. He should have known everything about the little shit. What size his underpants were. What his last thought was before he fell asleep; what his first thought was as he awoke. It would all be in the reports, the bottomless pile of buff that was sitting on the table in his flat, next to the half full bottle of Tsingtao. The bottomless pile of buff, that he had not had the time to read. He moved around the desk, past the girl. Her body, a peg to hang dreams upon.

"We are not infallible, we do not need to be. But a shit like you, well, there is another matter. I would be very careful from now on, Mr Restaurant Owner. You see, we now know your weakness."

The Senior Investigator running a hand across the desktop, two piles of banknotes falling into the wastepaper bin. Zhen straining against the Big Man's grasp; chair legs stuttering across the floor.

"You bastard. You fucking shit."

The flames gradually taking hold. White, to yellow, to orange. Piao pushing another pile of notes into the flames.

"Be careful Mr Zhen. For a man to know another man's weakness is a powerful thing. *It is a splinter in the soul.*"

The Senior Investigator retrieved the pistol from the floor, removing its nine-shot magazine. Walking to the door. With a nod, Yaobang released his arms and brushed past the secretary.

"You wouldn't consider joining me for a drink or two one evening?"

He smiled. The girl's eyes dead. His question left stranded like the dried noodle on his jacket lapel.

"I suppose not."

He opened the door and they walked out onto the landing. Their last view of Zhen, kneeling beside the bin, fingers picking in and out of the embers, trying to retrieve half burnt ten yuan notes.

★

They walked to the cars. The ancestors crying a fine drizzle . . . inescapable. The Xizang Road lost in a fine gauze of mist. Everything de-burred, smoothed. The cars seeming slower. Words too. Yaobang lit a China Brand, tipping the packet toward Piao. He'd been spoilt. A week of Panda's, the sweetness of their imported tobacco. He declined.

"This Xie, Boss, shouldn't be too fucking hard to find. I'll dig out his files and put a few of his likely hangouts on a list."

The Senior Investigator could taste the smoke from the cigarette hanging in the damp air. It felt familiar. It felt like home.

"The list, don't bother. I know where to find Xie . . ."

Far off, a moan, long, lingering. A freighter slipping blindly down the river. Piao wondering if its crew thought of the sun, hot and fierce, left far behind.

". . . he was arrested a month ago. He's in Gongdelin . . ."

"Sounds like the right place for the piece of shit. But he couldn't have been involved in the murder of Qingde and the others if he was fucking banged up in Virtue Forest, Boss."

"The tentacles of the Octopus can strike beyond the cave in which it is resting."

199

Yaobang threw the cigarette butt to the pavement with an anger of sparks. Treading on it as he passed.

"We should visit him, eh, Boss? A busy man like that in Virtue Forest. He probably gets very lonely."

Virtue Forest. Its name coming up again. Like a toothache, it demanded attention.

Fuck the cough. Fuck the breathlessness. Piao gave in and accepted one of the Big Man's China Brands, it tasting of every unfulfilled hope.

"Yes, it must get lonely in Gongdelin," he said through the smoke.

"We will pay Citizen Xie a friendly visit."

He warmed his hands with his smoke ladened breath. The car was cold. The flat would be even colder. He drove home.

Chapter 16

Reports. Type tripping over pages in a slow parade of dates, serial numbers, informants' details, internal/external visa authorisations, arrest and imprisonment data. There was little to be gained from the boredom of their reading, punctuated only by China Brands and pots of jasmine tea. Leaving him with a flail of a cough and a mouth that tasted of tea dust and callused leaf pickers' fingers.

Yongshe. Feng. Decai. Ziyang. It was as Rentang had said. All had been residents at Gongdelin. All had been habitual criminals, malcontents or insane. Strings of arrest details, charge numbers, hospital admissions . . . flowing from their files in rivers of type. Each life irrevocably leading to that one crime that the State deemed worth dying for. At the bottom of each report a thick red tick, signifying that each execution had taken place. The short walk. Forced into a kneeling position. The rifle discharging its load into the base of the neck. All had been executed by the bullet, a full day before they had been dragged from the Huangpu. Mutilated . . . every shred of evidence that could have identified them, torn, ripped or gouged from their bodies. Yet the protocols for the treatment of the bodies of executed prisoners were strict and always adhered to. Following execution, whether it was carried out in the grounds of a state prison or a high profile execution in a stadium, the bodies were take for immediate cremation. If the State so wished, relatives of the prisoner could claim the ashes. If the State did not so wish it, the ashes would be dealt with as the high cadre saw fit. The bodies of those executed, after all, were the property of the State. Of this there was no doubt.

Piao gathered the files. The faces, in grainy monochrome, lost in a shuffle of paper. Lives now lived only as serial numbers and as pixels on a VDU. The room was getting cold, the tea also. Piao pulled a blanket across himself, raising the cup to his lips. It's taste of long summer days, totally at odds with the hour. Also at odds and jarring, four men executed by the State and cremated on the fourth of the month. Four men, the same men, found murdered, mutilated, but pulled from the Huangpu on the fifth day of the month!

The Senior Investigator read one more report before he lay on the bed. To read the report taking minutes. To shackle sleep, longer. Much longer.

Ye Yang. Date and place of birth. USA passport number. Colour of eyes. Colour of hair. Marital status. A few dates of movements in and out of the country. Visa numbers. Gaps. Bare bones. He needed the flesh, muscle, skin. Ye Yang . . . a key to a lock that Piao could only guess at. Everything that he knew, everything that he didn't know, seeming to depend ultimately on gut feelings, without the safety net of knowledge or hard evidence. It was familiar territory for him, but it still felt unfamiliar. Dangerous.

★

He couldn't remember the instant that sleep harnessed him. The transition, stepless, from reading the reports to the papers scattering onto the floor. The cup in his hand tilting. The remainder of the tea, piss yellow, weeping across the rim of the cup and onto the sheet. Sleep was featureless. An expanse of time indented by nothing. When he awoke the tea stain had dried. He gathered the papers. Drank more tea. Washed and dressed. He was thinking of her when Barbara's phone call came.

"It's your day off. Why don't you show me Senior Investigator Sun Piao's Shanghai?"

His hair was still wet, uncombed, like noodles dyed in octopus ink. He smoothed it down with both palms.

"I will be outside your hotel in thirty minutes."

★

The day had a shine about it. A blue sky devoid of the bruise and graze of clouds. It was rare at this time of the year. The whole of Shanghai seemed to be taking advantage of the good weather. The Longs alive with people, and washing lines tethered across streets in waves and rolls of white linen.

The morning was spent at Yufosi, the Temple of the Jade Buddha. Further north, the Tomb of Lu Xun. And then down to Zhongshandong Lu, a trip on the river, two hours to where the Huangpu becomes the Yangtze. Piao in a white shirt, sleeves rolled up. The sun, a warm kiss across his skin. The city, just a backcloth to his view of her. Not for a second, his eyes leaving her. Missing nothing. The straps of her dress slipping across her shoulder. The lazy upturn of the corners of her lips. The ease with which she crossed her legs. Uncrossing them . . . the blush of pink on her thigh, fading to white.

They ate at the Xinya on Nanjing Lu. Spring thunder soup, white chicken meat and rice crusts . . . deposits of rice scraped from cooking pots and then dried in the oven, emitting sharp crackling thunder when served with the broth. Lacquered duck, the aromatic, melt-in-the-mouth exterior, the colour of honey and caramel. *Guiyu*, the mandarin fish . . . cut and shaped, cooked, half caramelised to resemble chrysanthemum flowers. Dragon's beard noodles. And for desert, lychee, kumquat and longan . . . 'dragon's eye'.

After lunch, driving southwest through the former French concession. The Longhua Pagoda, with its seven storeys of brick, wooden balconies and red lacquer pillars . . . resembling a wood screw being slowly turned into the blue of the day. In the park next to the temple they drank jasmine tea, made from cream flowers and black dancing leaves. A scent that secret words would have. The conversation light, stopping only when in the car on Zhongshanxi Lu, the traffic becoming a solid wall of panting steel. Piao cut down Tianyajiao Lu, moving north . . . the traffic coming to a complete halt within sight of the covered stadium. A slow-moving block of people on the pavements heading in one direction. A Liberation Truck pulled up beside Piao, a stream of olive green uniforms piling from it. Lean bodied and with shiny black hat peaks cutting across their eyes. Their features carved by the same artist from the same design. The Senior Investigator flipped his badge.

"Trouble?"

The driver stopped picking at his teeth, wiping his finger on the underside of the dashboard; straightening his posture.

"Not for us, Comrade Officer."

"Then for who?"

"Wang, him and two others. Today's the day they collect their prizes. It's in an hour's time in the stadium."

Piao thumped the steering wheel with the heel of his hand.

"Shit."

The driver smiled. Investigators . . . all braid and balls. Awake only when it was pay-day.

"Where have you been Comrade Officer, on the moon? Wang's is the execution of the year."

There was no room to turn. They would have to park and walk until they were free of the crowds and could get a taxi or pedicab. He revved the engine in anger, his eyes hard into the driver of the Liberation Truck.

"I have been investigating murders, Comrade Officer . . . and what have you been doing, investigating the cracks between your teeth?"

The driver smiled and wound up the truck's window, continuing to pick at his teeth. Piao parked and guided Barbara through the crowds, away from the stadium.

"What's wrong, where are we going?"

By now they should have been back at the Jing Jiang. Drinking coffee. Drinking Dukang. Her, him, away from everything else. The rest of the world beached and neatly hung on a hook.

"We must go, it is bad to be here."

"But why, it doesn't look dangerous. Look around, people seem to be having fun. There's a real buzz about the place."

The Senior Investigator increased his pace, pulling her behind him.

"No, no. It is not good. We must leave."

"But why?"

"We must leave. We must."

Barbara stopping dead. Wrenching her arm from his grip. A gap between them, the crowd pushing through it.

"What's going on? You're blocking me. We're having a great day and then you pull something like this on me."

Hurt in her eyes. Piao pushed his way toward her. Lowering her arms, placing them by her sides.

"The covered stadium, that is where they are going . . ."

His eyes leaving hers and looking over her shoulder at the reflection of his face in a shop window, the carnival passing by behind him.

A real buzz . . . people having fun . . . nothing dangerous.

". . . they are on their way to see a public execution."

★

The stadium was full, a capacity of twenty-five thousand seated. The Senior Investigator showed his badge once more. It was met by a salute.

"We can still leave. We do not have to be here."

Barbara shook her head. She was close to him, he could almost taste her lipstick; wanting to taste her lipstick.

"I need to see this," was all that she said.

"But why, when you do not have to see it?"

"I need to see this . . ." she said again. And Piao knowing, that sometimes truly to know death, it must be tasted. Not read about. Not studied. Not viewed on a cinema screen. But tasted. He nodded, and firmly taking her arm, they moved forward. They stood in the tunnel, in the shadow, away from the blind of spotlights. In the centre of the arena, a raised stage pooled in arc light and already studded with dark suited high cadre and polished and preened PSB. An open-topped lorry moved up the tunnel from the road. A deep throb of engine, belching diesel exhaust. It passed right beside them, filled with olive green uniforms. High cheek boned impassive faces, some fixed with black lensed glasses that offered back no reflection. At the top front, three figures. Two in white shirts, eyes looking down. Between them a taller man. Handsome, black jacket buttoned to the neck. Its cut sophisticated, not Chinese. On his shoulders, the white gloved hands of the PSB officers. The lorry plunged into the arc light. The officer's black lenses blazing white.

"His name is Wang Jianye. He was a high cadre, the planning chief of Shenzhen in the south. He accepted bribes of one and a half million dollars while he was a director of a municipal planning bureau. He was also keeping a mistress. They extradited him from Thailand to stand trial."

The lorry approached the stage and stopped, the PSB filing out. The three brought forward, marched from the vehicle; one of them supported under his arms, his legs folding beneath him. Wang moving more confidently. A sense of resignation glimpsed in each footstep.

"Who are the other two in the white shirts?"

"Officials. Tiny fish. Minor cadre. Wang is the big one. The highest ranking official ever to be tried and sentenced. Beijing is involved in an anti-corruption drive. There is much concern in the continued rise of economic crime. Senior officials have ordered that the campaign is to be pursued with a renewed vigour. Wang, he is the example that shows that the campaign is working . . ."

Piao lit a cigarette, offering one to Barbara. She declined.

". . . I have never seen an execution before. I have always been able to transfer to other duties."

She reached across and held his hand. His fingers, cold, rigid. Wang was pulled forward, flanked by two officers. An official rose and read out a list of his crimes in a voice that was harsh and over-amplified, pumped out over loudspeakers for the benefit of the crowd.

"Injustice! I am innocent!" Wang shouting out, his voice small. The crowd starting a chant of 'kill, kill.' And then it all moving so fast. Two PSB Officers forcing Wang's arms back, like flimsy black wings. Throwing him down onto his knees. The officers stepping back, but Wang remaining in position as if transfixed by the moment; the unfurling of the seconds that would end his life. A third officer marching forward, stubby rifle in hand. Bracing himself. The end of the barrel pushed firmly to the base of Wang's skull. Steel . . . so cold, kissing skin. A plume of smoke, silver-white, in a lazy twirl. Wang pitching forward. And then the sound. Not the sharp crack that Barbara had expected, more a thud that seemed to slam into her. That seemed to pinpoint, to package, every act of violence that she had ever witnessed.

"Jesus."

She felt herself jump. A numbness working its way up from her legs. Piao's hand tightening around hers. His other arm around her waist, leading her back down the dark tunnel, through the barriers, towards the road. Her face looking back across her shoulder towards the arena. The puppet limp body of Wang being loaded onto the lorry. A dampness spreading down the back of his jacket. A vomit of blood, scarlet, falling to green . . . dripping from his mouth and onto the grass. He would be cremated within two hours.

They were out of the stadium and into the road. The loud-speakers calling to attention the list of economic crimes of the next criminal to be executed. That he was an, 'obstacle to the progress of the economy . . . a maggot in the rice sack.'

The world had turned, night swept in on a wave of car lights. Everything different now.

Barbara's eyes narrowed in their glare.

"How many do they execute?"

"It is not known . . ."

Piao pulled his collar up. There was a chill in the air, the weather on the turn.

". . . but it is many. We have sixty-eight offences that are now punishable by death. Fraud, hooliganism, illegal share speculation, spreading superstition. The offences increase; the executions increase. At this time of the year we have many public executions at mass rallies."

"Why at this time of the year?"

The Senior Investigator led them into Xietulu, moving east. Snatches of PSB in doorways, readying themselves for the crowds to decant onto the streets. Piao hailed a pedicab and they seated themselves in the rear. Petrol and piss smelling cushions. Barbara's hand seeking his as the motorised rickshaw struggled to build up speed.

"You said this time of the year . . . there are more executions around now?"

The Senior Investigator removed his hand from hers and lit another cigarette, his features shunted sideways by the brilliance of the flame.

"It is nearly the Lunar New Year. It is a time for traditions. New clothes are bought, hair is cut, bills are paid. Lucky characters are pasted everywhere. Families will gather for a feast. Special dumplings and *niangao*, 'rising higher every year cakes' . . ."

He drew closer. Barbara could see the orange tip of his cigarette reflected in his eyes. His skin the colour of copper.

". . . the New Year is also a traditional time for settling outstanding scores. A traditional time for seeking vengeance."

A passing Pedicab backfired and she was back there, at the stadium. Wang falling forward, shadow shortening. The crowd silent. The PSB Officer stepping back. The smoke tumbling from the rifle's barrel. The tears fell and she could not block them, streaming down her cheeks as Piao's arm encircled her, his rough jacket smelling of loneliness and hope.

A traditional time for seeking vengeance.

How could such cruelty ever have become so institutionalised?

The Pedicab had built up speed. She closed her eyes. The flick of street light to street light, melting velvet through her eyelids. Each pulse taking her further from the stadium. How she wanted to be taken further from the stadium . . .

★

The Jing Jiang seemed as if it were another world; perhaps it was. Tourists, with their smells of soap, leather, perfume . . . and black market currency deals. Attentions already focussed to the next destination on their twenty-one day itinerary. Piao walked her to her room.

"Tomorrow, your visit to Gongdelin prison. I want to go with you."

He felt the weight of her request immediately burden him. Understanding the words, but not understanding the reason behind them.

"Why would you want to see such a place as this?"

"I need to put Bobby's death in some kind of context . . ."

A hundred reasons to say no. Barbara placing two fingers across his lips.

". . . you're not going to block me are you? We agreed to help each other, not cut each other out."

The coolness of her fingertips on his lips. He wanted to kiss them, bite them. She only removed them when he smiled. She unlocked the door. Switching the light on and slipping inside. Closing the door between them, a gap of a foot spilling pink light. Her head resting on the door frame.

"If you really want to help me, you'll do this for me . . ."

The door closing to a fine thread. Pink on pink. Her lips. Her cheek. Her fingertips.

". . . you'll do this for me and then dry my tears."

He didn't have time to answer; the door closed.

★

He was at the elevator when her door opened and she called his name; the smile still haunting her mouth.

"Thank you for a very special day, Sun. It meant a lot to me."

She opened the door a little wider. The side of her face stroked in pastels.

"The execution. It was just something that I had to see. Can you understand that?"

He nodded. Knowing. Sometimes you must give horror a reference point to know its face again in your life, or in the lives of others. She reached out, a hand moving to his arm, his shoulder, the back of his neck. Pulling him closer. Her lips on his. Strawberries brushing stone. A long kiss. A thank you? Friendship? It felt like more . . . he knew that it was more.

The door closed. He walked back to the open mouth of the elevator . . . already mentally drying her tears.

Black Shanghai Sedan on the corner of avenues . . . the junctions of streets meeting as one.

Black Shanghai Sedan . . . everywhere that they were. Engine running in a lazy pant.

He'd seen it, she'd seen it.

By the Temple of the Jade Buddha. Following them in a slow stretch from Zhongshandong Lu, as they had cruised the Huangpu until it became the Yangtze. As they had eaten lacquered duck at the Xinya, rolling it in a cigar of fine pancake, spring onion and earth red plum sauce . . . the black Shanghai Sedan, opposite, in the shadows. In the park next to the Longhua Pagoda as they had drunk tea, jasmine on her lips and on her breath . . . through the trees, the outline of the Sedan broken in a green on green melt.

He'd seen it, she'd seen it.

But no words. No questions, why?

★

Four telephone booths in the lobby of the Jing Jiang hotel . . .
EENEY . . . MEENY . . . MINEY . . . MO . . .
The more random the choice, the less the chance of it being bugged?
IF IT WRIGGLES LET IT GO . . .
The lobby telephones. They wouldn't bug the lobby telephones . . . would they? What would be the point, so many use them. How would they identify one caller from another?
EENEY . . . MEENY . . . MINEY . . . MO . . .
Cursing inwardly. The satellite phone that Carmichael had offered her, why hadn't he insisted?
Why hadn't she accepted?
MO . . . the booth on the far right.
MO . . . the second on the left.
MO . . . the first booth.

Waiting until the middle-right booth was vacant. Its mouthpiece still warm . . . pin beads of condensation on Bakelite. Mouthing Carmichael's private number to herself. Dialling direct. A bag full of yuan coins in her pocket, and a tight agenda in her head . . .

"Where are you telephoning from?"
"The hotel. The Jing Jiang."
"Jesus. Put the receiver down."
"Why?"

210

"Put it down, it will be tapped."

"I'm in the lobby, it's safe. It must be safe."

" Not safe. Safer."

"So its safer . . . and I need to talk and you need to listen."

Silence . . . in the background, an electronic beat pacing out the half seconds.

"So talk. Talk fast. No names. No precise details. Just generalisations. Got it?"

Silence . . . the beat stronger . . . quicker. A snare drum rim hit at double time.

"I want your unseen friends off my back. Understand?"

Silence.

"Was it your idea? It feels like your idea."

"You need support. There could be more to going missing than there appears. The other party could be trying to apply pressure. They know you're a mother."

"I'm a politician first."

"They know you better than you do. You're a mother first."

" I know what I am."

"Okay. If that's what you want."

"It's what I want. Also, there's others involved . . . watching. I want to prepare for any eventuality. Know what I'm saying? My friend, the comrade. Let's dig a little. Honey and shit, okay? And then prepare some packages for me to take to the picnic."

Carmichael laughing.

"Tough talking. Private arrangements. My area of expertise."

"Thought you'd like it. And the other little job I left with you . . . the groundwork and that shopping list?"

"Again, my area of expertise. My Christmas shopping is almost complete now."

A wash of white noise.

"Down to my loose change. See you soon."

"Remember, you're a mother. They will! Are you alright? Are you alri . . ."

Silence . . . the line dead. The ocean of static, still.

★

She held the receiver to her ear for sometime after the call was completed, listening for the tell-tale 'click' of a tapped line. A 'click' that never came. The silence, seeming to swallow her whole. And in her head, the only sounds in the universe, were lyrics from a song whose title she could not remember . . .

'. . . *you're gonna reap just what you sow* . . .
. . . *you're gonna reap just what you sow* . . .'

Chapter 17

Long after you left Gongdelin, 'Virtue Forest', it would remain in your mind. Asked to describe it, only one image would you be able to summon up . . . that of a clenched fist.

A vast and threatening clenched fist.

★

The car approached the great studded gate flanked by video cameras and armed security guards. A slither of light appearing down the centre of its length, both halves sliding open and spewing out a grey light fed by stained skylights and discoloured reflector shades, tethered by wire and dust covered cobwebs. Barbara had a sudden image of Jonah being swallowed by the whale. A sheen of perspiration forcing its way to her forehead, as the gates closed behind them, and the thump of bolts ramming into place. How could you ever get use to a place like this, even in five, ten, or twenty years? The noise of keys, of locks, of doors slamming.

"This is foolish. I should not have been persuaded to bring you. I should not have allowed myself to be . . ."

The Senior Investigator's fingers drumming on the steering wheel with each word spoken, with each word unspoken.

". . . remember, you are a member of the Washington State Parole Committee . . ."

Piao tapped the papers clenched in her fingers.

". . . it is all in the internal travel documents and permit of authority. It is unlikely that you will be challenged, being seen with me will be enough, but it is best that you should be prepared. Yes, best to be prepared."

Barriers to the front: red, white, candy stripes. Guards moving out of the office to the sides of the car. The peaks of their hats, like razor blades, slicing across the bridges of noses.

Barbara felt her stomach contract. A taste of oiled steel

213

across her tongue. The colour draining from her face.

"Documents."

Piao flipped his badge. A brief flicker of the guard's eyes. A snap of a salute.

"Park your car in Bay 13, Senior Investigator. An officer will take you to the Comrade Chief Warden."

The barrier rose. Piao drove through. They hadn't even looked at Barbara's papers. She dropped them into her bag, a sense of disappointment in her eyes. The Senior Investigator still muttering . . .

"I should not have allowed myself."

★

Chief Warden Mai Lin Hua's office was in a pleasant administration block as far as it could be from the long, beige rabbit warren corridors, the cells that studded them like tumours, and their contents . . . the crumpled heaps that they referred to as 'guests'. Guests. A name that bore none of the horror of not being able to leave Gongdelin's firm grasp.

Hua's desk was ordered, as was his face. A neutrality about it that would make it instantly forgettable within seconds of leaving his office. On the desk was a large photograph . . . two children of around eight to ten years old. It was hard to tell their age as they looked exactly like their father. Nothing in their features to hook onto, to use as reference points. They would also be instantly forgettable within seconds.

"Please . . . sit, sit, sit."

His English, jerky, bumpy.

"A privilege. A privilege. A colleague from America. Washington. We must get coffee. Yes . . . coffee. Americans like coffee?"

Barbara nodded.

"And then a tour. A tour. You must have a tour. We have prepared for you. It is not often that we have such an esteemed visitor. A foreign visitor. It was short notice. Very short notice, but we prepared."

She found herself smiling, like a fool, smiling.

"You have prepared?"

"The orchestra. Our twenty-five piece symphony orchestra. MaYi Ping has them assembled. He is the conductor. He
was musician on the outside. Yes, musician . . . and robber of
course. That is how he got to be in here. Seven years. Now he
just conducts. He learnt to do it here. Our dance troupe you
also see, yes? And our operatic tenor soloist and mixed chorus."

Barbara felt the smile dying on her face.

"Yes. Yes. We have many plans for our foreign guest Senior
Investigator. Go. Go. My Deputy will take you to see the guest
that you required. Your Officer Yaobang will meet you there.
We will look after our foreign friend. Go. Go."

He waved his hands at Piao as the door opened, and a man,
the Deputy, his face as gaunt as a switch blade, stepped into
the room and saluted. Chief Warden Hua beamed, his eyes
crumpled tight. Fleshy craters of imploded skin.

"Go. Go."

Piao smiled at Barbara as he passed her.

"Have fun."

"She will. She will," replied Hua, as he ushered the Senior
Investigator out, closing the door.

★

From an iron core of gantries and spiral open stairs wrapped
in a gossamer of meshed steel, radiated the corridors like the
spokes of a wheel. A brightness about them, a cleanliness that
seemed to be in a head-on collision with the horror of
incarceration. In the corridors, in the cells, the lights burning
constantly, day, night . . . boundaries of time blurred into just
one vast stretch of hard white light. The doors to the cells
were panelled with reinforced glass. Prisoners were required
to sleep facing the glass so that guards could watch over them.
If a 'guest' turned in his sleep, guards would wake him. A
swollen and infected ear was common amongst those who
had to sleep on one side for many years; in such cases you
might be permitted to turn over. And from the central core,
constantly, the salvo of doors slamming. Of screams, of threats.
Of lives left to stew in their own juices.

★

215

Xie was lucky, his cell had a small skylight. Through it he could see the clouds, sliced into even sized portions by the black thickly painted bars. It was a rare privilege . . . to be allowed to know the day, to be allowed to know the night.

A slither of sunlight had found the far wall. Xie sitting within it. Its sojourn across his face in a yellow edged gash. Elongating his nose. Slicing his lip. Cleaving his chin, neck, chest. His eyes were closed, only opening them when the silence was broken.

"You have visitors."

The Deputy nodded at Piao and moved toward the door.

"I will be outside."

The door closing . . . closed. Eyelids rising lazily across instantly alert eyes, yellow with sun. His movements, his look, reminding the Senior Investigator of a gecko warming itself.

"You've been drinking jasmine tea, Senior Investigator Piao. It smells sweet. It suits you . . ."

His arms slowly unfolding.

". . . and a woman. You smell of a woman . . ."

Eyes half closed, the yellow extinguished as he drew a breath, long and stuttering, through the flare of his nostrils.

". . . mmm, also sweet. So sweet. Not a wife smell, onions, flour, pissy knickers, tears . . ."

His eyes opened fully. Black. As black as midnight puddles.

". . . no. This smell is different. Skin lotion, restaurants, lace, pink nipples. What have you been up to Senior Investigator?"

Piao nudged the slop bucket with his foot; it grated against the tiled floor.

"I can only smell shit, Xie, and lots of empty hours."

The Big Man moved out of Piao's shadow to within inches of the prisoner . . . sniffing.

"Yeah, definitely shit, Boss. Almost unbearable."

Xie's mouth widened to a smile. Wet lips, shadowed tongue, resembling the deep stripe of a scalpel across taut flesh. The skin opening into an obscene fish-lipped pucker.

"It's not my shit you can smell. It's your own lives rotting on the vine . . ."

The smile remaining as he focussed his attention on the Big Man.

". . . a pity detective, but you were never the clever one, were you, or the attractive one? It was always your brother. Your little brother. So much praise, so much attention. And you on the outside always looking in . . ."

He stood, a taunt in his posture.

". . . you got your wish, detective. Now you can get all the attention. He's dead. Blown away."

"Bastard. Fucking bastard!"

The Big Man's head a hammer, forehead slamming down onto Xie's nose. Piao throwing himself in between them, shoving Yaobang against the door. The prisoner falling hard against the wall, slipping down it, hands across his face. Laughing. Removing the web of fingers. The bruise already storming across his nose and cheek. A slip of scarlet trailing from one nostril. Carving across his mouth, chin, neck. The Senior Investigator's hand firm against Yaobang's chest; it rising and falling violently with ripped breaths.

"Enough. No more."

"But how does he know about my brother, Boss? He must have been involved, the bastard."

The hand moving up to the Big Man's shoulder.

"These things get known. Anything that hurts a PSB Officer gets known by shits like this. He's feeding on you. In here they have nothing else to do. He was not involved, now let's get down to business."

Piao knelt beside Xie, the blood blotting into his prison shirt in an unfurling bloom of rust. And the smell . . . of pepper, of starched cotton, and of anger, hot and parcelled, to be opened up on another day.

"You have a half-brother, Liu Qingde, we want to talk to you about."

"He's dead."

Xie spat the words out as darts.

"How do you know that he is dead?"

"I know."

"And what else do you know?"

"That is for me to know and for you to have sleepless nights about."

The flow of blood stemmed, dried, like a cracked and arid riverbed down his lips and chin.

"Your half-brother, Qingde, I don't give a shit about. But the others who were killed with him and the others who have been killed since, these I do care about . . ."

Piao lit a Panda Brand, exhaling. The smoke writhing in the space between them. Xie would taste it. He would be thinking of the press of crowds on the Nanjing Road. Late night mah-jongg games. The fire of Dukang. He would be thinking of how great it would be to light his own cigarette.

". . . sleepless nights, I already have them and I don't like them. But the information that you are going to give me will be of help. Great help. If it is of use to you, view your assistance as a form of relaxation therapy. A very profound way of supporting another human being."

"Fuck off."

"That's not a very empathic response. Do I take it that you do not wish to enter into a therapeutic relationship with me?"

Not for an instant, Xie's smile waning.

"Fuck off."

Piao moved to the cell door. A shadow on the other side of the glass, the Deputy Warden, reaching for his keys. Holding a brief conversation, its words framed amongst the salvos of slamming cell doors, shouts disfigured in echo. A smell flooding in. . . . disinfectant edged in a sharp tooth of vomit.

"Everything ready?"

The Deputy entered the cell with two other officers; a nervousness snagging the corners of his eyes.

"I am against this."

Piao's cigarette, a warning, burning orange between his lips.

"But your superior, Chief Warden Hua, he is not?"

"No. No, he is not."

"Then get on with it. Your reluctance will be duly noted."

The Deputy nodding. The officers moving forward. Xie moving back.

"What's going on? Where the fuck are you taking me?"

Bare toes screeching across the hard tiled floor, as he was dragged from the cell. Voice swamped in the length of the corridor. Far away, a cell door opening, a cell door slamming shut.

Silence.

Piao lit another Panda Brand from the butt of his and offered it to the Big Man. He would not appreciate the subtlety of the imported tobacco, but what the fuck!

"Twenty minutes," Yaobang said through smoke.

"Ten," replied the Senior Investigator.

They shook hands.

★

Mozart's Symphony No.40 in G minor. Brahms' Tragic Overture. And a rendition of Ravel's 'Bolero' that outpaced itself, laying exhausted across the conductor's baton before it was half way through.

Barbara's face ached. Wincing as Ma Yi Ping raised the baton . . . a breath of relief escaping through her teeth as she realised that it was just to invite the orchestra to take a bow. Another bow, their sixth. She nodded. They nodded. She applauded them. They applauded her. Barbara stood, turning to walk to the door, her fingers already finding the Marlboro wrapper, only to be halted by the barrel chested tenor soloist marching past her toward the podium. She withdrew her hand from the bag, turning back toward her chair, preparing herself. The soloist, she knew, was a convicted con man. A rapist in the baritone section of the mixed chorus. Thieves amongst the sopranos. Ma Yi Ping tapped his baton. She sat, smiling the smile. The conductor smiled. The baton fell. The Mahler began.

★

Nine minutes.

The Big Man handed Piao a ten yuan note as the guards dragged Xie down the corridor and into the cell. Fresh blood on his face. Prison trousers ripped and trailing from his feet.

219

Pants around his ankles. White pearls of buttocks. A single rose bud of blood blooming at their heart and opening its petals. They laid him on the bed, as he struggled to pull up his clothes. Continuing to hold the broken belt around his waist with both hands. Defiance, humiliation, struggling for supremacy in that one simple act.

"Qingde. Tell us about him?"

Xie pulled his knees to his chest. A dark rust of dampness spattering the arse of his trousers. The stain growing, resembling the outline of Australia. But no words. Yaobang's shadow fell across the bed, the wall.

"Nine minutes. You lost me ten fucking yuan. I always get really pissed off when I lose a bet, but not as pissed off as the Bear down the corridor must be. That's what they call him. The Bear. Hairy bastard. Strong too. He'll be fucking pissed off. Nine minutes isn't going to satisfy an appetite like his . . ."

Yaobang lit a cigarette. It was as if everything about not being in a cell, not being in a prison, was summed up in the simplicity of that one action.

". . . they say he likes to take his fucking time. His last victim was a ten year old boy over in Pudong. They say he took at least four hours over him . . ."

Cigarette smoke creeping across Xie's shoulder. Warm beers, crowds, the perfumed tits of a yeh ji . . . they were all there in its smell, in its taste.

". . . in four hours you can do just about anything you want to someone. He killed the boy by slashing his throat. And then the bastard fucked him again . . ."

Xie's knees tightening against his chest. The words coming in a monotone flow.

"He was involved with a *wai-guo-ren*. American. A woman. I saw her once. She looked Chinese, but she wasn't. There were others, at Fudan. He would go to the university, pick up a parcel and deliver it. Two, three times a month."

Ye Yang. Heywood. Bobby.

Piao stood against the far wall. The painted stone, cold along the length of his spine. Outside, there was sun, he couldn't see it, but recognised its reality in the slither of light that slowly passed across his face. And as it did so, acutely aware that it cut him in two. One eye, schoolboy blue . . . the other, as dark as a hammer's head.

"Where did he deliver the parcels to?"

"Heilongjian, Harbin. Four hours out of the city in the Chang-Bai Mountains. A farmhouse in the snow fields. They had a workshop there. He had internal travel documents issued to him every month. They arrived by courier . . ."

He coughed. Snot, blood, tears.

". . . the foreigners have friends in high places."

The Senior Investigator had moved closer; Xie's smell, now of shit, a fine reek as sharp as a razor.

"A workshop. You said that they had a workshop?"

"Yes."

"The parcels, drugs?"

"Perhaps. He wouldn't say. Where there was money to be made, he was secretive. His work with the *wai-guo-ren*. He was silent, dumb. There must have been a lot of money."

"Or a lot of fear?"

Xie turned to face the Senior Investigator, features drained of skin tones. White on a white pillow, almost fading into it. Only the blood, now as brown as the deep tan of rich old retired men, marking the boundary of where face met linen.

He nodded. His tongue across ripped, salty lips.

"The foreigners at Fudan, you know who they were?"

"No."

"Have you heard the names Wei Yongshe, Hu Feng, Pei Decai, Yan Ziyang?"

"No."

"The woman. He talked about her, mentioned her name?"

"No."

Piao raised an eyebrow.

"No. No names. I asked him many times. I thought that I might get in on their operation, but they were keeping it small. He said nothing. I found out about the woman because I had him followed. It was a pay-off."

"Where?"

"The Peace Hotel. It must have been a good pay-day. He went straight from there to buy a Volkswagen."

"New?"

"Nearly new."

Of course 'nearly' new. Wasn't everything that they bought, everything in their lives 'nearly' new?

The Senior Investigator felt for his cigarettes, one left; it was broken in half.

"Detective Yaobang will stay with you for a while. You will give him every detail that you know about this workshop in Harbin. Everything that Qingde said about it, however trivial."

Xie moved his legs weakly over the side of the bed, sitting up. Beckoning Piao toward him. When within reach, grabbing his jacket collar. His strength surprising. Forcing the Senior Investigator to his level. Face against face. The dry river of blood stranded across his cheek and chin, coursing against Piao's stubble.

"I won't be in here much longer, Investigator, then I'll come looking for you. Or perhaps for those who are dearest to you. Yes. Yes, that is sweeter. Those who are dearest to you."

The Senior Investigator wrenched the hand from his jacket. Finger by finger. A button spinning to the floor.

Who was there to sew a new one back on?

He could hear Xie's voice as he walked down the corridor. It's calm thread of sing-song threats slicing through the madness of slamming doors, barked orders, whispered thoughts. It was only when he reached the central core where the corridors collided in a weave of steel web, that he realised that he could no longer hear Xie's taunts . . . that the words were repeating only in the confines of his own head.

★

"How was the tour?"

Barbara didn't look up from the pack of Marlboro. The cigarette drawn out, the white lifeline held firm between her slender fingers.

"I can't decide what the high point was. The Brahms, with a tenor soloist who conned a collective farm out of their diesel engines for ten tractors. Or the dance troupe whose choreographer robbed a drinks store with his dog, left the dog behind in the shop, and was later arrested after the PSB followed it back to his house . . ."

She lit the cigarette and pulled hard on its filter.

". . . yes, it was a fascinating tour. Remind me to get it included in next year's Thomas Cook's brochure."

Chief Warden Hua entered the room. He always seemed happy. Such people worried Piao. Happiness, it was a state that he himself had only achieved fleetingly.

"See Piao, see, your foreigner, we looked after her, didn't we, didn't we? Chinese hospitality."

The Chief Warden playfully poked Barbara in the back. She nodded with enthusiasm.

"You have been most generous, Chief Warden Hua. I will be sure to put this all in my report to my colleagues on the Washington State Parole Committee."

Hua rubbed his hands together frantically.

"Good, good, good. And you, Senior Investigator, you had a satisfactory meeting with our friend I hear, yes, yes?"

"Yes, satisfactory."

"You see, I told you, Piao, I know these people and you nearly didn't listen to me, did you? You didn't want to listen to me. Eh, eh? Put him in with the Bear I said, and hear him sing a pretty song. A canary. Just like a canary I said. I was right, wasn't I, eh Piao, eh?"

The Senior Investigator's attention momentarily drifted to the window.

"Yes, Chief Warden Hua, you were right. He did sing. He sang like a canary."

★

The Chief Warden walked them to the car. The Big Man was already in the driver's seat, wiping the inside of the windscreen with his jacket cuff.

"All right if I come with you, Boss? My car's fucking dead. Alternator I think."

"A hundred and fifty yuan, second-hand."

Yaobang started the car.

"Don't I fucking know it!"

The barrier rose. The main gate cranking painfully open beyond it. Outside it was dark . . . black. The floodlit interior of the bay escaping into the night in a graze of mustard and leggy shadows.

"Chief Warden Hua, four of the murders that I am currently investigating, you might recognise the names. Wei Yongshe, Hu Feng, Pei Decai, Yan Ziyang?"

Hua's smile uncertain.

"These names, yes, I recognise these names. Of course I do. But murdered, you are investigating their murders? No, no, no, this cannot be true? These men, all four, they were executed. Executed. Shot in the prison grounds and cremated. It is in the records. All in the records."

"Warden, these men were pulled from the Huangpu, chained together with others. Mutilated. I have positive identifications that this is so."

The smile on Hua's face now gone. Piao feeling a deep sense of satisfaction.

"You are wrong, Senior Investigator. Wrong. The bodies you have are not these men. Not these men. They are other men. Others. Be sure of your facts. The names you say have been executed. Executed. They are not your murdered. No, no, no."

He wagged a fat finger in the Senior Investigator's face.

"No, no, no Investigator. You cannot kill a man twice. You cannot kill a man twice."

But they had; the Senior Investigator was tempted to argue, but Hua had already turned away . . . the barrier in a slow fall behind him.

Chapter 18

Barbara saw his shadow before seeing him. Black. Hard edged amongst the winks of spotlights falling across her shoulder and onto the bar, also across the Scotch in her glass, one of many that evening. The trio of musicians lurched into an uncertain interpretation of 'Fly me to the Moon.' The shadow darkened; he was going to talk to her, throw her a line. There wasn't one that she hadn't heard before, but she couldn't stop him.

"I raise my cup in salutation to the moon. With my shadow we are three. Yet drinking is unknown to the moon and the shadows follow in my wake in vain. Let us honour moon and shadow nonetheless, for joy will last no longer than the spring."

The voice was English, neatly, precisely so. Barbara turned, squinting into the lights. He was blond. Most blond men seeming benign, safe. But there was an edge, a razor cut to this man . . . this blond. Something in the bottomless well of his eyes.

"A man who speaks with another man's words, ain't got any useful words of his own. That's what my ma use to say. And that includes words of poetry."

He smiled. It slithered with engaging attractiveness across his lips.

"It was not a poem. They were the lyrics from an old Chinese drinking song . . ."

He sat on a bar stool beside her. His smell of sandalwood in a head to head collision with her neat whisky.

". . . I'm Charles, Charles Haven. And you are?"

"I'm someone who likes drinking alone."

Barbara lifted the heavy glass and swirled the Scotch. The crystal, cold against the bridge of her nose, her forehead . . . looking through it. The world smelted gold and in flowing distortion.

"You are someone who has spent too long drinking alone."

One smile seemed to bind all three of the musicians together as they moved flawlessly into their next song; the organist kissing the microphone in an expressionless warble.

"I'd like to get you on a slow boat to China."

Too long alone. Yes, perhaps. Barbara didn't know what else to say to the blond man with danger in his face, except,

"I'm drinking Scotch."

"Then so will I," he replied.

★

Piao felt naked out of uniform. A sense of something missing. He checked his reflection in the tinted glass of the lobby entrance. A dark, almost unfamiliar figure to his own eyes. It was the first time that he'd worn the suit since his wedding day. He'd almost expected to see her face with every button that he fastened. The smell of her hair on its lapels . . . her soft words tucked into its top pocket. But they were all gone. Now, just a faint smell of dust and empty wardrobes.

"Ni nar."

Piao checking his pockets for his badge . . . finally finding it. The PSB officer nodding him past. Holding it in his hand as he walked across the lobby, has finger tracing the outline of the star at its heart. Red branded into gold. He walked the gauntlet of lights and into the bar. He could see Barbara. A smile on her lips. A glass held against her cheek. Reflections of amber against her skin. Beside her a man, his shadow across hers. Piao could see no features, just his body language. It shouted . . . you're already mine, you don't know it, but I do. The Senior Investigator turned to leave, a rip deep in his chest. But Barbara had seen him, her fingers across the man's shoulder, leaving her bar stool to greet Piao. His words coming out in a jumble when she was still some distance away.

"I was passing. I thought of you, and it came to me that you would appreciate me calling on you. To drink, to talk, maybe to eat? But I see now that you have a friend who is with you and so it is best that I . . ."

"You were just passing?"

"Just passing, yes."

"In your suit?"

Piao's fingers found his jacket button, fastening and unfastening it.

"My suit. In my best suit, yes."

She smiled that smile.

"It looks nice, you look nice."

The Senior Investigator felt the colour rising in his cheeks.

"But I will go now, you are with your friend."

"My friend? Oh, my friend."

She laughed. Its complexity indecipherable to Piao.

"No, no. Come and join us. He's English, an Englishman won't mind. They have good manners at hand for every occasion."

Barbara took his hand and led him to the bar. He felt like a child, dressed up and delivered to a birthday party that he didn't want to go to.

"Charles Haven."

The Senior Investigator grasped the outstretched hand.

"Sun Piao."

The Englishman had a firm grip. His nails trimmed, manicured . . . immaculate. A heavy gold ring, old gold, almost orange. The shirt cuffs pristine white; more gold, heavy cufflinks fastening them. The Senior Investigator sat on a bar stool, a glass already filled with Scotch within reach.

"You get to know each other. I'm off to powder my nose."

She smiled, a democratic smile to be shared by the two of them. And then she was gone . . . her glass next to Piao's, lipstick breathing its rim. A waiter placed a bowl of rice crackers on the bar top beside them. Haven picked one up, placing it in the centre of his palm, examining it minutely.

"So perfect. I cannot eat one. How could anybody ever eat something so perfect."

He placed it back in the bowl and turned to face Piao; it was the first time that the Senior Investigator had really looked at the Englishman.

"So, Sun Piao, what do you do?"

"I investigate."

"Investigate. And what do you investigate?"

Piao lifted his glass; the Scotch burning across his tongue.

"I investigate homicides. I am a Senior Investigator with the Public Security Bureau."

Surprise and a certain caution seeming to fleetingly cross Haven's eyes.

"I have been to China many times, but you are the first Investigator that I have ever met."

"That is good, but do not be disappointed. You obviously have done nothing wrong."

"Obviously."

Haven ordered another Scotch. The barman spoke a little English, awkward, stilted . . . but Haven ordered his drink in Mandarin, accent perfect.

"A Senior Investigator. You are very young to reach that exalted position, aren't you?"

Piao felt his defences rising. Turning into himself, checking himself out. It was second nature, developed in the dark alleys or longs of the city and in the interrogation rooms of Gongde-lin, but talking to a stranger in the bar of the Jing Jiang Hotel? Something was going on. Every sense whispered it, but he couldn't put a convenient tag on it.

"I was privileged. A good family. A good education. At university, a supportive structure with inspiring lecturers. Once in the PSB, the support of fellow officers, the Danwei, the encouragement of enthusiastic and brilliant senior officers was very comforting. I was lucky. I should not say it, but it is not always like this in my country. Life is now changing. Did you know that two thirds of our schoolchildren have never heard of Mao? Imagine. But ask them who Andy Lau is, and they will all tell you that he is a pop star from Hong Kong."

The Senior Investigator was playing it simple, playing the country boy flattered by the attention. Asking no questions. Drawing a splinter from the Englishman's heel. Scavenging a profile, information, from the questions that the man asked.

"You must tell me about your work. I insist. Who knows when my path will again cross that of a Senior Investigator of Homicide?"

He took a lighter, Dunhill, slim, gold, from his jacket pocket and lit a cigarette, English, Benson and Hedges. The smoke sweet; pictures of distant cities linked by silver jets, gleaming lives, filled Piao's head. Haven its ambassador. Everything about him was in order. Pristine. His eyebrows, his teeth, his finger nails. Piao had only ever seen people like Haven on the front pages of glossy American magazines. The Senior Investigator took a handful of rice crackers . . . so perfect. Tossing them into his mouth. Eating them noisily.

"My work, it will sound too boring to you. A Senior Investigator with the Homicide Squad of the Public Security Bureau, it sounds more than it is. If the title of a job could buy you drink, then I would own this bar."

"Come, Senior Investigator Piao, do not be so modest. I am sure that a city like Shanghai must stretch you to the full. There must be many interesting cases that you come across?"

"Interesting cases? Some, not many. We Shanghainese are hot tempered and we like to drink. You know maotai, Dukang?"

The Englishman nodded slightly through the smoke. His eyes pouring into Piao's. The Senior Investigator noticing that he never seemed to blink.

"Hot tempers, hot drinks, they are dangerous partners. Most of my investigations are simple. I have the murderer in two days, three days. Too much to drink. Too many yuan wagered on the mah-jongg board. Too much temper. Too close to a kitchen knife. Open and closed. Nine times out of ten it is one of the family. A brother. A cousin. As I said, boring . . ."

Piao's eyes burning in the smoke. Haven staring through it, still not blinking.

". . . but you, a businessman like you. Now there is a story to tell. Travel, restaurants, business meetings. And then there are the women. I suppose you could write a book or one of those stories for that little magazine . . ."

The Senior Investigator shook his head . . .

". . . I cannot remember its name . . . you know. Ah, the Reader's Digest, that is it. I like the Reader's Digest."

Haven shook his head.

"I am not a businessman. Looks can be deceptive. I am in the medical field."

"A doctor. Ah a doctor. This is a very venerable profession in our country. Very respected. Perhaps our meeting like this is fortuitous. I was unable to attend an appointment at a clinic earlier today. It is my fingers . . ."

The Senior Investigator placed his hand next to Haven's, tugging at the discoloured gauze.

". . . you would be kind enough to examine them? They are burns. I was in a very unfortunate fire."

The Englishman removed his hand to the glass of Scotch. A finger trailing its rim.

"I was under the misapprehension that any fire that burns fingers is unfortunate . . ."

He adjusted his tie, silk. It didn't need adjusting.

". . . you need to see a general practitioner. I specialise in a very narrow field and that field does not include changing the bandages on burnt fingers."

"A specialist. A very narrow field. It sounds very exciting?"

"No more exciting than what you are doing. You specialise in a very narrow field also. Murder."

The Senior Investigator smiled broadly.

"You are right, of course. I had never thought of it in that way before. I am a specialist also . . ."

He threw some more rice crackers into his mouth, lips open, crunching them loudly. Moving closer to Haven. The cheap cotton of his suit jacket brushing against the fine wool of the Englishman's blazer.

". . . I can tell you, this will get me a few drinks down at my local bar. With us Chinese it is not the job or the position, but it is the name that we call it that matters. From now on I will tell everyone that I am a specialist Senior Investigator in the narrow field of homicide . . ."

He slapped the Englishman on the back.

". . . I must thank you. You have a mind that is . . . is. Sorry, I cannot think of the words. How would you describe it?"

Haven rolled the Scotch in its glass. Amber light playing across his fingers.

"I have a mind that is very focused. A mind that can go to the very heart of a matter and then act decisively on it."

"Yes, that is how it is. I could not have put it in better words myself."

"You didn't."

Piao laughed, hoping that it sounded genuine. He moved even closer. His words across the Englishman's face; sensing Haven holding his breath from the garlic and ginger that was on the tail of each of the sentences that he spoke. The Englishman, he had no smell, except that which came from the glass and embossed gold of an expensive eau de cologne bottle. There was no sense of his body, of the animal inside the expensive suit.

"Actually, I have not been completely honest with you. My job as a Senior Investigator does have its moments . . ."

Piao picked some rice cracker from his teeth and slurped the dregs of his Scotch.

". . . take my latest case. Eight people mutilated, chained together and then thrown into the Huangpu. Very out of the ordinary for Shanghai."

"That would be very out of the ordinary for New York."

"My thoughts exactly, Mr Doctor. Exactly. I feel a little guilty about it, but it is exciting. When you are dealing with domestic murders all the time, a case like this can be very exciting to someone like me. Is this wrong?"

The Englishman studied his drink, raising it to his lips.

"Eight bodies, imagine. It is more murders than I deal with in two months . . ."

His mouth to Haven's ear. Invading his space. Piao could sense the Englishman's discomfort.

". . . of course, this is confidential you understand. It is even being kept away from our media. It looks like drugs. Who else would take the time and trouble to remove all identifying marks. Their fingertips. Smash their faces up . . ."

Lowering his voice to a whisper. Secrets, even more secretive when whispered.

231

".. . they had even gouged their eyes out. Imagine what people these are? Monsters."

"Or professionals?"

"Yes perhaps. Perhaps. Professionals with too much to lose. I had not thought of this. . . ."

Thoughtfully, dropping more crackers into his mouth.

".. . Barbara Hayes. Barbara. Sad. So, so sad. Her child was one of the murdered. An American national. It is causing the politicians bad heads. Migraines is what you call them, yes? Of course, she will not have told you yet. I am sorry, but people like me, police, we are clumsy. We are not used to being delicate."

Haven's eyes were mute; the bar lights reflections dancing around the dark stars of his pupils. Taking his lighter from his pocket, it's spike of flame flaring, the fireflies banished . . . his eyes, for an instant, the colour of a cat's caught in a full beam.

"I have known Barbara for only two hours, it will take me at least another two hours to know her complete life history . . ."

Sweeping a hand across his head, each hair falling exactly into place.

".. . but tell me, Senior Investigator, do you always catch your monsters, or do you not talk about your failures?"

Piao finished the last of the rice crackers. Perfection laid to waste.

"I do not have failures, Mr Doctor. And monsters, they are the easy ones to catch because they want to talk. They must talk. They have a hunger to be known . . ."

The Senior Investigator picked his teeth and then examined his nails.

".. . in China we do not have repeat killers, what you westerners would call serial-killers. That is 'official', you understand? But we still say of them, 'that never to be found out is never to be known.'"

Piao smiled, looking deeply into the Englishman's eyes and held up the empty rice cracker bowl.

"You should have had one, perfection can be very delicious."

★

"You've eaten all of the crackers . . ."

Barbara sat on the barstool, skirt riding high above her knees. Her index finger circling the inside of the empty bowl and then moving to her tongue. Across her lips . . . salt, sugar, sesame.

". . . but I guess that boys will be boys."

Haven picked up his lighter from the bar top and raised it to Barbara's cigarette. A dull click of electricity arcing, earthing. Piao could see its blue-white fork in the throat of the lighter an instant before the flame ignited. All of his life he'd wanted such a lighter. The Englishman slipped it back into his pocket.

"I had not eaten. The crackers, that was my hunger. I am sorry, I will order some more."

Piao moved a hand to summon the waiter, Barbara gently reached out and lowered it. Her fingers brushing his knee and instantly becalming the breath in his chest.

"No, Sun, that's okay. We've reserved a table in the restaurant on the eighth floor, why don't you join us for dinner?"

He wanted to, just to sit between them, to keep Haven from being alone with her. But the words came out differently.

"Thank you, but I will say no. I have an appointment. There is somebody that I must see."

"Are you sure?"

"Yes, I am sure. But thank you."

The Englishman was already standing, his jacket, his trousers, creases falling perfectly into place.

"Perhaps if the Senior Investigator had arrived earlier?"

The smile widened, like the jaws of an adjustable wrench. His voice now just a whisper into the Senior Investigator's ear as he passed.

"Perhaps you are someone who misses everything by just a few hours."

Yes, a life constantly missed by a few important hours. Rice falling through the gaps between the fingers . . . that was him.

233

And then Charles Haven was gone. Piao's last view of them as they slipped through the doors and into the hard light of the lobby. The Englishman's arm moving around her shoulder, and with it the memories jerking into place in the Senior Investigator's head in a series of pin-sharp stills. Of a wife lost in time, in rain . . . in the back of a Red Flag, an arm slipping around her shoulder.

Chapter 19

Piao rubbed the chalk from his fingers. The biggest murder case that the kung an chu had handled in twenty years and he'd been given an incident room the size of a toilet.

A line of thick chalk dividing the blackboard into what was known and what was not known. Into two distinct groups. Bobby, Ye Yang, Heywood, Qingde and Yongshe, Feng, Decai, Ziyang, having only two things in common: the blackboard that their names were written upon and the death that had them all in its sharp fold. Only one word breaching the dividing chalk line . . . Qingde. A carrier of parcels for the Americans. A guest of Virtue Forest with three other Chinese. Qingde.

Piao sat staring through the window and into the major incident room next door. A month ago it had been his, heading an investigation into the murder of a Friendship Store manager. Thirty telephone lines. Ten computer terminals. Four faxes. Even a stove for tea. Now he was investigating twelve murders with four telephone lines, one computer terminal, a fax that jammed . . . and no stove for making tea. He felt himself shake his head, warm his hands, even though they weren't cold. His eyes returned to the board . . .

And no motive. Where the fuck was the motive in all of this?

The room had a smell of unwashed bodies that had now gone home to flats with unmade beds. Again he felt himself shake his head. If he'd have had a cigarette left in his pocket, he would have lit it.

★

Liping had not needed any nudging. A walnut-eyed courier had delivered the box of tapes . . . streams of uncurling reel to reel. Questioning him had proven useless; he had returned their stares with eyes that permanently watered. A job as a

235

motorcycle courier in Shanghai's traffic polluted midday, was not to be envied. The anonymous office in the anonymous Security Bureau that the tapes had come from, would remain anonymous.

★

Ye Yang . . . her voice had surprised Piao. An all American girl. Cherry Pie and Southern Fried Chicken Wings. Nothing of the Chinese ancestry left in her. The almond eyes. The bisque complexion. The petal kiss of lips. The hair, bobbed, shiny and raven . . . all that remained. A shell, nothing that the Senior Investigator recognised as Chinese, filling it.

Along with four other officers he had listened to tape after tape. Family conversations. Business conversations. Friendship conversations. The spools in a slow carousel of tape slipping around steel posts. Building up a picture of her with each bronze loop. What she laughed at. What made her angry. How she said 'hello'. What she meant with the 'ah-huhhs' that littered her speech. Odd snippets of information about her, but none that helped him. No word that leapt out, that spoke of reasons, motives. Her voice only at the Shanghai end of the calls. Never Bobby's. No voice that could have been Heywood's or Qingde's. Just simple conversation following on from simple conversation, filled to the brim with tedium; no secrets, no plot, no agenda. And all of the time, Piao aware of the gaps, the days and weeks missing in the flow of the tapes. In the gutter of his stomach, the acid building . . . a sense of being fed the thick cut red meat. Safe, easy to recognise and digest. But where were the tapes that were the spacers, that were the gristle, the fat, the bits that would be indigestible? Ye Yang was not clean, he could smell it. Involved in something that was worth her murder. But the tapes were clean, nothing in them that even warranted a slap across the wrist. Nothing fitted.

Piao placed the last of the tapes into the box, sealing it. The sound of the adhesive tape pulling from the dispenser, stretching across the rift of cardboard edges, feeling almost comforting. Tomorrow he would write the memo and send it to

Liping. It would say, but in the massaged and diplomatic words that he had learnt were the common currency in dealing with cadre like the Chief . . . 'where the fuck are the other tapes?'

He expected a less manicured response back from Liping.

★

A single desklight illuminated his office at the arse end of the corridor. If status was determined by the view from an office's window, Piao should have been cleaning the ashtrays and toilets. The wall of an alley, just metres away. In the daytime, the occasional dog lifting its hind leg. At night, drunks. The vomit hanging from their lips in jewelled gasps. With such a view, why have a window there at all, he had often wondered? But he already knew the answer. There is no status in China. All are equal. If one has a window, all must have a window.

There is no status in China . . . just office windows with different views.

A note was attached to the telephone receiver. Piao recognised the scrawl. Reading it, leaving it in place . . . it would look as if he'd never seen it. Yun's memos were becoming more urgent, the colour of the ink that he used changing with the days. Green to blue . . . blue to black . . . black now giving way to red. Red, the colour of anger. Red, the colour of Detective Yun's acne. He couldn't wait to get hold of Piao's cases, poor bastard. He had the insensitivity to wear cast offs without a hint of embarrassment. Such men are dangerous. Such men could cause wars and not even know that they had done so. But the kung an chu was big, three blocks of offices pressed into service, grafted together by endless stairwells and corridors smelling of disinfectant and of paper being chased. The Senior Investigator could avoid Yun for weeks. It would not look like avoidance, it would look like bad timing, bad architecture. At least for the first week. After that there was the Danwei investigation. He would be suspended, sitting at home with a warm bottle of Qingdao beer. The investigation, rolling toward him, unavoidable. He should be preparing his case, defending himself against the tong zhi's charges. Zhiyuan

237

was coming at him with a cleaver and he was just standing there, frozen in the glare. But it was the way that he operated . . . had always operated. He would find his murderers. Pull the dirty linen from beneath the bed. Security involvement. Party collusion. All that he had hinted at to Zhiyuan on the foreshore of the river that night. The bodies of the eight, dead and cold at their feet. Everything that he had worked for, his career, his life, riding on it. It was a high risk, but he knew no other way. No other way, not now.

Through the window that looked into the alley, a drunk came alive in the spill of office light. He stopped for an instant, vomited and moved on.

All must have a window. There is no status in China . . . just office windows with different views.

★

The memo was brief. It was late . . . Piao had no appetite for words. The Big Man had no appetite for reading. The memo was well suited for both diets.

> *Charles Haven, English. Full Report.*
> *Visas, entrances, exits, internal travel.*
> *Who is he . . . what is he doing here?*
> *Squeeze the juice from the lychee.*

Piao went to Yaobang's desk, switching on a light, pulling open the large bottom drawer. Piles of paperwork that littered the desktop, toppling, sliding across each other. The contents of the drawer consisting mainly of food in various stages of consumption. It was the first and last place that the Big Man visited every day. And it was safe . . . a place only for the brave or the stupid. The Senior Investigator placed the memo in amongst a bag of half-eaten caramelised sweet potato fritters. Piao's stomach rumbled. He was hungry, but not that hungry. He closed the draw and turned off the light, walking down the corridor. Every lonely echo of footstep telling him that no one was waiting for him at home.

'Squeeze the juice from the lychee.' The Big Man would know exactly what Piao was after. Haven . . . the Senior Investigator wanted everything on him. His last thought before he slept. His first thought as he awoke. The size of his shoes. What side of his pants his dick hung on. The Big Man liked jobs of that kind, he was good at them. He liked jobs that he was good at.

★

5 . . . 3 . . . 42 . . . 42. The numbers coming as easy as breath itself. Knowing them now as well as his own telephone number. Also knowing her smile, her tears, as well as he had known any woman's. Other lives spilling into your own . . . it made Piao feel on edge, vulnerable. The receptionist at the Jing Jiang tried Barbara's room. Somehow he knew that she wouldn't be there. She wasn't. He put the receiver back on its cradle. It had been two days now. Unanswered telephone call dovetailing into unanswered telephone call. She was with the Englishman. Days spent with him. And nights? Yesterday Piao had stood opposite the hotel, two hours spent in drizzle that had eaten into his bones, his soul. He'd watched them coming down the steps, a taxi waiting. The Englishman's arm around her shoulder, his hand resting on her neck. Her hair falling across his skin. Barbara had not seen Piao. The Englishman had. For an instant they had looked at each other in a series of fast strobing snapshots, through the river of angry metal that fled between them in the road. And then he was gone, joining Barbara in the back of the taxi. It pulled into the flow, its horn blaring. Haven's arm moving around her shoulder once more. Barbara turning to him, smiling. The traffic folded, and they were gone.

The Senior Investigator had walked home, not knowing if he had stood outside the hotel soaked for two hours, to see Barbara . . . or was it to see the Englishman?

★

Piao didn't eat, the sheets needed changing, but he went straight to bed. Within minutes, asleep. The night fast, compressed into one dream. A quality to it that stabbed deep into the heart of the next day. He was driving down a street, Nanjing or Fuzhou? Looking through a smeared windscreen toward the pavement, frantically searching for someone. Barbara . . . even in the pit of sleep, aware of her perfume. Its bouquet, like the sweets that you ate when you were a child. His hand was on the horn. Faces in the pressing crowd, turning . . . slowly. Faces, their eyes on his. Each face was Haven's, only Haven's.

Squeeze the juice from the lychee.

Chapter 20

Little Brother, where are your little hands?
My hands are here.
They can grasp guns, they can fire, pow, pow, pow.
Little Sister, where are your little hands?
My hands are here.
They can do physical labour.
When the kerchiefs are dirty, they can wash them.

"It looks like a dragonfly."

The Chaic Zhi-8 squatted on the pad in a far corner of Hongqiao. Fat bodied. Stressed skin metal fuselage sprayed white. A red hot coal of the Chinese star burning above the windows of the flight deck. And like the petals of a steel flower that had not been watered . . . the six blades of the rotor drooping. It had the look of an object that could never hope to attain flight.

Piao helped Barbara through the rearward sliding door on the starboard side. The steps were high, her skirt also . . . his eyes following the curve of her legs into the gloom of the main cabin.

The rotors swung and strengthened, losing their individual form in a blur of grey. The Zhi-8 slowly rising. Piao folding his arms tightly across his stomach. A large breakfast and a large helicopter, not the best of ideas.

"No, it does not look like a dragonfly . . .' he said, hand across his mouth.

". . . it looks like airsickness."

He left her, Yaobang smiling, and made his way to the rear of the cabin, the sickbags. The Zhi-8's smell, that of every other helicopter that he had ever known . . . fuel, grease, and a thousand previous nervous stomachs.

★

It was a slow train of a journey. A Chaic Zhi-8 has a range of four hundred and ninety-seven miles using standard fuel with no reserve tanks, and cruising at an economy rate of one hundred and forty-four miles per hour. Harbin was a journey of one thousand seven hundred and seventy one miles. It meant re-fuel stops at Xuzhou, Shijiazhuang, Beidaihe, Shenyang. A sleep stopover at Tianjin. The Haihe . . . the Number 1 Hotel. Cold rooms. Cold food. Warm beer. Drop offs of equipment, sealed bags, an antique French bureau for a high ranking cadre . . . at Taishan, Chengde, Jinzhuo and Changchun, the town of the Eternal Spring and the home of the Number 1 Automobile Factory, makers of the Red Flag. Changchun reminding him of the saying that local citizens had . . . 'that to gaze upon the Number 1 Automobile Factory meant that you would never own a Hong-Qi, a Red Flag, yourself.'

Piao was certain that he never would.

★

Barbara out of earshot, the Big Man's voice dwarfed, words eroded by the muffled thunder of the rotors.

"You'll want to read this, Boss . . ."

He pulled an envelope from his inner pocket; horribly creased, tea stains, grease stains across its front. A Beijing postmark, dated three days ago.

". . . it's from Pan's old professor. Results of what he sent him from the bodies . . ."

Piao nodded. The envelope had already been roughly opened. Pulling the sheets, four pages typed and stapled, free from the wreckage.

". . . I only got up to the second paragraph. . . ."

Yaobang raising his voice as the storm of noise escalated.

". . . doctors. I couldn't understand a fucking word."

The Senior Investigator jammed himself against the bulkhead, stomach turning, twisting. Expecting nothing from the letter. But something about his body, bracing itself, that expected everything.

. . . midline incisions were made from the suprasternal notch to the

242

pubis. The sternum was split and there was evidence of bone wax application to minimise bleeding. The pericardium and pleural cavities were open . . . and the vena cavae, aortic arch, innominate vessels and pulmonary artery showed evidence of having been isolated . . .

Turning the page . . .

. . . the coeliac axis and superior mesenteric arteries had been dissected. The portal vein was also dissected and there were signs of cannulation to the inferior mesenteric vein to permit in situ portal cooling with alactate solution . . .

Again, pages turned . . .

. . . removal of the entire globes of the eyes had been achieved through standard enucleation procedures, with the rectus muscles divided on the globe side of where the sutures would, in normal circumstances, be applied. The oblique muscles were divided near their insertions to the globe. The remaining facial sheath was then dissected from the globe, thus freeing it.

The words, sentences, paragraphs, meaning little to nothing. Jargon. A maze of multi-syllables. Cold cut medical terminology. But still his chest thumping. Turning to the last page . . . a conclusion, a précis that even he could understand. Understand, but not fit into the shards of a case that seemed to lay in every direction. Piao looked up, lips paralysed. Barbara watching him. He folded the report, on autopilot . . . placing it in his pocket. Trying to hide the horror that he knew was written across his features. Trying to avoid her eyes. Looking out of the smeared window. In a series of swells, the land below rising. Mountains, their edges smoothed by drifted snow. His ears popping as the Zhi-8 took on more altitude. It was a harsh region. A country of tears and unheard cries. It was used to the sort of word that now screamed its way through his head. One word that was not even on a single page of the report that he had just read, but which should have been.

PINGFANG.

The Zhi-8's cabin was empty of cargo by the time that they reached Harbin, Manchuria . . . the Chinese-White Russian half-breed. Below, the Songhua River was frozen, a cleft of bone white embedded in grey city. Winter, unsheathed. Fifteen Celsius and falling. The weather closing tight its fist. The navigation of ships of up to five hundred tons would now be interrupted for the next six months. A winter with never a hint of compromise on its frozen lips.

It was late. The snowfields of Shangzhi, Yanshou, they would have to wait. They would still be there tomorrow . . . but perhaps the bite of the wind, the clench of the dropping mercury, would not be. Within minutes of landing the Zhi-8 was towed to a hangar, protective sleeves slipped over its rotors. A Liberation truck moved from the terminal, rendezvousing with them on the tarmac; sanctuary from a wind that sliced as viciously as a buzz saw. The International Hotel opposite the Natural History Museum, with rooms for eighty yuan a night, was twenty minutes away. They reached it in fifteen.

It was early, but nearly dark. By the time that it was dark, and still early . . . they were asleep.

★

Cold hotel.   Cold bed.   Cold dreams.

The steel interior of the Chaic Zhi-8's main cabin, ice. Everything stinging to the touch. Barbara sitting crumpled, hands drawn into sleeves. The instrument checks complete, the crew of three on the flight deck shared out the contents of the large cardboard box that Yaobang had brought on board. Reassuringly solid blocks of Marlboro and 'The Grand Old Drink of the South' . . . bottles of Southern Comfort.

"You said two thousand cigarettes and ten bottles."

The pilot looked impossibly young, growing a moustache in the hope of looking more mature. Clumps of isolated wispy hair, like gorse on a wind barren hilltop. The attempt had failed miserably. Yaobang grinned, meeting the pilot's gaze halfway. It took a stupid or a very brave man to throw anger at a smile.

"Half now, half when we get back to Hongqiao." The pilot stowed the cartons and bottles, priming and starting the three Changzhuo W26 turboshafts. Yaobang left the flight deck, still smiling. White horses of breath across his shoulders; strapping himself in, winking at Piao.

"It's not true what they say flight crews can count."

Laughing as the Zhi-8 laboured upwards, thrashing wildly at the sky. The pilot looked over his shoulder, smoothing down his moustache.

"Fucking PSB," he whispered, as he pitched the Zhi-8 to the southeast and the snowfields.

★

White kissing white.

The Zhi-8 was the only moving object in a landscape and sky welded into one. There was no horizon. No references to hint at the curve and throw of the topography.

The pilot lit another Marlboro. Sweet tobacco. Its taste, its aroma . . . ginger earth, cold coffee and cheesecake. Closing his eyes behind the Polaroid lenses. His hands freed of piloting, fully redundant . . . the Dong Fang KJ-8 autopilot now his fingers on the controls, now his eyes assessing the flight path ahead. Piao threw a chart across the pilot's lap.

"These are the areas that I am interested in."

He removed his sunglasses, squinting. His eyes, two knots tied in a length of string.

"Remote. There's nothing there."

"Nothing?"

"Well, just one guest house, three or four private zhao-dai-suo ski lodges, plus a few farms off the Shanghai-Yanshou road. Nothing else . . ."

The pilot threw a glance at Barbara.

". . . there are no tourists here. This is an area closed to wai-guo-ren."

Barbara drew deeply on her cigarette, returning the pilot's gaze. Regaining his composure, he switched off the autopilot, the Zhi-8 lurching momentarily.

"That's the guest house, it holds three hundred and fifty."

He pointed to a large black scar, still some distance away; taking them faster, lower, directly over it . . . powder snow in a frantic dance. The complex reminding the Senior Investigator of a scab on a pallid child's knee.

"The building that I am looking for will be as much as a thousand metres from any road. Wooden construction. Several outbuildings, but no animals . . ."

It wasn't snowing. Too cold. It hadn't snowed for a week. They were due for a little luck; this was it. The sky brightening, steel burnishing to blue. It would hold up. Piao's attention returned to the pilot's face.

". . . it is cold, all of the buildings will have fires, smoke from their chimneys. The one that I am looking for will not. There has been no snowfalls for a week . . . all of the other buildings will have paths cleared or footprints leading up to their doors. Ours will not."

The pilot shook his head, precisely replacing his sunglasses.

"Needle in a haystack. But it's your time. Your Marlboros. Your Southern Comfort. Just make sure the rest is there the moment we land back at Hongqiao Airport."

★

In Shangzhi County and Yanshou County, there is snow for a long time. From November to April the season is in full flood. Ski tracks from each door. Smoke from every chimney.

Three hours searching . . . but as soon as he saw it, he knew it. The house sitting broken in an endless expanse of untouched snowfield. A vast and dazzlingly bright duvet that had tucked itself up beyond the windows and across the roof, making it almost totally at one with its surroundings. No smoke from the chimney. No footprints or ski tracks to or from the door. One more fall of snow and the farmhouse would have been nothing more than another snow covered hillock, until the gentle thaw in late May. Too late. Too late.

The pilot was anxious. The drift deep. What obstacles might lie beneath its benign face? The Zhi-8 was equipped for a SAR role. He insisted that they use the hydraulic rescue hoist. It had a two hundred and seventy five kilo lifting capacity. Enough, even for the Big Man. The rearward sliding door hauled open. A world of violent noise. Buffeting wind . . . your breath stolen away. A knife-edge coldness. The outside imploding in upon them. And then Piao was in the air, twisting, dangling, dancing. A smell of grease, burnt electricity, lingering in his nostrils only momentarily. He pulled off the harness, fingers already numb. The drift up to his chest. Powder snow in a storm around him, stinging his skin. Blinding him. A shadow floating down from above him. Yaobang. And then another. Barbara. Tripping, swimming, stumbling, through the drift to the front door. The storm, the envelope of crashing wind and noise, instantly easing as the Zhi-8 pulled up and away. Piao wiped his eyes. He was sweating, but snow was everywhere. Down his neck. Up his sleeves. In his boots. He could feel its melt against the sweaty heat of his skin. Yaobang close behind, hauling Barbara in his wake. The door was not locked, but jammed. Yaobang's shoulder freeing it; falling inside with the drift. Snow scattered across a bare wooden floor . . . its timber as dark as black bean sauce. There was no electricity, the Senior Investigator switched on his torch, Yaobang following. Wavering beams crossing a simple room with doors leading off to three other rooms. A bedroom . . . two beds. Bathroom . . . washstand and a chipped and discoloured bath. Kitchen . . . stone sink, storage larder. In the corner of the main room an open trap door led to a full-size cellar, its floor, frozen earth. Its walls, stone . . . moss covered. The whole building smelling of wood smoke, pepper and honey . . . and of a winter in full stride. And in every one of the rooms, a deep silence, as if held in check by the tidal wave of snow that blanketed every window.

A long bench table dominated the main room. Across it and littering the floor nearby, a tumble of spilt and broken equipment. Microscopes, high intensity adjustable lamps, fine haired brushes, dental picks, two small vacuum cleaners with a series of small nozzled tools. Piao moved closer, lighting an oil lamp and examining the debris in more detail. Scalpels, enamel bowls, lengths of wire, spatulas. In frozen drips from the table . . . broken jars of epoxy and polyester resin, soluble nylon, PVA. Small tins of paint still sitting on the bench, a pallet with dried brushes . . . dried pools of colour. Ochre, black, yellow. In the corner of the room, lengths of planed timber. Jars of preserving fluid, varnish. Large plastic bottles of chemicals. Buckets of plaster of Paris and a thick dough . . . a grey mixture of alvar, jute, kaolin. And in the deepest shadow that even the light from the oil lamp could not illuminate, four sturdily constructed boxes treated and lined with polythene sheeting and layer after layer of crumpled soft brown paper. Whatever would be housed in them would be comfortable . . . very, very safe. They pulled on surgical gloves, a smell of latex and talcum powder filling the room.

"It's got to be fucking drugs, Boss, their own processing lab . . ."

Yaobang moved around the table prodding an index finger at whatever took his attention.

". . . they couldn't have picked a better place. No chance of anyone stumbling over this fucking place, not out here. And look at the distribution possibilities. Shit, we're practically in the USSR with Vladivostok just over the border. The coast of Japan's not much fucking further . . ."

He winked, shaking his head in admiration.

". . . fucking bright boys. They had it made."

'Fucking bright boys'. Piao pulled the Big Man's gloved hand away from the bench, smoothing it firmly to his side. And in a whisper, saying,

"If they were so fucking bright, why are they so fucking dead?"

The Senior Investigator walked around the bench, his eyes doing the probing.

"This is not drugs. I'm not sure what it is yet, but it is not drugs. I will work here, you check the other rooms. Look for the usual. I will look for the unusual."

Piao turned to Barbara, his voice low, but not knowing why.

"Look around if you wish, but please, touch nothing . . ."

248

He pulled the torch up, the beam firing her cheek. Her eyes sapphire.

"...Barbara, I know how hard that this must be."

She said nothing. He watched her as she turned, moving toward the bedroom, switching on her own torch. The words that he had just fired off, sticking like fishbones in his throat.

'So fucking bright, so fucking dead.'

★

Four chairs, two now on their sides, sat around the long bench, each at what would have been individual work stations. Individual processes in some anonymous, ritualistic production line. Now just a topple of damaged equipment. The order, the care, the finely honed procedures, swept to the rocks by the struggle that was still indelibly stamped on the scene. On the floor, almost hidden in the crash of glass, two stains had soaked into the runs of roughly nailed flooring. Worn and exhausted stains, the hue of dog shit left to dry and crumble. Blood. There would be more, the Senior Investigator knew it . . . when he really decided to look for it.

"Sun, in here . . ."

Barbara's voice from the bedroom, her back hard against the wall. The tears already in a slow fall down her face.

"...they're Bobby's."

Her eyes looking down, the bed meeting the floor in a deluge of creased sheets and strewn blankets. Nike trainers poking out from underneath them.

"You are sure?"

She looked up, smiling, crying. A strange combination of emotions to outsiders, to those who had not had their lives touched by such things, but not to Piao. The rain of death; the sunshine of at least knowing. He could see that she was sure . . . he didn't ask her again.

Piao swept his torch across the floor. Another stain, old blood on old wood, away from the bed beside the window, dark grey with drifted snow. She hadn't seen it . . . Piao took her arm leading her into the main room. Rescuing her, always wanting to rescue her. And yet knowing that it was already too late. He could feel the report that he had read, neatly folded in his inside pocket. It burnt. Yes, already too late.

"Home sweet home, Boss . . ."

The Big Man was sealing a plastic bag, toothbrushes, bristle to bristle, resting at the bottom. Another bag, sealed and labelled in his pocket, cutlery. Another two bags in his other pockets, a comb, a hairbrush.

". . . plenty of food in the kitchen. Mostly tins. About two weeks' worth. I reckon there were three of them . . ."

He held up the toothbrushes in the bag. Three.

". . . unless there were others who never brushed their teeth. Dirty bastards."

Yaobang grinned, his own teeth proudly clenched. Worn tyres that cried out for retreading.

"What are you doing, Boss?"

The Senior Investigator was kneeling, opening the blade of his penknife. He nodded toward Barbara, waiting for the Big Man to cross the room where she sat, blocking her view, before he gently scraped dried blood from the two stains on the wooden floor into separate polythene bags and sealed them. Broken glass, paper, a microscope, a desklight . . . Piao removed the debris from the arid brown pools. They were free of blood. The violence, had come first. The act that had thrown the objects from the table, second. A gap of perhaps hours between the two events. Hours . . . during that span of which the place had been cleaned, carefully laundered of something. The building isolated in its vast snow. The accumulation of equipment, materials . . . all for what? Cleaned, yes cleaned. The farmhouse now robbed of what they had meticulously set it up for.

Small places . . . look in small places.

He didn't clean in every corner, did others? The Senior Investigator leaned further under the table, focusing the torch beam on the film of fine dust; a buildup that clung to the edges of the large gaps between the floorboards. Across the latex of his fingertip, a dirt as fine as talcum powder. Reddish. The colour of fired clay, stamped under foot. He swept some into a bag, sealing it. Standing, straightening. His shoulders, his back . . . stiff, as if fixed with red–hot rods of steel. Piao moved toward the stairs that led to the cellar. Purpose in his walk, the Big Man following. The torch beam dancing across the cellar walls in dashes of brown, scarred green . . . resting on thick joists, the underside of the floorboards, and settling on the black rift of a gap edged in red dust. Moving the beam to the hard packed mud floor, where he could make out a small ridge of fine dust traversing a metre and a half length of the hard earth. Ochre on a rich black peat.

"What you got, Boss?"

The Senior Investigator bent down, removing his gloves, fingers trailing the dirt. Only two generations ago his family had worked the land and yet he couldn't remember the last time that he himself had run his hands through soil.

The red dirt doesn't belong here . . . neither do I.

"The dust was swept from the main room, upstairs . . ."

His fingers trailed through the dirt in faint waves.

". . . it fell through the large gap in the floorboards. There was much of it . . ."

His fingers smoothing the ochre ridge to a plain, a valley.

". . . the one who surprised them was very careful. Very neat . . ."

His fingers digging deeper into the blood hued dirt.

". . . this neatness. This hiding of a cold methodology in the chaos of destruction, does this neatness not remind you of something?"

In the valley of dirt, against his fingertip numbed with cold, the feel of metal. Metal, blue-green with the tarnish of millennia. A small button sized coin, its centre pierced by a square hole. Barbara and the Big Man over his shoulders, torch beams converging. The colour of the soil bleaching to pale grey.

"What the fuck's that?"

Piao stood, the coin sitting on his fingertip. An emerald blister of aged bronze. Turning it slowly in his fingers.

"That is *Mingqi*, a miniature burial item."

Barbara moving closer, her hair against the side of Piao's face.

"What does this all mean, for Christ sake?"

251

The Senior Investigator turned, the light from his torch across her face . . . features washed away, just a blank porcelain mask with only her eyes defined by their deep blueness.

"It means, Barbara, that you were correct. That none of this was about drugs. It means that all of this was about smuggling . . ."

Turning the coin gently between his fingertips. Over and over.

". . . your son was a smuggler of rare cultural relics and antiquities."

She was dreaming . . . a constant thrash of rotor blades beating air, interwoven into its cityscape. Walking down Nanjing. The sun on her back, as warm as a baby's mouth. Faces washing around her. Not one that she knew. Not one that she wished to know. A certainty that she would see him, as if she was working her way to a meeting, that had not been pre-arranged. On the corner of Shandong Lu, by the tea shop, Bobby was standing. Naked. Wet. Each footprint a puddle. A darkness spreading from his toes, his heels. Wanting to ask him why? A hundred times, why? But nothing came out, her lips wouldn't work. Her dream, but not her time to talk. He touched her shoulder, the warmth of the sun instantly dissipating.

'Ask him . . . ask him,' saying it to herself in her head. But he was already past her, joining the crowd. Their clothed bodies hiding his nakedness. Shoed feet, blotting, drying his foot-prints. The endless flow of people passed and he was gone. She walked a little further; the sun still on her back, but not warming her.

The beat of rotor blades unpicked itself from the back-ground and moved forward, encompassing everything. With each revolution, Bobby moving further away . . . losing him. Needing the pain as a reminder of him. Needing the pain to still hold onto him, but it couldn't be found in her dream. She woke herself, wanting to hunt it down and teethe on it.

★

The Sea of Bohai falling away. Crossing the Shandong Pen-

252

insula, rounding Mount Lao and its wooded hills. Qingdao in its grip . . . the town's back pressed hard against the Yellow Sea. Its beaches lost in darkness. Only the electric weave of street lights a witness to a population of one million. They were already losing altitude. Barbara rubbed her eyes, dust and unresolved dreams filling them. The Senior Investigator watching her. She could see him, as a child does, through the gaps between her fingers, just across the main cabin from her.

Ask him . . . ask him.

Acting on a dream for only the second time in her life, and both at her son's request.

"Tell me about Bobby?"

Piao feeling the question jolt him. Something that he recognised in it that was more than a question and more about a premonition.

"He was in a privileged position, and Heywood, to take many very special cultural relics . . ."

The Senior Investigator held out his palm, the button coin at its centre.

". . . I do not know exactly what they could have taken, but Mingqi such as this are found in the Emperors' tombs and longevity graves. In such places many important artefacts can be found that were buried there to help and defend the Emperor in the life after death. I have a contact in the Bureau for the Preservation of Cultural Relics. Such things they treat most seriously. A team will be sent out on the next plane to investigate . . ."

He smiled. A weariness stranding it across his face for longer than seemed justified.

". . . the Bureau for the Preservation of Cultural Relics has a large budget, they will not be dependant on hitching a ride for the price of a few packets of Marlboro and a few bottles of Southern Comfort ."

Barbara took the coin from his palm, a finger tracing its outline.

"How old would this be?"

"Two thousand years. Perhaps more."

He hadn't even blinked. The Senior Investigator took the coin back.

"The Bureau are very thorough, their investigation will tell us much. I still do not know about the girl, Ye Yang, and the others . . . the four who have died twice. What the girl's involvement in the operation was I cannot say, our reports on her are insignificant as yet. The other four are as weeds in the paddy field, they do not appear to be a part of what surrounds them. Time might make their story known."

"I've got contacts too. I'll ask the American Ambassador to get me a profile on Ye Yang and her family. I haven't wanted to do it. I guess I've been fooling myself, pretending that Bobby and the girl were innocent of everything. That their deaths were some sort of mistake. That they were drawn into something that was nothing to do with them . . ."

She stared out of the porthole, the lights getting closer, taking on more detail. Streets. Houses. Lives being lived.

". . . but the coin says it all, doesn't it?"

Still a question. Still an element of denial. Piao wanting to rescue her. He didn't answer.

Ask him . . . ask him.

Barbara looking across the cabin. The Senior Investigator averting his eyes, the report on fire in his pocket, and with it, a sense of knowing what was coming next.

Ask him . . . ask him.

"But you're not telling me everything about Bobby, are you?"

The promise of the dream put to the test. She wouldn't be able to read the report, but he handed it to her. At moments such as these you didn't want your hands to be free, you needed something, anything to hold onto.

"Pan, who examined the bodies, Bobby and the others . . . there were some points that he needed an expert opinion on. A clarification of some abnormalities. These examinations . . . what he found was beyond him . . ."

She was beginning to feel ill, a fever at the core of her.

". . . he was a professor at Pan's Institute and is now a government adviser in Beijing . . ."

Running out of space, the edge of the abyss, toes over it, looking down. The Senior Investigator's lips dry.

". . . much of the report is difficult to understand. Our medical professors, I am sure, are like yours, they attempt to explain things in unexplainable ways . . ."

He tried to laugh, it came out as a nervous cough.

". . . there are conclusions to his report. The four who were in Gongdelin and who it is said were executed, he found that they had been shot. But the entrance and exits of the bullet holes were disguised by the mutilations that they had received. The paths that led to their deaths, someone has tried to sweep them clean. Pan had missed this, it was not difficult in the circumstances . . ."

Her eyes were held firm, her gaze screwed to his. Attempting to prepare for the pain. Piao drew a breath, a tattered edge to it.

". . . these four and the others, including Bobby. Analysis showed that all had been anaesthetised. Opioids. Hypnotics. All had undergone a major medical procedure . . ."

The heartbeat in his chest, a thunder. Its echo in his inner-ears, his temples. Each word released to, and finding its way through its salvoes.

". . . Bobby, Ye Yang, Heywood, Qingde, the professor has concluded that their deaths were due to the trauma of these major medical procedures. That they were allowed to die on the operating tables following on from invasive surgical techniques. The mutilations, they were meant to hide this from us and to make our identification of the bodies more difficult."

Barbara's eyes, their hue shifting from turquoise to slate grey, and filled with questions.

"Medical procedures. Invasive surgical techniques. I don't get it. What are you saying, what's this professor saying? Why the hell should they have had operations?"

The Senior Investigator bit the inside of his lip. Untangling the words. Spitting them out . . .

"Their organs, they had been removed. Removed by surgical procedures. Removed systematically."

★

255

"Fucking helicopters."

Piao wiped the vomit from his lips. The rag, oily, causing nausea's wings to beat more rapidly. A hot hand on his shoulder. A smell of alcohol, candy and cough mixture, cutting through the reek of bile.

"Here Boss, drink. We thought we'd open a bottle. Check that it's what it says it is on the label . . ."

Grand Old Southern Comfort. The Senior Investigator took the candle ridged neck of the bottle and drank deeply. Slapping the Senior Investigator firmly on the back.

". . . some drinker, that pilot. Half a bottle. Half a fucking bottle in three snorts. The thirst of an Emperor."

The Zhi-8 took on more altitude. Shuddering. Piao shuddering. Taking another slug. Sugared Napalm. Wedging himself against the rear bulkhead. The Zhi-8's heartbeat deep into the small of his back.

"So Boss, what the fuck was that about?"

Nodding toward the centre of the cabin, Barbara Hayes . . . her eyes looking beyond steel and through the years. Piao had no appetite for words. Words. But perhaps they would still the nausea.

"Telling a mother how her son was slaughtered. Telling a mother that he died on an operating table . . ."

Another slug. Its heat expanding in his head.

". . . telling a mother that his organs were surgically removed."

Yaobang taking the bottle.

"That was in the report, Pan's old professor's report?"

"Last page."

"Last fucking page?"

Piao nodded. Head swimming, like a dog in a canal.

"Shit, sorry Boss. Never read a last page in my life. Always thought they'd be a fucking let down."

The Zhi-8 dropped. Piao pushing tighter against the bulkhead. Heartbeat racing the rotor's metal pulse.

"Not this last page."

Slipping to the plate floor, the Senior Investigator tracing the run of crescent moon welds with his finger.

"So what's it about Boss, what the fuck's going on? Operations. Organs missing. It feels like fucking madness."

Piao took the bottle. Finishing the bottle. Staring deeply into the label. Imagining himself in the buggy, passing the grand old house. Passing the grand old riverboat. Steaming just off the banks of the grand old Mississippi.

It feels like fucking madness.

Outside, beyond the metal confines of the Zhi–8, a constant flow of land. Formless wilderness, frontier, pecked into by the electric reasoning of villages, towns, cities. A flight from madness to sanity. From madness . . . the lands of the north east, the far north. The lands of the silent tears. The unheard cries.

PINGFANG.

"We flew over it, a tiny village. Thirty kilometres out of Harbin. Hardly noticeable now. Buildings, just buildings. And madness."

Letting the bottle slip across the metal deck in an arcing gash of colourless shards.

"They experimented on human beings there. Injecting them with deadly viruses. Freezing them, slowly. Observing the prolonged effects of frostbite. Dissecting them while they were alive. Conscious. Removing their organs."

"Pingfang, the secret Japanese research place during the last war. That's what you're fucking talking about, isn't it Boss?"

Eye contact enough. The Senior Investigator not needing words. Not needing to nod.

"You're saying that the bodies were experimented on, like there? Fucking cut up while they were still alive?"

Piao laboured to his feet. Across glass, making his way back to the centre of the cabin . . . to Barbara.

"Another Pingfang," was all that he said. Lands of silent tears. Lands of unheard cries.

★

She didn't talk. The rest of the journey to Hongqiao . . . a constant beat of steel wings through air. Her hand laced in Piao's. Sometimes tight, knuckles white; sometimes loose.

The sole barometer to what she was feeling. That, and the tears. His mother, his wife, and now Barbara. Women, a bottomless well of tears. He had often drunk there.

★

The car was waiting on the tarmac. They sat in the back, her hand still in his, not daring to let it go. A feeling that she would be washed away if he did. And every time that her gaze caught his, a flash. Like sun trapped in water.

The corridor of the Jing Jiang was dark. Silence, except for the city breathing. The sound of the key turning in its lock, a comfort. Inside the room, curtains billowing, tumbling as kites tethered by a fine cord.

Sometimes, a single thread is all that holds us to where we are and want to be.

She touched him. Undoing his shirt buttons. Her hands across his chest, down his arms; the shirt released to the floor. Not for a second her eyes leaving his, breathing in every feint of his irises. Breathing in unison. The buckle of his belt. The zip pulled open in a slow purr. Her hands moving down his flanks in a firm stroke; trousers, briefs, shoes, socks, kicked aside. He was naked and not trying to hide himself, his arms by his sides. Kissing him once on the shoulder as she slipped out of her dress, her underwear . . . silk moving down her skin to the floor. Nothing about her that wasn't perfect. Piao moved toward her, the pupils of her eyes widening. The breath torn on their lips. A shock . . . electricity as they held each other. She was heat against his ice. Softness against his hardness. She tasted of flowers and sleep. Tears and toothpaste. Drunk on her feel, her taste, her touch. He entered her before they had laid down on the snowfield of the duvet. Her legs around him in an unfolded whisper, a secret word. Everything that he was, had been, or would ever be . . . inside of her. The night, a seam of purple velvet and heaven. A catch of disjointed, out of time, memories and images.

She said only one thing as they had travelled the night together. One thing as her tears silently baptised his chest, as he had come inside her for the first time.

258

"Let me steal this moment from you now."

He had never heard more honest words in his life. He would have, should have, cried right there and then, but he didn't know how.

Chapter 21

Treat death as life.

The stink was rampant. Piao held his breath until he was deep inside the building.

The Headquarters of the Bureau for the Preservation of Cultural Relics straddled uncomfortably the borders of the Putuo District and the Changning District, in the far west of the city. There were no fences, but the district boundaries were there. And with them the disputes that divisions seed. The roads that surrounded the Bureau were clean. The road that it sat on, dirty. Rotting vegetables, paper, oil, shit, two dead dogs in the gutter . . . jawbones grinning. Which district would meet the bill of cleaning the road that sat exactly where the boundary fell? The argument had been running for two years.

Things move slowly in the People's Republic of China.

★

"How is your mother?"

Piao had known that the question would come. How would it not, from a man who had known her for more years than her own son? Fifty years. But still the Senior Investigator felt shame and humiliation. The Director's eyes fired with memory, and more.

"She was the most beautiful girl in Songjiang, as beautiful as you, Madam Hayes. And how she sang, like a canary. Did I ever tell you Sun Piao?"

He had, every time that they had met.

"She is well, but I do not see her as often as I should . . ."

It sounded as pretty as a bouquet of barbed wire; Piao feeling the need to justify himself.

". . . work keeps me very busy. I have important commitments."

The Director turned to Barbara, palms to the ceiling.

"And a mother is not an important commitment in this new world that we live in . . ."

The verbal slap across the face only eased as the Director poured the tea, hands shaking, and passed a cup to Barbara. A smile engraved across his face, as seemingly permanent as the words etched onto a pocket watch's inside case.

". . . you need to look at your life again, young Sun Piao. See what colour its eyes are. Your mother has been through a great deal in her life, all of our generation have been through a great deal. . . ."

He sipped the tea, the dainty cup held in fingers that were more bone than flesh.

". . . the Cultural Revolution was a ten year earthquake that people of your generation can never understand, but you should at least try. For your mother to be pregnant with the child of a foreigner. To be in love with a yang-gui-zi . . ."

The Director shook his head.

". . . lives split apart like bamboo. These were very difficult times . . ."

He swallowed hard . . .

". . . I would do anything to see my own father again, just to say to him that I understand."

To see his father again. The Hundred Flowers, the Cultural Revolution and the Red Guard's hatred of the 'Four Olds'. Old ideas. Old culture. Old customs. Old habits. There wasn't one family in the whole of the Republic that didn't have a tale to tell, that couldn't drive a tear from the most arid of eyes. Piao knew the Director's tale, it was worse than most. His father had been one of the country's most gifted concert pianists. One night the Red Guard had called . . . had hauled him from his bed. In a street in central Shanghai, not more than three miles from where they now sat drinking tea, his father's hands had been held firm to the road surface. A line of over two hundred and fifty Red Guards had marched across them in their boots. He had nearly bled to death that night, on the kerbside, but a skilled surgeon, whom the family had known had saved him. But not his hands. Not his mind. He had committed suicide six months later.

To see his father again. Just to say . . . I understand.

The Senior Investigator finished his tea, placing the cup and saucer firmly down on the antique desk. A punctuation mark begging a change of direction.

"Director, your team, when will they investigate the house near Harbin?"

The old man smiled, plough lines deepening around his eyes, his mouth. Piao had known him as a man in the spring of middle age. Skin taut. Eyes clear and fixed to the future. Seeing him now, it tugged at his own mortality. Knowing the feeling every time that he looked into a mirror. Every time, except the morning that he had woken with Barbara's hair splayed across his chest. Her breasts rising, falling, against his arm.

"A change of subject. You make a good detective Sun Piao. You would make an even better politician . . ."

The Director pushed a report across the desk.

". . . this is between you and me, Senior Investigator Piao. Madam Hayes was never here and this report does not exist. I give you this only because your mother is so good looking."

"Your team, they have already been to the house, haven't they?"

Director Chieh locked his fingers together and placed them on the desktop. A texture of gnarled tree bark resting on walnut veneer.

"We regard the smuggling of our national heritage, our cultural relics, as a serious problem. The Party and the government do not differ in this view and so our budget allows us to respond swiftly. As it so happens, it was most fortuitous that we already had a team working in the general area of Harbin. They were at the house just hours after you communicated with us . . . before you had even landed back at Hongqiao."

"What was a team doing around Harbin?"

The Director sipped his tea . . . a prop only. The tea itself had long grown cold in its cup.

"Pingfang."

Barbara saw Piao's irises widen, the words strand themselves in his throat.

"Pingfang, what is it, a place?"

"Our tragedy . . ." Piao replied, leaning toward her. She still smelt of that night and of a continent only partly explored.

". . . we have heard of your Dauchaus, your Belsens. You have not heard of our Pingfang. The west that you live in would like to corner the market when it also comes to human suffering . . ."

Dust in the room, its smell of old books, pottery fragments and glue.

". . . when the Americans liberated the camp from the Japanese Imperial Army, they guaranteed the freedom of those murderers involved, in return for all of the data that had been collected during the experiments on our citizens. Our experts believe that this made a significant contribution to medical research in the west."

"I'm so sorry."

Apologising for a nation. Straws in the wind. It sounded so meaningless as it left Barbara's lips.

"Memories fade, Madam Hayes; they were designed that way . . ."

Director Chieh's words, a welcome Band-aid applied over the running sore.

". . . but our case against the Japanese for compensation for what occurred, that does not fade. Our team at Pingfang has been collecting evidence for eighteen months now. It will be integrated into a report and a legal case will be brought against the Japanese government in the new year . . ."

He smiled. His face like a crumpled paper bag.

". . . not our usual field of work, but very rewarding to the soul. Very difficult for the soul also. Investigating your house in the Yanshou snowfields was a very welcome interlude."

Blood soaked into the wooden floor. A son's life ripped and spilt of its contents. 'A welcome interlude' . . . he made it sound like a tea dance. The Senior Investigator tapped his knuckles on the buff of the report.

263

"I have no time for paper, not with Liping sitting on my shoulder. What does it say, Director?"

Chieh stood, slowly, carefully. His posture, that of a question mark. His attention focused solely on Barbara. The old man had an eye for the women that time had not diminished. Does the bee ever lose its taste for the honey?

"Excuse me, my dear, if I slip into my lecturing mode . . ."

He smiled, she nodded.

". . . your initial report has been noted, Senior Investigator. And our own investigations, although brief, I can assure you were most thorough. As they always are . . ."

He studied his nails. A lifetime as an archaeologist had left its indelible print; the skin as yellow-brown as the soil of the Huang He's Great Loess Plains. The nails . . . thick, ridged, as tough as steel trowels.

". . . as you are already aware, Madam Hayes, your son was never officially in our country and I am not in a position to challenge this. Neither would I wish to. Swimming in the sea when you know that it is the season of typhoons, is a dangerous way to relax, if you take my point. And as your son was, officially, never in our country, he could never have officially worked for the Shaanxi Institute of Archaeology under the site director, Wang Xueli . . ."

The old man fingers formed a crooked, pointing spire.

". . . but, we know, Madam Hayes, that your son did exactly that . . ."

Barbara felt a jolt of focus. Chieh's words flowing over her.

". . . one of my archaeological inspectors, on several occasions, visited a very important site of a dig near the ancient capital of Changan . . . twelve miles out of Xian. It is the first extensive excavation of a Han Emperor's mausoleum in what we like to call 'the sleeping town of the Emperors and their wives and concubines.' Eight hundred tombs have been located on this single plain and although none of the royal tombs had been opened, there was a sense that the sleeping town should now be woken. Your son was a part of this process. One of the alarm-clocks. One of the first archaeologists involved. A gifted Han scholar I have been told . . ."

The Director turned, truth in his eyes.

". . . my inspector met him on two occasions. My department, this department, was the one to give your son a permit allowing him onto the Jing Di site."

She couldn't talk, tongue riveted in place by the simple truths that he had just spoken. Wanting to ask about Bobby. Mother things. But Piao spoke first . . . detective things.

"The coin that we found, was it a miniature burial item from the site that you talk about?"

Chieh took a small box from his desk drawer and opened it. The coin sat cleaned of earth on a bed of white cotton . . . blue-green bronze.

"The depth of your knowledge surprised me, Sun Piao. Your mother would complain that you were not the most accomplished student at school. But, yes, you are correct. The coin is a burial item, Mingqi. And, yes, once more, it comes from the site near Changan where the American boy worked. The fired clay dirt that you found at the house also confirms this."

"So, Director, do we know what it could be that was being smuggled from this site?"

The old man pressed a button and spoke overloudly into an intercom, it was answered within seconds by a meek tap on the door. A tall man entered the office, his face instantly forgettable; he placed a sealed wooden box on its end on the desktop and left. A box that was of identical size to the ones that Piao had seen in a corner of the house in the Yanshou snowfields. Chieh took a pair of cutters and snipped the wire that held the boxes sliding front in place. A thick, blood-red seal falling heavily onto the desk. Slowly the old man slid open the front of the lined box to reveal a crumpled padding of soft brown paper; Chieh's fingers pulling it out with care, laying it on the desk. His torso hiding the dark wood interior of the box. Moving aside . . . a gasp caught in Barbara's throat. A statue of a human figure, naked, armless. Slim, as a young boy. Soft muscled. Gently contoured. Terracotta . . . a fired clay of pale brown, almost pink. Hair, worn lacquer black and tied back into a tight bun. The face, beautiful. Hinting of a secret delight. A smile, generous, honest, across its open features. So different, but it reminded her of Bobby. He would have been around seven, going on eight, in a rush to grow up. Miami, a summer vacation spent on the beach. Hot days, long days, pierced with sighing Coca-Cola cans. Sand on his body. Watching him run toward the water, the surf falling across his shoulders, his back. As sleek, as glistening as a dolphin.

The Director was also smiling. His teeth as yellow as the sand on that beach in Miami.

"To see them is to smile, yes? In New York they realise up to fifty thousand dollars each on the art market. Ten of them appeared at auctions just one month ago. All were from the Jing Di site. Beautiful, are they not?"

Barbara nodded. Yes, they were beautiful. So was Bobby.

"We call them 'Men of Mud.' They are worth smuggling, do you not think so? Perhaps even worth dying for? Your son would not have been the first, Madam Hayes."

"Yes they are very beautiful, but worth dying for? No, they're not worth dying for, Director. I don't know anything that is worth dying for, except your own child."

He studied her eyes for several seconds.

"Yes, very beautiful, but perhaps you are right . . ."

He removed a pipe from an inside pocket of his jacket and tapped it hard on the window ledge. A litter of black tobacco decanted onto white paint.

". . . in March 1990 they were building a highway from Xian to Xianyang Airport, the road passed the tomb of Jing Di, fifth ruler of the Han Dynasty who reigned from 157 to 141 BC. The builders of the road noticed discoloration in the soil. They called us . . ."

The Director turned the pipe over and over in his fingers.

". . . ground tests revealed a total of twenty-four pits on the site. They contain the terracotta army of Jing Di, only the second imperial terracotta army to be found in our country. The first was the honour guard of over ten thousand life-sized soldiers that were found in the mausoleum of Qin Shi Huang Di, the builder of the Great Wall. At the Jing Di site, where your son had worked, only eight pits have so far been investigated. They contain over seven hundred figures. Seven hundred Men of Mud . . ."

He stroked a finger down the statue's cheek, its chest, the flat of its stomach. Barbara trying to imagine seven hundred smiles.

". . . as an Emperor during the Han period, Jing Di would have been considered divine. His people believed that he interceded with heaven on their behalf, their prosperity depended upon him. Too sacred even to name, as Emperor he would have been addressed by the words meaning 'foot of the stairs', the highest that a person could look in his presence. We know that the Han believed that the afterlife was a prolongation of this life, and so when life no longer possessed Jing Di, his mausoleum would have mirrored the magnificence of his residence on earth. Finely woven silks, musical instruments, food, drink, and an army to fight the Emperor's battles in the underworld . . ."

Director Chieh sat, fingers tracing the shape of the bowl of his pipe.

". . . the building of an army that might be required after death was taken extremely seriously. Jing Di, it is known, once accused his most loyal general of buying too many weapons for his own tomb. The man was charged with the intent of leading a rebellion against the Emperor in the afterlife. The general was imprisoned and humiliated. He was a proud and loyal officer. He starved himself to death . . ."

The old man passed a photograph across the desk; a deep pit, its sides rough and uneven. From out of its base, rows of heads sprouting like cabbages. Fired clay smiles floating on a sea of nicotine brown dust.

". . . Pit 17, it contained seventy terracotta soldiers marching behind two carriages drawn by wooden horses. An armoury of iron swords, shields, bows, arrows. The far end of the pit was filled to a height of two metres with grain. Then, as now, growing food to feed the masses was a national duty. A day after this photograph was taken, Pit 17 was filled in to allow farmers to sow wheat on the surface. A national heritage re-buried for a few hundred loaves of bread . . ."

He shook his head vigorously, the smoke curling around him in silver meanders.

". . . our inspectors have reported with frequency that the Jing Di terracotta site of twenty-four pits and the hundred foot high tumulus, that is the Emperor's actual resting place, were at the mercy of tomb-robbers. Our other Emperors' tombs also. Xuan and Wen, east of Xian. Wu, Zhao, north-west of Xianyang. These alone fall in an area that is around nine hundred square miles. How do we hope to guard such a vast area? Who is to say what is sowing wheat, harvesting corn . . . or robbing the graves of the Emperors and smuggling away our most prized cultural relics?"

Chieh tapped his pipe on the desk twice.

"We do not know how many Men of Mud have been smuggled from the Jing Di site. We do not know how many Men of Mud were at the Jing Di site! How many grains of sand are in your fist when you plunge it into a dune . . . see how they drift through the gaps between your fingers the more you guard against it and tighten your grip?"

The Director ran a fingertip across the fired clay face, between its eyes.

"Look at these Men of Mud, perfection. The beauty of nudity. Far superior to the ten thousand life-sized soldiers from the mausoleum of Qin Shi Huang Di, who had their clothes sculpted and painted onto them and who all looked the same. The Men of Mud were pieced together individually from four moulds, delicately painted, fitted with wooden arms, dressed in silk, equipped with weapons. And the face, look at the face. It speaks, feel its breath against your cheek. Over fifteen different expressions have been identified among the soldiers excavated from the Jing Di site so far. Unique. That is why so many would seek to own a Man of Mud . . ."

He slid the front of the box down. The smile eclipsed, as if a light had been dimmed in the room.

". . . your son was the latest in a long line who have died for the Men of Mud, Madam Hayes. In 1972 archaeologists from this department uncovered a graveyard of an estimated ten thousand prisoners who died building Jing Di's tomb. Shackles were found attached to the necks and legs of each skeleton."

Piao's eyes closed, just an instant, almost a flicker. Back on the river foreshore. When he looked up, Barbara was already at the door, opening it. A hand at her throat as she closed the door behind her, as if she was trying to rip chains away from her own neck.

Barbara walked into the corridor . . . ten minutes passing before she heard the footsteps on the dark marble, following her to where sunlight broke through the floor to ceiling windows. Footsteps, and knowing instinctively that it was Piao. You make love to someone once, and then you are suddenly able to recognise their footfall.

"I'm sorry, I just had to get out of there . . ."

She walked to the wall, leaning against it. Its marble facing bringing cool relief to the heat of her skin through her blouse.

". . . but at least we can now show that there is a cover-up going on. That Bobby was here in China and that someone high up is covering their arse. We've got the inspector that Chieh talked about, the one who saw Bobby twice. He can tell them. We must get a statement from him. And it was Chieh's department who allowed Bobby to work on the site. There must still be paperwork somewhere. There's also Bobby's trainers and the blood from the house at Harbin . . . the tests you had done already show that they belonged to Bobby . . ."

In a distant corridor, footsteps. A door opening. A door closing.

". . . we must take it to them, take it all. Show them. They'll understand now."

Wanting to hold her, but feeling himself back away. A distance, measured in polished marble floor tiles, increasing between them.

"Barbara, it is not possible to use the information that we have heard today . . ."

The words slipping from his mouth. Words already fed to him. Feeling like a mouthpiece. Nothing more than a message carrier.

"What the hell's going on here? This is what we've been looking for, isn't it . . . isn't it?"

Outside it had clouded over. Grey daylight filling the windows. He said nothing.

"Jesus . . . tell me that you don't mean it. Tell me that we can use this evidence?"

Piao talking, as if to himself.

"I was stupid. I should have known. When the Director told me that the report that he gave me did not exist. That you were never at this meeting. That what he was saying was just between him and me. I should have known. He was telling me, but I was not listening. It was killing the chicken to scare the monkey. A warning. All a warning . . ."

Trying to avoid her eyes.

". . . I said the same to Director Chieh as you have said, and then he told me. A directive had ordered him to halt the investigation, recall his team from the snowfields. All material evidence relating to the case is to be sealed and kept in the archives of the department. It has been expressly forbidden for any material to go beyond the gates of the Bureau for the Preservation of Cultural Relics."

She moved around him roughly.

"Do they know what they're doing? They're killing Bobby all over again."

"Director Chieh tried to trace the origin of the directive. It proved to be impossible. Chieh said that it comes from high up, very high up, the 'foot of the stairs . . .'"

Barbara walked toward the doors. The Senior Investigator following, not wanting his footsteps to make any sound. An apology in their silence.

". . . he told me about the house in Yanshou. It was directed that it be destroyed. Director Chieh's team burnt it. There is nothing left. The last thing that he said to me as I was walking out of his room, was for me to send my mother his most honourable regards."

A single smudge in a white universe. Burnt embers in melted snow. Stupid, stupid . . . and all that she could think about was Bobby's other trainer that they had left behind.

They drove, day fading. Taking Barbara back to the hotel. Walking her to her room. Not daring to touch her. Not daring not to. Needing to close the distance between them, but not knowing how to. She opened the door slowly and closed it slowly. She was gone and he walked home . . . rain falling in a drizzle.

Chapter 22

The high cadre's part is like that of the wind; the smaller man's part is like that of the grass. When the wind blows, he cannot choose but bend . . .

Imagine China as a giant flight of stairs. Each single person only knows what is on his or her step. No one sees the whole stairway from the top to the bottom. . . . it is too vast. The stairs beginning with a labyrinthine system of grades and ranks, into which each occupation has been divided by the Party. The twenty million cadres come first, twenty-four separate grades. On the bottom step of the cadre ranking are the ordinary clerks. Section chiefs, department heads . . . grades fourteen to eighteen. Bureau Chiefs . . . grade thirteen. Deputy Ministers . . . grade eight. The governors of cities and provinces . . . grades four and five. Above this, the clouds obscure the dizzy summit of the peak.

And salaries, each rank has a corresponding wage tacked to it. Eighty yuan a month for grade twenty-four. Three hundred and eighty yuan a month for a grade thirteen. Five hundred and sixty yuan a month for a grade eight.

In the PSB they have their own system of grades. Look at your boss's chair, that will tell you instantly what grade he is. A leather swivel chair? Then he must be above a grade thirteen. An upholstered chair, velvet covered? He is an official in the range of grades from thirteen to sixteen. If he is a grade seven cadre, his chair will be wooden with a cushion. Below that, a plain wooden chair without a cushion.

Rank, but not class . . . a stage set of shadows.

To prove this point . . . at an international conference on laser technology held in Beijing, the foreign scientists and Chinese professors of grades four and above, sat in the front six rows of the auditorium. In the back rows, professors of lesser standing along with junior scientists. In front of each place sat an identical white porcelain mug. An appearance of equality. But taste the scalding hot liquid in the white porcelain mugs in the front rows of the conference hall . . . fine tea. In the back rows . . . hot water.

Chapter 23

He'd rung her for three days now . . . no answer. On the fourth day her letter had arrived. Holding it to his nose, with its smell of some unnamed foreign and expensive perfume. The report that she had promised him on Ye Yang had CIA over stamped diagonally in red across the type. But it was the handwritten footnote in blue ink that he had read first.

'. . . where do we go now? I can't see any way through this mess, not any more. I'm thinking of going back to the States.'
BARBARA.

Piao's eyes turned to the parade of type. An urge to run to the Jing Jiang to her. But a glass barrier of duty restraining him. His eyes scanned the list of details, USA Passport Number, Issue Date, Birth Date. Height, Marital Status, Residence, Eyes, Hair, Basic stuff, just basic stuff. A photocopy of a black and white passport picture. Fine grain, high definition. The weave of her tweed collar. Each hair seeming separate. The words on a badge pinned to her lapel . . . 'I LOVE N.Y.' Chinese features, but an American girl. Lips pursed in a serious attempt at a straight face. Dark lipstick, bright red, Piao imagined. He read on . . .

RECORD ARCHIVES . . . CAMBRIDGE
UNIVERSITY, ENGLAND.
ENTRY: 2/10/1988   EXIT: 13/7/1992.

Y. YANG . . . First Class Honours Degree in Chinese
Studies and Archaeology.
Specialisation . . . the History and Archaeological Relics
of the Han Dynasty from 206 BC.

Y. YANG . . . Business Studies Degree in Accountancy
and Management.
Specialisation . . . Offshore Tax Strategies.

Clever girl. A high-flyer. Too high to be found in the mud of a
river foreshore. He read on . . .

DEPARTMENT Z14 . . . CIA PENTAGON
(Agent A.J. Moore)
FAMILY PROFILE:
YE YANG (Ref No. 20258423 AJM)
FATHER: JIANG YANG. MOTHER: XIAO YANG.

Fled Mainland China February 1966. Arrival in the
USA, New York, 7/3/1966.
Granted Refugee Status. Citizenship 22/6/1975
(42346867441)
Current IRS information shows a pre-tax profit for the
last financial year on the Yang's business, as five hundred
and seventy two thousand dollars. Assessment of their
properties and other assets stands at an estimated figure
of two point three million dollars. The profits were generated from the two antique/art galleries that they own
in the area of Fifth Avenue, New York. These comprised
sales, art assessments and consultancy work. The galleries
specialize on the purchase and sale of Japanese, Chinese
and Korean artefacts and relics.

Piao lit a cigarette, deep yanks on its bitter smoke. Ash falling
across the reports print. Absent-mindedly brushing it away as
he read on . . .

15/7/1992. Supreme Court Hearing
No. 005713556325.

Jiang Yang was charged with the importation into the
USA of rare Korean artefacts of great historical importance and cultural significance to the government and
people of South Korea. Extradition to South Korea
refused on the grounds of ill health. Custodial sentence
of two years imprisonment waived due to Jing Jiang's
general health. Died 3/2/1993 . . . Faith Hospital, Long
Island, NY. Control of the business passed to Song Jiang,
the only son. Ye Yang's responsibilities are as a buyer for
the two galleries and for several private collectors. For
the past two years she has specialised in the purchase and
sale of Chinese artefacts. Multiple entries to Mainland
China, Hong Kong and Taiwan . . .

9/6/1993, Beijing, Capital Airport.
15/7/1993, Hong Kong, Kaitak Airport.
30/9/1993, Shanghai, Hongqiao Airport. . . .

The list of entries went on for another ten lines. The profile of
a smuggler.

The Senior Investigator felt the anger tug at his collar.
More on this one report than he had received from the whole
collection of papers from his own Security, Luxingshe and
FITS. Fuck it, why should he have to go to the CIA to find
out information that should only have been a punch of a
keyboard key away from him? Piao reached into the thick
brown paper bag at his elbow. *Guo-tieh*. Fried dumplings
stuffed with cabbage and pork. They were a day old, the bag
would have more taste. It was his first meal in twenty-four
hours. It would do.

"What have you got?"

The Big Man blinked as he stepped into the light of the
office. He looked as if he hadn't slept. He hadn't.

"What have I got? I've got the fucking shits Boss. Didn't
get a wink . . ."

He grimaced.

". . . it's that fucking stall around the corner, the old mama. They should feed her dumplings to the rats around Suzhou Creek. That would kill the bastards."

Piao nudged his half-full bag of dumplings into the bin. Hunger is only in the mind, he told himself unconvincingly.

"Have any tapes arrived?"

Yaobang slumped in his wooden chair, two more years and he should be promoted up a few grades. Two more years and he'd get a cushion for his chair.

"Did Mao shit? Of course no more tapes arrived. We've only sent the Chief, what, ten letters? Called his iron titted secretary fifteen times."

Liping was a grade thirteen cadre. His cousin, the Minister Kang Zhu, a grade four or five cadre. High enough to shake any tree. High enough to free a few tapes snarled up in the system. Tapes that could mean anything, or fuck all. There was a block, somewhere. A person. A department. A political score to settle. An arse to cover. The tapes were being held back, not getting to where Piao needed them; Liping the gate, his only way to those tapes. The gate wasn't opening or not being allowed to open. The Senior Investigator unbuckled his shoulder holster. Placing it in the bottom draw of the cabinet, her words replaying in his inner ear as if they were now his sole motivation . . .

. . . *where do we go now? I can't see any way through this mess, not any more. I'm thinking of going back to the States.*

He would need a key, a special key, a strong key to unlock a special and strong gate. Piao walked into the incident room, the blackboard in the corner of his eye. Rows of names . . . a white slash of thick chalk dividing them. Two stories here. One, he was starting to untangle. Smuggling. Heywood, Bobby . . . the point of the needle. The ones who actually got the shit under their nails. Their fingers in the dirt. Qingde, with his contacts, his street knowledge. The internal travel documents that would be summoned up for him as if by magic. The courier. The local fixer. And Ye Yang, the mover. The one who made it all possible; the link between a run-down farmhouse in the snowfields of Yanshou and the art markets of New York's Fifth Avenue. Ye Yang, the one who snared the buyers. Ye Yang, the one who snared those with access to the relics that she required. Bringing both together in deals that were made in heaven . . . but in one that was made in hell. The last deal. And behind it all, a buyer who became a killer, or who had always been one? And confused within all of this, a reason for state involvement.

And the second story, that was still in knots, and tying him in double knots. The four who had been executed at Virtue Forest and then butchered once more before being left to the great sculptress, the Huangpu. Convinced now, more than ever, that these four were not part of the smuggling . . . that they were part of something else that had bound them in chains, leg to leg, neck to neck, with the others who had been.

He walked to the incident room door, his own office calling him . . . the blackboard also calling him, but ignoring it. Only as he went to pull the door to did he bow to its insistence. Wishing that he hadn't. For all of the fine writing upon it, seeing only a question mark. Just a question mark.

★

A loud voice in his office. Not angry, just clumsy, chaotic. The sort of voice that instantly reminded Piao of a very tall man trying to scrabble through a very small hole. Detective Yun . . . he recognised the precise placing of the words. The almost rehearsed sentences.

"Senior Investigator Piao, is he available?"

Yaobang was slumped in his chair, contemplating promotion and the cushion that would come with it. With an effort he rose, moving across to Piao's desk, his dumpling bloated bulk purposely eclipsing the Senior Investigator's jacket that clung to a corner of the wooden chair. The wooden chair with a cushion. Yun didn't wait for an answer, he never did, he worked only to his own agenda.

"It is just that I have been trying to meet with him for a while now. I get the impression that I am being avoided."

You are . . . we all fucking are.

From between the frame of the door and the beige wall, the

278

narrowest of cracks, Piao could see Yun. The detective could not see him. It almost feeling like a childhood game.

". . . he is to brief me on his current cases. Chief Liping wishes me to be in a position to take them over. I was assured that Senior Investigator Piao was in the building."

The Big Man spread his arms in surrender.

"No. No, he's not here."

"But surely, that is his jacket?"

Yaobang turned his head, in the corner of his vision the chair, the cushion, the draped olive green jacket.

"Yes it is, yes. The Boss was here, but he's not now. He had to leave in, in rather a hurry . . ."

He moved around Piao's desk, lowering himself into the chair.

". . . the Boss doesn't mind me using his chair when he's out, it's got a cushion . . ."

He bounced up and down on the chair as if road testing the cushion's plumpness; briefly glancing toward the incident room, a smile worming its way into the corners of his mouth. He couldn't see the Boss, but knew that the Boss could see him. He lowered his voice to a whisper.

". . . Senior Inspector Piao has the shits, the poor bastard. Through the eye of a fucking needle. The old mama's dumplings from around the corner . . ."

Behind the desk, Yaobang slowly reaching down into the bin.

". . . I warned him. Rat food. He wouldn't listen . . ."

The Big Man placed the retrieved brown paperbag on the desktop, with its islands of grease reaching out arms to encompass each other.

". . . now these, the best *Guo-tieh* in the area. Come, Yun, try one . . . try one. A man with fine tastes like you will recognise the subtle taste and texture that makes these dumplings superior . . ."

He held out the bag, nodding knowingly.

". . . they say that Jiang Zemin himself only eats these very dumplings when he visits Shanghai. There are rumours also, a very reliable source indeed . . ." he winked.

". . . that our beloved Prime Minister Li Peng, has some flown every weekend to Beijing by military helicopter."

Yun looked suitably impressed.

"Yes, they do look good and I did miss my lunch today. Paperwork. I like to keep it up to date."

"Here, Detective Yun, take the bag, please. I insist. Such devotion to work and to the People's Republic, deserves a reward. I was going outside for a break anyway. Even I can have too much of a good thing . . ."

Yaobang slapped a hand onto his own stomach and with the other pressed the greasy bag into Yun's palms.

". . . come. Eat. Eat. Think of our esteemed Comrade Prime Minister . . ."

Yun obliged. Grease glistening on his fingernails, on his lips, across his tongue.

". . . good, eh comrade? Have another. As you can taste, Deng knows a dumpling when he chews on one, that's for sure. My mother always said that you can tell a true leader by the dumplings that he eats. Mao use to eat crap, all dough and grease . . . and look what fucking happened to him!"

He ushered Yun out of the door, the acne faced detective unable to reply, his pitted cheeks swollen like overripe apples.

"No need to say anymore, Detective Yun . . ."

The Big Man shouted.

". . . I'll tell the Boss that you called. Enjoy your lunch."

He didn't look back.

★

Three reports arrived from central despatch as the afternoon died into evening. Three reports, each from different bureaus. Each sealed and addressed to Yaobang. Luxingshe. FITS. Bureau Six. One page making up each report. Black on white. All three reports identical and saying the same . . .

SUBJECT NAME: CHARLES HAVEN.
NATIONALITY: WITHHELD
PASSPORT NO: WITHHELD.

VISA NUMBER: WITHHELD.
OCCUPATION: WITHHELD.

Standard questions that would have been fully answered on any other requested report . . . all withheld. Piao's fingers drumming an anonymous rhythm on the desktop. Never had he seen a report such as this. In a country where information was oxygen, suffocation. Each report ending with the same statement.

ALL INFORMATION REGARDING THE ABOVE NAMED SUBJECT IS WITHHELD AND CLASSIFIED. ANY FURTHER REQUESTS FOR DISCLOSURE MUST BE MADE IN WRITING TO THE MINISTRY OF SECURITY. ACCOMPANIED BY A FULL EXPLANATION OF WHY THIS CLASSIFIED MATERIAL HAS BEEN REQUESTED.

"Shit, Boss, who is this bastard?"

The Senior Investigator avoided Yaobang's stare, slipping his shoulder holster on.

"A bastard with very good friends in very high places."

Chapter 24

He'd flipped the badge, stared the stare. The information had come. It usually did. The receptionist spilling it like rice onto a plate. When they had left. Where to. A car registration number. An address. Even directions. Three hours later he was in Hangzhou, West Lake. A house in the Geling Hills.

Piao parked the car and walked. The woods thick. Their floor a rough carpet of bronze needles. And the smell so clean, like laundry . . . like a new life. The guesthouse was low, modern. Glass and mellow brick. A little bit of Scandinavia transplanted into the People's Republic. Beyond . . . the lake, the city, the hills, the Tiesha River. Stacked one behind the other like shiny plates in a drying rack. The Senior Investigator waited for two and a half hours. When they arrived, the foreign car's headlights cutting between the comb of straight tree trunks . . . the lake was already fading to grey. Falling into a fold of darkness. The *Duan Qiao*, Broken Bridge . . . a vein of matt silver losing its form and strength, flowing into the lake. Steel into water.

Haven, dark suit, rounded the front of the car. Two winked flashes as he crossed the headlights, bleached white . . . his shirt, face, hair. A solid bust of white marble. His shadow, vast, thrown up against the canopy of trees. He opened the passenger door and Barbara stepped out, the Englishman's hand taking hers and then moving to the curve of her waist. Walking her to the front door. Reaching for the light; their figures thrown into black profile. Laughing. Kissing. Piao looked away. The pain upon him . . . sharp, suffocating in its pressure. Barbara entered the house as Haven went back to the car. As the headlights caught him, he stood motionless. His senses alive, reaching out . . . resembling an immaculate lizard, tasting the air. Looking straight in Piao's direction, eyes quizzing. The half smile that seemed to be tattooed to the corners of his lips.

Something on the wind, a realisation that all was not as it should have been, but not knowing what it was. The Senior Investigator not breathing, clearing his head of every thought in case it should taint the air. Haven moved out of the beam and reached into the car; the headlights dying in a lazy fade to black.

Piao waited for another hour. There was no reason to and he didn't know why he did. But perhaps that was the crucifix that an obsession was hung upon. Waiting. Waiting until the bedroom light went out and West Lake spilt into night . . . its shape only discernible from the curve of the Hubin Road skirting its eastern shores.

Let me steal this moment from you now . . .

Her secrets would be Haven's too. Her breath torn against his ear, his chest, his stomach. The Senior Investigator walked to his car. Pine rain on the breeze . . . and pain like a chasm filling him. Soaked by the time he started the engine; the headlights procreating an army of slanting shadows. Raindrops running down his face . . . a taste of pine in their drift to the corners of his mouth. He drove slowly. It took over four hours to reach the centre of Shanghai. Seeing her face with every beat of the wipers. And behind it all, the rain claiming everything. . . . the rain, and Haven.

Chapter 25

The cleanly swept alley was fifty yards long, six feet wide. The entrance that he was looking for leading into a communal kitchen and up a winding staircase . . . dark. A railing of chipped green paint, layered in grease. A smell of old cooking oil, kerosene, piss and babies' bottoms.

Zhiyuan, the Tong Zhi and Chairman of the Shiqu, his face resembling a partially deflated balloon . . . opened the door. Somehow he seemed smaller, less significant than when they had met on the foreshore of the Huangpu that night.

" Piao . . ."

He looked startled. In the black beads of his irises, the secret fear that every Chinese has when a uniform knocks on the door.

". . . what do you want? You should not be here. The investigation against you is next week. I am the principle witness for the prosecution."

"I know who you are . . ."

Piao moved foward from the darkness of the landing and into the light spilling from the room. Shadows rolling from his face.

'. . . and I know when the investigation is. I need to see you."

"You need me?"

He smiled.

"Me? You are desperate, Senior Investigator, and too late. The investigation against you will take place and you will be suspended from the Public Security Bureau pending a further investigation into much more serious state charges."

"It's not the investigation that I want to see you about, it's this."

The Senior Investigator pulled the file, white for murder cases, from beneath his jacket, holding it out. Zhiyuan

284

held-up a palm, a roadmap of deep lines all leading into cul-de-sacs.

"I do not want to see you until the hearing, Senior Investigator. There is nothing that you say that I want to hear."

Piao moved closer to the old man. It was cold, their breath tumbling into each others.

"But there is, Comrade Zhiyuan, and you have no choice but to listen to me. You are the Chairman of the Shiqu that includes my home. You are my democratic representative. My local voice to the ear of the Party, a voice that I need . . ."

The Senior Investigator brushed past Zhiyuan and entered the small room.

". . . obligations, comrade, they go both ways . . ."

There was little space for movement in Zhiyuan's quarters. The one room held four chairs, a bed, some stools, two dressers, a television, a table. Clothes on hangers hooked to the cords of window blinds. On the mantelpiece above the tiny fireplace stood a forest of photographs. Some framed, some not. All dusty. All faded. Comrade Zhiyuan with Mao, Zhou Enlai, Deng Xiaoping, Brezhnev, Castro, Jiang Qing, Nixon.

'Veteran revolutionaries only end up as monsters or ghosts.' . . . or faded photographs.

On the wall above the mantelpiece, framed certificates, red ribboned merits, gold embossed statements of honour and esteem from various Party organs. The Provincial Committees of the Triple Alliance of Peasants, Workers and Soldiers. The Central Advisory Commission. A letter of commendation from the Chairman of the Supreme Military Commission himself, Deng Xiaoping. But in place of honour, the only photograph that had both been dusted and its frame polished, a portrait of the Great Helmsman with a note written in his own hand . . .

'At first a fragrant flower can sometimes be mistaken as a harmful weed.'

Feted by the Party. A favoured citizen, Zhiyuan. And in the corner of his room, half hidden by the edge of the bed, a chamberpot . . . stained, chipped. Last night's urine, as orange as the juice squeezed from a tangerine.

"If you come to the laundry you must have stains that you wish to wash away Senior Investigator."

Piao's finger traced the smile on Mao's face, remembering the words, etched into every child of his generation's memory, over and over again.

From the Red East rises the sun . . . there appears Mao Zedong.

He turned from the fire.

"No, I have no stains to wash away, comrade. Read this."

The Senior Investigator dropped the file onto the table. Zhiyuan's eyes steady, not a flicker downwards.

"I have too much to read already. One more report from an officer who is working to his own agenda and trying to save his own fat job . . . why should I miss my sleep because of such a thing?"

"Because you believe that the State is pure and that the Party rides above such things as corruption. Because you believe that Mao still rises with the sun. Read this and tell me that all of these things still exist and that they are all true. I want to believe it also . . ."

Piao pulled open the folder, monochrome prints spilling across the table and onto the floor.

". . . twelve murders now. Twelve. The most important homicide case in the city's modern history, and Liping cannot get a few boxes of surveillance tapes released to me. Someone, somewhere, is stalling. I need the tapes, they might be nothing, they might be everything, but I need them. A comrade in your position could help me to just do my job, nothing more . . ."

Brandy in the Shiqu Chairman's heavy glass. He swallowed it, but no fire in his eyes . . . their emptiness panicking Piao.

". . . Liping knows things that he should not know, but I need his help. I need you to push him into giving it to me. You are my Shiqu chairman, it is my right."

"But there is more, Senior Investigator Piao. It is in your eyes."

And still no fire in the old man's eyes.

"Read the file comrade. Read the file. The eight that you

saw on the foreshore that night were missing their corneas, kidneys, their hearts. They had been removed systematically. Removed using surgical procedures. We have another Pingfang. A Pingfang in the centre of our city."

The Shiqu Chairman turned from the photographs, the past . . . Mao's smile still in his eyes.

"It is a thick file, Senior Investigator Piao. It will take me three hours to read it properly. Come back then and not before."

To walk for three hours on such a night is not difficult. There are stars, the river . . . the hotel. Piao stood outside the Jing Jiang, head back, counting the floors. Ten. Her room. Lights on, curtains drawn, as orange as Zhiyuan's urine. Barbara's room. He'd telephoned the front desk earlier.

'Barbara Hayes was at present in her room. Did he wish to be connected?'

So near . . . he could feel her, smell her, hear her.

"No. No I don't wish to be connected."

★

Zhiyuan's door was open, yellow light cracking around its frame. He knocked gently, no answer. It all feeling wrong. Reaching for his pistol . . . slowly, controlled. The metal seeming to burn in his hand. Slipping the safety. Moving through the gap, into the short hall, the room ahead opening up to view. Zhiyuan, slumped in a chair, papers scattered around him. A crazy paving of type and monochrome prints. The Senior Investigator's shadow overtaking him. Hand outstretched, shadow pistol wavering across the Shiqu Chairman's back.

"Put it away Senior Investigator Piao, it is not yet my time to die . . ."

Zhiyuan turning, the half glasses perched precariously on the bridge of his nose, a newly stoked fire in his eyes.

". . . the privilege of old age, dropping off to sleep. Now Senior Investigator Piao, make me some tea and tell me where I can find your Chief Liping on a Sunday? I have some tape recordings to free for you."

Chapter 26

An Eel on a nail . . . black, shiny. Pulled taut.
Skin stripped from flesh in one complete length.
Blood on the pavement, on knuckles, down fingers.
Black, white, red.

The lake was black, as if a bottomless shaft had been sunk through the heart of the earth. Clinging to its edge with jewelled fingernails, Liping's zhau-dai-suo ablaze with security lights. A Red Flag in the drive, its windows dead. Behind it another car, dark, skulking. Its shape lost against the bite of night. The Chief had guests, Piao hoped that he didn't mind two more. Eighty miles and three hours of travelling. It was tough if he did.

"Are we here?"

The Senior Investigator nodded, as he began to brake, then suddenly swerving from the start of the drive back onto the road, foot clamped on the gas. A punch of adrenaline nailed through his chest. Switching off the lights and engine, as he squinted into the darkness . . . the car free wheeling downhill for a further three hundred metres to the bend in the road. Pulling from the tarmac ribbon onto shale. Stones rattling against the underside of the car. A canopy of trees against the stars taking them to its breast. Zhiyuan coughed. Cheroot smoke, locked into his lungs and released in a coughing, stuttered fit of silver.

"What's going on?"

The Senior Investigator got out of the car, closing the door carefully. Noticing his breath against the sky. Noticing the rhythmic thump in his chest, the fingernails digging into his palms.

"There was a Shanghai Sedan in Liping's drive, a black one."

Zhiyuan leant against the car roof beside him, the cheroot bitter between his teeth. Its tip drawn from red to orange, almost yellow . . . the only feature that was visible in the comrade's face.

"Do you know how many Shanghai Sedans have been built. Black ones?"

"No I don't, but I'm sure that it is above the ten year quota figures."

Piao walked across the grass, the shale, onto the road. Keeping to the trees, the rough undergrowth, making his way to the side of the wide drive. The glow of Zhiyuan's cheroot following close behind. The fuzz of security lights blotting out the stars above Chief Liping's zhau-dai-suo.

"And tell me, Comrade Zhiyuan, how many Black Shanghai Sedans are there with double dents in their front bumpers from hitting a student. Killing a student?"

Piao's fingers travelled across the fender. One, two dents. Close together. Deep. Chrome already starting to peel in razor flakes of torn silver. He joined Zhiyuan at the line of trees that skirted the boundary wall. Shadows deep cut along its full length.

"It's the car . . ."

And in a sharp whisper,

". . . fuck them, fuck Liping."

Pulling the Shiqu Chairman by his cuff, a rocky path separating tree line from wall.

"Then perhaps you have enough evidence, Senior Investigator, if this is the car? We should go. I have contacts. I can make telephone calls. Insist on an immediate investigation. The truth will come out. I guarantee this to you. It is not proof of corruption, of murder, but it is enough to get a foot in the door and from such a position."

"Fuck a foot in the door. I want the whole mansion, not just a foot in the door."

On the other side of the wall, voices. Three, four, maybe five. And a fire. A roar of hunger in its throat. A marmalade fan of flames reflected against the uppermost canopy of the trees. Zhiyuan fell behind, feeling his way in a blind shuffle.

A hiss of a whisper almost hidden by the voice of the fire.

"We should go Piao. There will be nothing for us here. I have trusted comrades who we can involve. You should know when to let go."

No words. The Senior Investigator retracing his footsteps with certainty. No words. Guiding, half pulling the old man forward by his lapel. Stumbling onto Lake Taihu's foreshore. Bricks and steel growing out of silt and weathered stones. Dark, the only available light reflected across the wall from inside the garden.

"Shit!"

Piao tripping on a stone, foot in the water. Ice and electricity . . . shooting straight to his heart, his temples. He was cold, but sweating. Exhilarated, but terrified. A nest of tar barrels shadowed against the bottom of the wall. Stacking them up, and thinking of young women and their giggles, their smiled taunts.

Come give us blue-eyed babies Comrade Policeman.

Climbing up, hauling Zhiyuan after him. Looking through the gaps in the thick windbreak of pines. Liping, standing with another man half way down the garden. Laughing. Drinking. Looking on as three others fed the large fire pit with seasoned logs. White smoke. Flames, burnished to platinum in the security arc-light . . . fanning against their faces. All of them, looking as if they were cast from bronze. Climbing, the smoke. Crossing the wall, out across the water. White to black. And in the air, heady, nailing you in place, the smell of pine, petrol, and burnt grass. Zhiyuan hissed in his ear . . .

"There's nothing here. Look at them, they're drinking, laughing. Nothing worth a page in your next report Investigator. We are wasting time, we should go."

Piao stepping down with one leg, but a hand across the Shiqu Chairman's chest as Liping barked an order, interspersed with sips of Dukang, shiny on his lips. Men moving from the fire pit toward the house. Their shadows shortening as the Chief was left alone, ramrod straight and looking into the belly of the fire. The men returning in twos, carrying heavy bundles swathed in white sheets, polythene and rope. One at each end of each bundle. Four trips. Eight bundles. Eight thuds as each hit the earth. Thick cord being untied. Tape being pulled from plastic. Polythene unwrapped. Zhiyuan's lips against the Senior Investigator's ear, fire hot.

"What is this? What is going on?"

"Sometimes the ancestors smile on us. Sometimes they smile without a reason. Look, Comrade Shiqu Chairman, can't you see them?"

As he released the words, Piao feeling his stomach move up to his throat. His throat move up to his eyes. Burning. Too far away to make out details . . . faces, identities, names. Just the blank shapes of bodies. Skin. The shock of nakedness. Black pubic hair. Gashes . . . wildly huge, dark, gaping.

"They are people, comrade. People. Can you not see them?"

A count, half laughing . . . one, two, three. The first body thrown, tumbling into the pit. Into the fire. Its softness hitting the embers. A flight of sparks rising to the sky. Voices, words, lost in the song of the fire. Mocking. Joking. Taunting. Another body hauled up, swung, let go. Arms, legs, limp through space. Joining with the fire. The flames devouring it. Another body . . . Chief Liping re-filling his glass. The smoke from the fire changing colour, white to brown. Blood-brown. Its stench of dry tears, burnt meat.

"Recognise them?"

Zhiyuan saying nothing. Nothing. The vomit that forced, that spilt from between the tremble of his lips, down his shirt front, speaking for him. He took the old man to the water's edge, washing his face, his shirt, with cupped hands . . . gently, like a septuagenarian baby. The old man, trying to talk. Tongue numb, not working. Piao saying the words for him.

" See, it washes off, comrade, no stains. But what we have seen, that is forever. A stain on our souls. A stain on our lives. You understand?"

Cupping the water onto the old man's face. Across his eyes. His lips.

"You will act on it, tell of what you have seen, yes?"

At last finding his voice, the old man. Hoarse. Each word burnt in bile.

" Yes, for the sake of that Party in which I believe."

And all of the time from behind the high wall, laughter. Laughter, and flights of sparks filling the sky with stars where before there had been none.

★

Piao was already letting go. With every chevron that fled into their headlights and out again, aware that he was disengaging. It was the Shiqu Chairman's case now. Zhiyuan, his interface with the Party, his thorny presence into the various committee rooms . . . all would speed the control of it into his back pocket. Party business, that was what it had now become, what it always should have been. They would now become just a part of a process. Investigations. Hearings. Pleas. Trials. All leading to Liping's execution. Minnows swimming to the surface to fight for the job vacated by the old carp. Zhiyuan, for his trouble, would receive another letter of commendation to frame and gather dust. And the Senior Investigator of the Homicide Squad of the PSB? The Danwei's investigation into the official charges against him would be halted. He would retain his position, his rank and the perks that went with it. The cushion on the wooden chair. The meagre petrol allowance. Food vouchers. The new uniform every two years. Yes, he would keep his job, and with it, the nights spent in cars on surveillance; the Big Man picking his nose and adjusting his balls. The politics. The patting of the horse's arse. The four hundred yuan a month. Two years to save for a Forever Bicycle. Two years to save for a tv. And Barbara? She would go home. Tears and airport queues. There would be no confession at the trial. Nothing to cauterise the pain. No knowledge. No comfort. Just waste, waste for everyone, except Comrade Zhiyuan with his framed letter of commendation.

★

The drive back to Shanghai took over three hours. No conversation. Two stops . . . one to piss, one for the Shiqu

Chairman to throw up again. Piao walked Zhiyuan to his room. The smoke still in his nostrils, wood and black burnt flesh.

"The door, bolt it . . ."

The Senior Investigator tapped his knuckles on the thick brass lock.

". . . and sleep, you need it. You've had a shock, it might not feel like it yet, but it will do. Don't smoke, and drink a lot. Water . . ."

The Senior Investigator turned to the stairs, exhaustion, like a ball of clay, in his head. Wanting to close his eyes, but knowing what would happen when he did . . . smoke, flames, bodies, waiting for him like a bear-trap in the unlabelled hours of night.

". . . 9.00am tomorrow, I will come back then. We will make statements about what we have witnessed together. Who we saw. You will know who it is best to present these to?"

Zhiyuan nodded.

"Yes I will know . . ."

The door already closing.

". . . you have done well, Senior Investigator, I misread you. Thank you for your work. This will get you promotion and another one hundred yuan a month."

Piao turned back to face the Shiqu Chairman . . .

"And a velvet covered upholstered chair, comrade?"

But the door had already closed; brass lock snapping noisily into place.

Chapter 27

When the finger points to the moon . . . the imbecile studies the finger.

Only officials have telephones of their own . . . public telephones are in shops, offices, in the apartments of neighbours who are members of the Public Security Committee, the apartments of members of the PSB. In places where calls can be listened to by others. Reported about by others. The telephone. The most basic mechanism of government control.

A telephone is a privilege. There is a one year waiting list. An installation fee of four thousand yuan, a year's wages. Politburo members have their own special telephone exchange; their phone numbers beginning with the prefix '39'. Also a separate exchange for the military, the army. Their telephone numbers are strictly confidential.

Private numbers are not listed. Whole ministries are not listed. Telephone directories are sparse and in some cases are '*bu-dui-wai*' . . . 'not open to foreigners.' A one hundred and ninety page bright orange covered telephone book is issued by special subscription through the post office. There are no listings for individuals amongst its pages . . . just offices. The government, as part of its efforts to appear more open, for the first time issued a public phone book. Thirty pages give the numbers of public telephone kiosks. There are no listings for individuals in its pages. Central committee departments. Politburo members. Ministers. Their numbers only exist in the special exchanges, the private operators, the state of the art switching equipment; and in the little pocket-sized personal phone number booklets that the high cadre carry with them at all times. Constantly nervous that they might lose them.

Information is not a matter of money, but of connections. Information, like consumer goods . . . rationed out by title.

A quarter bottle of brandy . . . Greek. Four cheroots. Count-less pisses. Three abortive attempts at sleeping. At last Zhiyuan gave up, the smoke in his eyes, on his tongue, in his brain. He searched for his black book, its corners worn, polished . . . a smell to its leather covering of dried sweat, wood panelled committee rooms, powerful cadres. Fumbling for his half glasses. Index finger leafing through dog-eared pages and down the lists of numbers. A Beijing code. A prefix . . . 39. Mis-dialling twice. The third time it connecting immediately. Ringing over and over again. When it was finally answered, the crystal clarity of the line was unmistakable, unlike any other in the country that didn't go through a special exchange.

3:30am . . . a voice soaked in tiredness.

"Wei . . ."

"Zhang Chunqiao, comrade . . . this is Zhiyuan telephon-ing from Shanghai. I apologise for the hour, but my call is of the utmost importance. Very serious, comrade. Very serious."

"What time is it?"

Coughing. A flap of bedsheets. A sense of movement at the Beijing end of the line. The Politburo member sitting on the edge of his bed.

"It is 3:35 Comrade Chunqiao . . ."

The Shiqu Chairman breathless. Wiping the sweat from his palms on the arms of his chair.

". . . it is late, I know, but I have news that could not wait. Very important, comrade. I could not sleep."

"It had better be important Zhiyuan, I have a Politburo committee meeting at 9:30 . . ."

Coughing again, this time with the tiredness shaken adrift.

". . . so, you could not sleep and decided that I should not sleep also. Well, I think that you had better tell me what this is all about."

The smell of urine, its acidic bite watering his eyes . . . Zhiyuan pushing the chamberpot under the bed with the side of his foot.

"It is Liping, Chief Liping of the PSB. I have undeniable proof that he is implicated in the murders of eight people, possibly more."

★

The old comrades telephone was official property, owned by the Shiqu. Religiously Zhiyuan logged his call into the book beside it. His writing shaky, too much brandy, too much adrenaline, too little sleep. Every detail of the call noted. Duration, telephone number, who to, why?

To report concerns regarding Chief Liping of the PSB, and to demand an immediate emergency meeting with senior officials with the view to his arrest and charge for multiple homicide.

Comrade Chunqiao would move swiftly. He had an immediate grasp of the magnitude of what Zhiyuan was telling him. He talked of the implications, the outcomes to Liping and possibly others. He thanked Zhiyuan. He would act on the information forthwith. Telephone calls would be made; insistent that meetings would be held. Liping's arrest would be swift. A show trial would ensue. A trial that would clearly state to all, that the laws and expectations of the People's Republic of China applied to all . . . from peasant to Politburo member. Factory worker to the highest of cadre. It would end in a high profile execution.

The Shiqu Chairman felt a wave of relief wash against the anchors that tethered his soul. Perhaps, after all, the tune that he danced to was still the same. Perhaps the dance steps that had punctuated the doctrines and tenets that his life had been built on for so long, would not need to be re-choreographed.

Zhiyuan was to tell nobody else of Chief Liping's crimes and indiscretions. It could jeopardise the outcome of the arrest . . . put at risk the final decision of such a trial. Comrade Chunqiao thanked the Shiqu Chairman once more. Zhiyuan, once more, had carried out his duty to the Party, his duty to the People's Republic. It was now to be left to him and other members of the Politburo. Zhiyuan could rest assured that all outstanding matters would be dealt with. The telephone line went dead.

Zhiyuan had another brandy before he went to bed. Its fire on his tongue, its fire in his belly. He slept easily, the ghosts unpacked and passed on. Sleeping until 6:30am. A deep sleep. A sleep of celebration. Waking only to the firm knock on the door.

Ivory satin. Black hair.

She was called to the telephone by the a-yi at 3:50am. Moving from the side of the Minister, not disturbing his sedated sleep. Down the large flight of stairs, crossing the marble hallway and into the study in what seemed like a single flow of motion. Slight, almost insignificant of stature, but charismatic in every movement that she made. As if the simplest act had been choreographed meticulously and needed to be performed to perfection. The telephone to her lips, naturally red. Lips that changed their shape with the turn of the minutes, barometers of her mood. Pouting, dripping honey and kisses one instant. The next, whispering shards of glass, spitting nails.

"Comrade Chunqiao, Zhang. I had always assumed that you were the sort of man who had better things to do at this time of the morning than to make telephone calls to other comrades?"

He laughed. A laugh not too short to be interpreted as false, not too long to be experienced as vulgar.

"We missed you at the reception, Lingling."

"I missed being there and so did the Minister, his health would not allow it, as you know."

There was a respectable pause.

"How is the Minister?"

Another pause, the question left in the dust. It said everything and more.

"So Comrade Zhang, why do you telephone so early. Can't your lovely wife keep you in her bed?"

"I was wishing to talk to the Minister. A matter of great urgency and personal importance to him."

"I am afraid that to talk to him would be impossible, he is unable to take any calls at present. You may tell me. I have his full authority to deal with all matters that do not relate to direct Politburo issues and agendas."

A long pause, his breathing rapid. The line as clear as iced water. Lingling sensing the importance of what was locking his lips. She had the key to unlock lips, she always had. Totally confident in its ability to slip any lever. She laughed, more of a giggle. It sounded natural. It should, it had been practised often enough.

"Come comrade, you are not usually so reticent. So shy. One of your words is worth ten from any of the Minister's other colleagues . . ."

She lowered her voice to a whisper. Mischievous, like a game that children play in the dark.

". . . and if it is of great urgency and personal importance to the Minister, then it is of great urgency and personal importance to me also. Surely your silence is not an indication of your lack of trust in me?"

The key inserted, turned, levers slipping aside. And with it, certain, as night follows day, that his words would now flow. So certain, that she would have bet the life of her unborn child upon it being so.

Comrade Chunqiao spoke for ten minutes; there were gaps, silences, but she never invaded them. She had learnt long ago to manage silences, to hold them and nurture them for what they were potentially worth. The rewards coming in words that hadn't wanted to be spoken. Sticky words, sharp words, secret words . . .

"Thank you for your honesty Zhang. The Minister will be informed and I am sure will be most grateful. When the position of Deputy Minister is discussed, as it will be in the New Year, I know that it will be your name that will be at the top of his list. A good comrade such as you will not be forgotten . . ."

She laughed once more. Disarming. The threat hidden in scattered petals.

". . . and of course, I take it for granted that the Minister can rely completely on your total discretion regarding the issue that we have discussed?"

"Of course Lingling, of course."

"Then we have an understanding. Good. Please send my good wishes to your wife and you must come to dinner when the Minister is more himself."

"Thank you, we would like that very much. And please send the Minister our good thoughts for his full recovery. And our good health to you to, Lingling. How are you feeling, not overdoing it I hope?"

For the first time she sat, her hand crossing ivory silk to the slight swell of her stomach.

"Life, it is a wonderful thing. Sacred. To have a new life beating inside of you . . . I cannot find the words to really describe it . . ."

Life. Death. She had the rare ability to separate their intrinsic cycle. Owning one, discarding the other.

". . . thank you for your wishes, Comrade Zhang, and I can assure you that I intend to take it very easy indeed."

She waited for a few minutes after Chunqiao's call before pressing the two buttons; the telephone number programmed into the unit's memory. Drinking in the view, the moonlight fanning through the branches of the trees and spilling across the garden. The line connected, ringing just three times before it was picked up. To be answered so quickly, he could not have been asleep. Her words, few. To the point. No niceties. And then the call was over. Life. Death. Separate issues, but both breached within minutes of each other. The words of each still warm in her mouth. It was 4:00am. She would go back to bed now, sleeping to as late as she pleased. She intended to take it very easy. Her hand passed over her stomach. Life, it was a fragile weave that needed to be nurtured.

★

He placed the receiver gently back on its cradle and walked out onto the balcony. A rip at the base of the sky where the clouds ate into it; as red as bull's blood. The glow beginning to

299

tinge the surface of the lake. Texture pulling from the darkness. Detail coming into focus. His hand moving over the close crop of hair, the air refreshingly cold against his skull. Eyes moving to the fire, the pit of white-grey ash. Embers winking orange. And the smell . . . there was nothing quite like the smell of a fire in the morning's early hours. Some basic quality about it that travelled down the millennia and which sat at the primeval core of all of us. He stood on the balcony for some time, Lake Taihu dancing to a pale pink wash. The colour of his secretary's knickers. Chilled by the time that he stepped back into the room. Picking up the glass of Dukang and the telephone receiver . . . knowing by heart the number that he would dial. A man's voice at the other end of the line, instantly alert.

"It's Liping. I have another job for you."

★

Hot steel and horns, the traffic fixed motionless in exhaust fumes. Changle Lu closed where it joined Fumin Lu. Between the bumpers and the shimmer of heat from radiators, glimpses of blue print on shiny white tape. Police incident tape strung out across the intersection.

"Fuck it . . . Zhiyuan!"

The Senior Investigator threw open the car door, dodging between the cars under the tape. The Shiqu Chairman's room fifty metres away; between it and Piao, at least six patrol cars across the road, over the kerb and straddling the pavements. Some with headlights on. Blue lights lazily revolving. A scattering of PSB officers, photocopied from the same original. Olive green and brass. Peaks over eyes. China brands in the corners of their mouths; old jokes pissed from the opposite corners of their mouths. Piao running between them, his badge held high above his head, the Big Man already twenty metres behind. His cheeks, red balloons about to burst.

On the stairs the smell of blood, rust and honey, all mixed up with the aromas of cooking. Detective Yun was leaving the room. He looked pale, his acne bled to the colour of paper.

"Senior Investigator Piao. I have been trying to see you for

300

many days now. Your cases, Chief Liping would like me to familiarise myself with them."

"Zhiyuan, what's happened?"

"Are you alright, you look terrible?"

The Senior Investigator pushed past, Yun reeling against the door.

"Don't go in there, it is a terrible mess and this is my investigation. I said that it is my . . ."

"Fuck your investigation."

Nothing in the room had been touched. A brandy bottle, top unscrewed. Half glasses beside the bed on the table. Orange piss in a chamberpot, pushed half under the bed. It was dark, the curtains were still closed, the room lit only in fierce bursts of bluey-white. A Bureau photographer in a dance of half bends and stoops. A high pitched whine as the flash gun re-charged . . . a thump, a jolt as it discharged. Skin-tones blasted to the hue of ice. A spray of arterial blood across the hearth, the fireplace, over the mantelpiece . . . spotting the gallery of photographs. And against a bed leg, the back of Zhiyuan's skull.

The Shiqu Chairman lay in the centre of the room, on his back. A pool of blood, around what was left of his head . . . still soaking into the carpet. Glistening as each flash discharged. So much blood, so impossibly much. The two entry holes, an inch apart, in the centre of Zhiyuan's forehead . . . re-defined. Neat, incredibly neat. 7.65mm . . . type 64 rounds, rimless. Standard security issue. Their exits, wildly ragged, obscene. The rear of the cranium, a hole that Piao could have plunged both of his fists into. But it was the Shiqu Chairman's nose that held the attention in pincers. It wasn't there. It was missing. In its place, a rude black crater. Edges neat. A solid river of dried blood tethered from it in a deep flow across the lips, mouth, chin. A thick stripe of life flowed away, pooling in the shallow of the neck and across the chest in a ruddy reservoir.

"They've cut his fucking nose off. Shit Boss, why would they do that? Why the fuck would they do that."

Piao shook his head. So many questions, so few answers. A lump of bile in his throat the size of a mooncake. The photographer closed in . . . a flash thumped into the Shiqu Chairman's face. The Senior Investigator falling to one knee, palm across the twin lenses, pushing the camera aside.

"I need a torch, has anyone got a torch?"

An officer stepped smartly forward. Piao took the rubber sheathed torch and handed it to the Big Man.

"Hold it steady."

From an inside pocket he took a pair of tweezers, inserting them into Zhiyuan's mouth. Stainless steel rattling against enamel. Blood across his tongue . . . his teeth pink with it. The passage of the mouth stopped with blackness, solid. Piao poking his tweezers at it; the mass retreating further into the Shiqu Chairman's throat until he was able to, with a thrust, half impale it, half pinch it. Drawing it out slowly, carefully. Black becoming brown, becoming an angry butcher's shop red in the bright cut of the torches beam.

"Shit. What the fuck's that, Boss?"

Piao feeling as if barbed wire had been wound tightly around his stomach, around his heart. The nausea tearing at the back of his throat and across his forehead and chest, a sweat as cold as ice water.

"Get me a bag Yaobang."

"But what is it?"

"Just get me a fucking bag . . ."

Piao turned his head to look directly into the Big Man's eyes, voice lowered. The shock etched into his stare and instantly contagious.

". . . it's his nose. It's his fucking nose."

He dropped it into the bag and sealed it. The terror peaking and now coming down. Adrenaline spent . . . its loose change, a chill filling his chest, spreading across his body in a glacial fever. The Senior Investigator held the bag up to the light; blood smeared over the inside of the polythene in a grotesque mimic of a stained glass window. Another still to be added to the loop of film that would replay through the desolation of his nights. Reluctantly he placed the bag in his pocket.

"I think that you can take it that we have been warned."

The bar was chrome and glass. You ordered a drink, drank it, paid for it, moved on. No risk of getting comfortable. The beer was chilled, Thai beer, Tiger. As bitter as tears. The waitress' smile, chillier.

"This is it then Boss, you're dumping the case . . ."

His eyes avoiding Piao's, thinking that he knew what they said, but still not wanting to admit it.

". . . you said we've been warned."

The Senior Investigator stared across Yaobang's shoulder, out of the window. Everywhere feeling uncomfortable. Nowhere was home.

"They were giving me a message. Pulling Zhiyuan's nose out of his mouth made me hear it more clearly."

"So that's fucking it?"

The Senior Investigator finished his beer, catching the waitress' attention, within seconds, another bottle of Tiger placed next to his elbow.

"The eight from the river. The student . . ."

He tipped half of the Tiger into the Big Man's glass.

". . . Pan and my cousin, Cheng. Do you really think that I could dump the case?"

He shook his head.

"I was just saying that we had been warned. Nothing else. To be warned is to be told that you are close and getting closer. It is a good sign."

Across his teeth, the beer as cold as a corpse.

"Nobody saw us at Liping's zhau-dai-suo. I don't know how they found out about Zhiyuan, but I do know that if they knew about me, then I to, would be in the city morgue."

"But where the fuck do we go now?"

Piao looked into the beer, his own reflection distorted. Reaching to his pocket, pulling out a small, well thumbed book.

"We get some tests done on this, it's a telephone call log book from Zhiyuan's room. A page is missing, ripped out. Forensic might be able to pick out some details from the indentations on the following page. Beside that, I don't know . . ."

He hadn't eaten; the alcohol setting upon him with claws of velvet.

". . . I suppose we try to piece together the pieces that won't be pieced. Nothing makes sense at the moment, we must live with the chaos of not knowing so many things."

"Fucking Liping . . ."

Yaobang spat on the floor. Thick. White.

". . . the bastard's behind it all, Boss. The smuggling, the bodies in the river . . . the whole fucking lot, I know it. We should march into his office, now. Grab him by the balls and yank him all the way to Beijing to face the Politburo . . ."

He threw the glass of Tiger into his mouth.

". . . he's a fucking murderer. It's down to him that Pan's dead."

Looking deep into Piao's eyes.

". . . I want him screwed, Boss, you understand that, don't you?"

He could understand that, but he could understand other things also.

"Walk into Liping's office now and within ten hours they would be fishing us out of the Huangpu and putting our noses into tiny plastic bags. You know that, don't you?"

The Big Man nodded, a reluctance running through it like a vein through marble.

"I know, I fucking know Boss. It's just that it's so difficult. I miss Pan. I never thought I'd ever say it about the skinny little wanker, but I miss him."

Piao said nothing. It was a time to be silent, to drink beer. Words only coming when, his arm around the Big Man's shoulder, they had left the bar and the night air had hit him.

"We live with chaos and pray to the ancestors for some luck . . . just a little bit of luck."

★

A day off . . . but you're never quite off duty. Trying your best to trick yourself. Doing the ordinary things that others do, but in extraordinary ways. Sleeping, eating, shopping, walking, talking. But all of the time the case in the background.

Everywhere, and in everything. A jolt of fear every time a black Shanghai Sedan passes by. Tracking it. Expecting the car to mount the kerb, come at you across the cracked paving stones.

A day off.

★

Liping was already waiting for him.

"A holiday does not seem to agree with you Senior Investigator?"

"My mind was preoccupied with the Huangpu River case. I thought that I might as well be in here working at it."

Speaking the words, but all of the time, remembering . . . the smoke drifting over the wall and low across the lake water.

"A complaint from Detective Yun. You're interfering in his case, the homicide of Comrade Zhiyuan. You have an interest in the case?"

The Chief adjusted his jacket, pulling it taut. Eyes cast down.

"Haven't we all got an interest in the investigation, Comrade Officer Liping? Comrade Zhiyuan was an honoured member of the Party and was killed, apparently, for no reason and in an extremely gruesome manner."

"I know how he was murdered, Detective Yun has submitted his report to me. What is your interest in this case, Senior Investigator?"

Impatience tingeing his words.

"I have no particular interest in the case. I was just passing, Comrade Officer, and was able to offer Detective Yun my assistance."

"The death of Comrade Zhiyuan has complications attached to it. For you, Senior Investigator. For you . . ."

His lips clamped together, puckering, like a paper cut.

". . . the formal charges against you as lodged by Comrade Zhiyuan with the Danwei, these are to be dropped. He was the primary witness in the case. No Shiqu Chairman. No charges . . ."

The formal charges swept away. The danwei's hearing swept away. His career saved and all from one man's blood. But there would be more words . . . that was life. That was Liping.

". . . you will hand me your documents of authority. Your pistol. With immediate effect you will cease all of your duties. You will assure a swift handover of all of your current investigations . . ."

Out of the window, down the corridor, Piao could see Yun walking to his office. His acne blazing. His shoes dirty.

". . . Detective Yun will immediately take full responsibility for all of your cases. All files, material evidence, anything that relates to these investigations will be returned. You will not enter the kung an chu unless invited. And Piao, I assure you, you will be invited . . ."

Each word delivered as a hook, barb deep.

". . . your privileges as a Senior Investigator with the Public Security Bureau are withdrawn. You will assume the position of an ordinary citizen of the People's Republic of China. You will not travel beyond the city limits. Your car, Senior Investigator Piao, keep it. Where is there to run? Where is there to hide? The Street Committees will be my eyes. The processes of the danwei, the motivations of the Party and its servants, my fingers. Freedom within a bottle, Sun Piao. Freedom within a bottle. Enjoy it while you can . . ."

Yun stood at the door, smelling of mothballs and shit.

". . . Detective Yun will take detailed statements from you."

"I do not understand what is happening Comrade Officer Liping? If the danwei's hearing has been halted and the formal charges are not to stand, what is this all about?"

Chief Liping moved from the window. Monochrome melting into colour.

"You do not know what this is about, and you, a Senior Investigator?"

He smiled.

"This is about you being suspended from duty. This is about you needing a very solid and fully sustainable alibi for where you were and what you were doing on the night before last. This is about you being the prime suspect in the murder of our esteemed Shiqu Chairman, Comrade Zhiyuan."

Chapter 28

Six ten by eight inch prints . . . black and white.
One A4 typewritten sheet.
One brief, hand-written note.
They'd arrived in a thick woven manila envelope . . .

PROPERTY OF THE UNITED STATES OF AMERICA.
HIGHLY CONFIDENTIAL.

. . . the manila envelope in a cracked leather Diplomatic Pouch. Barbara popped the seal, removing the material. Fanning it across the coffee table. Averting her eyes from the courier, McMurta. He looked anxious, edgy. In turn, she picked up each print. The images, mosaic grained. Definitions in grey. Photos taken in low light with an exotically high ASA film. The apartment on Dong Hua Men Street . . . a few blocks east of the Forbidden City, Beijing. Other images, their lines as sharp as honed razors. High definition. Photos taken through a fine fibre-optic enderscope. The Xinqiao Hotel on Dongjiaominlu. A fine gauge hole drilled through the picture rail of room number 92 to the suite next door.

"Oh comrade."

A whisper. Perfumed breath across her nails. As she read the type. As her gaze returned to the photographs.

"Oh comrade."

Gathering up the material, slipping it back into the envelope. The type, the name on the bottom of the page and on the note, Carmichael . . . eclipsed in a manila shadow. The envelope placed back into the diplomatic pouch. He'd done well. Tough talking. Private arrangements. Shit and honey. Very well. She stood, handing McMurta the pouch.

"Pass a message on through your channels. Tell Carmichael

that he did well. Tell him that we'll talk. He'll know what that means."

Sure he'd know what that meant. And as McMurta left.

"Tell him not to worry, that we'll talk sooner than he thinks."

He left. An all-encompassing reek of tabac, slowly withdrawing its fingers. Barbara sat at the desk, finding the heavy cut glass of scotch in her hand. Across the mahogany grain of the coffee table, Bobby's postcards . . . read, re-read.

Yeah, tell him that he did real well . . .

Not reading them again. Going to bed. Sleeping. Dreaming. Dreaming of six ten by eight inch prints, with a comrade drowning in a wave of broken monochrome reticulation.

Chapter 29

"You look tired."

You look beautiful . . . thinking it, but not daring to say it.

"It is me who is the detective. How did you know where I live?"

Barbara winked.

"An American government official in China is not without influence Senior Investigator Piao. Now are you going to invite me in or do you really want me to cook this meal on the doorstep?"

She held out two shopping bags from the Jing Jiang's supermarket, neat, crisp, glossy and sharp cornered. Inside, a series of packages too perfect to want to open. He took the bags, hands brushing . . . aching to take each of the tips of her fingers, one by one, into his mouth.

"I never refuse a meal. Come in, I will try to find us two clean plates."

She stepped over the mosaic of letters and followed Piao into the kitchen. A room to inspire nightmares.

"I can see that you don't believe in wasting time over housework."

"Housework?"

"Yes, housework. Cleaning. Tidying up. Washing plates."

She handed Piao a dirty dish, grease on her fingers. Eyes searching for a tea towel that didn't exist.

"Housework, yes, now I understand housework."

He smiled, strategically placing the dish back into the sink that was piled precariously high.

"I am sorry. The mess. At my job I am very ordered. Every minute, every day. At home I have no order at all."

"I did notice."

She took his hand and pulled him to the sink.

"You wash, I'll prepare the food. If I can find a space."

Barbara cleared the table of empty bottles of Tsingtao, opened mail, unopened mail, reports, a half eaten mooncake. Unpacking vegetables from one of the bags . . . peppers, baby sweet corn, water chestnuts, chillies, cabbage, mushrooms, bamboo shoots. To cook for a Chinese, Chinese food. She was taking a risk. Coming here was a risk. Better to have cooked him a steak. Better not to have come here at all. To leave without telling him.

Again, the question that he had ignored earlier.

"You look tired."

His face away from her. The water from the hot tap almost drowning out the words of his answer. The steam across the window, blistering into tears. Never ask for anything; never show anything. So hard to change the scripts that our lives are built upon.

"I am being investigated. A Senior Investigator. Investigated."

Her knife slicing through the mushrooms. The hint of resistance and then the blade moving through the skin, the flesh . . . unobstructed.

"What for?"

"The tong zhi who raised charges against me, he was murdered. I am considered to be the main suspect."

Reaching for a red pepper. The knife inserted into its body, cutting around the green cap of its umbilical cord. Cutting away its base. Slicing its torso into equal-sized matchsticks. Juice . . . watery red, staining the chopping board.

"That's ridiculous. They're nuts. Once you give them your statement, where you were, what you were doing, they'll see for themselves just how stupid it is."

"You make it sound without complications. Americans do this. It is not like that, not in China. Not for me, not now."

Layer after layer . . . dark green falling, lighter . . . lighter. Steel edge moving through the heart of the cabbage.

"But it is uncomplicated. There was a murder. You were somewhere else. You didn't do it. See. Uncomplicated?"

Uncomplicated, the word sounded good. Something to crave for. Something that he had never known. A breath heaving, catching across his chest. Like when you were a child, the breath before you sobbed, whilst struggling to hold it all back. Piao turned both taps fully on. Torrents of ice cold and boiling hot water meeting on stained enamel. A shifting gate of steam moving upwards against his face.

"For them it is uncomplicated. I will be their murderer. I will have killed the comrade who could have dug a hole for them. They will be my executioners, another who could have dug a hole for them. They will have slit two chickens' throats with one slash of the knife."

He turned the taps off. Only the sound of her chopping the cabbage filling the room. She hadn't heard. Perhaps she wasn't supposed to.

"When you've finished the washing-up you can peel these onions," she said.

The Senior Investigator turned, foam across his forearms, the hairs swept into mimics of the traces that waves leave upon the wet sand of a beach.

"All of them, do we need so many?"

Barbara looked up, mischief plaited into her smile.

"No, but I just like to see a grown man cry."

⋆

Barbara's finger traced the outline of the face in the photograph. A heart shaped trail of hard colour through the dust. The face beautifully austere . . . a jigsaw of perfect features held in perfect unison. Suddenly feeling that her own reflected looks were the photograph's negative.

"Your wife?"

"My wife. Lingling."

Pulling her toward him. Pressing her against the wall. Fast, violently, as if anything less powerful would lose her. Let her slip away. Barbara's breath, five spice and lemon grass. Pepper sauce on her lips. Silk, cotton, her clothes . . . still warm, across the floor. Again, entering her to secret words. Breath on his shoulder, his neck. A tattered perfumed warmth. Earlobes pinched between teeth. Chest to chest. Sweat to sweat. The second time had been even better. He'd thought about it,

312

planned how he would touch her, rob her body of its treasures. How he would regain the territories that she had claimed on the first occasion that they had made love. She kissed him, as if it were a first kiss, a last kiss. Giving everything. With Lingling it had been so different, as if she was relenting, giving into something that was a part of a contract. Hard ink on hard paper.

"What you wrote about going back to America. I know that it looks impossible that we will find the killer of your child . . ."

His mouth against her neck, moving up to brush the outline of her jaw. The sweet fruit of her earlobes.

". . . but we will find out who was responsible. It is my promise to you."

Barbara's finger across his lips. A dam on the trickle of words. A sudden sense that they would be the last that he would ever speak to her. The last that they would ever share.

"Don't make promises that you can't keep Sun. They've got this case screwed up tight and both of us with it. Bobby's killer will never be found. We both know that."

Removing her finger. Replacing it briefly, too briefly, with her lips. But their taste had changed. Salt and airport lounge coffee. She had already said goodbye.

"I'm leaving for New York on Saturday with Charles Haven."

Chapter 30

. . . just a little luck.

Suspension . . . the shit on the sole of the shoe. The sandwich without the filling. Living as if his oxygen was slowly being turned off, starved. The strings that held him up, snipped one by one . . . collapsing. And then the shadow of Liping slowly showing itself in a campaign of victimisation. Spite. Piao, a Senior Investigator one day . . . the next being shaken down in the long by a group of PSB officers. Eyes hiding in the shadows of their peaked caps. Curses, jokes . . . on the tails of their bad breath. The shake downs soon becoming a daily occurrence every time that he left the flat. And then there were the unmarked cars following him. Faces that he didn't know. Eyes squinting under heavy brows. And then the litter, the shit . . . stuffed through his letterbox. The telephone ringing, day and night . . . all hours. Answering it to no reply. Or to the acidic chanting name calling,

Half breed . . . tell us stories of your wife.

Small cocks can only hold onto women for a short time.

before the telephone was slammed down. And then the silence. Silence like he had never known before. As if buried under a deep, deep fall of snow. And then the regular searches of the flat, day or night. The knock, harsh and invasive. Men in identically cheap linen suits. Concertina trousered. Hands that had been fiddling with their cocks minutes before, touching his belongings. Tipping his clothes onto the floor. Pulling pictures from frames. Papers from files. But through it all, they never finding what he didn't want them to find. They never would, never could. And in all of it . . . the last laugh. And then spaces, gaps, the uncertain, tricky freedoms that living in a bottle fool you with. Suddenly, no unmarked cars. No shake downs. No watching eyes. As if the world had turned a corner and had left you behind standing on the kerb. Left you, paranoid about feeling paranoid. A sudden sense of freedom. Freedom. But picked into its rich material, a constant sense of nowhere to run. Nowhere to hide.

★

The courier would not be questioned. No ordinary Bureau courier. No uniform. No obvious I.D. No words. Everything about him saying . . . 'don't even fucking bother asking.' Just the knock on the door. The parcel. The measured retreat back down the stairs.

Piao pushed the dirty plates to the far end of the table. The packaging of the parcel showing no indications of its origins . . . its contents, every indication. Ten spools of reel to reel audio tape. Dated, plus a coding of numbers from an anonymous government department at its centre. And under the word SUBJECT in thick black marker pen, a name . . .

YE YANG

It felt extreme, melodramatic, but he checked the telephone, the room, for listening devices before making the call. The flat had a smell, an atmosphere . . . a delicate balance of nuances that without being fully aware of he sensed and knew intimately. He would know if they had been into the flat, however careful they had been. But why take a risk? A risk is only worth taking when it was so calculated that there was no risk left within it.

"Boss, I've been trying to see you, but it's difficult. I managed to get my hands on a carton of Panda Brand. Don't ask any questions . . ."

A pause. An electronic flutter down the vertebra of the silence.

". . . that bastard Yun has been grilling me like a fucking lump of pork for two days, so I've not had a chance to get to you. Also, I'm being followed. I go for a shit, they go for a shit. I fart, they fucking fart . . ."

Yaobang lowered his voice, a hand shielding the mouthpiece.

". . . he's out to get you, Boss. The word is that it's worth a
promotion to him. The Chief and Yun are as close as two
turds in a toilet."

Piao closing his eyes for an instant. Pushing the panic down
from his head, his chest, his stomach. His legs aching with the
cost.

"The alibi?"

"Yun didn't like it, but I think he's swallowed it. All that he
said when I told him that you were with me at my house with
my two cousins that night playing mah-jongg was, 'why
don't I ever get invited?' The wanker."

A laugh as thick as banana toffee. Its freedom making Piao
feel envious.

"I need a reel to reel and a set of headphones."

"Sure Boss. I won't get them from the kung an chu, but my
neighbour will help, I'll use his. And I'll bring up the Panda
Brand. Why do you need the equipment?"

The telephone receiver slipping toward the cradle. Yaobang
only picking up the words as a whisper before the line
died.

"Just a little luck."

★

Piao let the smoke drift from his lips. Pouring the last of the
Tsingtao, a glance at the four empty bottles that the Big Man
had left behind. And two more packs of Panda Brand remaining . . . they would sweeten the hours, tame the boredom. He
put on the headphones. Laced the tape. Flicked the switch.
Adjusting the volume knob. The reels revolving, one slower
than the other. Mud coloured tape across the quicksilver of
the heads. And he was in the suite at the Heping . . . the Hotel
of Peace. August 11th 09:30am . . . a sharp metallic click as
the line connected. The UXT wire-tap triggered live. Ye
Yang, a girl far from home telephoning her family. The Senior
Investigator at first listening to everything. Every call, every
movement in the suite as the tape switched automatically

from wire-tap to the UHF transmitters housed behind the electrical points in two of the rooms. Everything. Ye Yang . . . showering, shitting, singing. He was there, right now, a part of the dead girl's past. Beside her as she soaped her back, flushed the toilet. He lit a cigarette and then another, as her routine was laid bare, cut to the bone. Developing a sense, after awhile, of when to fast forward, when to dwell. A sense of when to allow your mind to wander and when to focus. Listening in on her life. An electronic rape . . . with his finger on the pause button.

At 2:45 he switched the tape off and removed the head-phones. Sweat orbiting his ears in sticky bands. For the first time in five hours, aware of the traffic noise. Music from next door. An argument in the street below. All were normal, but now seemed new and louder. He walked to the Park of the People. Groups of fat girls practising their dance for the New Year's celebrations. Blue knickers peeping from red leotards. Damp patches under armpits. Smiles stamped onto lips claw-ing for breath. He ate ice cream and drank tea . . . a constant and nervous desire to get back to the tapes. The rest of the afternoon and evening, a blur of wearying voices and fast forwarded silences. Vast gaps in the tape . . . blank days that corresponded with the periods that Ye Yang was out of the country on business.

Night came, headlights moving across the flat's far wall. A pack of Panda Brand finished. The ashtray, overflowing. He'd burnt holes in the cigarette carton with each, before stubbing them out. The rough shape of a star . . . a five pointed star.

★

"Hi, how are you baby? I'm coming in on the five-thirty plane from Xianyang. Can you pick me up, I'm shattered?"

October 24th 1:35pm. . . . for the first time, Bobby's voice. Bubble gum and red Xian dust. Piao listened on for another hour; sleep weighted across his eyelids. At midnight, sleeping for two and a half hours. Reviving himself with a basin of ice cold water. Holding his face below the surface until his lungs were fire . . . his nose, cheeks, eyelids, numb with cold.

317

Turning on the machine, the tape slowly unloading its cargo from one spool to the other. Call after call . . . they never stopped speaking now that Bobby was back in Shanghai, back at Fudan. But always a care about what they said. Bobby never talking about his work. Ye Yang never talking about her work. Did they know that they were being taped? Had they been briefed about how to deal with it?

Nothing on the tapes that would get them a parking ticket. Nothing on the tapes that deserved death.

★

The morning sun was luke warm. Looking like a peach that had been squashed by a lorry tyre in the centre of the road, it spread across the sky in an orangey-yellow mash. Piao washed and changed his underwear and shirt. Pulling a jacket across his chest . . . a new cough, unfamiliar in his repertoire of many, tugging at his lungs. A cold, too many cigarettes? Whatever it was, the air made it worse. He stopped at a noodle shop, stumbling through breakfast . . . a bowl of rice soup, pickled vegetables, some potato noodles. Still feeling cold, his arms folded across his chest for warmth as he walked around the park opposite. Not enjoying the exercise, but doing it because he thought that he should. Under the trees old people were practising *tai ji quan* exercises. Slow measured movements. Septuagenarian alley cats stalking prey. He turned for home, aching. Buying a brace of Tsingtao on the way.

Through the hours, the measured orbits of the spools, through the taped conversations and telephone calls . . . a vocabulary emerging. Piao noting it down amongst the doodles and cigarette ash. Pulling the headphones off, angry with himself as he noticed the time. Eight hours without a break. The wall of electronically trapped words only breached by the flow of tea; his tongue coated in tannin, as sour as Sundays without children. He washed his face, returning to the table, eating a stale mooncake. Flakes, sugar brown, falling onto his notebook, across the words . . . 'the usual place'. References to the . . . 'gift being ready.' 'The gift can now he picked up.'

'The money for the groceries has arrived.' 'The van will arrive at the shop today for the groceries.'

Early December, and a flurry of such calls between Ye Yang and Bobby. A third American voice also taped . . . Heywood? Telephoning to confirm . . . 'that the gifts have been repaired. It took longer than anticipated.' And to, 'tell the owner that they will be sent within the next two days.' Constant references to the van delivering, the van picking up. Qingde . . . the courier? The Senior Investigator brushed his hand over the notebook, flakes of mooncake in a cascade to the floor. The conversations taken separately, as a string of sometimes just a few words, sounding natural and innocent enough. When put in context, placed together with a couple of dozen other such calls over a period of just a few weeks . . . taking on a pattern. A totally new feel. Piao now seeing them for what they were, clumsy and unsophisticated codes. Polished veneer over rotting timber.

★

"Ma . . . Happy Christmas."

Barbara's voice riding in the storm of a bad line in response. Talking about turkeys, presents, snow. Even in the fury of the electronic blitz, Piao recognising the closeness of Barbara's tears as each sentence tailed off. Another flurry of calls in early January, again in the middle of the month. More gifts ready. More groceries to be picked up and delivered.

Tape whipping against steel. The feed spool empty, the take-up spool spilling spirals of tape across the tabletop. Piao loaded the last spool and ran it . . . ears full of words, mouth full of mooncake. A different tape. A different atmosphere. Too different. Checking the label. A gap between the start of the new tape and the end of the last tape of two weeks.

Fuck it . . . games.

He was being jerked along, a dog on a lead. Spoon fed hours of tape that said nothing that he didn't know. And where there might be new material, important material . . . fucking gaps. Piao ripped the headphones off and threw them across the table. Grabbing a jacket and a pack of Panda Brand as he slammed the front door shut.

★

A wooden floored open air pavilion and dance floor had been erected in the heart of the Park of the People. A jazz band of six musicians, their average age sixty-eight, playing . . . 'When the Saints Go Marching In.' Strings of light bulbs. Red, white, blue, yellow, hanging in the breeze above them. And with it, the smell of beer and mothballs. A thick collar of onlookers crowded around the floor watching the dancers. The weaves, feints, sweeps and dips of the ballroom. Heads swivelling sharply, snapped back on long necks. Hands held high in steeples of rigid fingers. Piao bought a beer and watched the sharp profiles cut shadows from the pools of coloured light. Dancing . . . everything about it fascinating him. He was a child of the Cultural Revolution, dancing had been forbidden.

"Senior Investigator Piao, it is a surprise to see you. I did not imagine you to be interested in ballroom dancing. Let me introduce you to my wife. Da, this is an ex-colleague . . ."

He halted for a split-second, his acne, blue cratered in the lighting.

'. . . this is a colleague of mine, Senior Investigator Piao."

The woman was as pretty as a pressed duck. Her head seeming to balance on the platter of a deeply frilled polyester collar. She held out her hand, Piao took it politely and shook it; only at this point that he recognised the man who had performed the introductions. The man in the black suit, white frilly shirt topped off by an extravagant red bow tie. Detective Yun . . . the pucker face smoothed and ironed by the fades of coloured lighting.

"My sister-in-law does not have a partner Piao. It would be very welcome if you could take her for the next dance."

A small woman stepped forward, a puffball of baby pink chiffon. A smile cutting her face in two . . . a melon slice of teeth too white to be real. Panic gripped the Senior Investigator's chest with sharp talons.

320

"But I don't dance."

"Nonsense, Piao, nonsense. Lili will show you how."

She wrenched the Senior Investigator onto the dance floor; only just enough time to drop his beer bottle onto a table. The next few minutes, a kaleidoscope of trodden toes, awkward hands, hurried instructions, and the odour of armpits and five Yuan perfume.

"You are doing very well, Senior Investigator. Very, very well indeed."

Yun at his side, snapping, twisting his wife to the left. Her frilled collar lifting across her face in the breeze. Twirling around the Senior Investigator and his partner in an exhibition of intricate steps. A fugue of sweeps and dips.

"Da and I enter competitions when work allows . . ."

Another sweep past Piao, orbiting to the other side.

". . . we dream of one day winning an international competition."

Yun smiled, it looking like a black slit in a hessian sack.

"Move to the left, the left," the puffball muttered, jamming her foot against Piao's and wrestling him into a new tack. Yun at his shoulder, leaning across to make more importance of what he had to say.

"See, see. You are getting the hang of it. Wait till the next song, a foxtrot, a little faster. It should suit you . . ."

Closer still, almost whispering.

". . . she's a wonderful dancer, isn't she? A good cook too. And not a boyfriend on the horizon."

He winked at the Senior Investigator. Piao feeling his stomach fall to his clumsy feet. Moving his hand to a less sweaty position on the puffball's nylon strapped waist. Hearing himself say aloud . . .

"I'm not surprised."

But the words lost as the band struck up with an up-tempo arrangement of . . . 'New York, New York.'

★

The positioning of Yun's table was unfortunate, directly under

321

a strand of crimson red bulbs. The detectives face looking as if his acne had exploded in unison.

"I need to interview you," he confided to Piao.

"I had Yaobang in yesterday and the day before. He provided a very sound alibi for you. Very sound. Too sound. I totally believe it, of course, but Chief Liping . . ."

Yun shook his head and loosened his bow tie, stroking the velvet.

". . . beautiful material. Made in England you know. Quality, sheer quality."

"Chief Liping," Piao reminded.

"Yes, yes the Chief. Sometimes not the most understanding of men. Sometimes not the most trusting of men, as you know. He believes that Yaobang is covering for you. He has insisted that his cousins be brought in and questioned. Also questions put to you and Yaobang's Neighbourhood Committees. 'Someone's prying eyes will know if you were in or you were out', he says. 'Someone's listening ears will be able to say if you were at Yaobang's home that night'. No, no he is not a very trusting man at all . . ."

Yun held the beer bottle high, draining every last drop from it.

". . . to be so untrusting must be a terrible thing."

Piao nodded as he stood.

"I must go, it's getting late."

"Already, Senior Investigator? But the band will be performing a selection of songs from South America after the break. It is the highlight of the evening. The cha-cha-cha, the tango. Lili is marvellous when it comes to the tango . . ."

The puffball giggled and looked shyly away. Yun leaning across the table, hand half covering his mouth.

". . . Lili and the tango, it is hotter than chilli sauce in August."

Nylon, rudely pink chiffon and the tango . . . it was not a combination that had ever fired his fantasies of unbridled passion. Piao said his good-byes. As he passed her chair the puffball pressed her address, scribbled onto a scrap of paper, into his hand. It took the Senior Investigator until halfway home to find a rubbish bin. Dropping litter on the street could get you a very hefty fine.

★

Another day.   Another beer.   Another tape.

"Left before you were awake. The traffic was jammed right up to Fudan's gates. I've been running late all morning. There's ten minutes before my meeting with Lazarus and the Principal. Thought I'd phone quickly just to tell you that I love you."

Ye Yang, stretching, yawning. Piao could imagine her as the tape unwound, sable hair against her cheek. Dark nipples riding over the horizon of the silky peach bedding. Lips against the telephone receiver in a sleepy kiss.

"Love you too," she whispered.

Piao retreated to the bathroom. The water in the hand basin, as cold as ice. 'Love you too.' Her words creating within him a pain as hot as molten steel. Drying his face. The fever tempered, tamed. He opened a beer. Little else on the tape, except for background noise . . . a shower. And Shanghai Radio playing . . . a phone-in, 'Citizens & Society.' Calls of complaint to Cheng Xi Yuan, Executive Vice-President of the Shanghai Post & Telegraph Administration.

> CALLER – 'My telephone is terrible, it doesn't work well.'
> CHENG – 'We know that there are problems and are doing our best to rectify them.'
> CALLER – 'What?'
> CHENG – 'I said that we know that . . .'
> CALLER – 'I can't hear you on this terrible phone, there's something wrong with it!'

Piao fast-forwarded, listening into the faint race of highly accelerated sound. An instinct developed of when to pause the onrush. Finding himself eavesdropping in on a one-sided conversation, braced with gaps and scaffoldings of deep

323

silence. Ye Yang on the telephone . . . the voice hers. The silences the caller's . . . no indication of who it was. He fast reversed the tape, picking up the start of the call; a discreet electronic double click, as it switched from UHF room bugs to the UXT wire-tap. The call was pre-arranged, it would have had to have been. Ye Yang picking up the telephone and instantly knowing who it was who was calling. But no names said. Her voice veined with nerves. Nothing from the caller. Silence. The girl launching into a diatribe. The curtains of her anger flung back. Words, so rehearsed . . . giving an instant sense that she had talked this call through a thousand times. In the shower. In the elevator. In her sleep, and still had not perfected it. Overstretching for each word. And nothing but coldness coming from the other end of the line. An emotion spreading from Ye Yang that Piao had been unable to label, until now. That of the small fish for the very first time, seeing just how wide the big fish can open its jaws. Terrified. Ye Yang was out of her depth, and terrified.

"I know that we had a deal, but we took special risks to get these gifts for you. Do you know what would happen if we got caught?"

SILENCE.

"But why should you care."

SILENCE.

"The price has gone up. It's no good threatening us. We have them, you want them. Triple the price and they are yours. That's business. We have taken the risks."

SILENCE.

"They are perfect. I went out to the workshop myself last week to see them; better than any other example that has reached the market up to now. I guarantee that you could treble the price that we are asking."

SILENCE.

"Screw you. Say something. Have we got a deal?"

SILENCE.

"Have we?"

SILENCE.

The telephone receiver being put down by the caller, then

Ye Yang. Switch back from wire-tap to room bugs. A sound of breaking glass, smashed pottery. The diminutive Ye Yang's voice a roar through the mayhem of a tantrum.

"Fucking arsehole. Fucking, fucking arsehole."

Her last words. The remainder of the spool empty. Just a consistent spill of white noise as faint as a constant intake of breath. But Piao not hearing it, his senses already on rewind; moving back, focussing on the clear sound that had spiked the silence just before the death of the telephone call. Just before the silent caller had hung up. A dull click. Electricity arcing, earthing. Instantly knowing the sound. Fast reversing the tape . . . a dozen and a half clicks. Listening over and over again, volume turned deafeningly high. But not really needing to, just confirming. Positive that he had labelled the sound correctly from the very first time that he had heard it.

All of his adult life he'd wanted a cigarette lighter such as that. Electronic. Slim. Gold. Dunhill. A dull click . . . and the blue-white fork of electricity in the throat of the lighter the instant before the flame ignited.

A dull click.

"Fucking got you," Piao said, as he switched the tape off.

He opened his last beer and lit his last Panda Brand, not finishing either. Exhaustion, on a tide of alcohol, nicotine and exhilaration . . . laying him to waste. A sudden sense of numbness. He slept the sleep of a baby, the first time in weeks. Dreaming of pink chiffon, Dunhill cigarette lighters . . . and the Englishman, Charles Haven.

Chapter 31

Renmin Square . . . People's Square. Floats of flowers. Tableau of the Great Helmsman. Red Stars. The Long March. Tsingtao Beer. And flower petals of every colour to walk upon.

A small funfair had been erected in the centre of the confusion. Roundabouts, slides . . . the relentless hammer of a generator chewing lumps from the music playing tinnily from the loudspeakers. On the breeze, a heady cocktail; the smell of kerosene, burnt dust and overcooked food. And also on the breeze, flights of red, red petals . . . resembling cherry lips.

Piao watched as Chen and the children passed him once more on the carousel. With each revolution, their waving lessening. So many promises to take them out, so many cancellations. Each fixed revolution of the painted, chipped, horses and pandas, now easing his guilt.

He sipped the warm beer, watching as Yaobang stumbled over an electric cable, pressing his way through the crowd. Food in both hands. Snatching bites as the crowd thinned and thinking of bites as the crowd flooded around him.

"Good stuff, Boss, some American students have set up a food stall next to the float celebrating the Great Leap Forward . . ."

He raised a handful of sausage, bread, onions and grease stained paper to his mouth. The bite squeezing a thick slug of mustard from the mass and onto his fist. A plump amber tear. Its slow fall onto his tie almost defying gravity with its grace.

". . . they call them 'hot dogs'. Shit name, but they taste good. You should try one, Boss. It beats a lunch of beer and cigarettes."

Determined not to feel guilty, the Senior Investigator immediately lit up another China Brand.

"What have you got for me?"

Yaobang rubbed a hand across his chin. Ketchup on stubble.

"What have I got?"

A laugh, reigned and weary.

"What have I got? Nothing but fucking shit and more shit. Daily shakedowns by every cross-eyed officer in the Bureau. Twice yesterday. The day before, three fucking times. Tipping out every drawer, every cupboard. They even went through the rubbish bins. They won't fucking do that again in a hurry . . ."

Piao feeling the weld of anxiety settle onto the centre of his forehead. They had only to nudge occasionally and show that they were there. Remind you that you were in a goldfish bowl within a goldfish bowl . . . within a goldfish bowl. No need to get too heavy when there is nowhere to run. When there is nowhere to hide. Telephones tapped. Street Committees noting every coming, every going. Travel permits required for movement beyond the boundaries of the city.

Where is there to run. Where is there to hide.

Another laugh. Ketchup, mustard, across his teeth and lips.

". . . and Yun, the bastard, over me like a fucking rash. More questions than the spots on his face . . ."

Yaobang pulling closer, his eyes alert to everything. A whisper on onion breath.

". . . he doesn't believe me. Nobody believes me, or you."

The carousel slowed, stopped. Children slipping down the sides of painted horses, into parent's arms. New passengers climbing aboard. The carousel labouring into a lazy revolution. Horses . . . rising, falling. Music . . . tinny, distortingly loud. Building up to speed in a wavering, undulating tempo. The Big Man clenched his fist. As large, as white as a dinner plate.

"They're squeezing, Boss, so fucking hard that there's only pips left."

"What have you got for me?"

The fist unclenched.

"Shit, don't you ever give up, Boss?"

327

The Big Man pulled a paper from his inside pocket and handed it across the bird shit stained table.

"Forensics, by the back-door. They came through this morning, Boss. They got a telephone number from the indentations on Zhiyuan's telephone log book."

Piao's eyes chasing down the print. The number prefixed with a '39'. A Politburo number. A Beijing code following. A thump in the Senior Investigator's chest as the adrenalin punched in.

"Turns out to be a fucking heavy tong zhi, Boss, an old friend of Zhiyuan's. Zhang Chunqiao."

The Big Man leered. Bread, mustard, flesh-hued sausage, hard packed into the gaps between his teeth.

"I used another back-door to get a check on Zhang Chunqiao's line. I've an old friend who's an operator. It cost me three packs of China Brand. You're buying, Boss."

"Three packs, and you call that friendship?"

"It is when you hear what fucking shit he has dredged up . . ."

Yaobang pulled the paper from the Senior Investigator's fingers and turned it over. More grease. More mustard and ketchup. More numbers.

". . . twenty minutes after Zhiyuan called his old buddy Chunqiao, the comrade made a call of his own at 3:50am, a call that lasted for eight minutes . . ."

Piao could see the number. Another tong zhi. Another Politburo member . . . a prefix '39'.

". . . do you recognise the number, Boss?"

The Senior Investigator studied it, knowing that he should.

"No, but you thought that I might?"

"Only if marriage is for life, I guess, Boss . . ."

He bit on the hot dog, bread and paper on his tongue, both tasting the same.

". . . it's your wife's number. Minister Kang Zhu's residence in Beijing."

The world seemed to jolt. Silence pressing onto his inner ears, and in its wings the sound of rain. Across Piao's face. Across the paintwork of the Red Flag. And his last glimpse of her. An arm, a hand heavy in gold rings, slipping around her shoulders. Her face slowly turning away. Jolted once more, Yaobang's words pulling him back.

"Eleven minutes later at 4:01am a call was made from Kang Zhu's residence to this number . . ."

The Big Man stabbed at the paper.

". . . it's a Zhejiang code, a Hangzhou number . . ."

Piao already knowing what was coming, bracing himself for the wave.

". . . Taihu Lake. A zhau-dai-suo registered to the Minister, Kang Zhu. Ring any fucking bells Boss?"

Remembering the smell of the smoke from the burning bodies.

"Liping."

No more than a breath from Piao, Yaobang nodding. The Senior Investigator finished his beer. As warm as dishwater and with the taste of dishwater.

"Chunqiao. Kang Zhu. Liping. Join the dots and see what fucking picture they make . . ."

The Big Man licked his fingers clean of grease. Lips shiny.

". . . the murder of Comrade Zhiyuan. So does my telephone operator get his three packs of China Brand, eh Boss?"

"Has he got any more information for us, calls from the zhau-dai-suo?"

"More. Isn't this enough? Any calls out of the zhau-dai-suo would have been beyond the operator's area. I haven't got old friends who are operators in every fucking province."

Piao looked deeply into the empty beer glass; streams of foam, slower than clouds in a summer sky, falling back down the glass.

"No, not three packs. Four. He did well."

He clinked his beer bottle against the Big Man's.

"Done, Boss. What the fuck would we do without the back-door?"

"Be four packs of China Brand better off?"

Yaobang examined his nails.

"What is it with Liping, Boss? Shit, he's the Chief. The law."

The carousel was slowing to a standstill. Piao moved forward, small arms reaching out for him. Arms that needed him.

"Liping uses the law as a dog uses a lamppost, for support, not illumination."

The Big Man nodded; he didn't understand what it meant, but it sounded about right.

★

Wet kisses. Warm arms. Piao bit his lip . . . saying good-bye and not daring to promise to meet for the New Year. Ice creams, parades, cuddles, tears . . . better not to let them down. To make promises to children and then break them, is to mortgage your soul.

★

He was running late. Darkness bruising the rooftops. The lights from the fair ripping at the advancing night. Walking at a pace.

"The reception, you got hold of a guest list?"

The Big Man running beside him.

"There was one in the duty office for security checks, Boss."

"And?"

They were on the corner of Weihai Lu and Chengdu Lu, Piao looking for his loaned car. Yaobang for the next food stop.

"The name you gave me, it was high up on the list Boss. A very favoured foreigner . . ."

His attention drawn by the noodle shop, a handful of doors down on Chengdu; the next hour of his evening planned. Already deciding what to order. Baozi dumplings, rice noodles, steamed buns, Sanpijiu draught beer.

". . . to be favoured must be comforting, eh Boss?"

"I wouldn't know. Who invited him?"

Yaobang was already crossing Weihai Lu. The road frantic. Thunder on wheels. Shouting at the top of his voice. Piao hardly able to hear him.

330

"Liping. Liping invited him. You'd better hurry Boss. You're fucking late."

★

Red Flags. Red Banners. A dog pissing up against a wall.

The reception that he hadn't been invited to was held in the Shanghai Conservatory Arts & Crafts Institute . . . an austere and unsmiling building just off of Huaihai Lu. Pigeon shit and dressed stone. Its toes paddling in the gutters that flowed from Fumin market, just a block away.

Guests were arriving. Red Flags, pennants unfurled. Floodlights across gloss black paintwork and flaming chrome. Security, a hand resting inside their jackets. Chauffeurs running around bonnets to open doors. Piao pulled at his collar, the dress uniform that he had hurriedly changed into, a series of snags, tugs, and rubs. Joining the queue of jocular, cement chinned Russians and gnarled Politburo Members. At the front of the line, American voices. Behind them a brace of Italians . . . the men preening themselves, the women as moody as rain clouds in July. The private jets from Beijing's Capital Airport were busy tonight. Piao had walked, leaving him with the legacy of a thirst that was big enough to drown in.

The anomaly of being suspended from duty, a murder suspect, yet dressed to the hilt, a back-door invitation to the customary pre-New Year reception . . . encouraging him to light another cigarette. For no apparent reason, his eyes were drawn to the road. Through the exhaust smoke and its sting, a figure briskly walking toward the Institute from Fuxingxi Lu. Elegant as a pin. Rounding the traffic, cutting the search of headlights, Charles Haven. Already unbuttoning the black cashmere coat, pulling off soft leather gloves. A hand brushing through the steel wire of his hair. Moving past the open doors of the Red Flag limousines. A nod to the plainclothed Security Officers. The line of queuing guests ignored. A smell of expensive cologne and toothpaste as he walked by, almost brushing against Piao's shoulder. At the main door, Liping, skin weather-tanned, as brown as the mahogany of the heavy double doors, beckoning the Englishman through. Greeting him with a double-handed shake of the hands. Shepherding him inside, arm across his shoulder. A smart throng . . . languages, perfumes, cleavages, all vying for ascendancy. The doors swinging closed. A sudden stab of pain in Piao's stomach; he hadn't eaten since the morning. It took the Senior Investigator another twenty minutes of queuing before he could walk through the same doors.

★

Hazel hen, 'flying dragon' . . . served with mushrooms, *hericium erinaceus*, from the walnut forests. Duck smoked over tea leaves and camphor wood. Smoked yellow river carp. Frogs legs with grains of Huajiao spice, orange rind and spring onions. Rice flower birds preserved in spiced honey. Ravioli stuffed with crab-spawn, steam cooked and served in quinlong . . . bamboo boxes. Long tables. Starched white linen. Silver serving dishes. The banquet placed onto white bone china. Sauces of sunflower, damask, saffron . . . racing into each other. A line of waiters in dress white. Sleepy faced, shoes scuffed . . . eyeing the food hungrily. Serving with a controlled animosity.

Piao settled for carp, smoked in Suzhou. It had come a long way, the least that he could do was to eat it; his appetite left behind at the back of the queue to get into the reception. And all of the time watching the Englishman, glimpses of him between the stroll of guests. Haven not eating, just drinking still mineral water. Sips, lips hardly wet. Close enough, at times, to hear the odd word of his conversations with high cadre and Politburo members. His Mandarin, perfect . . . spoken with the distinct accent of the Shanghai-bred, but with an edge of elegance that could never be emulated by the Shanghai-bred. The Senior Investigator placed his empty plate on the buffet table, orange pepper sauce on his fingers. Sucking them clean. Drinking the remainder of his Dynasty white wine, its taste soured. Changing to a glass of the red. It was no different; as tart as limes and bad news. Moving through a glut of French diplomats. Cologne and garlic. The path to the Englishman clear. Haven alone in the desert of the centre of the hall. Piao, hearing the heels of his boots against the solid oak flooring. Hearing himself talk, and hating it . . .

"To be invited to such a reception, you must have friends in high places?"

There was a gap of a few seconds before Haven turned. Every movement smooth, as if rehearsed.

"Senior Investigator. The detective who burns his fingers. You are in good health, I hope?"

Piao raised his hands.

"Burns heal."

The Englishman didn't look at them, his attention focussed over Piao's shoulder as he looked for the next person to talk to.

"Some burns do not. I thought that you had been suspended, Senior Investigator?"

Piao moved closer, the Englishman, a complex recipe of smells. Foreign cologne, dry–cleaning fluid, peppermint breath. But beneath it all, the odour of the animal ready for its feed. A keynote, faint but high pitched . . . Civet.

"You seem to know a great deal about me, Mr Haven?"

"A reputation for brilliance and now for self-destruction, and a stubbornness to succeed well at both. Who could resist knowing about you, Senior Investigator?"

Piao wished that he had a drink, not for the alcohol, just for the glass . . . something to keep his hands busy. A mask for nerves; his fingers already giving him away. He buried them deep into his pockets.

"And I thought that I was investigating you, Mr Haven."

"Me, Senior Investigator. Why would you want to investigate me?"

Smiling, but darts in his eyes, like a distant arrowhead of crows worrying at the horizon.

"Because you murdered Bobby Hayes. Also Ye Yang, Heywood and Qingde. In our country that is enough reason to want to investigate somebody. Do you not think so? Tell me, Mr Haven, do you have a cigarette that I could kindly have?"

The Englishman reached into his inside pocket. A gold

pack, hard and neat cornered. Tobacco as sweet as brown sugar.

"And a light please?"

The lighter was already in his hand, manicured fingers across the gold block. A dull click. The electricity arcing. Gas ignited. The flame spiking blue, building to pale yellow.

"Thank you, English cigarettes are very good. Very sweet, like yellow wine. And your lighter, it is very beautiful. I have always wanted such a lighter as this."

Taking back the lighter, his eyes meeting Piao's for the first time. Ice on ice.

"Do you often accuse people of four murders in such a novel fashion?"

"No. I have never investigated a man who has committed four murders before."

"And, of course, you can prove your accusations, Investigator; witnesses, forensics, evidence. Remember evidence?"

"No. Officially I cannot even prove that you are here in our country, that you have ever been in our country. Officially you are not standing here now. We have less on our files about you than I can dredge up on Deng Xiaoping with the push of a single button. I just have a feeling about you."

The Englishman brought the mineral water to his lips, teeth magnified through the bottom of the glass.

"I didn't think so. You are a dreamer, Investigator Piao. You should know that 'feelings' do not hold up well in courts of law."

"Of course you are right, Mr Haven, but it will come, evidence is like that, it builds like bamboo scaffolding, very slowly. And murderers, they are like monkeys, the higher they escape up a tree, the more that they show of their arses."

Haven closed the narrow gap between them; his words warm on Piao's cheek. But chilling. So calmly said . . . so well wrapped.

"But I am not a monkey, Senior Investigator. Monkeys do not swap New Year gifts with Senior Politburo members. Perhaps you should be scared."

An invitation . . . but everything in Piao's stare rejecting it.

" I will wait, Mr Haven. I am very good at waiting. Wait and let the evidence show itself. Play the games that we PSB are good at. You will wish to leave our country, but you will find delays that cannot be explained. Ticket reservations will be cancelled from computer screens. Your credit cards will be rejected for no apparent reason. Stolen articles or illegal substances will be found in your hotel room, in your suitcase."

The Englishman turned to walk away, but before he did, whispering words through clenched teeth. Words precisely hewn from ice.

"You have no idea what you are getting into, Senior Investigator, a simple policeman like you. Get out before this swallows you whole."

Haven twisted leisurely through the perfumed throng of guests. The silky swerve of the lizard. Within seconds he was lost to Piao's view in a press of Armani and overzealous braid.

One last glance as Piao made his way from the reception hall, their eyes meeting in a brief snap, as bitter as frostbite. Haven turning, continuing his conversation with a Mao suited clutch of Politburo members. Laughing. Glasses clinking.

Piao walked home, watching every shadow. The Englishman's words, a constantly repeating hiccup in his mind.

Get out before this swallows you whole.

★

Five calls, cut off in tears. Angry words. Slammed receivers. The anxiety of each conversation spilt across Piao's table in an ashtray full of cigarette butts and a sentry of empty Tsingtao bottles. He called the number again, knowing it by heart. Asking for the room number. The line connecting, ringing, picked up. Her voice . . . already knowing who was calling.

"I don't need this, not again, Sun. Not again. I don't want to argue anymore. I don't want to cry."

Piao closed his eyes, sucking in a breath and pushing the urgency, the panic down. Reaching for each word, polishing them. Listening to Barbara's breath as he spoke and trying to gauge her emotions by the rhythm of her exhalations against the mouthpiece. Seconds of silence . . . and in it, the echo of his last word. And faint, ever so faint in the background of the call . . . a glass being filled, a cigarette withdrawn from a pack and being lit. The dull click of a lighter.

Clawed fingers racked the wall of Piao's stomach, his legs feeling as if they were set in concrete. A sudden realisation that Haven was in the same room as Barbara. Through all of his calls, in the room with her.

"You're wrong, Sun, he's not like that. Charles could never hurt anyone. He's going out on a limb to help me find Bobby's killer . . ."

Silence again, snapped by her voice breaking. Eyes filling. Tears . . . warm, salty. They would taste of good-byes and of the Englishman's cologne.

". . . we're leaving on Saturday. Please don't call me again. I don't think that I could stand it."

Seconds of silence, and then,

"Sun, I won't forget you."

And she was gone, only the electronic pulse in the telephone's earpiece remaining.

★

It was late. Out of cigarettes. Out of beer.

Piao slept, deep, bottomless. Dreams of broken bodies bleeding mud and airport lounges smelling of disinfectant.

He integrated the sounds into his sleep. A key slipping into a lock. A door opened. A door closed. Footsteps in the hall. A precise and careful footfall. And then the adrenaline thumping in. Hard across his chest. Shifting up the back of his skull. Finding himself instantly awake and slipping out of the bed. Naked. Pulling the shoulder holster out from underneath the bed. Its leather, cold against his thigh . . . diamond etched pistol butt, colder in his hand. Slipping the safety. Moving to the wall. The footsteps closer. A shadow, cutting its shape across the carpet. In one movement, stepping from behind the door, taking the intruder's neck with his forearm. Maxim-pattern silencer of the type 67 hard against the bone at the back of the intruder's ear. Everything in his posture expecting a counter move. Nothing came. A scream only – muffled, cut short. Piao pulling his arm away and up. A figure, dark, slight . . . toppling, spinning from his grip toward the bed. Perfume in his nostrils. And in his eyes, the familiar curve of lips that he had once kissed. Her hair falling in a curtain against the side of her face, like ink spilt across paper.

"Lingling."

His wife. One of only a few times that he had been able to say her name since she had left.

"It's good to see you, Sun."

A sudden flush of embarrassment, he reached for a towel to cover himself, pulling it around his waist. Hiding himself from her, as if they had never been intimate.

"It's good to see you. You're looking well."

She smiled, reminding him of frost across a window. Taking him and every detail of the room in within a single glance. She would see that he hadn't shaved. See that he'd been drinking and eating crap. And her, every detail of her . . . immaculate. He felt miserable in his shabbiness.

"Have you come back?"

She didn't answer. And suddenly wishing that he could snatch the words back as soon as they had left his mouth. Stupid. So stupid. Replacing the pistol in its holster and pushing it under the bed. Glancing out of the window as he stood. It was raining. Hard, relentless rain. Below, in the street, a Red Flag parked. The rain across the jet of its paintwork. Engine still running. Looking back at Lingling . . . rain in her hair, just like that night. Of course she hadn't come back.

"Sorry about being so dramatic. I was going to write and send these by courier . . ."

Her eyes lowered, for the first time Piao noticing the thick file in her hands. Porcelain white fingers spanning the thick black characters banded down its front.

OFFICE OF THE MINISTRY OF SECURITY.

". . . but it was important that I made sure that these were put directly into your hands . . ."

She halted for a second, raising her head slowly. Her tongue across her lips. Eyes on his. He knew the look so well. So odd to be re-experiencing its icy blast.

". . . I wanted to see you and so I used the key. I was surprised that you hadn't changed the lock."

He felt like laughing, crying. Both emotions suddenly, confusingly, feeling a hair's-breadth apart.

"Why change the lock? I have nothing left to steal."

She passed him the file, her hand brushing his. His wife. So obvious now that she hadn't come to see him . . . she had just come to lever him into position. Nothing changes, except for the names of the days. The Senior Investigator broke the file's seal, pulling back the flap. Inside, two spools of tape. Glancing at the labels; they plugged the gaps in the run of tapes from Ye Yang's hotel room. Also in the file, a series of papers. Computer printouts, reports. On the top page a passport sized photograph. Photocopied. Grainy. Charles Haven. A smile on his lip, like dog shit on a doorstep.

"These are from the Minister? It was Kang Zhu who sent the other tapes by courier a few days ago?"

She straightened her dress. Raw silk, foreign. A year of his wages could not have purchased for her such a dress.

"I gave you the other tapes. I give you these. The Minister knows nothing of this. The Minister is to know nothing of this. The whole point is that he be kept out of your investigation. Do you understand?"

"I understand, but I can't guarantee that anyone can be kept out of my investigation. When it comes to murders . . ."

She moved across to him, taking the file from the tabletop. Pulling it to her breasts . . . both arms wrapped around it.

"Then I take this back. And the next murder you will not be able to investigate because it will be your own . . ."

She turned to the window, eyes blocked in the jigsawed light spilling through the fine blinds. Mocha. Black. Mocha. She had always turned when there was a truth. As if her eyes could not stand its glare.

". . . I am trying to save two lives here. Kang Zhu's and your own, Sun."

"The Minister has an involvement in the case that I am investigating?"

She didn't answer. Her lips like a child's, pursed, closed.

"He must realise that any involvement in these murders would mean the death sentence to one in such a position of authority as Kang Zhu."

She whispered it to the bamboo blind, the window that it shaded catching her breath in slips, dots and dashes of matt grey . . . fading as quickly as they had formed.

"He is already serving a death sentence."

She walked to the door, the file still clenched over her breasts. Piao moving to bar her way, an arm across the narrow hallway, his other hand holding the towel around his waist. His wife, yet she smelt of a rich high cadre.

"Give me the file. I will not implicate the Minister in my investigations. This is not to save Kang Zhu's arse, this is to appease the victims and their families."

A ghost of a smile haunting the corners of her bud lips.

"And this is not to save your own life, Sun?"

"I don't know, perhaps it is. Perhaps seeing you has shown me how much I have already died. It is not something that I like."

She released her grip and he took the file. Walking to the door, she opened it. Her hand falling into his, metal at its heart.

"The key to your door. I will not need it anymore."

He watched her glide down the flight of stairs. Across the long to the Red Flag, its door being opened for her. Watching it drive away. Rain bleeding across the black desert of its roof. Not once did he see her look back. It was only when the limousine was out of sight, Piao opening the flat's windows wide to purge the smell of her perfume, the odour of a septuagenarian's mouth across hers . . . that he realised that he had not wished her well in her pregnancy. He closed the windows, shaking from the coldness that was inside him. The tears cutting down his face with the intensity of a welder's neat beading. And with them, the words repeated, like an endless river of pain.

"It should have been my fucking baby . . . it should have been my fucking baby."

★

He sat for an hour, still in his towel. Drained, as if a plug had been pulled on him. Unable to move. File on his lap. Key in his palm, piercing the flesh white with a reassuring pain. Calm while she had been there. Only now being washed by a tidal wave of emotion. Finally he moved, with speed, with resolve. Discarding the file on the bed and the towel on the floor. The shower water, as cold as good-byes. Shaving, beard stubble peppering the soap. Scrubbing his face, his body, with unnecessary force. Watching the foam run down his legs to the discoloured plug-hole. It washing away . . . her with it. His wife.

He dressed, nearly putting on his uniform until he remembered, with a painful nudge of reality, that he was still suspended from the Bureau. For breakfast, four cigarettes and a Tsingtao. Reading the file until he had finished another two. One hundred and four entries and exits in and out of the People's Republic of China within the last five years. Haven was a busy man with a penchant for airline food and terminal queues, as well as gold lighters. The Senior Investigator's finger trailed the computer data. Characters . . . times, dates. Matrix dotted meaningless information . . . structures built from precarious black specs. His attention drifting to the top of the page; darker print, larger dots.

CENTRAL INVESTIGATION DEPARTMENT.

A name that he'd only come across once before. West of Beijing, driving to the Fragrant Hills during a brief secondment to the City Central PSB on Beichizi Dajie. An old colleague pointing with a cigarette, at a drab unmarked building just beyond the old Summer Palace.

"The Institute of International Relations . . ."

With the words he had spat a shred of tobacco from his lip. It had stuck to the inside of the windscreen. Piao

340

remembering how he had been unable to tear his attention away from it.

". . . it belongs to the Central Investigation Department. Top Secret. So secret that most of us Chinese don't even know that it exists. They spy on foreign countries. Send operatives abroad under the cover of diplomats, journalists, businessmen, attachés. They do special jobs."

The car had turned, the building pirouetting behind Piao's shoulder. It had been a summer's day, the sun cutting across his eyes in a shutter of incandescent white.

". . . they say that the Central Investigation Department is so important that it comes directly under the Party Central Committee, not the government. And if they want you they can get you transferred out of any Danwei."

He had spat more shreds of tobacco, Piao hearing the sound only.

". . . it's obvious that they don't fucking want us."

Piao remembered having nodded . . . and waiting. Waiting for the sound of his colleague's next spit.

The Senior Investigator's finger trailed off the side of the page. Moving to the next report . . . typed. This time prisons, lao gais. Prisoners' names, numbers, crimes. The dates, times, locations of their executions. Piao's eyes following his finger back and forth, from the report to the computer data on Haven. Thousands of executions across the whole of the Republic . . . Haven in China for every one that had occurred in the Shanghai and Beijing city areas. Coincidence. Narrowing it down . . . finger moving through the lists of internal travel visas extended to Haven. He had been in the city of Shanghai or Beijing as each execution had been carried out. Not one missed. Coincidence?

Last entry in the report. Four executions. Location, Virtue Forest. The prisoners . . . Yongshe, Feng, Decai, Ziyang. Piao closing his eyes, just an instant as he exhaled. Checking the computer data for an answer that he already knew. The Englishman was in the Republic, in Shanghai when all four had been executed.

★

The reel to reel tapes confirmed only what Piao had already assumed . . . informing his assumptions. Haven was Ye Yang's buyer of the Men of Mud. The girl, squeezing the pips and raising the price with every telephone conversation. The Englishman's silence, a threat that could be cut with a steel wire. But the material from the Minister Kang Zhu's office, his and the Central Investigation Department's involvement, Haven's frequent periods in the Republic slotting into the lists of state sanctioned executions . . . what of these? What meaning did they hold?

At the bottom of the file a few more papers remaining. Haven's, passport details. Financial profile, long, anonymous lines of figures. Intimidating. Coldly powerful. More than a hint of how wealthy he was. A single A4 sheet rested, creased, at the base of the file. Computer print. Grey, on almost see-through paper. A list of state hospitals, most of them well known; spread throughout the whole of the People's Republic. In thick cuts of biro, four firmly underlined. Two in Shanghai. Two in Beijing. Hospitals of excellence, teaching hospitals, whose rigours and skills fed the rest of the People's Republic. At the bottom of the page, indented in black upper case bold and also underlined. A name. A title that he didn't recognise, towing it into position, midpage . . .

CONSULTANT SURGEON CHARLES HAVEN.

Picking up another Tsingtao. Warm to the touch. The concentration seeming to press itself on the inside of his skull.

"Fuck. Fuck."

Executions. Shanghai, Beijing. Haven's movements. Teaching hospitals . . . also in Shanghai and Beijing. The Englishman . . . a surgeon, a consultant. A jigsaw of important things, only of important things. How he hated jigsaw puzzles. He finished the beer, thinking of refrigerators that would really chill a Tsingtao. Thinking also of what his grandfather had once told him . . . 'important things, they only become important when you discover their importance for yourself.'

★

The Senior Investigator's interview with Detective Yun was harrowing. Pushed and guided by Comrade Officer Chief Liping's unseen hand. Meticulously, a frame-up being swung and manhandled into place. Piao being shunted to the dark edge of the abyss, in a meeting punctuated by lukewarm tea and snatches of the acned detective's views on the rumba, the polka . . . and the tango. It was all very friendly, almost jovial. But it was obvious in which direction the current was flowing. New witnesses had 'unexpectedly' come forward from Zhiyuan's neighbourhood, people of good reputation and fully paid-up Party cards. They placed the Senior Investigator in the vicinity of the old comrade's flat in the early morning of the day that he was murdered. One even had Piao running to his car and driving off at speed.

The result, for the time being . . . he was to remain suspended. Not allowed to go beyond the city limits. Serious charges were in the process of being drawn up. Yun ended the interview, standing, his finger snapping down on the tape recorder. Walking to the door. The light reading the Braille of his acne like a barcode.

"Lili, my sister-in-law. You remember?"

Candy floss. Baby pink chiffon. The puffball. Yes, he remembered Lili.

"The New Year dance at the Shanghai Mansions, very prestigious. We had wished to invite you, with you escorting Lili. But of course, under the circumstances, you understand?"

Perhaps clouds did have silver linings? The Senior Investigator pulled the door open, stepping into the disinfectant tainted air of the corridor. How long would it be before he wouldn't be allowed to open a door at all? Saying nothing to Detective Yun as he left the interview suite. Walking out of the kung an chu and into a midday devoid of any clouds at all.

Chapter 32

The package was small, fastidiously wrapped. Just Piao's name handwritten on the tight brown paper. He slit the tape and carefully unfolded it. She had saved everything, packaging, string, paper . . . why was he still saving rubbish for his wife? He screwed the wrapping into a tight ball, throwing it against the far wall. It felt good.

At the heart of red and gold marbled paper and the fine layers of tissue . . . a box. Rectangular, polished wood, as pink as a woman's lips. Inside, velvet. At its centre, a cigarette lighter. Recognising immediately that it was identical to Haven's. Running a finger across its flawless solid gold sky. Underneath the base of the velvet lining was a chamois leather pouch and a simple buff message card. It was written in black ink. Each letter a flourish of serrated edges.

A gift. For someone who also appreciates perfection in all of its forms.

The Senior Investigator held the lighter, flicking it on a half a dozen times. A half a dozen dull clicks, in a rapid volley. Studying the flame. Almost white, almost invisible. It would be easy not to see the flame at all; a man could get badly burnt. Watching it die, the instant that he removed his fingertip from the flush gold button. Reverently placing it back in its box. Closing the lid. Walking to the high cupboard of spilling drawers; the very bottom one jerkily pulled open. Inside, pictures of his wife. Mementos of their wedding. Her letters to him. The whole drawer holding her smell, as the mind holds the memory.

"Perfection," he whispered, as he placed the box deep into the drawer and closed it.

He pulled his jacket on and walked down the stairs and into

the long. A cerulean mid-morning. Clouds scant, like spilt rice. A day for parks. Bottles of *Jiu* . . . and a niece's and nephew's warm hands.

Chapter 33

The Big Man was drunk and ecstatic. His words, slurred skid marks, fuelled by a complimentary fusion of pre-New Year celebrations and good news. Good news that had been worked for, nothing better.

"Wu, I've tracked the scrawny little shit down. It'll cost four packs of Panda Brand Boss."

What didn't cost two packs of Panda Brand?

Piao said nothing. Listening to the voices, the laughter, the words of the drinking song in the background of the telephone call,

> *'If wine were not beloved of the Heavens,*
> *Those Heavens would not contain the star of wine.'*

"The day after we pulled those bodies from the mud, when the doctor was so fucking helpful, he was driven to a government zhau-dai-suo in Jiading District, near the Dachang Airfield. He's been moved around regularly ever since . . ."

The Big Man stopping to overfill his mouth with beer. Piao could picture its foam dripping from the young detective's series of chins.

". . . they've even provided the doctor with his own fucking car and chauffeurs. The car's a black Shanghai Sedan."

A sudden sense of a bottomless disappointment, almost palpable. Piao almost having to steady his feet.

"If Wu has been entrusted to them he will be dead by now."

Yaobang laughed. In the background of the call, the drinkers, their song, reaching a climax of premature ends,

> *'If wine were not beloved of the Earth,*
> *Its fountainhead on earth would not exist.'*

346

"But that's why I needed to talk, Boss. I saw the little shit my-self two hours ago. Wu isn't dead, they've got him in another government guesthouse north of the city in Baoshan . . ."

The Big Man halting briefly to drink again. Piao could hear the beer gurgle to the back of his throat, the rough material of his cuff wiped across his mouth and stubble.

". . . for them to do that, Boss, the doctor must be fucking important. Too important to kill, too important to let loose."

The Senior Investigator losing the rest of Yaobang's words in the swell of drunken singing,

'Only when draining all the pleasures of the moment is a man happy; therefore never leave the golden goblet standing empty in the moonlight.'

Piao put down the phone. He would have joined them, but he'd run out of beer.

Chapter 34

In the crowd, a man . . . static in a swim of torsos. His back, hard against the shop window; the glass as grey as smoke, twisting with a flow of reflections. The crowd thinning.

"There, crossing the road."

Tight against the shop fronts, following him through the growl of traffic. Bumper to bumper. A metal corridor, shape shifting, edging forward in exhaust fumes. Catching him at the junction of Changshou Lu and Jiangning Lu. Yaobang taking the old man's arm by his skinny wrist, forcing it behind him and up to just below the nape of the neck.

"Very unprofessional them letting you go out shopping by yourself . . ."

Doctor Wu's lips twisted to form a shout, the Big Man's other hand coming around, clamped across his mouth, forcing it back down his throat.

". . . make a sound and I'll break your fucking arm."

Wu's head snapping around, seeing Piao; questions and pleadings in the pale amber of the old man's eyes. The Senior Investigator answering at least one of the questions.

"It's true, doctor, he will break your fucking arm."

The long was dark, sunlight never entering it. Just impressions of shadow, chrome, and birdshit. The car couldn't be seen until you were almost upon it.

"Fucking dogs."

The Big Man kicked out at the stray that was pissing against the front wheel of his car. Missing it, but it yelped out of the long as if he hadn't. Wu was pushed into the front seat beside Piao and handcuffed to the inside of the door. Exhaust fumes choked the alley, the Big Man lighting a cigarette, handing one to Piao.

"Hey, Boss, why is it always my car that dogs piss on."

The Senior Investigator engaged the gears. The car in a death rattle.

"Why not," he said in China Brand smoke, as he drove out of the long, piercing the heavy traffic on Haifang Lu.

★

Night folded in . . . the windscreen scrolling midnight colours. Across the clasp of Wu's lined face, beats of yellow street light. Yaobang in the back, examining his tie in the pulses of available lamplight. Breakfast stains. Lunch. Supper stains. Piao driving, always knowing the plan. Always knowing that Wu wouldn't talk, but firing the questions anyway. Always knowing that the old man would need an incentive. Now moving south and then east. Dangerous thoughts. Dangerous games. That incentive, nearing.

"That night on the foreshore, there was something that you recognised."

Moving across the Wusongjiang, scarred in bridge light reflections. Ripples stitched in mercury.

"Only that you are dangerous, Piao. I said it that night, didn't I? A rogue. Now take me back, I will be missed. They will come for me. They will come for you."

"They will not come for you yet, doctor. Whoever 'they' are, only call at the zhau-dai-suo every two days. We have eyes also . . ."

Headlights, full beam, spearing the shadows.

". . . forty-eight hours, doctor, and I will only need forty-eight minutes with you."

In the back, the Big Man flexed his fingers, joints popping.

"And I will only need forty-eight seconds."

From Hongkou, stealing into Yangpu. The refineries south of the Zhonghua Shipyard burning off their gases. Through the gap in the window, a taste of its heat on air. The sky singeing to a deep copper hue.

"Was it the identities of some of the bodies that you recognised, or what had been done to them?"

A smile. A nervous cough from the old man.

"What were you telling me that night in refusing to examine them, Mr Senior Police Scientist?"

"Walk away Piao, while you still have the legs to do so. I also said this to you. Walk away. It is not yet too late."

Above the steelworks, black spanning into black . . . arms reaching from both sides of the Huangpu in a proposed handshake of girders, rivets and concrete. The New Yangpu Bridge, unfinished. Between the wide gap where the stretching spans had not yet arced and embraced, a spit of cold ivory stars. Piao moved onto the highway, just constructed, just opened. The slip road for the bridge twisting up and away to the left. A puzzle of barriers, cones, heavy plant, workers' huts, pre-fabricated site offices, fenced stock depots.

"The name of Haven, do you know it . . . Doctor Charles Haven?"

"It is not too late Senior Investigator. Walk away, go home to your bed and bury your head under the sheets."

At speed, spinning the wheel, taking the long curve up onto the slip road. The bridge nearer. The stars nearer.

"But it is too late, doctor."

Wu's eyes in the slashes of floodlight . . . panic tethered in sepia. Pulling hard on the wheel as the slip road uncurled onto the concrete surface of the bridge. An arc-lit racetrack, sprouting a forest of cones. Far ahead, picked out by the headlights like white sutures piercing in and out of raw flesh, a double barrier marking the point where steel and concrete became chilled air and a deep drop to the Huangpu's invisibly black wash.

"Are you mad Piao? The bridge is not yet complete. You cannot pass over it."

The accelerator floored. Steel screaming. The parapet racing past in a thudding strobe of grey pierced with dark grey. The old man pulling on the taut handcuff chain, fear breaking through the flimsy material of his calmly delivered words.

"What are you doing, Piao? You will kill us, don't you understand . . . you will kill us all."

The Senior Investigator catching Wu's stare, that of a rabbit

350

in the centre of the road the instant before the wheel comes down. And the old man catching the look anchored at depth in Piao's eyes. Chilling him to the heart. The doctor's voice, a scream above the shriek of engine.

"Pull over . . . please, please. What do you want of me?"

City lights running between the braces of the parapet. Cold, so cold.

"I want you to talk. To tell me what it is you know." Wu, one eye on secrets. One eye on truths. Screaming now,

"They are powerful, too powerful for you. I cannot talk. I am a man of principles. What they are doing has gone too far. I do not agree with it, but I cannot talk."

"That is something that I have heard before. Tell me something new, old man."

"For me to say will mean my death. Your death."

Double barriers marking the edge of the span, a gash in the night . . . dominating the horizon. Slicing towards them.

"Sometimes I feel as if I am already dead, don't you, doctor?"

Piao pulled the wheel, skewing the car around the first barrier. Blurs, the night cut in long knives. Tortured rubber. A city running distant. A swerve, a skid . . . violent and set in snatches of Wu's face, glistening sweat. The second barrier sprinting in elongated whites, extruded, luminous reds. Brakes floored. Headlights finding blackness only, as they thumped to a halt. Engine stalling. A silence that pressed on the ears with a cold and certain firmness; broken only by the rhythmic tears of breath across the old man's teeth. Fishing in his pocket, throwing the keys to the cuffs onto the Big Man's lap. Yaobang untangling himself, straightening his uniform. Making his fingers work. Finding the lock in the handcuffs with shaking fingers. Pulling Wu from the car, onto the bridge. It was cold. Breaths from lips. In an instant, sweat drying. The doctor adjusting his tie.

"A wise decision Senior Investigator. At last, a wise decision on your part. Nothing could have been gained by such a foolhardy act."

"Bring him."

Piao already rounding the front of the car. His shadow thrown across the rutted span and into darkness. The Big Man tugged on the chain, Wu stumbling after him. Ridged concrete grafted over rusted steel rodding and girders. The edge of the span, its very lip . . . five metres away. Knowing that the river was far below, but unable to see it. As if it didn't exist. Just a hole. Deep. Black.

"His legs."

Yaobang pulled the doctor toward him, removing the handcuffs. Picking him up bodily. Cradling him. So light . . . just a bag of bones. And with it, remembering his own grandfather. Carrying him, bed to toilet. Bed to toilet. The cancer holding him in its grip. Wasting him. Ravaging him. So light . . . just a bag of bones.

The edge of the span. Taking one of the doctor's legs each. Piao, Yaobang, on their knees; the coldness of the concrete running up their thighs. A weak struggle as they held him by his ankles over the edge of the span. His body in a violent swing. Shirt, vest . . . riding up over his stomach, his chest. Behind his head, jacket flapping. Loose change, in a fall into blackness.

"That night on the foreshore, what did you recognise, their identities or what had been done to them?"

Nothing. Just dribble in a long thin spit from his lips, set against the backdrop of city . . . a necklace of living light.

"Talk. I will drop you, doctor."

Wu, forcing his head up. Eyes locked with Piao's. Finding the words. The breeze as sharp as a splinter, stealing some of them away.

"You . . . a dangerous fool, Senior Investigator. I am old . . . not drop me. You would not dare . . . execute you . . . be finished. Stop. Think. I am . . . city's Chief Medical Exami . . ."

His head dropped with an exhausted snap. The lights of Padong hurtling, streaking in a violent barcode.

"Talk. Tell me what you know?"

A sound. A laugh? Humour in even this, or the escape valve of horror?

"Nothing to say. Do not . . . stupid, Senior Investigator . . . immediately . . . pull me up."

The world in a violent lurch. A half scream, choked, snatched by the wind. Piao letting go of the doctor's leg and standing. A groan of effort as Yaobang took the full weight of the old man.

"Boss?"

But the Senior Investigator ignoring it. Just staring down at Wu. A puppet set against a backcloth of nothing, almost all of its strings cut. A patch slowly expanding around the doctor's crotch. Darker. Darker. Spreading down to the trouser waistband. The urine in a sheet flow across the heaving stomach. The chest. Coming off the chin, the cheeks, the tip of the nose, the forehead . . . in a shower fall. Caught against the cityscape like a scatter of jewels. Deep thudding gags of inhaled breaths. But no words. Piao knelt, hands on the Big Man's hands. Slowly, carefully, strongly, peeling the large fingers, one by one, from the doctor's ankle.

"Fuck, Boss, what are you doing? We can't, he's the fucking city's Chief Medical Examiner."

The Big Man's grasp slipping, sliding away from him. In his head, already rehearsing the mannequin's fall. The plunge . . . losing focus, losing form as it bit into darker darkness.

"No, Boss. No . . ."

Below, from the old man, coughs, cries, splintered words. Lips bathed in a mixture of piss, sweat, tears, dribble.

"Talk . . . talk . . . I will . . . talk, tell you."

Seconds of silence before Piao spoke. Recognising the words, but not his own voice.

"So tell me?"

"Tomorrow . . . you see, tomorrow. Come . . . clear. Everything . . . know everything. God help you."

Seconds of silence before Piao spoke again. Recognising the words, and this time the voice also.

"Haul him up."

Walking the doctor back to the car, the old man pulling a cuff across his face.

"What you did to me back there was not n-necessary,

353

Senior Investigator. I am a man of principles. I am a m-man of moral direction, of p-principles . . ."

Across the front of his shirt, a sash of vomit. Trousers pissed. But the words rock calm. The eyes, steady.

". . . what you did was w-wrong. You should have appealed to those qualities in me. I just needed to be c-convinced that I could speak of these things that I have come to loathe and yet remain s-safe. I have a f-family also . . ."

His breath becoming even more tattered.

". . . there are many ways to persuade, Senior Investigator. Many w-ways. Many ways to court."

Gently, sitting the old man in the Sedan. The Senior Investigator pulling a blanket around his shoulders.

"Eight are dead, Doctor Wu. I do not have time to court. I want a witness, information. I do not want a wife. I already have one of those."

With the words, Piao suddenly and intently aware that the night only smelt of hard things. Things that would not submit. Concrete. Steel. A river that could not be seen. Only hard things . . . and he now at their hub. Yaobang replaced the handcuffs on the doctor's wrist, locking him to the inside of the door. Lighting him a cigarette. Turning on Piao. Fire and questions in the Big Man's eyes. And in a whisper, as sharp as swarf,

"What the fuck was that about? You wanted to kill him?"

The Senior Investigator walked to the lip of the span. Words, questions . . . stranded. Below, the river, lost in darkness. His toes over the edge, balancing on his heels. So easy to die. At that moment, so easy to die. Head filled with the numbness that decants into it when horror has been exorcised. When suicide becomes so easy, one small step. Too easy. Meaningless.

"Tomorrow," he whispered to the night, to the river, before turning and walking back to the car.

"Well doctor, it looks as if you will be my guest tonight. I hope that you like chicken?"

Wu coughed politely.

"Then I should tell you that I am a vegetarian, Senior Investigator."

A smile on Piao's face as he drove back down the bridge and onto the slip road. And to the night.

"I thought that you might fucking be, old man."

Chapter 35

The New Year.

Debts are paid. Peace made with those with whom relationships have been strained or broken. Sweetness and new life filling your home.

At the centre of the main room, a table . . . now an altar. A pig's head, a chicken, a fish, and a New Year's cake resting upon it. In the avenues, young children parade their new clothes; bright colours, red, blue, green, but mostly red. Gloves, hats, scarves, little things giving so much pleasure.

New Year's Day, and everything is sweet. Tea must be sugared. Lychee and dragon's eye eaten. As well as lotus fruit seeds, persimmons, grapefruit, crystallised ginger. And flaky cakes, as well as *niangao*, the traditional 'rising higher every year cakes.' On the streets, spanning the longs, lucky characters are pasted up. The promise of sweetness and new life to fill your home.

And in the hearts of the high cadre and the *dahu*, the new money people . . . the fixers, the shunters, the dealers? Business as usual.

★

To the minute they arrived on time, two unmarked ambulances. Tinted windows. Pulling into the rear, the business end of the Number 1 Hospital, with its skips and overflowing dustbins.

"Say nothing," Wu hissed, as a door slid open and they boarded. Moving off at speed. Headlights fanning into Suzhou Beilu. In the rear of the ambulance, other pale faces. No conversation. No smoking. Attention drawn in.

The New Year. Eating, dancing, music, hands holding somebody else's. Bottles of wine, bottles of beer. Faces passing by in long tangled chains. None looking back. It was as if he and the ambulance didn't exist. Perhaps they didn't. For the rest of the journey he studied his fingers, his palms . . . the confusion of road-map lines, none of which led anywhere.

★

They skirted the outer wall of the Municipal Prison and entered by the south gate. In its blinding white blaze, diffused shapes of ash metamorphosing into a welcoming party of guards and wardens. Piao kept close to the doctor, through a maze of corridors; bare brick walls and puddled concrete floors. A line of single discoloured light bulbs cutting the darkness . . . and the sound of footsteps in unison. The sluice room was in the new block, still smelling of paint hurriedly applied, drips frozen in mid-fall. A double bank of olive green lockers ran down the centre of the room. The hospital staff moving toward them, removing their jackets. Opening the lockers in a cacophony of pressed steel onto pressed steel. Wu pulled at the Senior Investigator's jacket, the corner of his lips twisted in a whisper.

"Here, do everything that I do."

A gown, a hat, starched white. Piao took them from the locker, removing his coat and slipping them on, hiding his shoulder holster with the locker door. Feeling out of place. Feeling stupid . . . even as a child, hating dressing-up games. Turning to see the green garbed figures pushing through the high rubber double doors into the next room. The Senior Investigator followed, Wu at the line of sinks, hands in a scalding cascade of water. Steam across his spectacle lenses.

"Wash your hands, do all that I do, exactly."

Piao watched and followed, soaking his hands and forearms in the fierce deluge. Pushing the hibiscrub dispenser with his elbows . . . catching the pink slug of soap in his palms. Working it into a lather. Rinsing it off. Hands dried under the airflow. Helping the doctor on with a pair of surgical gloves; Wu in turn helping him. The last figure moving through the rubber doors. A clap as they swung and met in an eddy of medicated air.

"The rest of them are wearing green, we're wearing white?"

Wu snapped the top of a glove in place and picked up the sterile pack of instruments.

"Very astute, Senior Investigator. You will, no doubt, also detect that we are about to go through a different door to the one that the others used. Now keep close, do as I do or we will not be able to, to, how do you say it?"

"Put the shit back up the horse's arse, doctor?"

The old man opened the door at the far end of the sluice room and walked into the short corridor alive with chisel-edged shadows.

"Exactly Senior Investigator. Exactly."

★

At each window of each cell, a face. Hands clenched around bars, black. Fists, white. Piao's eyes moved down the six-storey block, the lengthy runs of stone, square and precisely cornered, making up three sides of the vast inner compound. A face, fists, at each window. Wincing as his eyes caught the banks of floodlights . . . tracing the blue-white beams down to the two pools of fierce light that transformed midnight into midday. In one area, the helipad . . . a fat black blowfly of a Zhishengji-9A 'Dolphin' Helicopter in PLA Air Force insignia, at its centre. And then the second area of light pinpointing a group of figures around a low podium . . . the warden, officials, guards. Papers in the high cadre's hands. Sawdust, as brown as shit, across their polished toecaps. A cigarette being lit, laughter, loud and jarring from the Zhishengji's crew . . . and in its fallout, Piao's whisper.

"What is this? What's going on?"

Wu standing back, anchored to the penumbra.

"Wait. See. Investigators are good at that, yes?"

The doctor was enjoying the power. Piao joined him in the shadows, a sudden sense of the leather shoulder holster that he was wearing and the steel of the pistol that was slumbering within it. Yes, he would wait. See. He was an Investigator, he was good at that.

A drizzle had started its fall. Fine, but demanding, soaking every exposed area of skin. The crescents between cuffs and gloves. Collar and hairline. The warden barked an order; in no mood to get wet. And then everything accelerated. Four guards followed closely by two others carrying rifles, pulling one prisoner and then another from the darkness, through the shadow and into the blind of arc-light. They looked lethargic, sedated. Feet dragging. Four toe trails through the sawdust. The prisoners propped to attention as the warden read out their crimes. The sentences. Giving the order. The prisoners forced to their knees. Guards advancing. The rifle of one pressed firmly into the back of a prisoner . . . the rifle of the other stubbed at the base of the second prisoner's skull. A shot. Another. Muffled sledgehammer blows of decibels volleying between the detention blocks. Twin tongues of smoke licking skyward in a lazy tumble from the ends of the rifles' barrels. Piao closed his eyes, the colour behind them, maroon . . . shot through with two silver spikes. When he opened them again the bodies had folded forward. The guards turning them onto their backs. Blood pumping from underneath them in a torrent across the sawdust, threatening to turn the whole compound into a thick black lake. Wu moved into the arc-light. The crumpled bag lines of his face bleached clean. He looked twenty years younger, the Senior Investigator could almost imagine a man in his prime. A husband, a father, a lover . . . not just a dried up old man.

"Come, Senior Investigator. Death calls us."

The warden and the officials, already walking briskly toward cover. For the first time, Piao noticing the smell that rain has, not unlike tears . . . cordite on its wing. And also the smell of the warm blood across the sawdust. Stepping forward into the noon, eyes squinting. Following the old man.

"Come doctor. Death calls us."

"Don't talk, just do everything that I do."

Piao knelt in the sawdust. Blood everywhere. Soaking through the gown, through his trousers, to his knees. Already imagining the strawberry stains that he would have to wash from his own skin. Watching every move that Wu made.

Watching the instruments that he picked up and wielded. A stethoscope. A small torch. Mimicking his actions in the hunt for any signs of life. A pulse. A pupil dilating. But nothing that showed that life hadn't fled within an instant of the rifle shots being discharged. Watching as Wu pulled a long needle from the sterile pack. No hesitation . . . pushing it deep into the prisoner's temple. Piao feeling a vice of pressure clamp across his skull. Reluctantly drawing a needle from the pack. Its steel in the arc-light, as bright as glass. Hesitating.

"Do everything that I do."

Hesitating. Wu's eyes, nervous. A glance across his shoulder at the guards looking on. A fierce whisper.

"Do it. Do it."

"Do it yourself, doctor. Death calls you."

The guards moving forward. Wu shifting uncomfortably on arthritic knees . . . hissing.

"For God's sake, do it. It's just a needle. He will not feel it, he is dead. Do it, or we will join him."

Hesitation, and then the Senior Investigator pushing the needle. At first the skin taut, puckering, pimpling in . . . and then giving way in a single plump grape of blood. Bile at the back of Piao's throat. Shining the torch into the prisoner's eyes. Nothing. Their colour, yellow-brown, fading away . . . sand through fingers.

"He's dead."

The Senior Investigator catching the reflection of his own eyes in the blaze of the old man's glasses.

"Of course he is dead. The front of his head has been shot off."

Wu closed his bag, nodding to the guards. Their hands pulling the bodies up and across the compound. Thin spit trails of blood leading back into the new block.

★

Skin on steel. Steel on skin.

They didn't waste any time. Two teams, gowned green, drawn from the blank-eyed ambulance passengers, now consummate professionals. Cutting the clothes from the bodies.

360

Bathing them. Applying a wash of iodine yellow antiseptic from sternum to pubis. From forehead to cheek. A team working on one of the dead prisoner's eyes. Muscle hooks. Curved enucleation scissors. The steel blades inserted along the lateral orbital walls. The tough, rubbery optic nerve between its razor-edges . . . cutting close to the apex of the orbit. The globes, the eyes removed. Placed in sterile containers, in McCarey-Kaufman tissue culture solution. Extensive endothelial cell death avoided. The sterile containers sealed and packed for transport. The second team working on the remaining body; a scalpel racing in a midline incision from xyphoid notch to pubis. A cruciate abdominal cut, deep, just above the umbilicus, allowing extended exposure. Towel clips applied to each leaf of the abdominal incision, folding the flaps back to the flanks of the torso; skin on skin. Working fast . . . controlled, but fast. The c-portion of the duodenum dissected by a Kocher manoeuvre. Both kidneys finally removed en bloc. A cylinder of inferior vena cava, attached ureters of fifteen centimetres length included. The kidneys separated, packed . . . placed in cold storage preservation units.

Tasks performed, as if they were the cement between the bricks . . . team members broke away, returning to the sluice room. Lockers opening. Gowns discarded. Some moving back out to the compound in a procession following the organ packs. The Zhishengji thudding into life. Rotors slicing through air and arc-light. Wind, dust, and thunder . . . it rose out of the grip of the floodlit compound. Wind, dust, thunder . . . abating. Lost in the night, darkness closing around it in a tight fist. Moving north, over the city. Nothing left of what had occurred except the witness of green tail lights fading by the second.

★

The operating room was empty, just Piao, just Wu. And on the tables, holed and discarded . . . two white bodies. For the first time the Senior Investigator noticing their faces. Young, early twenties. Too young for age's etch of lines. For grey hair. For an instant, just an instant, the Senior Investigator closing

361

his eyes. Monochrome stills welded together in photoflood blue-white, filling his inner vision. Eight faces of mud. Eight bodies of mud. Lacerations, holed flesh, eyeless eyes . . . as the shit hued mud was washed aside. Piao opened his eyes, the breeze from the air-conditioning across his teeth in a sickening taste of iodine, hibiscrub, and spent helicopter fuel.

"This is what happened to the eight that we found in the Huangpu, isn't it?"

Wu, slowly peeling back his surgical gloves.

"They had their organs stolen and you knew, didn't you, doctor?"

Raising his head, his spectacle lenses blazing white in the operating lights.

" 'Harvested'. We call it 'harvesting' the organs."

"Harvesting? No, doctor. No. Harvesting is about wheat, summer days and working together in the fields and trying to get a peek down the front of the girl's work overalls. That is harvesting . . ."

Piao waved a hand toward the bodies.

". . . this is not harvesting. This is murder. This is rape."

Wu removed his theatre hat, his spectacles, polishing their lenses with it. Saying nothing. The Senior Investigator took the glasses from Wu's hands, holding them up to his eyes. A world of smeared, dragged colours. And the bodies, melted into baby pink blobs. The sculptured crimson strokes of the scalpels diffused, whispered away. Piao removed a blemish from one of the lenses with a pinch from his shirt front and handed the spectacles back to the old man; his voice low, calm, but with a cut-throat edge of purpose.

"Tell me what you fucking know about this harvesting, or we will complete our sightseeing drive across the Yangpu Bridge."

Wu leant against the stainless steel of the operating table, his cuffs brushing dead skin. The holed, dissected body, disregarded . . . just so much waste by-product, to be discarded.

Somebody's child. Somebody's son.

"People like you."

362

The old man averted his eyes from Piao, replacing his glasses.

"People like me, what doctor?"

"People like you are smug. You are young, in good health. You think nothing of those who are not. Can you even imagine what it must be like to suffer from kidney failure . . . to be told to go home, wait for the telephone to ring to tell you that a replacement kidney has been found? And all the time, knowing that such a call will never come. Or for your eyesight to slowly degenerate into a blur, into blindness. Knowing that with a transplanted cornea you could see your wife once more. The faces of your grand-children . . ."

The old man waved an angry arm across the corpse.

". . . this is what that is about. Giving life. Giving hope."

"No doctor. This is not about giving life. This is about taking it away. Giving no hope . . ."

He moved closer to Wu, so that the old man could not mistake the look in his eyes.

". . . for fuck sake, look at them and tell me that this is about life, that this is about hope?"

Wu looked away.

"And what should we do, waste these organs, incinerate them . . . is that what you want? Be sensible, be realistic. We execute over ten thousand prisoners a year, their bodies belong to the State, we can do what we wish with them. And what we wish, is to use them in a responsible way so that out of bad can come some good. I ask you, Senior Investigator, is it unreasonable that out of so many necessary deaths we should choose to give so much life?"

"Tell me how it works. Tell me how we can give so much life to others from death?"

Piao's eyes on the pale face of the prisoner, hardly able to accept that it was the man whom he had seen being dragged from the detention block and shot in front of him. A face without eyes. So much humanity ebbed away with their loss. Hardly able to accept that this face had ever been loved, kissed.

"I do not understand what you require, Senior Investigator?"

Moving closer still. So close, the doctor would be able to steal his breath; it would smell of anger restrained and in chains. It would be of a sadness that no words could ever colour in.

"I want details. Everything that you know about this trade, I want to know. Not your viewpoint. Not a lecture on the ethics of it. Details. Just details."

Wu removed his glasses, fiddling with them nervously. Details . . . there is pain in just details. The veneer rubbed down to the bare boards of truth.

"You must realise that what I am going to tell you is a state secret. It is knowledge that few people in our country know. It is knowledge that is not known beyond our country. Ethics committees outside of the People's Republic would not understand. They would not be able to dissociate a post-execution process from the execution process itself. In our country it is a different situation."

"How different?"

The old man's finger traced along the edge of the stainless steel operating table.

"Prisoners who are to be executed are not asked for their consent before donating organs, neither are their relatives. Families of the prisoners are held under house arrest until the execution has been completed, until they are allowed to come and receive the ashes. They will not be told that organs have been removed. In the rare cases in which relatives are asked for their consent, if they do not give it they will be threatened with large bills for the prisoner's food and for the cost of the bullet that will be used in the execution and for other expenses . . ."

The old man paused before continuing, waiting for the sharpness of Piao's tongue. He said nothing.

". . . once a prisoner is shot, from a legal point of view he is no longer a human being. He is just an object that is now the property of the State. The authorities will have known what blood group he is. They will have already matched his organs up with a recipient for them."

"But they wouldn't be able to plan that far ahead. The execution would damage organs. Bullets don't obey orders."

Piao's gaze drifting to the far table. The body. The shot received at the base of the skull, exiting through where the left cheek had been. A crater of horrifying size. The eye, the nose, half of the mouth, teeth, jaw . . . consumed by its ravenous hunger. A ragged bite, the colour of a car's tail lights moving down a black tunnel.

"But some bullets do obey orders Senior Investigator."

The understanding thumping Piao in the solar plexus. A hit and run leaving him breathless. Hardly able to form the words.

"The prisoners are shot to order, aren't they? If the surgeons want their eyes, they are shot in the back. If they want their kidneys, they are shot in the head."

Wu moved across the room.

"The demand for organs is extraordinary. At present there are more than two thousand provincial centres in the country with prisons that carry out executions. All of the organs from these we can use, but to do so we have to be organised, professional. It is necessary that we plan ahead."

"So this is planning ahead?"

"You fail to understand Senior Investigator. If you require a kidney we can obtain one for you within four hours, harvested to your personal medical details. A prisoner shot at 11am . . . you will receive your kidney by 2 pm. In any other country in the world you would have to wait for days, weeks, months, maybe even years. In most countries the wait would be too long and you would die."

The old man cleaned his glasses once more; they didn't need cleaning.

"We have sick people coming to us from all over the world. Coming to China. Coming from Europe, America, Asia. For a single kidney they will pay up to one hundred thousand dollars in cash. Imagine Piao, it is regenerating our hospitals. It is bringing many, many millions of dollars into our economy from people who would simply die in their own countries."

He attempted a smile, the result, pathetic.

"The eight that we pulled from the river, you recognised them, doctor, didn't you?"

"I recognised what had been done to them. I recognised that someone had tried to cover this up by mutilating them."

"You recognised them, didn't you?"

"Only four of them I recognised."

"Which four?"

No answer. Carefully placing the spectacles across the bridge of his nose.

"So I shall tell you, doctor, shall I? You recognised the four Chinese who were executed in Gongdelin. Yongshe. Feng. Decai. Ziyang."

"Yes, I knew them. I was the one who pronounced them dead after their executions at Virtue Forest. The last that I saw of them was as they were being loaded into a lorry for cremation."

"They weren't used for organ donation?"

"No. They were unsuitable for harvesting."

The thump of rotor blades beating air invaded the room from the courtyard; a resonance humming through the stainless steel of the operating tables and the glass fronted instrument cabinets.

"A blighted crop, yes, doctor? It must have hurt to have to reject the few hundred thousands of dollars that their organs would have brought to our needy economy."

"There have been some problems. Screening. Tissue matching. Our quality control has had to improve as many of our prisoners are executed for drug abuse and can carry hepatitis and other viral infections."

Quality control, the sound bites of the report writer, the economist. They were talking about somebody's child, somebody's son. And yet Piao could only think of factories, of cars, refrigerators . . . of bicycles.

"And what did your quality control say about these four doctor?"

"There was drug abuse."

"And?"

"Hepatitis . . ."

366

Wu halted momentarily, weighing up the words before they dripped from his lips.

". . . one had HIV."

The Senior Investigator whistled. Long, low . . .

"But Doctor, HIV doesn't exist in the People's Republic of China. It is a disease of the capitalist system."

"You are correct, officially, Senior Investigator."

"And un-officially?"

"Un-officially, HIV does not care about political systems. It does not stop at checkpoints. It is becoming a problem that is 'awkward'."

"Awkward? An interesting description of HIV, Doctor Wu. But it's not the only 'awkward' problem, is it?"

Piao walked to the door, opening it . . . thundering noise, untethered, piling in upon them. Switching off the main theatre lights; the large reflectors diluting from white, to yellow, to orange, to black. Wu caught in the darkness, fumbling, following the Senior Investigator's words out into the corridor.

"Four people that you witnessed being executed, Doctor Wu, and sent for cremation. Too infected for their organs to be used for transplantation. And then they are found on the Huangpu's foreshore, organs stolen. Bodies mutilated to hide what they have been through. Unsuitable donors. Damaged goods."

They were back in the compound, but Piao was thinking of a street market, any one of a hundred street markets. Over-ripe fruit. Bruised vegetables. A braid of sharp voices. A boy again, hand in hand with his mother. From her purse, counting out the fen coins for the damaged and dented tins sorted from the series of large bins. Damaged tins, dented tins . . . always someone willing to buy. Cut price offers. No questions asked.

Piao's lips to his cupped hands, cupped hands to the old man's ear.

"You have a black market, doctor. Someone stealing the organs that you steal. Someone who doesn't give a fuck about quality control. Someone who will take organs that shouldn't

367

be taken. But there were four others who were dead on the foreshore that night doctor, also robbed of their organs. Three were foreigners, remember? Three who were not a part of our judicial system and who were not executed by the State. You recognised that also, doctor. Another reason why you didn't want anything to do with the case, Senior Police Scientist and you wouldn't even fucking touch them."

"I know nothing of these things, Senior Investigator. Nothing about black markets. Nothing about what you found on the foreshore of the river that night. I only know of our state policy to help those who cannot help themselves."

Another Zhishengji lifting slowly, sluggishly, as if afraid of heights. Scattering the compound in a strobe of blue-green, orange-red lights.

"What happens when demand outstrips supply, doctor, do you execute more prisoners to make up the shortfall of organs? Make laws that apply the death sentence to lesser crimes? Or just kill anyone who happens to get in the way?"

Wu pointed to the Zhishengji as it moved across the roof of the far detention block. The night sky taking up its spewed colours and dampening them.

"There are three patients waiting in the Number 7 People's Hospital in Zhengzhou. Two are high-ranking army officials, the other a businessman from Hong Kong. By morning they will have received their organs. Their new lives will have begun. Imagine, Senior Investigator, how they will feel? Imagine how you would feel? Like a new pocket watch on a golden chain of good luck."

For an instant, before anything moved, no sound, no colour. The Senior Investigator staring through the old man's spectacle lenses and deep into his eyes. The old man actually believed his own words.

"Yes, Doctor Wu." Piao whispered, ". . . a pocket watch on a golden chain with a broken heart hanging from each link."

★

A cut of headlights through darkness. A sweep of a turn. Reverse lights bleaching brickwork as the second ambulance backed into the inner compound, pulling up hard against open double doors. A stretcher loaded carefully into its interior; a cocoon of chrome and white aertex blankets. Just a prisoner's face visible. Pale. A pin-cushion of cropped hair. Heavily sedated . . . his only movement, the roll of the REM snared eyeballs under their lids. The doctor shifted uncomfortably beside Piao, waiting for the question as the stalk of wheat awaits the scythe.

"Who is he? Where are we going?"

"We go back to the hospital and then you will know."

"Know what, doctor?"

Wu raised a hand to his mouth, shielding his lips.

"Keep your voice down, Senior Investigator. I have said too much already. I will say no more. No more."

"I want some words from you, Wu. Names. Loud words. Loud names."

"No. No."

The old man's eyes flaring behind his glasses.

"Nothing more, I owe you nothing more."

The ambulance pulled out of the south gate, into the streets. The New Year. Crowds, lights, voices . . . laughter from mouths crammed with food. And with it, remembering every New Year that he had spent with her. Every single one. How they had always made love on that night as if it were a ritual, as if it would be for the very last time. And then eating oranges, watching the juice dripping onto her breasts. Oranges. As if it would be the last one that he would ever eat.

Savour the taste . . . one day it will be.

★

The body prepped, anaesthetised. Its torso held in a vice of blind albino theatre light. Looking down upon it from the viewing gallery. A globe of flesh, white, featureless. Its skin seeming as flat, as hard and barren as an ice floe.

Wu and the Senior Investigator squeezed into the back row, tacked onto the end. Every other seat in the gallery taken by young, bright-eyed medics. Some with pads, pens poised. Others with text books open across their knees. Below, the lights dim. Gowned personnel moving in the theatre in a choreography of precise measured paces and actions. Rehearsed procedures. On the table beside the body, the instruments being laid out in a flawless ballet.

"The prisoner that we brought here, what do they want of him?"

No answer. Just a cough from the old man. The measured response, a shutter to hold in place the fear, the secrets.

"Why him?"

Again, the cough.

"Speak, fuck you. Why him?"

A hiss of words, garlic and ginger on their breath.

"He is young. He is fit. These are the reasons. And he is available. His situation makes him available . . ."

Looking down, eyes hidden, but in his words, a distinct edge of shame.

". . . this I do not like either, as I have said, I also have principles. Principles are not just the property of the PSB, Senior Investigator . . ."

Pointing at the prisoner. Young. Fit. Available.

". . . I am co-operating with you for this reason only. Because I disagree with what we have here, not because I was held from a bridge by my ankles. You understand?"

Piao not able to hide the sarcasm in his tone. And not wanting to.

"I understand. You are a man of principles. Now tell me what is going on here?"

Doctor Wu half standing to go.

"You do not need me here, not now. It is too dangerous. Too stupid. I have brought you to this place, that is enough. I have given you enough."

"Stay."

Piao's hand firmly on the old man's shoulder, pulling him back down into his seat.

"But."

"Stay. Fucking stay, man of principles."

The Senior Investigator's hand a vice, his stare, like spot welds holding the old man in place. Below, the stage set. No one moving. Green gowned surgical staff standing in position. On hold. Waiting. The double doors to the theatre opened in an exuberant burst. A slap of rubber meeting rubber. Yellow light in a brief spill. And slicing through the space a tall figure, fully gowned in white. Tight hood embracing a full visor. The face, a harvest moon of shifting reflection. A stride rampant with confidence. An instant and all pervading sense that this was a man who could preserve or despatch any life.

On the operating table, the body now masked in tight folds of green canvas. A vulnerable rectangle of flesh running from sternum to lower stomach, from nipple to nipple. Four television monitors in the viewing gallery flicked into life. The conversations amongst the audience of viewing doctors and consultants, falling away. A close-up. Scalpel meeting skin in a firm paced glide. A single tear of blood following its path. The cut becoming a crimson plumb line. Becoming a track. An ugly puckered gape. Beside the surgeon an assistant, a thin wireless microphone across his mouth. A constant commentary relayed through to the gallery. Surgical techniques, cuts, clamps, medical procedures . . . every pass of the surgeon's fingers set to a stream of emotionless words. Piao's eyes moving from the crisp monochrome of the monitors and focussing on the ruddy wound stabbing the torso. Blood in smears and fine droplets across the surgeon's gloves. One kidney and then a second, eased from the viscous cavity of the clamped incision. Taken gently, as if they were newly born kittens, from the surgeon's hands and out of the theatre. The words rising like a wave inside Piao; hot, saline. Almost impossible to whisper them . . . when they needed to be shouted.

"What's going on here, he's taken both kidneys. The surgeon's killing him. Without a kidney he'll die?"

Wu removed his glasses. Eyes watering.

"The surgeon knows what he is doing, Senior Investigator. He has performed this operation many, many times before. That is why so many of our best medical students and surgeons are attending this demonstration. We desperately need more surgeons skilled in these techniques in the People's Republic."

"A demonstration? This isn't a fucking demonstration, this is cold blooded murder."

"No, not murder, Piao. You can live for twenty-four hours without a functioning kidney. They will sew the prisoner up and take him back to his cell. Tomorrow he will be executed."

The words fouled up in a tangle of lost thoughts. Piao's attention returning to the theatre below, the trolley already being wheeled out of the spotlight to a sterile side room. Silent . . . rubber across scrubbed white tiles. Another trolley, chrome bright, moving through the double doors past it. Almost touching. Already anaesthetised, a septuagenarian patient.

"What is this?"

The old man wiped his eyes, replacing his glasses. Waving the Senior Investigator's next question away. Below, the precise dance unfolding. Bodies never touching, paths crossed, but not blocked. Re-sterilised steel. Re-adjusted lighting. The surgeon re-emerging from the sluice room. Monitors in a petit mal of activity. A slow zoom to focus on a blade of surgical steel meeting skin. The cut . . . the commentary.

'The iliac vessels exposed retroperitoneally through an oblique incision, ten inches long, in the iliac fossa . . . the oblique muscles divided in the line of the incision and the peritoneum reflected upwards and medially.'

Parallel lines on a monitor. Incisions in grey. Dissections in grey. Blood in nondescript midtones.

'The renal vein anastomosed end-to-side to the external iliac vein and the renal artery anastomosed end-to-side to the external iliac artery.'

Chess moves in steel.

'The ureter is implanted in the bladder, ureteroneocystostomy . . . through an anterior cystotomy with a submucosal tunnel to prevent reflux. The right kidney being implanted in the left iliac fossa and vice versa, to facilitate the vascular anastomoses.'

Lights fading up. Eyes moving from monitors to the theatre below. Incisions in red . . . dissections in red . . . blood in a blazing primary.

'The wound is now closed, without drainage where possible. An indwelling catheter left in the bladder for up to five days. A 'living kidney', unlike the twenty to forty per cent of cadaver kidneys transplanted, will function immediately. Urine output over a twenty-four hour period will be expected to be in the region of five to two hundred and fifty one.'

★

Wu was already standing, moving up the small flight of steps to the exit. Piao at his shoulder, his words, a blow torch across the old man's cheek.

"Why, for fuck sake, tell me why?"

The doctor turned.

"He is General Zhang De, a Deputy Chief of Staff of the People's Liberation Army."

The Senior Investigator immediately knowing the name, the reputation, and the series of litmus tests that determines a senior official's real authority. The time and the place that a man joined the Communist movement. Was it before or after the Long March, the two year trek in 1935 and 1936 that shaped the People's Republic? Did the cadre serve in Yanan, the Communist wartime cave headquarters, or did he work on a less prestigious assignment as an undercover agent in the Kuomintang or 'White Area'? Was he a member of the Red Army or just a civilian party official? The 'tests'. The rites of passage. General Zhang De passed them all.

"His residence is within the shadow of the West Wall of the Forbidden City. He is a grade four cadre. The recipient of many commendations. He owns two Red Flags. A Japanese made colour television set. In his kitchen he has an American refrigerator. He shops at Number 53 Dong Hua Men Street, the 'Peking City Food Supply Place'. The store is only for the

373

Republic's highest ranking officials. Members of the Communist Party Central Committee. The heads of the eleven Military Regions which command the People's Liberation Army . . ."

Piao had heard of the store. Large yellow croaker fish, big enough to feed a banquet table of twelve. Frozen prawns from the Bohai Gulf. Whole sides of Sichuan pork. Fat wives queuing for fat husbands. Yes, Piao knew of it.

". . . such a cadre as this general, when they become unwell they are powerful and insistent in their demands. They get what they require, what they want. They get what you have seen. Fresh 'living kidneys', harvested solely for them. Harvested just minutes before they will receive them . . ."

Wu, silent as the streams of excited, enthusiastic medics clutching their notebooks, passed on their way to the exit. Looking down, ignoring their eyes. His whisper, as hot as crushed chillies.

". . . this is why I talk, just this. Not what you and your baboon did to me on the bridge, but what you have seen here."

The old man's hand, worn skin, flicking toward the theatre below . . .

"The prisoner, the boy. He was nineteen years old. His crime was that he stole two tractor tyres from the collective farm that he labours on. But it was not his crime that brought him here, to this. It was his kidneys for harvesting . . ."

The old man, shifting from foot to foot. As if words were weights. Sentences shackles.

". . . his real crime was to be young and healthy with kidneys that cross-matched with a seriously ill high-ranking cadre. And that he was available . . ."

Silent again, as another group passed, moving through the exit.

". . . with such kidneys as his, to steal a grain of rice would have been enough to get him executed. I am a moral man, this I do not agree with."

The Senior Investigator slumped into the nearest seat. Out of touch with his body, except for the vice slowly being tightened across his temples; his heart riding a tide of palpitations. Wu pulled open the door, his words in a fading trickle as he moved into the corridor beyond it.

The door slowly closing behind him.

"Walk away, Piao. Run away. Or perhaps it will be you who will provide the next harvest."

★

The last image . . . an incision's crimped edges being drawn together by bridges of suture. A furious line, as red as the narrow banded seal around a pack of Marlboro. So neat, the surgeon finishing the work himself in a balletic trip of catgut, needle, tweezers, scissors. Taking his time. An obsessive competence being exerted. To the last, displaying a flamboyance in the skills that he possessed . . . that were much more about the surgeon's needs and less and less about the patient's. Finally, laying aside his instruments, the job finished. Walking to the doors. Already removing his gloves, loosening the gown from around his neck. Pulling the hood from his head; the blond-silver hair, burnished steel in the light. Removing the full-face visor, behind it . . . Charles Haven.

For an instant, no more, stopping and looking up toward the gallery. No longer the lizard, more a snake . . . a snake the instant before it strikes. He turned and walked through the theatre doors, its rubber on rubber applauding him. Piao found himself standing; no memory as to when exactly he had left his seat. Legs uncertain, but already moving him toward the steps, the door.

★

A torrent pouring from the tap, scalding hot. The steam in a constant plume across Haven's face and the mirror . . . half of his features confused, indistinct in the fogged reflection. His arms parting the cascade, enjoying the burn of the water. Haven half turned, his face speaking of nothing.

"Why am I not surprised to see you, Senior Investigator Piao?"

"Because I am self-destructive, stubborn."

375

The Englishman smiled, turning off the tap, facing Piao. His eyes alive, missing nothing. Taking in the door, the windows . . . assessing if the Senior Investigator was alone. Smiling again, satisfied.

"You received my little gift?"

Piao reached into his inside pocket, removing the box of polished wood . . . opening it. Black velvet. At its heart, the gold of the cigarette lighter catching the light in its grasp. Sliding it across the work surface towards Haven. The Englishman dried his hands and removed his gown, before allowing himself to take back the box.

"Your investigation . . ."

"It is over," Piao cut in, moving to the door that led into the corridor; gently prising it open by half an inch. A crack of strip lighting, polished floor . . . and two men, thick set, leaning against a beige wall. A joke about a passing nurse's fat arse, still on their lips. Snorting laughter. The strain and bulge of their market stall jackets over shoulder holsters. Piao let the door slip closed.

The Englishman ran his manicured fingers across the top of his skull, his hair falling perfectly into place.

"You have come to arrest me?"

No fear. Eyes unblinking and the colour of ball bearings.

"No, not arrest you."

"Then, Investigator, Barbara Hayes and I will be leaving on our flight for New York which leaves in . . ."

He checked his watch.

". . . exactly four hours' time."

"No you will not, Mr Haven. Even in China, men who kill four people do not catch aeroplanes and just fly away."

The Englishman dropped a crumpled ball of used tissues into a bin by his feet.

"I can get one hundred thousand pounds to you within forty-eight hours, Senior Investigator. It will come through Liping. Of course, I will expect to be on my flight to New York. No delays. I will also expect you to hand all material relating to your investigation of me to Liping. He will know what to do with it."

"As he did with the bodies of Bobby Hayes, Ye Yang, Heywood and Qingde."

Haven turned slightly, light from the window tracing his cheek in crimson.

"For someone who is self-destructive, you have done well, Senior Investigator. You can end this a wealthy man . . ."

He pushed the polished wooden box across the worktop, against Piao's fingers.

". . . and you get to own the cigarette lighter that you always wanted."

Piao pushed the box aside, the Englishman's eyebrows rising to form question marks.

"You don't want the lighter, do you . . . or the money?"

"No."

"Liping told me that you would be like this, that you would not be bought off. I didn't believe him."

The Senior Investigator eased the door open once more.

"You should have believed him . . ." he whispered as he stared through the crack. The two men, CID or Bureau, still leaning against the wall. Another joke on their lips. Piao had heard it before. It was funny, but only when riding on the crest of six bottles of Tsingtao wave.

"I am curious to check if I am correct. The Americans and Qingde, they were smuggling cultural relics for you. Men of Mud. Ye Yang was pushing the price up. A tough woman. A stupid woman . . ."

Haven adjusted his collar. His tie.

". . . with the aid of Liping's security men, you went to the workshop in the snowfields, seized them and took them back to Shanghai. Back to a hospital operating theatre. You waste nothing. To just kill them in the snowfields would have meant wasting their organs. Hundreds of thousands of dollars on the transplant black market . . ."

Seconds. Seconds. Watching the Englishman. Fastening his cufflinks.

". . . raping them of their organs. On your operating table, letting them die . . ."

Watching him. Buttoning his jacket. Smoothing down the lapels.

". . . they would have been alive when you operated on them. Living organs would fetch more dollars . . ."

Haven lowering his mouth to the drinking fountain. The water on his lips, hardly wetting them.

". . . and then they were mutilated. Thorough. Carrying it out yourself . . ."

Haven smiled.

". . . it would have been very freeing. None of the rigours of the precise surgical techniques that you are normally bound to. Freeing . . ."

Watching him. Lacing his shoes. Precisely. An operation of fingers surely too delicate to fashion violence. A sense of the Englishman's anger, but of it immediately being cut short by him re-adjusting his tie.

". . . a mistake. The only part of the murders that you did not perform yourself was the disposing of the bodies. That you left to Liping's security officers. They chained them to four others and disposed of them in the Huangpu. The incinerator was on the other side of the city. The river nearer . . ."

No reply. But watching the Englishman's eyes. Waiting for a fray in the fabric. But nothing . . . just a clock ticking out its life. A confidence about the man. A sense that he was strapped firmly, safely, into a harness of insurance. Knowing something that the Senior Investigator did not. Piao reached into his jacket. Fingertips finding the polished steel sleeping in its shoulder holster. Cold. Re-assuring.

". . . and the four prisoners that they were chained to, legally executed in Virtue Forest. Their organs were infected, but still taken by you for the blackmarket. No tell-tale links between the two groups. Just coincidence. No deep meaning in this to Liping's men, chaining these two separate groups together and disposing of them in the river, rather than incinerating them. For men like these there is more meaning in the bottom of a bottle of Tsingtao. But for you, Mr Haven, a mistake. The first, the only, mistake . . ."

Watching him. But nothing to see of Haven, except the preened exterior. But inside Piao, the anger rising. A wave of hot tears and the compulsion to act them out.

Just shoot him. Here. Now . . .

". . . the Minister Kang Zhu, Comrade Officer Chief Liping, they were understanding of your mistake. Smiling Chinese faces pouring more drinks. But what is there for a westerner to read in the smile of a Chinese?"

Nothing in the Englishman's eyes. Baptisms of truth, and yet nothing.

Just shoot the fucker.

". . . and all of the time they were thinking the unthinkable. What if the threads were tracked back by one stupid, misguided person . . ."

The Englishman turned to the window, moving toward the briefcase that sat close to the door. Friends in high places will only put up with so many mistakes. Was he still a favoured foreigner, or had he become a loose end to be tied off? The Investigator, just his being there . . . said no. Someone was aiming Piao in his direction. A clockwork toy, just doing what it does. He would have to watch his own back now. But always a step ahead, that was how Haven worked. Not waiting for revelations. Never surprised by surprises. A step ahead.

Piao spread his arms, his contact with the pistol in his jacket, with steel . . . lost. Naked. Naked and vulnerable.

". . . I have given you the invitation to talk. To be known. To be found out. You have not found the words, but neither have you found the outrage. A serial killer who wants to be known, but not found out. But the ocean does not advance and recede in the same instant . . ."

Piao pulled the pistol from its holster. Grotesquely dark. Rude. Black. An instant smell of light machine oil, polished metals . . . and death. Slipping the safety. Finger firm down on the Type 67's spitcurl trigger. Haven's eyebrows arching in surprise. Moving back against the wall, hands falling into each other. A cradle of fingers not as relaxed as the pose suggested.

". . . I am going to walk you out of here. My pistol will be in your back. One fucking move from your men and I will put enough pressure on this very sensitive trigger to put a hole in you the size of a mooncake . . ."

Moving forward, the tip of the 67's silencer, grazing against the fine material of Haven's jacket.

". . . your men will follow, I know that, but it will not be so difficult to lose your CID in the longs of Hongkou . . ."

Pushing the pistol firmer against the Englishman's ribs.

". . . and then we will drive, and drive. North. Two, three days from now we will turn up at a small village and report to the local office of the PSB. At first they will not believe what it is that I have to say. Murders. The smuggling of cultural relics. In a village where the theft of a pig or a shovel is a major crime, this will cause much excitement. Everybody will want to be a chairman. Many telephone calls will be made. Officials will be drawn in from the next town, from the nearest city . . ."

Piao prodded the Englishman with the pistol.

". . . when wolves in their sleep smell the closeness of the deer, they awake with a great hunger. It will be their obligation to examine the case. It is cold in the north, the weather breeds people who are patient. Truths will come slowly, but they will come."

The Englishman's checked his watch, hand moving to the door knob.

"I have a flight to catch and Barbara to meet in forty-five minutes. It is against my principles to let a lady down."

"Walk into that corridor and I will shoot you."

Piao poked the pistol violently into the Englishman's side. Steel grating rib. Doubling up . . . pulling his hand from the door and to his flank. Face black with anger. But nailing it in place. Reasoning the venom from it, but storing it away.

"Shoot me . . . shoot me and you would be dead within ten seconds."

His eyes darting left, indicating the corridor beyond the wall, the two men standing in it. Smoke and stale jokes. Pistols holstered.

"It might be worth it."

"Suicide, for what, to provide a truth for Chinese justice?

Don't be so naive. You are the only one left, Senior Investigator, everybody else knows how rotten the system is from the top of the pyramid down. Everyone. Everything is for sale. Rock bottom prices. The People's Republic of China . . . a whore for a packet of Benson and Hedges. A state secret for a bottle of Teacher's. So what is worth dying for, Senior Investigator? Do you really think that killing me or bringing me to trial will end the transplant industry in your country. That it will stop the prisoners being executed and their organs from being harvested?"

The curve of steel against Piao's finger. Its tension. Squeezing it . . . the 7.62mm round, his anger. At that moment wanting to kill Haven; the Englishman with that rare ability to convince that everything that you touched or believed in, was covered in shit.

No words left anymore. Just kill the fucker!

Haven feeling the barrel of the pistol against his ribs expand, as if it was about to discharge. Holding Piao's stare in check with his own. Pointing to his top pocket. Moving his hand slowly towards it, the Senior Investigator almost mesmerised. Pulling a tie from it. Draping it over Piao's pistol . . . over the Senior Investigator's hand. A PSB tie. Food stain upon food stain across it. Yaobang's tie. Without doubt, Yaobang's tie.

"Yes, Senior Investigator, you are definitely someone who misses everything by just a few hours."

"Where is he?"

Haven pushed the pistol away from his ribs. The Big Man's tie slipping to the floor.

"He is safe, but if my associates do not get a telephone call from me thirty minutes before my flight leaves Hongqiao Airport for New York . . ."

"Where is he?"

Leisurely Haven walked across the room, picking up his briefcase.

"The string of barges opposite the north river entrance to the Jiangnan Shipyard in Luwan. He is on the furthest of the barges into the river."

A shiver. *The Huangpu*. Piao holstered the pistol.

"Then we have a deal, Senior Investigator Piao. I get my flight to New York, you get your fat deputy back . . ."

He stooped, picking up Yaobang's tie.

". . . and he even gets this back. It will be as if nothing ever happened."

Haven hung the tie over the Senior Investigator's shoulder. Piao pulling open the door and walking into the corridor; the two heavies stiffening. Jokes, smiles, falling from their lips. Their hands reaching into the insides of their jackets. The Englishman raised a hand and they relaxed, like pit bulls who had been thrown a bone. Still ugly, but well behaved ugly.

"I shall pass your best wishes on to Barbara Hayes, Senior Investigator . . ."

And then, almost in a whisper.

". . . I shall miss China."

Piao started his walk toward the elevator.

"Go and get your flight to New York, Mr Haven. Go before I change my mind."

Chapter 36

An anonymous rhythm drumming on the roof of the car. Rain incessant, insistent. Crowds in shop doorways, snaking, tight to the shopfronts, pressed hard against plate glass windows. Piao parked in Wanpinglu and proceeded on foot, half running. The downpour stinging, drenching him. Down his face in rivulets, off of his nose, his chin, across his eyes. And all of the time, a hole in his shoe . . . his foot, as wet, as cold as misery.

He hit the embankment and the climax of the New Year celebrations began, as if his reaching the Huangpu had triggered a switch. Down river, the Bund, a stream of rockets spurting skyward. Raking gold traces. The river as yellow as mustard seed. Another thunder, the river now as red as capsicums. Piao moved into the crease of shadow, down the embankment. From the steps, jumping onto the first barge; arm thick ropes threading through the bobbing, weaving caravan of rising iron pontoons. Fastened to heavy steel ring shackles fixed into the stone wall of the embankment in a weep of rust and algae. Beads of rain across his face, mimicking the primary colours of the rocket bursts. On his hands and knees; the roll of the river transferred through the cast iron hull of the barge, centring on his forehead. Numbing it. A swell of nausea flooding over him. They would be waiting for him on the last barge, knowing that he would be coming alone. Yaobang was here, he knew it . . . it was a trap, not a lie. He threw up. Fear or seasickness, he wasn't sure, and did it actually matter now that the options had all run out? More rockets, the sky thumping too violet, the clouds purple. He moved to the rolled lip of the barge, face to the sky, mouth open . . . the rain on his tongue in a taste of gunpowder, rusted iron, and every word that he had ever wanted to say, but hadn't. Thinking of a limousine on the road to Hongqiao

Airport. A jet being turned around, re-fuelled. The dull click of Haven's Dunhill cigarette lighter. Barbara's legs in a long lazy cross. And tonight . . . he could die tonight. He could die any night, so what the fucking difference? The difference being a red-hot rivet of shock, in the sudden realisation that he no longer wanted to die.

Standing uneasily. Looking out to the centre of the river along the uneven string of barges. An iron chain with each link providing its own white knuckle ride. Jumping across the crushing gap. The metal deck rising up, meeting his feet. Another gap, another. The river sandwiched in between rolling buffers of scarred iron . . . its waters in quick changes of hue as rockets streaked skywards, arced and fell. This time tangerine. This time blazing white. The night torn. Thick smoke linking cityscape to cloud base.

Piao slowed as he came to within five barge widths of the last pontoon, taking some breaths, calming the feverish thoughts in his head. His sweat mixed with the driving rain. The tide, now on the turn, each wave as plump as a pregnant woman approaching full term. Leaping to the next barge as it fell between waves; burdened by its bundled, tarpaulin and roped load. Losing his footing, falling. Grabbing the rough weave of heavy cords. A fierce rope burn across his palms, the colour of a crimson lipsticked mouth. Hauling himself to his feet, his thoughts already moving ahead. If they were as good as they should be, they would be well prepared and waiting for him. If they were half as good as they should be, they would already have seen him . . . and would be watching him now. Traversing the humps of cargo. The barge falling, its sister rising, jaw against jaw in metallic whelps. The river squeezed between them into fluorescent azure needles as the arc of the rockets reached their zenith, falling back upon themselves in a shower of sapphires. Barge to barge . . . Piao moving across, half jumping, half scampering. The light plunging to black. Cityscape, river, barges, melting into each other in degrees of grey. When the sky lit again in a flood of cherry-red, he could see the last barge moored tightly against the buoy. And a man, Yaobang, blood on his forehead, matting his hair . . . tied against the cargo hold. Checking the shadows, double check-ing; just the Big Man, no one else. Pulling his pistol and keeping low, the Senior Investigator jumped the gap to the neighbouring barge. The roughness of his cuff across his eyes, wiping away the shutter of rain. Checking the magazine, the spare nine shot detachable box in his pocket. Slipping the safety. Rockets falling in sparks . . . and everything exploding to grass green. The river. The rain. The deepest mounded folds of the tarpaulin. Rounding the puddled hillocks, eyes straining. A constant salvo firing in his chest; expecting to see a shadow peel from a shadow. Metal in its hand. A breath of flame, as a round was let loose from a snub-nosed pistol . . . but nothing.

A clear view of Yaobang now. The bind of ropes around his wrists, around his ankles. Shaking his head as unconsciousness loosened its grip. For an instant, light fading into grey, then the darkness plunged aside . . . everything, a blinding gold, as sharp as citrus juice. Dropping onto the fierce roll of the last barge. The rain in sheets of gilt. Moving toward the Big Man . . . words on his wet lips, but nothing coming out. His eyes widening, wild, staring past Piao, across his shoulder. Behind the Senior Investigator, a figure rising up, arms straightening. Piao instinctively diving to the left, the bundles of tarpaulin breaking his fall. Twisting. Both hands already wrapped around the Type 67's rectangular butt. Letting off two shots, chest height. A squat figure, blood-red in the vermilion light, folding, then falling hard against the iron of the deck. Head in a sickening concussion. Pistol skidding through the shallow puddles. Rain streaming onto his face, eyes open . . . but dead. A damp blot, almost black, spreading across the front of his jacket and double-holed shirt. A thud . . . and the sky was white, blazing. Transforming iron into ice. River into glacier. The shadows around the bow uncovered and with it, a grey smudge left stranded, shape shifting. Two, three flashes, as the man knelt, stood, ran . . . discharging his pistol. Piao picking up his sprint against the scuds of ferry lights, pin-line of the 67's sight chasing the running man's torso. Opening up with two bursts. One short, clipping off a mooring point. Its sparks, freezing white. The other shot holing the flapping tail of his coat. Letting loose another two shots . . . the rimless rounds finding their targets, hip and stomach. Punching him violently into the gap between the barges. The Senior Investigator running to the curled iron lip, about to look over into the slice of river when the hand reached up, as tight as a shackle around his ankle. Falling, losing balance, the iron of the deck racing up in a crunching blow. Piao's fingers bleeding, scrabbling for a handhold as the weight of the man pulled his legs, almost up to his groin, over the side of the barge. Looking down, the man's face silver with sweat and rain. The river below, black. Aware of the shrieks of fireworks all around, but seemingly far way. The only noises inside him, heart thumping, and the clatter of memories being assembled like train carriages to parade before him. A smell of gunpowder, raw sewage, and the cheap cologne of the man whom he was about to die with in the Huangpu. But in an instant it happened . . . seeing the sister barge rear up on the belly of a fat wave, the gap narrow. Rust iron jaws closing around the man's shoulders in a sickening squeal of metal against metal. His immediate loss of grip on Piao's ankle and on the welded angle iron that his other hand had been fastened to. The Senior Investigator hauled his legs up and over the barge's snarling lip. All of the time watching the man's face, the glaze of surprise in his eyes. Always surprise. Even as the barge's jaws closed around his skull in an embrace of bleeding rust, flaking paint, and memories, thoughts, life, spilling in a slow plume of scarlet . . . watching the man's face.

Piao turned toward Yaobang, nothing in the Big Man's eyes this time, but raising his bound hands . . . raising them, three fingers shaking and extended. Just three fingers. Three. There was one more left alive and he would be behind Piao. He had to be behind.

The Senior Investigator spun, keeping low. It was already too late. The noise, the pain, laced with fire. Two shots thudding into his lower back, punching him across the deck; colliding with Yaobang. Watching his pistol jolt from his hand. Watching his own blood, as warm as a summer night, curve and swirl into the rusted puddle around him. Everything . . . sounds, shapes, the rain against his face, edged in a new reality. Both close and distant, both serrated steel and plush velvet. Piao looked up, a man in front of him, chrome bright, pistol in his hand. Rain and light playing across his skull . . . Comrade Officer Chief Liping.

The sky crashed to indigo and Liping advanced with purpose, his footsteps making no noise. His words far away, as if being whispered down a long tunnel.

"Stupid Piao. You were my best Investigator. Always so clever. Too clever. To be too clever can be a disadvantage . . ."

Kneeling in front of Piao. The Chief's eyes, the warmth of blood flowing from his own back and yet tasting it on his tongue; the total that was the Senior Investigator's universe. And yet only thinking about Liping's knee resting in the puddle. It would be wet. It would be as cold as ice.

A man could catch a nasty cold . . .

". . . I saw myself in you. I tried to guide you. Encourage you. Warn you. Like a father with a precocious child . . ."

Liping placing his pistol on the deck; matt black on a river of reflection. The colours dying from cornflower blue to slate. Reaching into his pocket, pulling the blade of the knife from its body with over-precise care. Its honed edge catching the light.

". . . it hurts doesn't it Senior Investigator, to know a truth, to die for it? To know that it will die with you. Dying, that is what you are doing Piao. Will you do that cleverly as well, Senior Investigator?"

Liping reached forward with both hands, slowly, deliberately, as if to embrace the precocious child. Taking hold of Piao's right ear, at first gently . . . the grip increasing to the pinch of a vice. His other hand, the knife moving across the Senior Investigator's face. Coming to rest with its cold cutting edge hard against the pinch of flesh that joins earlobe to jaw. And with it, blood in a thick tear down the side of Piao's neck. The blade just at rest for a second or two . . . before striking violently upward in a sawing action. The knife pulled away across the Senior Investigator's line of sight. A wash of intense pain and sickening warmth flowing down Piao's collar to his shoulder. Liping holding the trophy between two smudged, bloody fingers. The ear, smaller, neater than Piao would ever have imagined. And yet knowing that he should be screaming with the horror, clutching with both hands to the side of his burning face. To staunch the pain, to dam the river of blood. But everything was dulled and there was no strength . . . the Senior Investigator could feel it slipping away from his back, burning hot onto cold iron. And all of the time, the rain drumming against his skull; marking the flight of each second.

Chief Liping spoke, each word remote and separately packaged. Washing the blade of the knife in the puddle. Replacing it in his jacket and standing as he did so.

"You have been a grub in the rice bowl, Senior Investigator Piao. So nearly ruining the banquet . . ."

Raising his hand, the pistol fisted in it. A single accusing finger of anodised steel.

". . . but now it is over."

The finger tightening, about to spit its venom.

A shot . . . its crack almost eaten by the anger in the skies overhead. Liping toppling sideways, as if he had been fashioned from an overextended pile of children's bricks. The pistol and Piao's ear, falling from his hands. The jaundiced white orbs of his eyes rolling up . . . dead before he hit the iron deck. Only when he was lying on his face at Yaobang's feet could you see what had felled him; the wound, the hole as large as a dumpling at the base of his skull. Blacker than his eyes. And the red ribbon flowing from it, across his neck . . . into the puddle, until the puddle was made up only of blood. Piao watched the flow of blood for some time, it reminding him of a kite's gentle tail riding the breeze, until the shadow of the man standing in front of him eclipsed it.

Haven knelt, his eyes so dark that they couldn't be seen. Two smudges holing his face . . . just like the eight, just like Bobby's. And all of the time, the rain, falling in the deep crease of shadow between them.

"You do not seem surprised to see me, Senior Investigator?"

388

The words, like a distant bell, weaving into the punch and slap of waves against the iron hull of the barge. Piao didn't answer, his attention like flotsam and jetsam . . . adrift and moving out of reach.

"But you wouldn't be surprised would you?"

Haven's fingers trailed through the puddle, the consistency of paint. Picking up the ear and holding it in front of the Senior Investigator's eyes. Placing the ear on his lap. Blood across his fingers. In the amber light, as brown as shit. Wiping them down the front of Piao's shirt.

"Failure is a new experience for you, it will take time to sink in. But of course, there will not be time for any new experiences to sink in. You are bleeding to death. In an hour, perhaps less, you will die . . ."

Just words, so many sounds following each other in a meaningless dribble. Piao adjusted his head slightly, all of his will power taken up and spent. Trying to look past the Englishman's shoulder to the river. To the pretty pink-coloured waves.

". . . you want to know why I killed Liping?"

Haven had taken his hand, carefully unfolding the fingers of his clenched fist.

"I was the loose end that he was supposed to deal with. A pity. He never realised that he was a loose end also. A loose end that I wanted to tie off . . ."

He smiled.

". . . I would say that he's pretty well tied off now, wouldn't you, Investigator?"

Haven wiped clean the butt of the rifle, the stock, the scope, with his handkerchief. Taking Piao's hand. Carefully, so carefully, modelling it around the pampered timber. As soft as the caress on a fat girl's thigh. Collecting the spent cartridge case and dropping it a few metres from the Senior Investigator's feet.

"Another loose end, the Minister, my business partner. You want to know why Kang Zhu has turned against me?"

Piao looking down at the rifle before staring into the Englishman's eyes; feeling their fire melt into his. Speaking the words, but his own voice so unfamiliar to him.

389

"Not paid."

Haven laughed, the inside of his mouth as red as over ripe cherries. He patted Piao's hand closed.

"Oh, he was paid, Senior Investigator . . ."

Standing, the light clotting ruddy around his head and shoulders.

". . . and now he is collecting the interest . . ."

He lit a cigarette. Smoke lost in smoke . . . as the stream is swallowed by the river, the river by the sea.

". . . so, Senior Investigator, this is how it looks. You were obviously acting out a vendetta towards your Comrade Officer, Chief Liping. It was well known that he was looking into very serious charges against you. You saw it as personal. You lured him here on the pretext of making a full confession. Yes, that sounds promising, we'll keep that bit in, shall we? But, of course, your Chief was no fool, he brought two men with him. There was a fight. Terrible. Bloody. Violent stuff. Nobody survived. No loose ends . . ."

The Englishman checked his watch. Still ahead of schedule. The night sky, a confetti of stainless steel sparks.

". . . I have a lady to meet. A flight to catch. And you, Senior Investigator, you have a death to die. Just like your fat friend . . ."

He kicked Yaobang's feet.

". . . as dead as a fucking dog."

Without looking back, Haven moved across the stagger of barges, the Senior Investigator watching their rise and fall; the hurdles of smoke icing the water, drifting across the rust of iron pontoons. A passage slicing through primary colours. Watching him. Watching until there was nothing left to watch. Piao's head fell back against the Big Man's leg, eyes filled with sky and a glimpse of Yaobang's face. As white as the full moon . . . unconsciousness smoothing out each feature. And the rain still driving in spears. And the blood . . . everywhere he looked. The blood.

The New Year was coming to an end. Rockets falling to earth. Crowds dispersing. Beer bottles in the kerb. The odour of sweat and of money spent that couldn't be afforded. The sky now darker than any other that Piao had ever seen. Looking up, hearing himself say,

"See the stars, they've come out tonight . . ."

The pin-pricks becoming smudges, as his eyesight failed. Only the pictures already in his head illuminating the black desert that reached out towards him. Her eyes. Her smell. Her hair. The way that her lips slumbered in a half smile . . . the secret that she alone seemed to know and would never give up. And through it all, a silver jet slashing toward a silver life, in a silver city, inhabited by only silver people.

Go and get your flight to New York Mr Haven . . . before I change my mind.

The palm turned to a fist . . . Piao at its centre. So dark, so black the night. Fathomless, and with nothing left in it for him. And all of the time the rain falling, a constant stream. As if God was pissing on him.

Chapter 37

Can you not see the waters of the Yellow River descending from the
Heavens, hurrying irrevocably down to the sea?
Can you not see that the high hall's gleaming mirrors are
saddened at the sight of your white hair?
Silken dark at dawn, by dusk it is like snow.

Fragments of unconsciousness, blunt, safe edged. Shards of consciousness, honed razors. Words shunting into place, as if snipped by shears from tinplate. Vague images, thoughts. His mind, a butterfly on the breeze, unable to settle on the bloom of any one idea. And then the morphine kicking in; carrying him on its warm roller, further, further out to sea. Away from the rocks of reality and the hard beach that had stranded him.

Looking up at the sky . . . stars and paramedics faces. Being carried across the buck of barges, the movement seizing his head, entering it in a sickening swirl. A glimpse, like a snapshot, of Yaobang being carried beside him strapped into a steel framed crib; his face, like crumpled paper. Across his forehead, a black crescent moon of a scar . . . no longer bleeding. And all of the time the rain. On his tongue. On his eyes. A sweetwater baptism. Reaching out to hold the Big Man's hand, the rain dripping from his knuckles, but the nylon straps denying him.

"Get your arm down, you'll hurt yourself."

Everything in degrees of blue. High on the embankment the ambulances, the patrol cars, lights revolving. Sirens opening their mouths. Doors slamming. Body bags zipping. Buildings racing through the smoke grey of the ambulance windows. The paramedic's face, bone and canvas taut skin, watching over Yaobang. So close that you could smell his life. His attentions turning to Piao. A sting as he put a line into his arm; taping it into position. The Senior Investigator reaching

out his hand again, across the Big Man's forehead. The paramedic forcing it down, tucking it under the nylon straps.

"Don't care about him. You're dying . . . care about yourself. Understand? You're dying."

★

A holding room of light and fogged pain. The bed hemmed
with rails. Tubes into him. Tubes out of him. Next door,
through the glass, in the hours between the minutes . . . the
theatre being hurriedly prepared. A surgeon, masked, waiting
. . . smelling of hibiscrub. Arms reaching down to examine
him with latex coated fingers. Running across his cheek to
where his ear had been. Traversing his back and probing with
a lover's gentleness at his stomach, his diaphragm. The lights
in fierce strips, as intense as an August noon in Kunming . . .
throwing blade-edged shadows across the surgeon's face, side
shifting his features as he pulled down the mask. Haven.
Golden and whispering words as if they were secrets, in
breathy gaps across Piao's face.

"You should be dead, Senior Investigator. Tough little bastard, aren't you? But let me assure you . . . you are dying.
Severe internal damage, kidneys, liver, stomach. So much
chaos from two little bullets . . ."

The words stopping for a few dripping seconds. Piao praying that they would start again for the coolness of their breath
across his brow.

". . . you made me miss my flight after all. Somebody wants
you to live very badly. They insisted on the very best surgical
team that money can buy, and so here I am. Very, very
inconvenient . . ."

Haven so close, cheeks brushing. The whisper as soft as the
breeze through the topmost branches of the trees.

". . . so, Senior Investigator, what is it to be, should I help
you to live or should I help you to die? The latter is easier and
more accommodating. I could catch the next plane if you die.
But to live, the repair work necessary . . . it could mean that I
would miss tomorrow's flight also. What to do, what to do?
Perhaps a little of both, eh?"

393

He turned his face and it glowed. Looking back to Piao, tongue tracing the inside of his cheek. Eyes as blue as a schoolboy holding a bag of sweets.

"Are you worth that much, Senior Investigator, another cancelled flight?"

Opening the door. Outside in the corridor, PSB officers seated, pistols slumbering across their laps.

"If the darkness has no end, then you will know that I decided to catch the next flight."

He left, a nurse entered, hypodermic in her hand. A needle fashioned from light. Feeling the darkness travel up his arm, to his shoulder, his neck, to the epicentre of his forehead. Expanding its warmth. The darkness filling his head. Black swirling black. And with it, the words . . . 'as dead as a fucking dog.'

★

Black. Red. Orange . . . yellow. White. The darkness blistering in episodes of unrelated consciousness. White. Yellow . . . orange. Red. Black. The light in agonising fades to timeless continents of unconsciousness.

He was a siphon. Tethered by tubes in . . . delivering blood, sustenance. Tubes out . . . flushing away piss, puss, waste. The hours measured by the puncture of hypodermics into his arm. The minutes, by the drips of the colourless liquids down the lines from the bottles suspended above him. Body, mind . . . separated. Only coming together in the clashes of panic as he felt the tide of morphine that held him, wane. The knives of pain, unsheathed, and carving at him. And then the release of the hypodermic. The slow float of the mind separating from body. Thought separated from action. Finding a part of himself in the far corner of the room, high against the ceiling; looking down on that other part of himself, that part held together by sutures. And in some islands of consciousness, aware of the change in the light, as a parade of faces that he once knew, gathered around the bed. Splinters of conversation stranded in mid-air. Barbara's fingers running through his hair, as cool as stream water. Remembering her holding him. Guiding him inside of her. The flex of her pupils as he had come. Her hair across his face. The smell of shampoo and of a cold bed made to sweat.

"You'll be all right now. Charles has done his best. It's up to you now. Fight, Sun. Fight."

Her long walk to the door, its sigh as it closed. Wanting to shout, but nothing coming out except for a string of echoes in his head. And again, the blackness gathering him into its deepest pocket.

★

Time, as syrup. Days losing order.

A group around the bed. None of them shadows that he could recognise. But knowing that they were officials. Cadre. Their smell of paper clips and foreign shoe leather. Clasping hold of some of their words as if they were lifelines in the storm of a sea.

"You should make a statement, Senior Investigator Sun Piao. Your record is exemplary. A statement would be in the spirit of your service with the Public Security Bureau . . ."

The nearest had leant forward, a gold tooth set at the front of his mouth. A convex reflection of the world with Piao, bandaged, at its centre.

". . . you are dying, clear the good reputation of Comrade Officer Liping. You still have family alive, do not let your shame spill onto them. Come, whisper your confession to me now."

Raising his head from the pillow. Blood on his lips. Lips to the cadre's ear.

"Fuck off," Piao had said.

Remembering their panic as he had fitted, haemorrhaging. The lines flushed full . . . a glorious red. An alarmbell cutting across the chaos. The nurse's footsteps. The injection. The sleep, thick and troubled.

★

Aware, over time, that they were cutting back on his medication. The sea of morphine receding. The pain roosting, feasting on him. More conscious of the procedures that he was the

395

focus of. Dressings around his head, his torso, being changed. Drips removed. Sutures snipped and pulled adrift. Slowly, a feeling of turning out from himself. Noticing his surroundings and a myriad of little details. Aware of the empty thirty bed ward, that only he occupied. Three exits. One opposite his bed . . . twelve paces of the sturdy nurse's legs away. The other two exits at either end of the ward, both over forty-five steps away. Outside each, PSB Officers. Brief glimpses of them as the doors swung. And their smell . . . of cold tea and hot crutches. And sometimes he could even hear them. In-depth conversations about nurses' tits. And stories about himself also . . . Sun Piao, who was once a Senior Investigator with the Public Security Bureau. And their summing up of his situation, an instant before one broke wind . . .

"Why bother fixing him up, they're gonna fucking shoot him anyway?"

★

"You have surprised us, Officer Piao . . ."

The Doctor pulled the drapes around the bed. Privacy, although the other twenty-nine beds in the ward were empty.

". . . you will live and make a good recovery."

He drew the blind, the sunshine across his face making Piao wince.

"How good a recovery?"

The voice that he now owned, foreign to Piao.

"A good recovery, for someone who had complete renal failure. One kidney shredded, the other detached and severely damaged. You were lucky. You are strong and had the benefit of a first class consultant surgeon . . ."

He turned, adjusting the tempo of the drip.

". . . he called a specialist in to attach your ear using micro-surgery techniques and carried out the repair work to your colon, stomach and diaphragm himself. He was even able to procure the organ for you. Most people, including high cadre, would have died on the operating table waiting for it."

"Organ?"

The Doctor smoothed his hands across his white coat and

adjusted his stethoscope. A ritual that every doctor that Piao had ever come into contact with practised.

"The organ. The kidney! You have been the recipient of a living renal donation. The match was perfect and the transplant went well. You are a very lucky officer. Very lucky indeed, Piao. Do you not think so?"

It was some seconds before he could speak. The young doctor's white coat already disappearing through the double doors opposite.

"Yes, doctor. Very lucky."

★

Another five times the group of officials came. Never giving their names. Never answering questions. Just asking them.

"Your investigation into the murders of the eight found in the Huangpu was a farce. You were looking for state security involvement and the complicity of high-ranking officials where there was none."

"It is all in my reports."

"You fabricated evidence and bullied witnesses to say things that suited your arguments. That suited your own views and ideologies. And you befriended a foreigner, a woman, an American government official, in the hope that this would enhance the authority of your stance."

"It is all in my reports."

"You attempted to taint the venerable reputation of Comrade Officer Chief Liping when you realised that he had seen through your traitorous accusations against the State, its officials and its people."

"It is all in my reports and at the bottom of the garden in Liping's zhau-dai-suo."

"Words, words. Your reports just condemn you. Charges against you for the murder of Comrade Zhiyuan were about to be formulated and pressed. You blamed your Commanding Officer. You lured Comrade Officer Liping to the river and shot him. There is no argument . . . the weapon was in your hand when you were found."

The statements and tirades had continued. On his state of

mind. On his methods of interrogation, signed affidavits from the criminal, Zhen, and the prisoner, Xie. Comments on his unorthodox methods from Chief Warden Hua and Detective Yun. Another signed statement from the city's Senior Police Scientist, Doctor Wu . . . words that spoke of the ordeal that Piao had put him through. Of the Senior Investigator's psychotic behaviour. Of his apparent death wish. They cited his failed marriage and the loss of his wife to a senior Politburo member as the basis for his disenchantment, his traitorous thoughts. She was now pregnant, having the child that Piao had always wanted . . . it was no secret. The shame. The intense upset and loss of face; powerful enough to unhinge the most responsible of citizens. All were given as proof of the Senior Investigator's mental breakdown. His violence increasing as the psychosis deepened. It could not be denied. It was all a matter of record. Catalogued. The Senior Investigator had used his illness and its accompanying violent behaviour to great effect, acting it out on a Comrade Officer who had done nothing but support and promote his protégé. And the woman, the American whore . . . what had Piao acted out between her milky thighs, between the yang-gui-zi's perfumed sheets?

Again, the gold tooth taking the lead.

"Confess, Senior Investigator. You will feel better for it . . ."

The other officials nodding, like so many little trained dogs.

". . . we know everything. A confession is for you, your family. It is not for us. We are offering you a chance to save your family's face. Why should they suffer a lifetime of no privilege's because of one like you . . ."

The gold tooth closer; the universe in its reflection.

". . . come, speak, Senior Investigator. There is nothing that we do not know."

"It is all in my reports . . ." was all that Piao replied.

They left. Twelve paces to the double doors opposite his bed. Piao counting each one. He never saw them again.

A week later, he was walking. Doubled over. Catching his reflection in the orb of a polished door knob . . . a question mark in a painful shuffle to the window. His strength in an unpredictable ebb and flow. One instant, in celebration of the vigour flowing into him. The next, in tears, as weak as a baby as he was lifted back into his bed.

★

The windows of the ward looked out onto Hongkou Stadium. Beyond, the Gonghexin Road lined on both sides with factories panting sallow breaths into the evening sky. He was unaware of any hospitals in this area, only the occasional rumour of a military hospital that was used for 'special cases'. Psychological cases. Another term for 'forced re-education'. Perhaps this was it?

In Hongkou Stadium the floodlights were alight. Brash, bullying, bleeding mercury onto the substantial crowd ringing its interior, surrounding the patch of green. The football players, dots. The game already started. A hazed mushroom of light glowing above the stands, pushing against the hospital building; nose to glass, across Piao's face. The window was locked but he tried to open it, again and again. The nurse, less sturdy legged than the others, stopped re-making the bed.

"We lock them. Patients throw themselves out."

Piao backed away from the glass and into the deep, high-backed easy chair, hearing it huff as he sat, taking up the contours of his body. Closing his eyes. Smells, sounds, colours. It was all there . . . the roll of the river under the flat hull of the barge. The blade down the side of his face. And the Big Man, crumpled, discarded, now only so much waste. His deputy, his ears, his eyes, his friend. Dead.

"I didn't want to jump. I just wanted to listen to the crowd, to other voices."

The nurse turned, uninterested. She'd heard those words many times before, but still they jumped. Now they locked the windows.

★

Another week. Another. No newspapers, books. No radio. Watching people in the streets below. Counting the minutes

399

to the nurse's next round. Rehearsing the usual exchange of words with the doctor as the dressings were removed. His ear healing, but still as blue as his eyes. The scars across his back in haphazard and organised train lines, running into junctions; red and raised. The dressings changed. Smudged brown to white. The doctor walked away. Last words before the night crashed around Piao. The last words for thirteen hours.

"You're well, Senior Investigator. Very well."

Looking out from the window, people in the street walking on stilts of fragile, elongated shadows. Quick footsteps, taking them on their way home.

"Very well. How well is very well, doctor?"

The door pulled open.

"Well enough to be executed?"

The door pulled closed, question unanswered.

★

Comrade Prosecutor Weishi knew him; he knew Comrade Prosecutor Weishi. Nods in corridors. Faces across polished meeting tables. Names falling within the same sheaths of reports. A relationship of shared points of contact, shared criminal targets . . . the rituals and niceties of being on the same side. But never bottles of Tsingtao clinked together. Never arms over each other's shoulders as drinking songs were bawled out. Prosecutor Weishi was not that sort of man. Neither was Piao.

The room was small, dominated by the bulk of the Prosecutor. A mountain of tumbling flesh swathed in a tight black Mao suit. A fine fabric, superbly cut, hand stitched. Only the Paramount on the Nanking Road or Beijing's Hung Bin, near the old Foreign Legation Quarter, could produce such quality. A suit to appear in most citizens' dreams, but never to appear in their wardrobes.

Piao sat, a large desk between them. The Prosecutor's virgin pad, with his fistful of sausage stubbed fingers resting across it. And his smell, lancing . . . sweat, as sweetly acidic as balsamic vinegar. Weishi swept a hand across his forehead; the perspiration that glazed it constantly, transferred to his palm and onto the pad. Its outline reminding Piao of the shape of a country. Australia, India, England? It didn't really matter which, they were all so very far away.

"So, Senior Investigator Sun Piao, tell me your story. Everybody charged with murder has a story."

The Comrade Prosecutor looked uncomfortable, far too fat for the chair that he was perching on; in plump black cotton, buttocks dripping over its edges. Two chairs would have been better . . . the Prosecutor was not built to sit on a fence. The phrasing of his question, its very tone, it was already clear which side of the fence he was slipping down onto.

"I don't tell stories. If you want stories, Prosecutor, go to the Xinyihua Opera."

Weishi bit his fat cherry of a bottom lip.

"This is difficult for the both of us, Sun Piao. Do not make it more difficult than it already is."

The Senior Investigator laughed, unable to remember when the last time had been.

"Difficult for the both of us; what is it that you really want?"

"The truth. Nothing more, nothing less. Every detail of your investigation. Every shred of evidence that you accumulated and which went towards founding the accusations and charges that you made."

"It's all in my reports."

Prosecutor Weishi reached down, with difficulty, retrieving a slim briefcase from the floor. Dark brown Italian leather; its rich brown smell losing out to Weishi's odour. Reaching inside. Dropping the thick pile of reports onto the desk.

"Your reports, I have read them. Now I need to believe them. I want you to say the words. Your eyes will tell the tale."

"The eight that we found in the Huangpu, they had no eyes. They had no tale to tell."

Prosecutor Weishi picked up his pen and wrote the date on the top of the pad, beside it, a large number one.

"But they have you, Senior Investigator Piao, to find out and speak the tale for them, don't they? Now tell me with your eyes, what their eyes would have spoken."

The interview lasted four hours. Full of repetition and glasses of warm water. Five other meetings of similar length followed during the next eleven days. And then a gap of over two weeks. No explanation. Every hour of that time spent reviewing each and every answer to every question that had been posed to him.

★

It was a different room, even smaller. Prosecutor Weishi in the corner, dominating it. Sitting. So huge . . . granite. As if he had always been there. As if the walls of the hospital had been erected around him.

"Liping's zhau–dai–suo, the garden. We dug it up . . ."

He halted to light a cigarette, knowing that Piao would want one, but not offering him one.

". . . we found nothing."

The smoke rising across his face.

". . . and the tapes and transcripts that you insist were hidden in your flat, they are lost. There was a fire. Nothing was saved."

A fire. Piao fumbled for the words, but they fell like loose change through his fingers. A fire. The tapes. The transcripts. But only thinking of his wedding pictures. His best suit. Headlights smeared across the room, fanning across Weishi. His stance becoming more formal. His words more framed and gilded with an authority that was usually reserved only for the courtroom.

"The charge, amongst others, of the cold-blooded, premeditated murder of Comrade Officer Chief Liping. I have found no evidence to overturn the charge made against you. I do not believe a word of what you have told me, Senior Investigator Piao. The trial will be held on the tenth, a week and a half from now. It will, of course, be followed by your immediate execution . . ."

The world imploding . . . everything shunted in with a jolt. The ceiling. His breath. The walls. His words. A feeling, not

402

unfamiliar, of being stuffed into a deep and dark back pocket. Prosecutor Weishi stood, moving to the door, wiping the sweat from his brow with the flab of his palm.

". . . Chief Liping was a good friend. A close and personal friend. You understand?"

And he was gone. His smell, a sweet reek, remaining . . . reminding.

"I understand."

It took hours until he could sleep. Hours until the Prosecutor's stink could be driven from his nostrils.

★

The car was a black Shanghai Sedan. Blank plates. Tinted windows. Two men inside, tight eyed and sleepy lipped. They would be the remainder of the CID team; two of their comrades spent on the rust iron of the barge, felled by Piao's rimless rounds. These would be the men who had killed his cousin and the student. Also Comrade Zhiyuan. These would be the men who had murdered Pan and his brother, the Deputy Investigator. Yaobang, the friend whose burial Piao had been forbidden to attend. He got in the car. The sweat starting its run down the side of his face. Weakness reaching into him, seizing his brain in a lurching carousel. The car smelling of danger and unclean underwear, and of June roses past their best showing. Slowly, it pulled away; Piao doubting that he would ever smell June roses again.

June . . . the fortnight when the 'grain is bearded'.
The weeks of the 'plum rains'.

The car moved from Zhejiang and into Jiangxi. A residential area just beyond Jingjiang; high-walled mansions, corralled and tamed woods. A district devoid of ugly government buildings. Neither were there any courthouses in such a place as this. But executions?

Beyond the village hemmed in by the mountains, the road broke like a twig. Paved carriageway into rutted dust. The woods darker and less tame. A window was partially open, but

403

Piao could hear no birdsong. A gravel drive splintered from the track, and at the end of its lazy meander sitting awkward in the olive shadows, a mansion of beige stone and heavily hung trellis work. Hanging from it, roses large and brooding, like blood-red kisses.

The air was rich. Piao's first steps beyond the corridors of the hospital for three months . . . the combination nearly intoxicating him. And the smells so complex, washing away the residue of antiseptic and polish. All at once, he could smell the earth, as brown and as bitter as dark chocolate. The grass, freshly rained upon. And the apples, holed and bruised, lying rotting on the ground. An a-yi waited at the door, Piao following the CID across the courtyard towards her beckoning hand. There was no one behind him, he could have run, the tree line thirty, thirty-five metres away. Weighing up the pros, weighing up the cons. He wouldn't have made ten metres before they caught him. It was painful, but he was the weak one, they the strong. It was reality. Reality, the only commodity there had never been a shortage of in Piao's life.

The house was dark. His pupils widening to take in the detail. Wood panelled walls. Oil paintings; thick paletted colours stabbed into form. Polished hazel oak floors. Islands of salmon pink, powder blue; Chinese and Persian carpets. And from the leaded windows, a simmer of light.

The elderly a-yi left behind. The CID officers now leading . . . at the end of the corridor, stopping at heavy double doors. Waiting for ten, fifteen seconds before knocking lightly. Smoothing down their hair. Tightening ties. A voice . . . bracing themselves before pushing open the doors. Perspiration on the polished brass door plates. Piao entered, the doors being closed behind him. The large room was dark. Heavy drapes across the windows. Rows of books and oak furniture. A smell of dust, old age, money, and piss-stained underpants. A long and ornate desk, leather topped, gold embossed tracery. And behind it, a darker shadow cut into the shadows . . . a man carefully, intricately peeling an orange. The smell of dust and urine submitting to citrus.

"Sit down, Sun Piao, you must still be very weak. Sit.

404

Although we have never met, I do feel that I know you so very well."

Piao remained standing, not knowing what to do with his hands.

"You don't know me. It's my wife that you know, Minister Kang Zhu."

Eyes getting use to the gloom, picking out the trace of gold rimmed half glasses. The widow's peak of hair slicked back into a tight black cap. The crab fingers unfurling the orange from its peel; an unbroken ribbon, lengthening. An umbilical cord linking fruit to desktop.

"Then I should tell you something about your wife that I know, but which you do not know, Sun Piao . . ."

In the Minister's hands the orange taking on a secret sensuality; Piao knowing that in his own hands, it would just have been food. The thought making him feel clumsy, half a man, but a whole failure.

". . . your congratulations are in order. Last week Lingling had her first ultrasound scan. The baby is healthy. It is a boy. Ten thousand ounces of gold."

Piao felt his heart sink. Thankful for the darkness of the room, as a flush instantly spread across his face.

It should be my child. My son. Nemma bai – nemma pang. Too painful to remember . . . too painful to forget.

The orange peel falling from the fruit and onto the desk. Zhu breaking the flesh open, evenly separating the segments. Juice down his fingers.

"A silence is worth a thousand words . . ."

Juice on his lips.

". . . have some, Sun Piao. Come, take an orange, it would be good for you. You must build up your strength."

He held out a palm, the segments served on its trenched plate. Piao looking past it to the faint reflections on the half-moon lenses of the Minister's glasses, to his eyes.

"Forty seconds and you've proved that I was right to hate you all of this time. Just forty seconds. That must be a record, even for you, Minister?"

"No, no it is not a record . . ."

He laughed, short and without humour, sounding like a hammer beating on a car panel.

". . . but let us not get personal, Sun Piao, this is not the time for such things."

"Then what is this the time for?"

Zhu leant back in his chair. The juice from the orange, sticky on his fingers. In turn, sucking each one clean.

"Today is the seventh day of the month. Soon it will be the tenth, the day of your trial and of your subsequent execution . . ."

He removed the last of his fingers from his mouth. It glistened with saliva. Examining it as he spoke.

". . . this is the time for the making of deals . . ."

The folder was already on his desk, the Ministry seal sticking to it like a bloodstain. He nudged it toward Piao.

". . . a full pardon on all of the charges against you and any charges that might be pressed in the future relating to your investigation. There is also a letter of authorisation from the Comrade Secretary of your Danwei that will allow for your temporary transfer to the Central Investigation Department. You will note that you have been promoted by several grades, your pay adjusted accordingly. Also included are purchase authority slips for an apartment, furniture, clothes, a new car. A very generous package."

Behind the glasses, the mercurial brightness of the Minister's eyes. The prospect of a child could light up even the most weary of eyes when you were, *Ni-ai* . . . 'drowning with love.'

"Deals have two tongues, both sharp. What do you want from me, Minister Zhu?"

"Very astute, Sun Piao. From you, yes, we do want a little something from you. The Englishman known as Charles Haven, you will kill him for us."

"For you Minister, you want him killed for you."

The smile was slow. A calculated slither bending Zhu's mouth into a harsh sickle.

"Yes, Senior Investigator, I stand corrected. You will kill him for me, but yourself also. The Englishman murdered your own cousin, your deputy and your friend, Officer Yaobang.

The Englishman left you to die on that barge in the middle of the river. And your American government official, how safe is she with such a monster . . ."

Zhu folded his hands together. Fingers, a sharp weave of thinly veiled bone. Imaging those dry twigs across her breasts. Raking through her hair. Guiding her hands to the shrivel of his cock. Imagining her name called by the old man as he came. Lingling. A cracked bell of tuneful syllables hung with thick spittle and the smell of ammonia.

". . . this American, I hear that she is very beautiful, that is, if you like American women. Personally I find their looks similar to a sky in the summer. Bright, but empty. Featureless. But I was told that she had legs like the necks of swans and breasts that you would not get bored with. Tell me Sun Piao, how many times did you fuck her, once, twice, ten times? Whatever it was, it was not enough, was it? You still think of her whenever you smell fresh bed-linen. Whenever you get an erection, do you not?"

Piao moved closer to the desk, at last, something to do with his hands . . . bracing them on the leather, edged with gold tracery.

"Killing Haven for you, Minister, this is more than just covering tracks, tying up loose ends, isn't it?"

It was in Zhu's eyes. Truth. As pale, as indistinct as a cataract. But still truth. And with it, Lingling's words, as she had talked about the Minister that night in Piao's flat. The file, the tapes, tight in her hands.

He is already serving a death sentence.

Her breath on the window, fading with the death of each word.

"This is in your blood, isn't it? Revenge. What could a man like Haven have done to deserve such anger, Minister?"

Pain in a ragged flight across Zhu's irises. For the first time discomfort seeping into the Minister's posture. There was a full minute's silence before he spoke.

"In collaboration with several other Politburo comrades, I was keen to develop an organ transplant service in our country . . ."

407

Squirming in his seat, the leather creaking.

". . . Charles Haven was brought in to head a team that would do just that. Develop a service. Train our own medical personnel and surgeons in transplant techniques. To produce a network that would cope with our own internal demands and sell our services to foreigners wishing to come here for transplants. Using the organs of prisoners was inspired. Haven is a very brilliant man. He achieved all that we wished, plus more. He became a most favoured foreigner . . ."

A glass of water at his elbow, the Minister picked it up, coughing, drinking it dry.

". . . we offered each other the courtesy of favours. We made many deals . . ."

Zhu placed the glass down onto the desktop, his finger distractedly tracing its rim.

". . . I was one of the first that he operated on, along with several other influential Politburo members. I received a living kidney from a prisoner who was due to be executed the next day. The transplant technique went extremely well. Post operative recovery was quick, smooth. Exceptional for a man of my age, I was told. But I had not realised that our screening of donors and their organs was so inept . . ."

Removing his glasses. The corners of his eyes glistening like jewels.

". . . I had not realised that HIV was so widespread in the People's Republic and that you could be infected from a transplanted kidney . . ."

Not giving Piao the pleasure of seeing him wipe his eyes. Replacing his spectacles, blinking back the tears.

". . . it was only when Lingling found that she had my baby in her stomach, the many blood tests, that it was discovered that she had contracted the HIV Virus . . ."

An icicle around Piao's heart. Lead in his guts.

". . . I did not know it, but I must have been carrying the virus for those years. I infected Lingling, your wife. Lingling, the mother of my child to be . . ."

A buzz invading Piao's head. Hot, deep, dangerous. The

anger pushing out in all directions against the inside of his skull.

". . . HIV is not conscious of rank. It does not stand around in corridors awaiting an appointment. As for me, it has been diagnosed that I now have AIDS. My immune system is fully depressed. A month ago I had a major operation to remove a cancerous tumour from my insides. They found many others. I have very little time left . . ."

He poured some more water, sipping it.

". . . yes, you are very astute, as I said earlier. This is personal. This is revenge . . ."

He pushed the folder further across the desk, its edge against Piao's fingers.

". . . the Englishman. You will kill him for me. For your wife and the child. And for yourself, Sun Piao. And for the others whose faces you see every time that you close your eyes."

"But I'm not a murderer. I'm not an assassin. And I don't give a fuck about you, Minister."

Zhu switched on a desklamp; hard light, as yellow as amber. For the first time seeing the wasteland of the Minister's face. The eyes sunken into potholes.

"But yourself, Sun Piao, you are about to be tried and executed. Do you have the capacity to think of yourself? It is sometimes more difficult to do than hating others."

"A high cadre, a fucking Politburo member who is a part-time philosopher. History is full of such dangerous combinations. Millions of graves can testify to that."

Zhu pulled the folder back to the centre of the desktop; his fingers parched leather. The ministerial seal like a red-hot coal beneath them.

"An anger to take you all the way to your execution, Senior Investigator. But kill the Englishman, Charles Haven, and you can claim back your life. Lingling will need you. Listen . . . she will need you. That is what you have wanted to hear every day since she left you, is that not true?"

Leaning across his desk, breath as sour as unfermented wine.

"Your life is fading by the minute, Sun Piao. Kill the Eng-lishman. You do it. You know him. You have the anger. Kill him and live. Kill him and you will be protected by the law from the charges that are held against you."

"The law? What does a man like you know about the law, Minister, except that others follow laws and you make them and break them."

A cough rattling the Minister. Deep. Dark. A storm of the soul escaping through a gaping mouth. Lips as tight as elastic bands stretched to their limits.

"Kill him. Look what, look what he has done to me. Kill . . . kill him."

Looking deep into Zhu's eyes. Tears, in weak tracks down his cheeks. From his lips, spittle, on fine filament dribbles Silver-white and flecked scarlet, dropping down to the desktop.

"No, Minister. I will not kill for you. Or for me."

Zhu's cough ploughing deeper, suddenly halting to a sharp intake of breath. A barbed hook that rolled his eyes. That made his crab fingers scuttle across the desk, seeking some unknown purpose. On his lips, down the front of his shirt, as thick and as deep hued as plum sauce . . . blood. Instinctively, Piao running to the double doors, thumping on them with both fists. Hearing his own voice in a guttural shout for help. Instantly, the two security officers swept into the study, sweeping the old man into their arms. His spectacles in a slow tumble to the floor. Blood and thin laced vomit, across their shirts in an angry scar. An immediate reek of bile, vinegar and gamy, filling the room. Mutterings from Zhu's lips, loose and mouthing against the security officer's chest as they swiftly ran him from the room and into the corridor. A door open-ing, closing, at the very end of the corridor. And then silence. Complete. Unbroken. As silent as if the world itself was hold-ing its breath.

*

Piao slept for five hours, seeming like five minutes. Aware of the constant activity at the end of the corridor. Comings, goings, from Kang Zhu's room.

He awoke worried into the dark. Never as black. Sitting on the end of the bed . . . Lingling.

★

Morning. The sky lemon, when she rose kissing him . . . tasting of salt and strawberries. Her words few. Last words. Almost thrown away as if they didn't really matter. As if she had never doubted that he would agree to what she would ask. The Englishman, Haven, what he had done to the eight in the river. To the Minister. To herself . . . the HIV, the slow boat of death. What he had done to Piao . . . his trial, his execution only days away. So many venerable reputations to be soiled by his wrongdoings; reputations pulled through the mud. So many to lose face. Such loss of face. Yes, he had to be killed. There was no other way. The Senior Investigator would, of course, do as the Minister had requested . . . save himself and kill the Englishman. She kissed him again, this time longer. Sweeter.

"Haven. Kill him, Sun. If not for the Minister, then for me."

She had smiled, and automatically he questioned the words that he knew that he wanted to say. Each one a fishbone in his throat.

"I am not an assassin."

Lingling closed the door, walking silently to the room at the end of the corridor. The smile slipping from her face.

★

The day was one of uncomfortable silence. Sleeping, as it took him. The nervous naps of a cat dozing on a window ledge high above the ground. Dreams of only hard things. Spiked things. Food served at regular intervals by an elderly, toothless a-yi. Outside of his room, the measured pace of security officers. And inside of his room . . . a constant awareness of the corridor and the Minister Kang Zhu's bedroom at the dark end of it.

Seeing Lingling only once during the whole of that day. A glimpse, brief and desolate, as she had run the length of the corridor. Her bare feet making no sound. Both hands

411

clasped to her face. Tears bleeding between the gaps of her fingers.

★

Dust angels moving through a splinter of morning light.

The a-yi left . . . Piao' s eyes adjusting to the darkness of the study. Moods, textures, filling the room to its brim. Everything the hue of mahogany and bitter chocolate, except Lingling. Her back, hard against the bookshelved wall . . . wearing white. Completely in white. The colour of death. At the centre of the study, the carved desk had been removed. In its place, a heavy chromium plated stand, resting upon it, a dark wood coffin. A re-touched Kang Zhu only partially filling its large gaping interior. Hair slicked. Cheeks rouged. Lips painted. More a septuagenarian clown than a Minister of Security.

She moved from the bookshelf towards the casket. Her perfume, Chanel . . . invading. A sharp stiletto piercing other scents. The scents that Piao always associated with death. Wet earth. Long standing puddles. Rusty railings. Fallen fruit. She stood at the coffin, her crimson tipped fingers braced on its carved wood and gently tapping to some anonymous rhythm. Speaking across its mouth. Speaking across the body of Zhu. Again, the question . . . more forthright this time. It worrying Piao that she felt no need of levers in her words.

"Will you kill the Englishman for me?"

For me. The Minister's dead, but Lingling taking up the reins of vengeance.

"I am not an assassin."

For a second, her fingers still, before moving to the window and pulling the drapes aside. Piao shielding his eyes as the room flooded ice-white. Details . . . noticing details. The fingerprint grain in the wood of the coffin. Gold titles on the spines of the leather bound books. 'The Water Margin'. 'Rulin Waishi'. 'The Family'. 'David Copperfield'. And Zhu's eyes, looking like black scratches under glass. Mascara smeared and charcoal pencil underlined. The Senior Investigator's gaze drawn to the residence's gardens, a verdant fist . . . at its centre

412

a man. Paper pale. Across his forehead a jagged scar. Yaobang. Beside him, the shadows of two security officers.

"As you see, not dead at all . . ."

Flexing her fingers, she studied her nails, gesturing toward the window, toward Yaobang. As if remarking to a girlfriend about a handbag in a shop display.

". . . he will be executed, maybe his organs harvested, if you do not kill the Englishman . . ."

A head-on collision of emotions. Both extreme, both opposite. Alive, Yaobang alive. A thump of joy in the Senior Investigator's chest. And in the other corner, regret, loss . . . already starting a process of grieving for him. The Big Man's life in the palms of his hands, yet about to leak between his fingers.

"No, I will not kill for you."

Lingling moved around the foot of the casket.

"Sun, you are making me do things that I do not wish to do. Turning me into someone that I do not want to be . . ."

It was raining outside. On the window, the snare-drum rhythm of its fall. The security officers still standing over Yaobang. His hair wet. Its square cut fringe, spiked, as serrated as a bread knife.

". . . that is what men do to women. You turn us into other things. The bits that you do not want, we become. The things that you will not do, we do for you . . ."

Heavier, now the rain. On the trees. The leaves. On the grass. Over her shoulder, Piao watching its streaked, grey fall.

Wash everything away, please wash it all away.

She was reached into her pocket, in her fingers a piece of paper. Unfolding it slowly. A computer print-out. Its words unveiling a more personal horror. A premature shiver taking hold of Piao.

". . . this is from your specialist at the People's Military Hospital. The results of your latest blood tests . . ."

Taking it from her fingers. Everything with an edge. Hues. Smells. Textures. Feeling the thickness of the paper between his fingers. The print raised infinitesimally above its surface. But not reading it. Not needing to. Knowing that she would tell him. With certainty . . . knowing.

413

". . . the transplant organ, the kidney that you were the recipient of at the hands of Charles Haven. It had come from a living donor. A prisoner who was infected. The Englishman would have known of this . . ."

Outside, still the rain. Seeing its flow in rivulets from Yaobang's nose and chin. Seeing its fall on every individual blade of grass. And above, the sky moving in a seamless shutter . . . the colour of amalgam spat into a sink.

". . . the prisoner had HIV. You have HIV . . ."

She smiled. A lipsticked gash. The sky falling. Piao feeling for a chair as his legs melted. A blurred snap of a glance, out of the window to the gardens. It was still raining, but the Big Man was out of its fall now and nowhere to be seen. Out of its fall, safe and dry. Safe.

Chapter 38

See . . . the waters of the Ghost Month fall on the dry earth.
See . . . we burn the incense. We make the offerings.
We appease, pacify the spirits of the ancestors.
See . . . still the rice does not grow.

The rain . . . here she came again. Every day. As if earth were turning to ocean. For weeks now. Months?

Piao sat on a log, its fall in a constant wash down his face. Each drop, a snare beat, drumming the strength back into him, where before there had been none. In the corners of his mouth, its taste . . . bitter tastes. Only bitter tastes.

He followed her journey from the main body of the house, a glide in black, leaving no witness to her passage on the sodden lawn. A large, dark umbrella above her head, like a brooding cloud. And then she was with him, standing over him.

"It is time," was all that Lingling had said.

★

During the ride to the airport he had read the slim file. Arrangements. A hotel room. A car. The airline tickets. Expecting a flight to the United States of America. Gleaming people in gleaming cities. A jolt of surprise pinning his back firmly to the velour upholstery of the black foreign car.

A flight, one way . . . to Capital Airport, Beijing.

★

On the flight, as they had spanned the garden city of Suzhou, the silk city of Wuxi, Zehngjiang on the Long River Delta, following the straight cut of the Great Canal and crossing the ancient Marshlands of Hebei . . . he had removed the last two items from the file. A large and detailed article from the provincial newspaper 'The Daily Weekend' and a computer listing of Visa details and internal travel permits. The subject . . . Haven.

As Piao had drunk tea, scalding and bitter, and the CAAC flight had turned across the frayed edge of the Sea of Bohai . . . his finger ran down the pale grey lines. The Englishman re-entering the People's Republic just over a month ago. Forward travel onto Kunming approved and stamped, basing himself there ever since. Kunming, with its reputation as a transit centre for drug trafficking and its major hospital, the Kunming Court, renowned as a centre of excellence. Just days ago, the internal travel permits showing that Haven had entered Beijing. A return flight, CX 251, to the United States of America, reserved . . . and just days away. So smooth his movement in and out of the People's Republic. So smooth his internal travel within the country, from province to province without question. It was obvious that he was still a 'favoured foreigner'. Still a man who had friends in very high places.

The article from The Daily Weekend was a copy, from a copy, of a copy . . . grey on grey and barely readable. It debated the new liberalising changes to the law that the National People's Congress had approved and which had come into effect in January. Among other provisions, it allowed the authorities to seek out alternatives to the use of the firing squad as a means of carrying out state sanctioned executions. It named a doctor, Wang Jun, a director of a hospital in the south-west of the People's Republic, who, since a few months ago, had been experimenting with the most reliable method of putting people to death. The work had been thorough. Exhaustive. His teams of doctors trying out a never-ending wave of drug cocktails on convicts. Slowly, slowly . . . narrowing an efficient death down. The main concerns, the main criteria being that the lethal injections should not damage the victim's internal organs that could be used for transplantation. The final batch of criminals had thanked the director and his team, as they had voluntarily presented their arms . . . sleeves rolled-up, ready. All had seemed calm. Not one had been tied to their stretchers. Twenty-two had been injected by the doctors. Twenty-two had died. Each death individually monitored by colleagues holding stopwatches and clipboards. Levels of pain accompanying death, duly notated and described. The timings of how long it had taken to die, fastidiously recorded. Death had ranged from three minutes forty-five seconds to just fifty-seven seconds. This was seen as being dependant on whether the criminal was lying down or sitting up. But more so, on what cocktail of drugs had been administered. Mixture No.1 or Mixture No.2. Within days of the final trials, Hu Jiankang, Director of the Intermediate Court, had approved the use of Mixture No.2 as the 'preferred dose' of the State, for what he had termed as, 'a kind of euthanasia'.

Director Wang Jun's pioneering work in this field was much praised and was now being studied at national levels to see if it should replace the ritual of execution by a shot to the base of the head or into the back.

Piao had sipped the tea, now cold, tasteless . . . as the jet had turned, dropped, whining on its initial approach towards Capital Airport, fifteen thousand feet below. Through the window, heavy cloud. Black on grey. Grey on black. Nothing of the world to be seen. And knowing, before he had even read it, what the footnote in Lingling's handwriting would say . . .

'Doctor Wang Jun is the Director of the Kunming
Court Hospital.'

Kunming.
Haven.
Friends in high places.

417

Chapter 39

The interpreter was working on the last page of the computer data. A fall of Chinese characters toppling down its length, spilling from page to page. Her finger, steady, manicured and baby-pink tipped, scanning across the black laser print, cross referencing.

"Have you traced the email?"

Moving slowly across the cutglass vista, Carmichael glanced back toward Barbara Hayes. Removing his spectacles. Polishing their lenses on his tie. His eyes so small, so impossibly small. He resembling a Gucci garbed Winnie the Pooh.

"Hot mail addresses, false data, and re-routed through at least four systems. It could have come from anywhere . . ."

He smiled. His eyes only coming alive once he had replaced his glasses.

". . . I've narrowed it down to the People's Republic."

Barbara stared out of her office window across the 'City of Magnificent Distances', to the Potomac. It could have been any river at the onset of night. The Thames. The Seine. But more so the Huangpu; perhaps it was, in so many ways. She raised the glass to her lips and drank the wine. Australian . . . flowers and honey, but strangely soulless, empty. Looking out of the window to the streams of cars, tail-lights slashing . . . fleeing home to the white and affluent north-west quadrant of the city. Weatherboard twee and stucco chic; worrying about their kid's college fees and the hardcore porn found under little Billy's bed. And in the south-west and south-east districts, blacks dreaming about getting a job. Where the fuck the next ten dollars was going to come from and what the hell had ever happened to the American Dream.

"Madam Hayes, I have finished."

Barbara turned to focus on the interpreter; Chinese-American, with the looks that spanned two different worlds . . . fusing them together in soft tans, silky blacks and features crafted by a much more delicate palette knife.

"What are they?"

"Hospital records. Confidential hospital records . . ."

The interpreter's nail scored through a chain of characters, identical on several papers.

". . . this is headed the Shanghai No 1 Hospital, the Huangdong."

Barbara dipped her fingertip into the wine and onto her lip.

"What sort of hospital records?"

"Lists of transplant organ donors. Lists of the organ recipients."

Ask her. Ask her.

Barbara looked toward the far window. Toward the voice. Bobby, naked and wet. His finger drawing darkly on the sea of condensation. Circles. One, two, three, four . . . interlinked.

Ask her.

His voice, so clear, but his lips unmoving. Beyond him, beyond the glass of the window, a vista in grids of multi-coloured electric. Everyday, Christmas. His face drinking it in . . . sightlessly.

Dreaming . . . just dreaming?

Barbara pointed to the characters outlined in marker. Fluorescent pink, as bright as cheap candy. Already knowing the answer that would come.

"And these?"

"Names, Madam Hayes, as close as they can be to the original American names. This one will be the name of Professor Heywood. This one, the name of Robert Hayes."

"Bobby."

The interpreter nodded.

Ask her.

Barbara drank some more wine.

"What do the records say about Bobby Hayes?"

419

The interpreter's fingernail moved from character to character.

"He was a donor. Heart, living kidneys, corneas . . ."

She turned the pages, cross referencing; highlighted candy-pink to highlighted candy-pink marker pen.

". . . his kidneys were transferred to the No 7 People's Hospital in Zhengzhou for immediate transplantation. The corneas were kept at the Shanghai No 1 Hospital and were both used for corneal grafting on the same recipient two days later. There is no further mention of his heart."

Ask her.

"The recipients, do we know who they were?"

Pages being turned.

"His kidneys were transplanted into two recipients. They must have been very important officials. Their names have been withheld."

"And the corneas?"

A veil of ebony hair across her face, the interpreter brushing it aside. Her eyes, rubber balls, dancing down the characters and pages.

"They went to an American national . . ."

Tying in the patient's reference number to a computer billing invoice. Tapping it with her knuckles, as smooth as cowry shells.

". . . the bill, it was paid in cash, forty-five thousand dollars. The corneas went to a child, ten years old. Adam Michael Irving. There is an address in Philadelphia. Also a telephone number."

Barbara took the page to her desk, tracing out each individual digit of the number with her fingernail. The telephone number of the boy that now saw through Bobby's eyes. Picking up the receiver. Dialling. And then silence. Silence marked and measured by the thump in her chest. Listening, and finishing the wine, warm and weak, but immediately craving something stronger. She cut the call off before it connected, knowing that if it had been answered, it would have been answered by him. Him. A ten year old boy. He would be blond . . . also knowing that. And with beachball blue eyes.

Bobby's eyes. She put the receiver down, moving to the drinks table, pouring a large Teacher's into heavy crystal. Gold into silver. The ice cracking as the spirit made contact. Raising the glass to her lips and drinking it in one. Pleasure and pain, the Scotch. Fire and ice.

Ask her.

"Bobby Hayes, his heart, kidneys, and his corneas, who removed them?"

The interpreter turned pages, eyes following the meander of her own fingernail; as certain, as convinced as a scalpel's deep glide.

"A consultant surgeon. A Doctor Charles Haven."

Eyes burning, Barbara turned to the window, but Bobby had gone. Just the circles left; tears of condensation bleeding through them.

Dreaming . . . just dreaming?

"Is there anything else, Madam Hayes?"

Barbara placed her hand in a gentle print across the glass where Bobby had traced. She could feel him,

"No, I've finished. I appreciate your help, thank you."

The door closed. The room empty. The world empty. Just tears filling it. Picking the sheets of data up from the desk as she left; the brief cover note with its faint smell of China Brand cigarettes. She could imagine him writing it. She smiled, placing them in her attaché case. Turning off the office lights.

"Thank you, Sun Piao," she whispered, as she moved toward the elevator.

★

Walking . . . a perfect day torn apart. A sky in tatters. Sun, but rain on its coat tails. You could smell it, feel it. Wanting it to come and pass, but it was digging its heels in.

Barbara hurried her pace. Walking nowhere, but everywhere. Past familiar cafés. Seeming unfamiliar. Everything at odds. Only turning back to the office, resolve in her pace, when the tail of music wagged from the open doors of the bar.

421

'The moment I wake up,
Before I put on my make-up . . .
I say a little prayer for you.'

Sometimes everything, anything, takes on a meaning.

★

Pushing the intercom.

"I need someone checked out, Carmichael. All the way. And traced. I need him tracked with a daily update. Whatever it costs. Whatever deals have to be made. He's in China at present. I'm not sure where. If its Shanghai, it will be the Jing Jiang Hotel. If it's Beijing, the Diaoyutai State Guest House . . ."

Through the window, the sky moving toward darkness in a steady flow. Almost liquid. Yellows to mauves. Reds to purples.

"Friend or foe?"

Barbara's eyes followed the curve of the Potomac, the George Washington Memorial Highway hugging its far shore in a lazy flex of traffic.

"Foe."

She could hear his fingers already tap-dancing across the computer keyboard.

"You said 'him', so it's a male?"

"It's a male."

" An American National?"

"No."

She heard the slap of the keys slow, fall silent.

"Not one of us, so what is he?"

The sun falling like a stone toward the horizon. Barbara left with no certainty that it would ever rise again.

"He's English."

"As English as fish and chips. Scones and jam?" Barbara smoothed her hand across the glass, city lights blooming smeared beneath it.

"No, Carmichael, as English as 'Jack the Ripper'."

Chapter 40

THE GHOST MONTH, *GUI YUE* . . .
THE SEVENTH LUNAR MONTH.

Do not be devout, for during this time the ghosts of hell will walk the earth. Do not be devout or it will be a dangerous time to travel. To go swimming. To get married. To move to a new house.

Do not be devout, for during this time if your husband should die, your wife, your father or your mother, if your brother, sister, or your own child should die . . . you shall not bury them. You will preserve the body for a funeral, a burial, a month later.

Long weeks. Longer days.

So many things not to do if you are devout. So many things to do if you are.

On the first and fifteenth days of the ghost month you will burn ghost money and incense . . . to appease, to pacify the spirits. On the first and fifteenth days of the ghost month you will prepare food, carefully, intricately, offerings to be placed on tables outside your home . . . to appease, to pacify the spirits. On the first and fifteenth days of the ghost month you will bathe, dress in your best clothes and visit the Taoist temple . . . to appease, to pacify the spirits.

Death, it is a sensitive issue. Do not talk of it . . . do not hint of it. Longevity, you talk of. Death is taboo. Be careful, so careful when pronouncing the number 'four' . . . in Chinese it sounds so like the word for death. Do not give a clock as a gift, it is a sure sign that somebody will die. Should you write a will, it will be impossible for you to find a witness to your signature upon it. If you give flowers, always give red flowers, never white . . . white, the colour associated with death. The purchasing of life insurance, this is to be avoided. And if you are to take a holiday or to move home, always seek out the many wonderful geographical names that litter the People's Republic, as confetti does at a wedding. Happiness Valley. Paradise Road. Heaven's Gateway. The Boulevard of a Thousand Joys. When visiting the United States of America, go to the many beautiful National Parks that the country has to offer. Except one, always avoiding one . . . Death Valley.

And on the seventh day of the seventh moon, falling during the heart of the ghost month . . . *qingren jie*, lovers day. Cards. Chocolate candies. Restaurants. A day of love in a month of ghosts.

Do not be devout . . . too devout. It may pass you by, the ghosts stealing it away.

Chapter 41

BEIJING, THE PEOPLE'S REPUBLIC OF CHINA.

A man moving against a wall of sheet mirror-glass. Moving through the traffic of Chang'andongjie . . . an artery of a city chewing on the fumes of one million cars, ten thousand buses, fifty-five thousand taxis, one and a half million motorcycles. Still distant, but unmistakably, Charles Haven.

Closer. Outline firming. Features, shifting, settling into place. Eyes, surprisingly blue. Furiously blue. And hair, blonder than Piao had remembered.

Memories of memories of memories. How they fool. How they convince.

The Senior Investigator lowered the pocket binoculars and rubbed his eyes. Sleep, not so much a natural act now, more a butterfly that refused to be netted. Watching as the Englishman pierced the shadows of the pavement, entering the Bank of China. Days now . . . trailing him on a leisurely journey. Hospital to hospital. Bank to bank. Government office to government office. The boredom and weariness building. Paralysing. Disabling. Flowing through the Senior Investigator's arteries into his muscles and the cortex of his brain. Doing a job that would have required the deployment of thirteen PSB officers if it had been a Bureau operation.

Surveillance . . . an art in which mistakes cannot be erased. Piao, pulling every trick from a deep bag of experience. Changing his jacket frequently, extremes of colour. Glasses, sunglasses . . . worn, not worn. Sometimes a tie, a collar. Sometimes a tee shirt, a vest. Hanging different keepsakes in the windscreen of the hire car and changing them frequently. Lucky charms. A Dragon. A miniature football shirt. On the top of the windscreen itself, see-through plastic stickers with different boy's and girl's names on it.

Peng & Ye. Yan & Miao. Zhou & Lili.

Changing them frequently also. Anything to deceive the quick glance of the target being followed. Hints that his eyes would catch that would pacify any suspicions. Operating at an almost subliminal level. Subtle messages, whispering to his sub-conscious . . .

See, you are not being followed. His jacket is a different colour. The windscreen of the car has different names upon it . . . Hong & Wei. A dragon hanging from the rear-view mirror, not a plastic Coca-Cola bottle. See, he wears a tie, not a tee shirt. And sunglasses. Relax . . . see for yourself, you are not being followed.

★

It was an hour and a half before the Englishman emerged to an afternoon dying on its feet. Hot rivers of traffic from Qianmenxijie, Tiananmen Square, Dongdandajie . . . south, towards the Park of the Temple of Heaven. An hour and a half, waiting . . . sweat, in slow trains down the back of his shirt. Watching the bank's revolving doors revolve. Parents, children in tow, leaving the Palace of Museums. Three hundred and ten thousand objects dedicated to the political indoctrination of the people.

An hour and a half, Piao thinking only about a gap in time and place in which he could kill a man.

Keeping a respectable distance. Parking beyond the line of trees, the perimeter fence. Through binoculars, smudges focusing into hard edges . . . watching as Haven returned to the Diaoyutai State Guest House. Walking up the steps of one of the many villas dotted around the leafy grounds of what was the site of the Imperial Residence some eight hundred years previous, the villas . . . reserved only for the most noteworthy of foreign guests. Immaculate. The Englishman looking as if the day had not held in its teeth a humidity that almost bled sweat. A day in a life, marking its passage by the grubby rings of grey soot that it bequeathed to the inside of shirt cuffs and to shirt collars.

A glint from a brass and glass door, and Haven was gone. Piao parked, walked. The Qianmen Hotel two blocks away. Three hours sleep. A shower, as cold as misery. Shaving, cutting himself. Blood in a flow, and unable to staunch it. *Fuck, fuck . . . why won't it stop!* In the mirror, half misted, a face staring back. Hardly recognisable. Tracing the scar around his ear. Across his stomach. Its ache in red seams down his back. Feeling and looking like the jigsaw of an old man. Plunging his face into the washbasin. Ice and hotel soap. The water flowing over its rim. Again, again . . . vigorously washing his face, his hands. Wanting, needing to wash so much away. Until the pain, the decisions, the shadows of acts not yet carried out . . . were gone. The hotel soap in a crudely printed wrapper. The hotel soap making him smell of pink roses. All day, of pink roses.

★

Picking up Haven's car on Salihelu. Prompt, 10:30am, as usual. Black, German . . . Mercedes. The morning light, like sliced lemons across its paintwork. Hot, humid, the air already with a sting in its tail. Thoughts of a shower, ice cold. A kill, flame hot . . . orbiting the Senior Investigator's attention. Through the glare, following the Englishman to fixed points in a day, measured by pools of boredom . . .

11:00 to 12:15 – On Beichizidajie, the Public Security Department.

12:35 to 1:45 – Capital Hospital, north on Dongdanlu.

2:00 to 2:55 – Lunch at Fengziyuan, 'The Horn of Plenty'.

3:15 to 4:10 – The Jianguomenwai Diplomat Compound off of Ritanlu.

4:30 to 5:20 – Beijing University and Qinghua Technical College.

The black Mercedes pulling north towards Nanhai, negotiating the junction at Qianmenxijie. Traffic in a smoked shuffle as the sun fell through the concrete tangents and aerial forests of the city. The Senior Investigator on autopilot. Brief glimpses of Haven in his interior of leather and glass. Piao trying to see him as stone . . . just a target to knock down. But failing miserably. Only imagining the swift act. The blur of action. Form, colours, in a haemorrhaging wash.

A knife . . . *yes, a knife would be best.* A series of 'pops' as it pierced jacket, shirt, skin. Resistance, as it pushed through flesh. Grating bone. Seconds, it would be, the knife up to its hilt, his fist against the silk of the Englishman's shirt . . . before the bleed. Seconds, to stare into a man's eyes whom you are killing. Seconds, to contemplate what noise it would be that would prise his lips apart, as the wave of blood rolled up his shirt. Cream to crimson.

Knowing how it would be. Intimately. With certainty.

It was dark when the Mercedes pierced the sanctuary of the Diaoyutai State Guest House . . . and was lost to sight. Dark, as the Senior Investigator drove across a city splintered in harsh neon light.

★

As straight as an arrow, the Fuxing Road . . . leading onto Xichang'anjie, Dongchang'anjie, Jianguomenwai. Out of the city, into the city, out of the city. Spearing Beijing, pinning it in place. A tarmacadam stick through the belly of a wriggling fish. Lanes of traffic, racing hot . . . angry.

Piao put his foot down. The Mercedes four cars ahead, on Qiamendajie, feeding onto the carriageways, moving east. A seamless dip into madness. Chromed psychosis. Jamming into the next lane, horns all around him. Swarming motorcycles in wild flight. No rules in this driving, just muscle. In the Mercedes, its air-conditioned wave, Haven, running a hand through his hair. He was going to be late. Ten, fifteen minutes, but late all the same.

Fuck this traffic. Fuck Beijing. Fuck China.

Across the carriageways, low enough to see the rivets, a jet, sprinting up from Capital Airport. Gaining height now as it stretched south-west towards Wuhan. The great cotton growing plains of Hebei would be under its wings . . . the invasion route of the Northern Barbarians as they made their way to the Yellow River Basin, tempted by the shining lights of civilisation. The ancient capitals of the Celestial Empire, Luoyang and Kaifeng . . . the silver jet's footsteps. The Yellow Mountains, Heavenly City Peak, Immortal Peak, Flying Dragon Peak . . . umbilical cords of recognition. Piao lit a China Brand, drawing on its bitterness. Pulling his gaze from the sky and back to the tarmac. Better to concentrate on the road. Silver jets fleeing to silver cities, were for silver people. For him, the piss puddled longs. The tattoos of cabbage leaves squashed underfoot. The streets choking in their own smoke.

So many places never to see, an itch that you can never hope to reach.

Ahead, a Toyota pick-up, mud and chrome dented fenders . . . pulled violently across two lanes, separating Piao from the Mercedes. Horns, brakelights, a flock of motorcycles startled into a weaving dance. In slow motion, one going down. Angle between bike and road surface pressing more acute. A hand taken off of the throttle and held up, warding off fast metal. Wheels coming down fast. The Senior Investigator floored the brake. Arms locking, bracing as they bit hard.

"Shit. Shit."

Thumping the wheel with both palms. Fumes, heat haze . . . rubber tainted. And through it, watching the Mercedes drift away. Haven lost. Tail-lights in a fade from scarlet to palest pink. Fading, fading, gone.

Forty minutes for a paramedic crew to fight through traffic, knotted and growling. For a motorcycle and a pick-up truck, to be removed from the lanes. For the road to be swept of glass, mud, twists of metal trim, and sawdust put down. Piao having to drive halfway to Tongxian, shadowing the Great Canal, before being able to head back west towards the city centre. Midday now, and the shadows shortening. The highway cutting between Baliqiao and the distant city . . . a sweep of greyed spikes, points blunted by a mustard haze of pollution. At the debris littered junction with the Wenyuhe and the Chaobaihe, the traffic slowed, staggered, stopped. No apparent reason, just the secret life of heavy traffic. The Senior

Investigator lit another cigarette. Winding down the side window. Smoke escaping across the outside of the windscreen. Looking around, the heat haze rippling metal and flexing concrete. Through car windows, faces, puffed and pink. Releasing the handbrake as the string bead traffic loosened and slowly broke up. Clear road glimpsed between bumper to bumper. As he eased the gas, black seeping into the corner of Piao's vision. A car, squat and glossy . . . cruising. Opening out into a sprint of jet laced in tart lemon splinters of reflection. A Mercedes, in the next lane, easing next to him. Its driver in a nonchalant sideways glance at Piao. Palm on chin, the Senior Investigator in a vacant sideways glance back at the other driver, before the realisation.

Haven. Fuck it . . . Haven.

A high tension wire hooked up, eye to eye. The Englishman shorting it. Foot clamped down on the accelerator.

Piao. Fuck it . . . Piao.

A dash of black sprinting into silver, as the Mercedes gunned. A second, two, three . . . before the Senior Investigator reacted. A buzzing, deep, hot, invading his inner ear, as he careered his car across the lane. Fifty metres ahead, the Mercedes, lost in exhaust and skidded rubber. A smell, heady, sickening . . . like burnt caramel. Like a belly full of too much toffee apple. Everything accelerating, as if he was stationary, but the world itself was racing. Headlong. Unbalanced. Everything now with a razor edge. Everything now liquid, and with the hue of mercury. The game over. Ripping the adhesive names, Zhou & Lili, from inside the windscreen. Tearing the miniature club football shirt from the rear-view mirror. The game over. Unshocked, as he realised, without even a hint of hesitation . . . that at last he could kill.

Ahead, the traffic building. A wall of heat rippling metal. The Mercedes slowing fast. Brake lights bleeding ruby, as it skewed across the lane choking in its own smoke. A door flung open. A figure in white momentarily glancing back. Running. Running, against the stream of heavy traffic moving with resolve in the opposite direction. White against red. White against blue. Black . . . yellow. A curtain shimmer of heat leaving the tarmac. Pluming from bonnets, roofs. Shrink-ing him. Swallowing him. Piao also running. Under the soles of his shoes, the burn from the road. Instantly, sweat in a sheen across his face, his arms. Sprinting, drawing every ounce of energy to his legs; already starting to labour. Shins, ankles, knees, turning to rusty iron. Calves, thighs . . . concrete. A running man chasing a running man down a broken corridor of slow-moving glass, plastic, chrome. The gap between them measured in dirty number plates and worn treaded tyres. Each windscreen burning from a sun held at midday . . . cadmium. Everything feeling as if it were in the process of being gilded.

The highway rising across a grey junction of traffic, static in exhaust fumes. Ahead, thirty metres, forty . . . the Englishman. Legs, torso, head, distorted by the shimmer of the road surface as he ran from the bridge's apex and down its gentle incline. A monochrome matchstick man, shifting against a wall of col-our. Piao's lungs bursting. Fire and lead. The slope tugging at his stride, pulling him down like a magnet. Sweat in streams . . . down his face, neck, chest. Aware that his thoughts were drifting, like feathers on a breeze. A glimpse across the parapet, below, a string of schoolchildren, five, six year olds, hand in hand and being led across the junction of snarls and belching smoke. Anywhere but here . . . at that instant wanting to be a child. On a swing, a slide, in a play pit. Crossing a junction, hand in hand in hand, with other children. Anywhere but here. And other thoughts, random and fired by delirium. Only one image holding. The Englishman, at his feet, dead. Centre of forehead, an unbleeding hole from a single round.

So neat. So very neat.

The distance between them, not closing. As if an invisible hand were holding them apart. As if that hand didn't want blood on it. A moan of horns as Haven vaulted the barrier, parting the on-coming traffic. Waves of motorcycles curving, folding around his sprint. A mechanical waterfall engulfing him. Ahead, the slip road where the Tonghui River turned snakelike, meeting up with itself. The Senior Investigator fol-lowing with gasped breaths. Oil and dust. Catching his foot on the top of the barrier, falling . . . gravel, stinging into the heels of his palms. Bleeding in deltas down his wrists and onto his shirt cuffs.

"Fuck. Fuck."

Mentally pulling himself up, but wanting to stay on the road, clasped to the narrow central reservation. Starting to walk. Starting to run. In his mouth, the taste of blood. Face to the sky, pulling on breaths as if they were chains tethered to anchors. The sky . . . just knife-cuts of cloud in a cerulean wash, but praying that it would rain. Rain. Cold and relentless, like that night on the stained iron deck of the barge. Ahead, Haven. A stutter of glimpses through traffic. Shreds of white, riding in, riding out of focus through a bow wave of exhaust fumes. Moving down the slip road and onto the rough ground . . . the shadowed ground, beneath the spans of the flyover. Sunlight, shadow, back into sunlight. Haven, a chameleon of caramels and creams. Beyond the flyovers and the constant sigh of eight lanes, a series of dirt tracks. Government run yards hemmed by a holed wire fence. A topography of trash tips and snubnosed mountains. The Englishman already amongst them, in running relief against their detritus. Snared in the reflections of oil slicked and rainbowed puddles. Piao, through the gate. Corrugated iron shacks. Black dogs pissing gold. Bent men . . . dull-eyed. And the heavens achingly blue. Ridiculously blue. Broken only by the lonely scratch of a single telegraph wire, threaded between poles. Curve to curve. Curve to curve. Curve to curve.

The track finishing in a cul-de-sac of dust, patches of black oil, snatches of exhausted grass. The Englishman already climbing, falling, negotiating a series of rubbish dunes. Looking around. A snatch of a glance . . . worried. Face catching the light. A sheen of sweat, as if he were fashioned from stainless steel. Piao stopping on the rough path, almost collapsing. Doubled up. Lungs . . . hotplates. Breath across his lips in a hot fan. Looking up, Haven, like an albino spider. Feeling for his pistol, its butt, but drawing his hand away from it. So easy to kill, now. So easy . . . but wanting to see his eyes. Needing to see his eyes as the round discharged. Punching, buzzing through material, skin, flesh, bone. So easy; too easy.

And now he was running again, meeting the mountain. A jolt of surprise as it unveiled its face, its features. Ripples, waves, walls of electronic trash. Circuit boards. Computer parts. Television components. A technological ocean, receded and beaching a highland range of hitech carrion. At its boundaries, its beaches of bare earth, loose knots of women veiled against a merciless sun. Hands heavily gloved against the razor edges. Busy fingered and quick-eyed, as they stripped the precious metals, silver, copper, brass, sometimes gold . . . from the never-ending electronic flood. Recovered metals. A twelve hour day would earn the rice, the noodles, a few vegetables, to feed five . . . as long as they were not too hungry. To feed five and to put away a few fen for days when the dragon's breath was too hot.

Just a view of the bottom of the Englishman's shoes, his arse, jacket flapping, the back of his head . . . as Piao looked up. And a sky, cloudless and fired. An avalanche as Haven reached a snubnosed summit. The Senior Investigator, arm across his face protecting himself from the fall of razor sharp corners. His forehead in a blaze as something hit it . . . the blood, slow and full, running back into his scalp. Climbing, clambering to the top. Watching, wide-eyed, breathless, as the Englishman stumbled down a broken incline. Each foot riding the back of a slow, controlled slip . . . and into a short and scissored valley, before he started another climb. Instinctively, it seemed, knowing where Piao was; looking up and across, on his face a smile. Chisel cold. The Senior Investigator stumbling down the deep fall. Arriving in the valley . . . spit, blood, on his lips. And words, whispered, shouted. Ripped with frayed breath.

"Fuck you. Fuck you."

Climbing again, each hand hold, a cut. A sense of everything moving in oil, slowed, silent. Against a candied scratch of cloud, the Englishman pulling himself up to a fractured and spiked plateau. Running, running. White turning to black in the fierce blind of sun. Piao following, in a delirious chase through a colour bleached landscape. Stopping, pulling his pistol. His hand shaking uncontrollably . . . hardly able to carry its weight. Moving to a double grip. Hand over hand.

Centring himself. Calming himself. Panning with the sight. A running man . . . black on white.

"Fuck seeing his eyes."

The trigger squeezed, round loosed. On a sharp bridge of electronic scatter, a spark of fire. A thud, in echo, playing out its shout over and over again. Missing Haven, but causing him to twist violently. Losing his footing and dropping. A wheel and blur of arms, legs, down the cutglass crag. For a while, laying motionless in the deep crease of valley shadow. Piao running. Pistol aloft. Exhaustion miraculously dissipated. As the white suited figure stirred. Sat. Stood. The Senior Investigator in position above him on the clip of the summit. So easy, but again, wanting to see his eyes before killing him. As if scripted, the Englishman raising his face. The Senior Investigator steadying his pistol for a head shot. An easy shot. At last, his eyes. But no satisfaction in the viewing of them. Nothing of worth within them. Piao's finger in a slow, deliberate squeeze. Waiting for the gentle click that you hear an instant before the hammer strikes its blow. The gentle click that travels through the pistol's metal body and into your hand . . . centring into the inside of your wrist. Faintly exhilarating. Faintly terrifying.

Slipping . . . below Piao's feet, component boards, switching units, terminals, keyboards, spent VDUs. A high ridge crumbling into its individual constituents. His pistol sight in a tremble. A waver. A jolt. Violent blurrings . . . Haven, an off-white elongated smudge. Slipping . . . arms pointing upward. Piao desperately trying to pull them down, back on target, as his feet struggled for a firm stance. But aware, the bitterness palpable, that he was already falling backward, away from the Englishman and down the other side of the ridge. Pistol sight aiming at the sun. Blurs, thuds, a violent carousel of dangerous motion, freeze-framed in twisted colours. A shot discharged, let loose. But its crack already fading into a darkness marbled with scarlet.

★

The darkness . . . a second, a minute, an hour? Pulling himself up, over the truncated ridge. The landscape transformed, but the pistol still in his hand. Tight, knuckles white. Wet with blood. Reaching the top of the ridge, looking down into the gash of valley. The Englishman gone.

★

In the shower, a man standing. Washing his hair, face, body. Concentrating on his hands . . . cleansing them again and again. Thoroughly. Intricately. The soap, the foam . . . red to pink to white. In slow, plump drips, from his fingers, his forearms. Down his torso, his legs. One, two, three languid revolutions around the waste hole and gone.

A telephone rang and Charles Haven stepped out of the cubicle, its door already open . . . a pool of water across the marble floor. A white linen suit discarded. Half dry. Half wet. Rips, bloodstains edging them like lipsticked mouths. Walking to the table. A puddle beginning to form where he stood naked, slowly sinking into the thick piled carpet. Listening with an extraordinary attentiveness, then unleashing the words. Anger, raw and unrefined . . . undiluted. The very edge of a razor blade. The very edge of a madness.

"Comrade, don't piss in my ear and then tell me that it's raining. I need him dealt with tonight."

Silence. Ten seconds. Fifteen. Twenty seconds. Unafraid of silence. Never seeking to fill it. When he spoke again it was more deliberate.

"You owe me. Understand? You owe me."

Examining the cuts on his hands as he listened. Still bleeding. An hour and they were still bleeding. Wondering if they would ever stop. Wondering if they were a sign . . . stigmata.

"Use him if you want. How many birds you kill with one stone is up to you. Just get him out of the way."

His anger cooling. Dabbing a tissue at the gouge that centred his palm. The shape of a harvest moon. Scarlet.

"Tonight. And they are reliable, I have your assurance on this?"

Squeezing the tissue into a tight ball, dropping it to the floor.

"I will trust you when it is done, comrade. This is the start, a new arrangement. We are both still feeling our way. Trust has to be earned, and it has to be paid for. I have paid you. You now have to pay me. Tonight will be your first instalment."

Haven placed the receiver back onto its cradle with unnecessary care. Walking back into the bathroom, the shower still running. Entering its cleansing sting. A curtain wall of water around him. Again and again, washing his hands. The soap, the foam . . . red to pink to white.

No end to the flow of blood. No end, until tonight.

Chapter 42

The door to room 57 was thin, flimsy . . . they made swift work of it.

Noise. Movement. Feet over splintered wood. Piao instantly awake. Adrenalin jolting through him. Black from black. Three bodies, four? Moving against him at speed. Unaware of his own actions, but feeling his feet on the floor. Hand reaching for the worn leather holster . . . the pistol. Rough hands. Strong, violent hands. Steel coming down upon his arm . . . instantly knowing that his wrist was broken. Pain, a ravenous hound leaping, centring its attentions, fangs sharp, on his temples. Feeling the blood, in freeflow, stream down his hand; tingling as it ran, as it fell from his fingers. The weight of a man on his chest. Arms. Legs. Fingers, callused, tasting of salt and sugar, thrust deeply into his mouth. Lips tearing. Gagging as a rubber ball was pushed roughly inside. Adhesive tape ripped from a roll. Bound around his head, mouth, feet, knees. Arms bound at the wrists, elbows, behind his back. Chest, stomach . . . heaving. Breaths in snuffs and spasms. Standing him on his feet. Kettledrums beating in his ears. No words, not a single word as they lifted him, carried him from the room and down the corridor. Doors ajar. Gaps with eyes. Watching, but no one helping . . . the silence thundering. Carrying him down the fire exit stairs. Outside, to the narrow alley, smelling of petrol and piss. A car sitting in darkness, starting up. Burning bright. The alley illuminated. Stilt-limbed shadows crossing each other in a thrash of movement. One, two, three, four of them . . . glimpsed in graduations of grey. Throwing Piao onto the floor in the rear of the foreign car. Two of them sitting on the back seat above him, using him as a mat. A constant smell of cigarette butts, rubber, adhesive tape . . . and one of the fuckers with dogshit on the sole of his shoe.

A journey. Thirty minutes, forty? Trying to calm his panic. Concentrate on breathing. Calm. Calm. Priorities . . . just to breathe. No ball shoved down his throat. Think only of mountain tops. Wide spaces flowing with a firm breeze. Think of cormorants startled and in flight . . . their black torn wings over skies marbled silver. Think of anything, except the rubber ball thrust half way down his throat.

★

Gates leading to gates. Metal set in metal. Corridors intersecting corridors. Lone, discoloured light bulbs. Brickwork . . . green, damp. Feet on concrete. Piao's toes dragging inbetween the pairs of dirty shoes. And from his fingers and onto the floor, a spatter trail of blood, like the petals from red roses.

The room that he was taken to was large. Windowless. A table. A metal framed bed, bolted to the concrete floor. A large, chipped enamel bowl . . . witnesses to the last inmate, streaked in shit along its bottom. The adhesive tape cut from him. The ball pulled from his mouth. With the gasp of air, an acrid taste of rubber and glue. The vomit flowing in a thin stream from his torn lips, baptising his acquaintance with the enamel bowl.

The smaller of the men, a Bai Country Lisu, as mean featured as the leftovers of a banquet, moved forward directly under the single light bulb, holding a handkerchief. Gently, he dabbed the Senior Investigator's lips. Across the white cotton . . . spit, blood, vomit.

"Strip."

Piao refused. They stripped him, roughly. Examining, searching him. Tending to his arm. Binding it. Re-dressing him. In silence. All in silence. They turned to leave.

"Haven, is this who you are working for?"

The Lisu turned. His face, a fish skeleton picked clean. He smiled, the steel door closing on it, cutting it adrift.

Piao, shouting,

438

"I am protected from what you are doing by the late Minister of Security. By Kang Zhu. There are papers, official papers. You cannot prosecute me. You cannot harm me. Check with your fucking Party advisors and your superiors. It's official. You can't touch me, I'm protected."

The door closed. Metal set in metal. Bolts sliding into place. And through the small security grill set deeply into the door's heart, a voice as thin as rice paper.

"Protected? Words. Paper. How easily they are blown away, Senior Investigator."

Chapter 43

The sixth meeting. The last meeting. The Beijing Hotel. A private suite on the top floor. Electronically swept. Furniture removed. A round table at the very centre of the main room. Four chairs. The delegate and negotiator from the People's Republic of China. A personal secretary. The delegate and negotiator from the United States of America. Another personal secretary.

"Comrade Dun, we wish to conduct these negotiations in a swift and positive manner. The President, as conveyed to me by the Vice-President only two hours ago, wants these matters settled . . ."

Pouring a glass of water. Slowly. Deliberately. Raising it to his lips. Dun knowing that all of the eyes in the room were upon him. Feeling their heat, but only thinking about water. Why Chinese water tasted so good; American water tasting of nothing. No character.

". . . Comrade Dun, it is becoming increasingly apparent that you do not recognise the seriousness of the problem that confronts your country."

Putting the glass down onto the tabletop. Once, twice. Watching the rings of water skate on the deep lacquer imprisoning the walnut grain. Watching them run into each other. Link into link.

"But we do not have a problem, negotiator. It is you who have a problem. It is you who have been the initiators of these contacts. Of these discussions. The mouse chasing the cat."

In the answer, a cul-de-sac that they had been down so many times before. The negotiator meeting the comrade's smile.

"Shall we be solution focused rather than problem

focussed, and call our negotiations a means by which we can create answers for both of our countries. Developing a relationship that will provide us with a garden from a desert?"

Comrade Dun smiled. Perfect teeth, engineered with the support of American dentistry.

"Beautifully phrased, negotiator. Beautifully. Your President, your Vice-President, they would be most proud of you. But, of course, you are correct. We should be swift, positive with our negotiations. Swiftness and decisiveness, are these not excellent bedfellows? Of course they are, and it is to the advantage of all of us that a garden be planted. But we must be sure, must we not, negotiator, about whose land this garden is on?"

Another smile, folding onto his lips like a delicate, but well designed and thought out piece of origami.

"Perhaps you should continue from the very organised note pad that you constantly tap, negotiator. Continue with swiftness. With decisiveness. And a sense of the planting of gardens in the mind . . ."

The negotiator's pen froze in mid-arc, desisting from tapping the note pad. A burn of anger, but controlling it and drawing it in. Finger running across the type of the next page. A clear agenda in black print on white paper. A clear synopsis of what was wanted and of what would be given up in return. *Black and white.*

"My government's starting point is an attempt to solve two difficulties. The first being the high levels of hepatitis, HIV, and later AIDS, being introduced into the United States of America as the results of undergoing organ transplantation in the People's Republic of China. Estimates on our part, through the relevant government departments, suggest that eighty per cent of those visiting your country for the transplantation of organs, are either American nationals or people who will visit the U.S. within the next five years. Twenty per cent of these will become infected from the organs that they have received. An estimated fifty thousand infected people crossing back into the United States of America over that same five year period. A very significant figure that will be multiplied tenfold as they infect others. A half a million infected people. A very significant figure that will result in a major drain on our resources. Figures that, as I recall, you did not, and do not now, dispute, Comrade Dun?"

Placing the glass down once more. A triad of water marks. Geometric. Balanced.

"Figures . . . smoke through trees. What is there to dispute in figures? What is there to dispute in something that has no substance?"

An answer heard a hundred times. A thousand times. Continuing. The negotiator's finger travelling to the next string of type. The next bead of words.

"Our second difficulty concerns my country's shortfall in quality human organs for transplantation. Demand simply outstrips supply . . ."

The negotiator stopped for Dun's input. There was none. Just the glass of water to his mouth.

". . . we saw the answers to these two problems as lying firmly in your, that is, the government of the People's Republic of China's sphere of influence."

He waved a hand. Graceful in movement, as the wind is through the tall grasses. But giving a sense of a wind that would never stop, until the grasses, one by one, were all blown down.

"Please, please continue. You are doing so well with your synopsis of what has occurred over our last five meetings. You have made it sound so like one of your soap operas."

Anger at the gate, but the negotiator bolting it firmly in place. Moving onto the next phase of notes.

"We approached you with the idea of developing a meaningful partnership between our two great nations. One that would allow my own country to have a hand on the steering wheel, that will allow us to support your country in the running of your organ transplant programme through the provision of technology, expertise, and of highly-trained personnel in the key areas of production, screening, cross-matching, and quality control. We also approached your government as a prospective and major source in the provision of human organs for transplantation. A prospective source that would make up for the gaps in my nation's needs in this area. That would reverse the shortfall that we have been experiencing."

Comrade Dun laughed. Controlled. A humourless grate. The negotiator had heard it before, and knew what it brought. The cane across the hand. The salt rubbed into the wound. Knowing how it would be replied to also. What words would be chosen to cushion its sting . . . calm its ache.

"But, negotiator, what of your cries of moral outrage? The human rights issues? Your disgust as a nation about how my country comes by its human organs for its highly successful transplant industry?"

Feeling it. The sting. The ache. The truth . . . the cane across the hand. But not showing it.

"It's just business, Comrade Dun. Just business . . . as it always is. Counting dollars. Counting yuan. Whether it's in DC or here in Beijing. Whether it's capitalism or communism. It's not about human rights. In the landscape that you and I move in, comrade, there is no such thing . . ."

Through the far wall of glass, carpet to ceiling, the sun high now, at its zenith.

"And your free American press, they will see it in this way also. Just business?"

The negotiator walked to the window. A view across the Imperial Palace, Beihai Park with its Hall of Breaking Waves, its Temple of Eternal Tranquillity. A view to Lishinanlu. Fuxingmenwai and the Military Museum of the Chinese People's Revolution. Beyond, the Altar of the Moon and Yuyuantan Park. Their colours stolen. Washed away. Cover on cover of monochrome vistas, like white sheets drying on a hundred allies' washing-lines.

"Forget the press, comrade, they will not see it at all. As we have discussed, the arrangement between us will be distanced from our government, and I would suggest, your government also. An agency with no overt governmental links will be set up to handle the operation from beginning to end. Cradle to grave, so to speak . . ."

Against the glare of the window, the negotiator, a negative.

443

". . . and if the press see something that they shouldn't see. Know something that they shouldn't know. We shall pressure, and all underneath a deep cover, an impenetrable blanket of denial."

"Denial. Yes, denial. We are good at that, are we not? The currency of the politician . . ."

He laughed, a ribbon of colour mixed in with it this time. Banging his glass down onto the table. Arms outstretched. Hands demanding an answer to the question.

". . . so, we know what it is that you demand of us. The harvested organs of our executed prisoners. Clean, screened, un-infected. But what is it that we receive in return? As I have said at our previous meetings, negotiator, money is not enough for what you desire from us. In such an instance as this, we require much more than just what the mighty dollar can give us. Much more."

Turning from the window. Walking toward the table.

"This will be sent to your Politburo at the completion of our meeting. If we are able to agree upon details . . ."

"Details?"

Steel, the negotiator's face. Pressed, de-burred and buffed.

"The price for which you will sell to us the organs for transplantation."

Again, the laugh.

"Ah, there we have it. What price a kidney, a cornea. What price a human heart?"

The negotiator pushed the bound file across the table. Its travel smearing the four linked rings of watermarks.

"This is what the United States of America is prepared to offer the People's Republic of China in return, Comrade Dun . . ."

Sitting. Opening the file to its first page. The seal of the United States of America. The Vice-President's signature. The next pages. The deal. What we get, what you get. Point by point, taking the comrade through them.

". . . in return for what I have outlined, a high degree of control in your organ procurement programme, especially in the areas of quality control and screening, and for a large quota of these human organs to be exported to the United States of America for use in its own transplant programme. The numbers that we require being as itemised on pages six and seven of Appendix A . . ."

Comrade Dun turning pages. Fingers moving carefully down lists of numbers. Human organs. Tapping the bottom of the page. A thin, long, slow whistle escaping from his lips. It saying nothing, and saying everything.

". . . the Vice-President, on behalf of the government of the United States of America is prepared to offer the government of the People's Republic of China the following. Firstly, we will lend our full support in denying the illegitimate regime of Nationalist Taiwan membership of the United Nations. If necessary, through our use of the veto in the Security Council. Secondly, we pledge our full support to the People's Republic of China in its dealings with Tibet. Immediate recognition will be given by our country to the twelve year old boy, Gyaincain Norbu, as the reincarnation of the revered Panchen Lama, as sponsored by the People's Republic of China . . . in preference to the child, Gedhun Choekyi Nyima, who is supported by the exiled Dalai Lama and his faction . . ."

Not a word or its deepest meaning lost upon Dun. Quite a prize, the wresting of the spiritual control of Tibet, once and for all, from the exiled Dalai Lama. Turning more pages, the comrade pulling the smile inward.

". . . thirdly, we will use our best endeavours to bring the People's Republic of China into a more liberal focus in the eyes of the American people and world opinion. Particularly in the area of human rights, and your remarkable progress in the field of organ transplantation . . ."

Saying nothing. His fingers moving across the embossed state seal. Stars, eagles, stripes . . . flowing under their tips.

". . . fourthly. The post of Head of the Secretariat of the United Nations, the Secretary General, is a position that is held for a term of five years. It is appointed by the General Assembly on the recommendations of the Security Council. The Secretary General of the United Nations is soon to start

445

the last year of his term of office. The new Secretary General of the United Nations, we guarantee, will be a citizen of the People's Republic of China . . ."

Dun's fingers gliding from the embossed seal to the signature of the Vice- President.

". . . fifthly, finally. Your controversial application to host the Olympic Games here in Beijing. The Olympic Committee, as you know, is due to vote upon this matter very shortly . . ."

The negotiator gently closing the bound file and fully meeting the comrade's gaze.

". . . we can guarantee that your bid will be successful."

The ink of the Vice-President's signature flowing in swirls, tight curves, broken slashes . . . beneath Dun's fingertips.

"Tempting. So tempting. Perhaps we have the beginnings of a deal, negotiator. As you said, it's just business. The counting of dollars and of yuan. Come, let us now talk of mere details. The price of a kidney. A cornea. The price of a human heart. Perhaps the price of ten thousand human hearts."

★

A full pack of Marlboro. A carafe of water, replenished three times. Hours . . . in smoke. Tracing water marks on lacquer. Hours . . . tracing details. Together, moving from the table to the spacious side room of full length windows and leather furnishings, personal secretaries left behind. The sun, a decaying blood orange, spilling its ruby hue across the carpet, the far wall. Across the comrade's face. As he spoke, pouring the coffee.

"I thought that a little privacy would be welcome. These are rather delicate issues. Sugar?"

The negotiator declined.

"May I say how refreshed you are looking after your visit to my country just a few months ago, negotiator. Our climate obviously agreed with you. Welcome back to the People's Republic of China. Let us hope that it agrees with you this time also?"

"You know that I visited Shanghai?"

"Of course, negotiator, of course. A pleasant trip. A productive one?"

446

The American government official, Barbara Hayes, sat, crossing her legs.

"Yes, it's been a long time since I took a vacation."

"Good, good. A holiday. Everybody should have holidays. Next time that you are in Shanghai you must visit my family. Our house overlooks the Huangpu River, the Bund. Beautiful. Beautiful. It is a very fascinating city, changing dramatically, as dramatically as you women change your minds and your faces . . ."

Passing her a coffee, even though she had declined. Sipping his own, while watching her.

Yellow eyes above a fondant ice porcelain horizon.

". . . so, negotiator, it would seem that your country wishes to have a full involvement in our transplant industry and also in our organ procurement programme. A 'window of opportunity', as you Americans like to call it, seems to have arisen. And as we are going through much change ourselves with our programme at present, it would appear that the timing could not be better. Perhaps you had heard, the main driving force and architect of my countries transplant industry has now, regrettably, moved on. Our esteemed Comrade Minister Kang Zhu."

"Yes, I had heard."

Suprising herself. Words without the narrowing of the eyes. Words, without a blush.

"A window of opportunity, negotiator. Yes, a window of opportunity."

His eyes not leaving her. The comrade placing his coffee cup and saucer back onto the table. Bone china on wood. The sound seeming to jar the room. Standing, walking to the window. Filling a fresh cup.

"But what of you, negotiator. How would I, we, be certain of your commitment to the objectives you have so eloquently outlined. You will understand, I am sure, that we need more than words on little pieces of paper . . ."

He tapped his attaché case. Inside, the price of ten thousand human hearts.

". . . what are words, but words after all. With meanings that as yet we do not know. And with other words in long queues, waiting, ready to replace them. We need something more solid. We need someone in a position of authority who will view us in a positive light and who will express this in all of our future negotiations . . ."

Not bothering to sit. His shadow, across the room, across her.

". . . in this area, I felt that you might need, now how shall I say this without offending you? A little more involvement. A little more incentive?"

A snare tightening. Circle of shiny steel wire about to snap closed. She could feel it.

"But of course you are involved, aren't you? How silly of me. A government official of the United States of America who has had such an intimate relationship with a Senior Investigator in the PSB. And an Investigator, who, I might add, remains a major suspect in several very violent murders, including that of his own Chief, our esteemed Comrade Liping. A Senior Investigator who has very complex links, through his wife, to our late esteemed Comrade Minister Kang Zhu. Such a government official as this is very involved. Look at the implications. The interpretations. People can be so cruel, especially in politics. People can be so keen to make judgements . . ."

Saying nothing. Her heart in free-fall, but saying nothing.

". . . and what are we, as his masters, to make of such a Senior Investigator as this? Obviously, such a man as this we must keep at arm's length . . ."

A whisper, fused with caffeine and garlic breath.

". . . or keep him so close to our bosom that we know even when it is that he breathes."

The move. The snare. Feeling it trip. Feeling it bite.

". . . well, negotiator, let me inform you. We hear his breaths, we hear his exhalations. He was arrested some days ago, and held in the custody of the People's Republic of China. But do not worry, your Senior Investigator, he is safe. Even protected. Protected by an old man's authority that reached even beyond the grave. Protected by words on pieces of paper . . ."

Comrade Dun, moving from the window toward her. She had not realised how ugly he was, not until this moment. And with it, reflections . . . how ugly she had become?

". . . but as I have already said, words are fragile. Pieces of paper could be blown away. And there are accidents to consider. Who can legislate for accidents. Serious accidents that might befall a prisoner?"

He leant over her. Close. Smelling of ambition and a spent ocean of sperm.

". . . to advance, negotiator, we would need you, how do you say it . . . in our pocket. Perhaps this is now the case, yes?"

The negotiator, Barbara Hayes, pushed the cup and saucer aside. Coffee in a swirled grainy spill over the cup's brim and across the saucer. Opening her attaché case. Hand automatically finding the thin file. Opening it. One by one placing the ten by eight inch monochrome prints on the table. By now, knowing them intimately herself. Watching the comrade's eyes as he discovered them for himself. The fades and washes of his irises. The dilations and contractions of his pupils. Almost tasting how he would feel. The balances and weighing up that would be tethering his every thought. How, in a thousand random, hijacked seconds, she had rehearsed this moment . . . again, again, again. Tasting how he would feel. Watching the ordered procession of his gaze. Photographs from the apartment on Dong Hua Men Street. The suite in the Xinqiao Hotel. Dun and the young man merging together in pepper grain. The comrade's hands on the boy's body, like leather on silk. Pushing him down. In the boy's fingers, the buckle of Comrade Dun's belt. The zip of his flies. Pants, around his thighs, knees, to his ankles. The boy's head pushed down. Down. In his hand, in his mouth . . . the limpness of Dun's cock warming hard, hot.

"He's eighteen, the same age as your daughter. His name is Lo, but you call him by a girl's name, Lihua. Which I believe means, 'Strength for China'? He's a student at the university where you occasionally lecture. What is he studying Comrade Dun?"

A polite cough. Recovering himself. The passions pushed

449

back into place, but in his eyes, razor wire. His pain, his anger, almost tangible. She could smell it on him, aching through his every pore.

"What is he studying?"

"He is a first year student in politics."

"Politics . . ."

Feeling herself smile.

". . . you seem to be giving him a very apt lesson, comrade. If you're going into politics its good to know what its like to be fucked beforehand . . ."

Drinking his coffee, the colour returning to his face in a gradual wash, but the reek of pain and anger, unabating. Tough talking. Shit. Never enough. She pulled a small envelope from the file, opening it. Handing the document to him. The balm after the burn.

". . . it is already deposited in Taipei, the Bank of Taiwan on the Chungching Road. The account number is enclosed."

So many noughts following a single number. He had never seen so many noughts. Comrade Dun looked up, catching the blaze of her eyes.

"Tell me, what is it that you require, negotiator?"

'Require' . . . a strange word from a politician. She knew the lesson. Require nothing. 'Insist'.

The note was already prepared. So much, coming to this moment. Two names, as simple as that, scratched in ink. Black on white. The comrade would know why they were on the slip of paper. Words not necessary. Letters would only fog, syllables confuse. He would know what to do about them. Two names.

CHARLES HAVEN.
SUN PIAO.

She stood, sliding it across to him. Fastening her attaché case. Knowing that inside of it she already had the price of a human heart . . . the price of ten thousand human hearts. Waiting an instant as he read the note. Noting the recognition in his eyes, like a bushfire moving through trees. Walking toward the door. Toward the elevator. The dying sun, tangled in her hair.

"I'll be in touch comrade, about what else I 'require'," she said. The lift doors trembling shut.

★

Barbara refused the comfort of the open doored limousine and walked. And walked. Chang'anjie. Jiaominxiang. Chang'andongjie. Park of the People's Culture. Nanhai. The Jade Basin. Onto the footpath that hugs the Beihai, the North Lake. Day revolving into night . . . and everything left with a subtle brush of gold. At one point thinking that she had seen Bobby, naked, wet, on the other bank of the lake near the Five Dragon Summerhouse. Walking the footpath toward the Screen of Iron. Looking at her. Staring. Where his eyes had been, nothing. Just tears of blood.

Dreaming . . . just dreaming.

Chapter 44

Rain and neon . . .

A sharp pull into Dongzhimenneiajie. The traffic splitting out of the Worker's Stadium in slashes . . . scarlet, lemon, white. End to end. A plunging saw-band of steel.

Staring into the rear-view mirror of the BMW hire car, Haven eased the revs, slipping into the outside lane. That feeling of being watched. Being followed. Of some impending pivotal event about to be unleashed . . . haunting. The adrenalin rush, now easing to a walking pace. The Englishman passing a hand over his forehead; sweat, cold, clammy. He would have lost them. If 'they', actually existed. In this traffic, he must have lost them. Calm. Collected. Lighting a cigarette. Marlboro. Sweet tobacco, sweet America. The loose ends tied off, double knotted. He should congratulate himself. The last thorns plucked from the rosebush, and without a single prick . . . a single bleed. But an uncharacteristic slither of un-informed paranoia stalking every hour of every day that he had been in Beijing. He exhaled, shaking off the feeling, as he joined the straight flights of dual carriageway. Capital Airport, just another twenty-nine kilometres. But even with the nico-tine, a nagging sense of something about to fall. To crash.

On the far runway of Capital, a silver jet would be in the process of being re-fuelled, cleaned, re-stocked. Flight CX 251 . . . each air mile to London, and then after transfer, to New York, being punctuated only by whisky miniatures.

Haven guided the BMW across to the slow lane. There was no hurry, fate is not a butterfly, it does not fly away. The world was a peaceful golden garden, and he, a golden picknicker within it. He lit another cigarette.

★

Across the huge departure lounge of Capital Airport, through the weave of torsos, a finger pointing . . . pale, crimson tipped. "There."

★

Assassins, they are not apart. They have other roles also. Other hats to wear. Fathers. Sons. Lovers. Once they were even children. Babies spilling from the womb. They are neighbours. They eat. They shit. They laugh. Cry. Brushing past you in the market. Sitting next to you in the cinema. Slash of knife . . . a job. Taut cross of ligature . . . a day at the office. Snub-nosed alley hit, measured sniper shot . . . squeezed in between taking the children to school and a light lunch of peanuts, pickles and pumpkin soup.

Assassins, a job like any other. Just another step toward the pension. No sweat, no adrenalin rush . . . even the pulse rate barely raised. Returning to the office. Paperwork in triplicate. Pencils to sharpen. Paperclips to replenish. The job finished. Leaving in time to meet the children from school. On foreheads, kisses. Carrying their lunchboxes. Asking how their day was. Daddy.

Assassins . . . they are not apart.

★

They stood together for twenty minutes, in silence, before he moved. Briefcase and belly. Middle-aged and Mao suit. Slowly across the departure lounge, but only when the flight had been called. Flight CX 251 to London.

People rising from red-clothed contoured foam seats. Stay-pressed slacks and sensible shoes. Hotel soap smelling. Carrier bag carrying, filled with obscure rice spirits that would never be drunk. And rising slowly, grey silk and gold. Moving against steel and glass . . . Haven. Joining the back of the queue. There was no hurry . . . fate is not a butterfly, it does not fly away.

Fingernails to lips. Crimson on crimson. Watching, as the two intersected in grey and black. An assassin at work, black. Moving on the target, grey. Briefcase slamming into the side of the Englishman's thigh. As the other hand, instantaneously, silver at its heart . . . sprinted and stabbed. A third size hypodermic emptying its load into his numbed leg. Haven's weight shifting. Rubbing his thigh. Swearwords twisting onto gaping lips, aimed at the back of the black Mao suited middle-aged Shanghainese, as he walked, even paced, towards the gates. Steel and glass. Opening. Closing. Seconds, just seconds . . . and he was lost in the crowd.

The queue advancing. Hostesses in red. Fixed smiled. Ginger breathed. A manicured hand extended. The Englishman reaching into his jacket for the boarding pass, but the dizziness already upon him. A call that would not be ignored. Flowing from his leg. Deep. Certain. Centring, warm and numb, across his forehead. Behind his eyes. The world tilting. Falling. Rushing. Hard-edged slashes. Whites into white. A thud as the floor met him in an anvil of even sided, identical marble tiles. Immediately, faces above him. A static orbit of concern against an arched cathedral ceiling; high-bowled lighting. Thinking that the stars were really fashioned from pressed steel. Watching lips, talking. But hearing no words. The world and all that it was and contained, safe behind a glass wall. Head falling to one side. Shoes, seating. Floor. Running out of focus across the length of the departure lounge. And nearer and nearer, carving across it, two men running toward him either side of a wheeled trolley stretcher. Chrome. So bright. So bright. Feeling the dribble run free from the corner of his mouth. Its course across his stubble. Silk collar in its bubbled flow. Feeling himself being lifted. The pillow under his head . . . feeling like concrete. The airtex blanket thrown over him, with the dead weight of slabbed stone. Blurs on blurs. Vision tunnelling. Hard light. Soft edges. All honed from peeled chromium. Only as he felt the piss flow, his bowel collapse in an urgent panicking warmth, smelling the acrid taint, the reek of his own shit . . . did he realise. And with the realisation, a scream, but locked into his own head now. His world, solely, him. With no means of communicating beyond the boundaries of his own skin. The muscle relaxants, the inhibitors . . . kicking in. Switch by switch, his body closing down. And through it all, replaying, over and over again, even in the ocean depth of his initial panic . . . the assassin's precise move. The kill. The leisurely black Mao suited walk to the departure lounge gates. No hurry in his pace. No nervousness in his posture.

A professional hit. A mute death dealt out to him with such efficiency. An efficiency to be wondered at, even admired. His keen curiosity still intact. Wondering what had been used . . . Mixture No2? He would have smiled, if he could have . . . the very irony of it. Injected with the very same cocktail mixture of drugs that he had been one of the architect-bartenders of. Even as breaths faltered, taking a professional pride in its smooth flowing passage. Its cold and systematic ruthlessness.

Counting the seconds, as if it were a personal experiment. Stopwatch and clipboard in hand.

THREE MINUTES THIRTY-TWO SECONDS.

A compromise of Mixture No2, or death would have tied its knot by now. An assassin who does not assassinate? A kick-start of panic nailing him in place. A drug designed to kill that does not kill? He was being delivered. Delivered.

Moving out of the terminal building. Strapped tighter into the steel cot. In its thin plated chrome, elongated reflections of a clear blue sky.

FOUR MINUTES EIGHTEEN SECONDS.

And now pure panic. Boundaryless. Bottomless. Filling all that held him to life, and life to him. Delivered . . . to what?

★

'Point, and then view it all as if from Heaven,' the comrade had said. Yes, he had been right, but still she regretted it. A wall of glass. Barbara moving against it, slowly, as below the chrome bright cot was loaded into the rear of the unmarked ambulance.

In Beijing Military Hospital, the elected and cross-matched recipients of his kidneys would already have been prepared. An army general. A local high-ranking party official. Between them, sharing a tether on life of one hundred and thirty-five years. In Guangzhou's Zhongshan Medical College, the men who would receive his corneas were already in situ. Hong Kong businessmen with wallets stitched open. Dollars in a steady, unabating flow. Model patients, each last one of them . . . they had insisted on only one matter. The kidneys, the harvested corneas that they would receive, they must be fresh. Living.

Delivered. Delivered.

★

'Point, and then view it all as if from Heaven,' the comrade had said. Yes, he had been right, but still she regretted it. It wasn't enough. It could never be enough.

Chapter 45

HONGQIAO AIRPORT, SHANGHAI . . . THE
PEOPLES REPUBLIC OF CHINA.

One week later.

Ten cleaners in a line with mops, moving in unison across the
floor of the airport. A sweep to the east . . . a sweep to the west.
A sweep to the east . . . a sweep to the west. Half of the vast
floor, scuffed grey. Half of the floor, a mirror sea of reflections.
Strip lights. Indicator boards. Neon signs. As if that portion of
the world had suddenly been tipped upside down.

★

So early . . . the first shuttle flight of the morning. Passengers
decanted and free from the luggage-laden carousels and the
press of braided, peak capped customs and permit inspectors.
All except one. An hour later, a steel partition door sliding
back upon itself. A figure. Alone. Moving through the officials; their ministrations left indelibly on his internal travel
visas. Stamps of black on white. Red on white. Green on
white. Stopping for an instant and looking back. Folding the
papers neatly and placing them in his inside pocket. When he
started to walk again it was at a faster pace, traversing the line
of cleaners at a forty-five degree angle. Walking from wet to
dry. A straight trail of footprints making for the far exit.

A single car was parked on the slip road outside. Through a
condensation misted windscreen, instantly recognising the
lone passenger. Recognising the carton of cigarettes, sharp
cornered and bulky, poking out of the top of the carrier bag.
Marlboro. Yaobang already feeling for his box of matches.

A series of jolts as the window wound down. Helping it
with his thick fingers.

Focussing on the commuter's face. The scarring around the eyes, mouth, nose. The right wrist and hand, heavily bandaged. And his posture . . . the way he moved. Whispering of dark rooms. Metal framed beds. Truncheons of hard, black rubber. And questions, over and over again . . . the same questions

"Shhhitttt . . ."

Like a sigh.

". . . what happened Boss, walk into a fucking door?"

Piao pulled the carton of cigarettes from the plastic bag and tossed it onto the Big Man's lap.

"Several doors. Over and over again"

Cellophane, cardboard . . . ripped. A match . . . struck. Two cigarettes lit. Yaobang handing one to the Senior Investigator. For a while, seconds uncounted . . . not talking. The smoke around Piao in a shifting question mark.

"Where the fuck you been, Boss? I tried to get news, but not even the offer of bottles of Japanese whisky could loosen a fucking lip."

Silent. For the first time Piao noticing freedom. Big things at first, in bites. The coldness. The sky. And then the little things, in nibbles. The litter in the gutter. The belch of ten thousand factory chimneys.

"Where the fuck you been, Boss?"

Piao pulled deeply on the Marlboro's butt, holding the smoke down. Holding so many things down. It burnt. Rounding the front of the Sedan. Pulling open the stuck door and getting in. Hiding the pain, as best as he could. Always hiding the pain.

"Haven. He got away. I didn't get to kill him."

"Well, Boss, somebody fucking did . . ."

Yaobang tapped the envelope in the dashboard well.

". . . or perhaps this is for something else?"

The envelope reeked of government. Of box-like offices. Of pressed suits over threadbare underwear. The Senior Investigator ripped it open. Inside the envelope . . . things expected, things unexpected. A life folded in Manila. A letter from the Danwei and the Ministry of Security, retracting all charges against him. Absolution from the murder of Liping and the Chairman of the Shiqu. Release from any further charges that might spring from his investigation of the eight who were found in the Huangpu, or from any of the events surrounding it. Sticky, tricky, legal words, that he would have to examine and perform an autopsy on at a later date.

Digging deeper. Food, clothes, furniture vouchers . . . to be spent at the Friendship Store. Deeper still. A purchase voucher for a car, second-hand. Of course! A slip to draw his wages, his backpay. Another slip, informing him of his promotion of two grades. Waiting for him, an upholstered chair, velour covered. Another slip . . . noting his promotion and awarding the relevant rise in pay. One hundred yuan a month. Zhiyuan, the old bastard, how right he'd been. And on yet another slip, an address of a new flat rented on his behalf. His new home. A road just off of Wenmiao. Views of the river, if you went up onto the roof and stood on tiptoes. A road off of Wenmiao. He was going up in the world, or was it down? A road off of Wenmiao, an area littered with middle-ranking cadre and nodding Party brown-nosers. A road off of Wenmiao . . . they were already trying to block him in. Package him up. Keep him safe. Keep him sweet. A last draw on the cigarette, flicking it out of the car window. A fury of sparks, before it faded and died.

Deeper still. A floppy disc. Removing it. Turning it over and over in his fingers. Its blunt, rounded corners. Its safe edges. Its inoffensive demeanour. How could death come in such a neat and innocent looking package? He lit another cigarette. It tasted better than the first. It always did. Always would.

In the bottom of the envelope, a smaller envelope. So different from everything that had surrounded it. Pastel against harsh monotones. Handwriting against type. Perfumed page against the hints of ink and stationary cupboards. Lingling. For an instant, the thought, the constant question within himself . . . is she coming back, does she really want to come back home? Reading it, and as he did, instantly aware that there was nothing at the bottom of the page about her wanting to come back.

'. . . the blood tests, the doctor's reports, the files from the hospital.
They were prepared at our request. They were lies.
You do not have HIV. You never had HIV."

Cold. Numb. For seconds, not able to move. Not able to breathe. And then the slow thaw of relief. Of release. As soft, as warm as a deep swelling wave of morphine.

The car coughed into life, settling into an uncomfortable shiver. Yaobang finishing his second cigarette to the last strands of tobacco.

"So, Boss, good trip?"

'Good trip' . . . a question to be answered, but not yet.

The car rolled and Piao wound up the window. He would be going to the flat now, on a road just off of Wenmiao. A home that he had yet to know. Behind the door, nothing but the mechanics of a life. Behind the door, no perfumed letters. A life, re-visited. In his fingers, the floppy disc in idle orbits. Taking hold of it more firmly. Bending it, until the black casing bruised grey . . . snapping with the caustic high note of plastic.

His last link to the man who was Haven. His last link to the woman who was . . .

Winding down the window. In two separate jig-saw halves, letting the plastic, now valueless, slip from his fingers. Death, sentenced by data, in tumbled falls into the stained gutters.

Cold. So cold. But leaving the window down. Pulling the jacket on the back seat around himself. Reaching to fasten the collar, but the button missing. The button still missing. And who was there to put a new one on? Moving toward Yichuan Park . . . the spike of the trees, the carve of the walls, softened, blunted by the early morning smog. The breath of the Yellow Dragon. Gleaming cities. Gleaming people. Never further away. For a second, closing his eyes as the soundless, matt landscape, fell past his window.

A button missing. He would have to learn to sew.